Praise for #1 *New York Times* bestselling author

NORA ROBERTS

"When Roberts puts her expert fingers on the pulse of romance, legions of fans feel the heartbeat."
—*Publishers Weekly*

"You can't bottle wish fulfillment,
but Nora Roberts certainly knows how
to put it on the page."
—*New York Times*

"With clear-eyed, concise vision and a sure pen, Roberts nails her characters and settings with awesome precision, drawing readers into a vividly rendered world of family-centered warmth and unquestionable magic."
—*Library Journal*

"Her stories have fueled the dreams
of twenty-five million readers."
—*Entertainment Weekly*

"Roberts' style has a fresh, contemporary snap."
—*Kirkus Reviews*

"Characters that touch the heart, stories that intrigue, romance that sizzles—Nora Roberts has mastered it all."
—*Rendezvous*

Dear Reader,

Every memorable romance needs an irresistible hero—and no one can deliver that man quite like *New York Times* bestselling author Nora Roberts. This riveting collection tells the tales of three such fascinating men of mystery... and the women who steal their hearts!

In *This Magic Moment,* the ambitious Ryan Swan has only business on her mind as she makes her way to the remote home of Pierce Atkins. Yet how is she supposed to work with this mesmerizing man when all she can think about is the way he looks at her—and the way he kisses her?

Search for Love is the story of one woman's journey to discover her family roots. But Serenity Smith never expected to encounter the arrogant Count de Kergallen, nor to be so attracted to the man. From their first heated glance, though, she is under his spell....

What would you do if you found yourself on a darkened beach in the arms of a dangerous stranger? Morgan James gets the chance to find out in *The Right Path.* But will she survive the passion and peril that mystery man Nicholas Gregoras brings into her life?

These classic romantic suspense tales are sure to enthrall until the very last page and leave you wanting more!

The Editors

Silhouette Books

NORA ROBERTS

MYSTERIOUS

Silhouette Books

Published by Silhouette Books
America's Publisher of Contemporary Romance

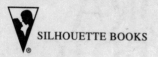

SILHOUETTE BOOKS

Recycling programs
for this product may
not exist in your area.

MYSTERIOUS

ISBN-13: 978-0-373-28161-9

Copyright © 2008 by Harlequin Books S.A.

The publisher acknowledges the copyright holder
of the individual works as follows:

THIS MAGIC MOMENT
Copyright © 1983 by Nora Roberts

SEARCH FOR LOVE
Copyright © 1991 by Nora Roberts

THE RIGHT PATH
Copyright © 1985 by Nora Roberts

This edition published by arrangement with Harlequin Books S.A.

For questions and comments about the quality of this book, please contact us
at CustomerService@Harlequin.com.

Visit Silhouette Books at www.Harlequin.com

Printed in U.S.A.

CONTENTS

THIS MAGIC MOMENT

Chapter 1

He'd chosen it for the atmosphere. Ryan was certain of it the moment she saw the house on the cliff. It was stone gray and solitary. It turned its back on the Pacific. It wasn't a symmetrical structure, but rambling, with sections of varying heights rising up here and there, giving it a wild sort of grace. High at the top of a winding cliff road, with the backdrop of an angry sky, the house was both magnificent and eerie.

Like something out of an old movie, Ryan decided as she shifted into first to take the climb. She had heard Pierce Atkins was eccentric. The house seemed to testify to that.

All it needs, she mused, is a thunderclap, a little fog and the howl of a wolf; just some minor special effects. Amused at the thought, she drew the car to a stop and looked the house over again. You wouldn't see many like it only a hundred and fifty miles north of L.A. You wouldn't, she corrected silently, see many like it anywhere.

The moment she slid from the car, the wind pulled at her, whipping her hair around her face and tugging at her skirt. She was tempted to go to the seawall and take a look at the ocean but hurried up the steps instead. She hadn't come to admire the view.

The knocker was old and heavy. It gave a very impressive thud when she pounded it against the door. Ryan told herself she wasn't the least bit nervous but switched her briefcase from hand to hand as she waited. Her father would be furious if she walked away without Pierce Atkins's signature on the contracts she carried. No, not furious, she amended. Silent. No one could use silence more effectively than Bennett Swan.

I'm not going to walk away empty-handed, she assured herself. I know how to handle temperamental entertainers. I've spent years watching how it's done and—

Her thoughts were cut off as the door opened. Ryan stared. Staring back at her was the largest man she had ever seen. He was at least six foot five, with shoulders that all but filled the doorway. And his face. Ryan decided he was, indisputably, the ugliest human being she had ever seen. His broad face was pale. His nose had obviously been broken and had reknit at an odd angle. His eyes were small, a washed-out brown that matched his thick mat of hair. Atmosphere, Ryan thought again. Atkins must have chosen him for atmosphere.

"Good afternoon," she managed. "Ryan Swan. Mr. Atkins is expecting me."

"Miss Swan." The slow, barrel-deep voice suited him perfectly. When the man stepped back, Ryan found herself fighting a reluctance to enter. Storm clouds, a hulking butler and a brooding house on a cliff. Oh, yes, she decided. Atkins knows how to set the stage.

She walked in. As the door closed behind her, Ryan took a quick glimpse around.

"Wait here," the laconic butler instructed and walked, lightly for a big man, down the hall.

"Of course, thank you very much," she muttered to his back.

The walls were white and draped with tapestries. The one nearest her was a faded medieval scene depicting the young Arthur drawing the sword from the stone, with Merlin the Enchanter highlighted in the background. Ryan nodded. It was an exquisite piece of work and suited to a man like Atkins. Turning, she found herself staring at her own reflection in an ornate cheval glass.

It annoyed her to see that her hair was mussed. She represented Swan Productions. Ryan pushed at the stray misty blond wisps. The green of her eyes had darkened with a mixture of anxiety and excitement. Her cheeks were flushed with it. Taking a deep breath, she ordered herself to calm down. She straightened her jacket.

Hearing footsteps, she quickly turned away from the mirror. She didn't want to be caught studying herself or attempting last-minute repairs. It was the butler again, alone. Ryan repressed a surge of annoyance.

"He'll see you downstairs."

"Oh." Ryan opened her mouth to say something else, but he was already retreating. She had to scramble to keep up.

The hall wound to the right. Ryan's heels clicked quickly as she trotted to match the butler's pace. Then he stopped so abruptly, she nearly collided with his back.

"Down there." He had opened a door and was already walking away.

"But…" Ryan scowled after him, then made her way down the dimly lighted steps. Really, this was ridiculous, she thought. A business meeting should be conducted in an office, or at least in a suitable restaurant. Show business, she mused scornfully.

The sound of her own footfalls echoed back at her. There was no sound at all from the room below. Oh, yes, she concluded, Atkins knows how to set the stage. She was beginning to dislike him intensely. Her heart was hammering uncomfortably as she rounded the last curve in the winding staircase.

The lower floor was huge, a sprawling room with crates and trunks and paraphernalia stacked all around. The walls were paneled and the floor was tiled, but no one had bothered with any further decoration. Ryan looked around, frowning, as she walked down the last of the steps.

He watched her. He had the talent for absolute stillness, absolute concentration. It was essential to his craft. He also had the ability to sum up a person quickly. That, too, was part of his profession. She was younger than he had expected, a fragile-looking woman, small in stature, slight in build, with clouds of pale hair and a delicately molded face. A strong chin.

She was annoyed, he noted, and not a little apprehensive. A smile tugged at his mouth. Even after she began to wander around the room, he made no move to go to her. Very businesslike, he thought, with her trim, tailored suit, sensible shoes, expensive briefcase and very feminine hands. Interesting.

"Miss Swan."

Ryan jolted, then swore at herself. Turning in the direction of the voice, she saw only shadows.

"You're very prompt."

Confused, she stopped. "Yes. Yes, he is." She found herself staring again.

Pierce smiled as he stepped down to her. "He phoned an hour ago, Miss Swan. Long-distance dialing, no telepathy." Ryan glared before she could stop herself, but his smile only widened. "Did you have a nice drive?"

"Yes, thank you."

"But a long one," he said. "Sit." Pierce gestured to a table, then took a chair behind it. Ryan sat opposite him.

"Mr. Atkins," she began, feeling more at ease now that business was about to begin. "I know my father has discussed Swan Productions' offer with you and your representative at length, but perhaps you'd like to go over the details again." She set her briefcase on the table. "I could clarify any questions you might have."

"Have you worked for Swan Productions long, Miss Swan?"

The question interrupted the flow of her presentation, but Ryan shifted her thoughts. Entertainers often had to be humored. "Five years, Mr. Atkins. I assure you, I'm qualified to answer your questions and negotiate terms if necessary."

Her voice was very smooth, but she was nervous. Pierce saw it in the careful way she folded her hands on the table. "I'm sure you're qualified, Miss Swan," he agreed. "Your father isn't an easy man to please."

Surprise and a trace of apprehension flickered into her eyes. "No," she said calmly, "which is why you can be sure of receiving the best promotion, the best production staff, the best contract available. Three one-hour television specials over three years, guaranteed prime with a budget that ensures quality." She paused a moment. "An advantageous arrangement for you Swan Productions."

He moved then, and Ryan saw that he stood on a stage. He wore black and blended with the shadows. With an effort, she kept the annoyance from her voice. "Mr. Atkins." Ryan went toward him then, fixing on a trained smile. "You have quite a house."

"Thank you."

He didn't come down to her but stood on the stage. Ryan was forced to look up at him. It surprised her that he was more dramatic in person than on tape. Normally, she had found the reverse to be true. She had seen his performances. Indeed, since her father had taken ill and reluctantly turned Atkins over to her, Ryan had spent two entire evenings watching every available tape on Pierce Atkins.

Dramatic, she decided, noting a raw-boned face with a thick, waving mane of black hair. There was a small scar along his jawline, and his mouth was long and thin. His brows were arched with a slight upsweep at the tips. But it was the eyes under them which held her. She had never seen eyes so dark, so deep. Were they gray? Were they black? Yet it wasn't their color that disconcerted her, it was the absolute concentration in them. She felt her throat go dry and swallowed in defense. She could almost believe he was reading her mind.

He had been called the greatest magician of the decade, some said the greatest of the last half of the century. His illusions and escapes were daring, flashy, unexplainable. It was a common thing to hear of him referred to as a wizard. Staring into his eyes, Ryan to understand why.

She shook herself free of the trance and started. She didn't believe in magic. "Mr. Atkins, my ogizes for not being able to come himself.

"He's feeling better."

"Perhaps."

He was looking at her too closely. Ryan forced herself not to fidget. Gray, she saw. His eyes were gray—as dark as was possible without being black.

"Of course," she continued, "your career has been aimed primarily at live audiences in clubs and theaters. Vegas, Tahoe, the London Palladium and so forth."

"An illusion means nothing on film, Miss Swan. Film can be altered."

"Yes, I realize that. To have any impact, a trick has to be performed live."

"Illusion," Pierce corrected. "I don't do tricks."

Ryan stopped. His eyes were steady on hers. "Illusion," she amended with a nod. "The specials would be broadcasted live, with a studio audience as well. The publicity—"

"You don't believe in magic, do you, Miss Swan?" There was the slightest of smiles on his mouth, the barest trace of amusement in his voice.

"Mr. Atkins, you're a very talented man," she said carefully. "I admire your work."

"A diplomat," he concluded, leaning back. "And a cynic. I like that."

Ryan didn't feel complimented. He was laughing at her without making the smallest attempt to conceal it. Your job, she reminded herself as her teeth clenched. Do your job. "Mr. Atkins, if we could discuss the terms of the contract—"

"I don't do business with anyone until I know who they are."

Ryan let out a quick breath. "My father—"

"I'm not talking to your father," Pierce interrupted smoothly.

"I didn't think to type up a bio," she snapped, then bit

her tongue. Damn! She couldn't afford to lose her temper. But Pierce grinned, pleased.

"I don't think that will be necessary." He had her hand in his before she realized what he was doing.

"Nevermore."

The voice from behind had Ryan jolting in her chair.

"That's just Merlin," Pierce said mildly as she twisted her head.

There was a large black myna bird in a cage to her right. Ryan took a deep breath and tried to steady her nerves. The bird was staring at her.

"Very clever," she managed, eyeing the bird with some reservation. "Did you teach him to talk?"

"Mmm."

"Buy you a drink, sweetie?"

Wide-eyed, Ryan gave a muffled laugh as she turned back to Pierce. He merely gave the bird a careless glance. "I haven't taught him manners."

She struggled not to be amused. "Mr. Atkins, if we could—"

"Your father wanted a son." Ryan forgot what she had been about to say and stared at him. "That made it difficult for you." Pierce was looking into her eyes again, her hand held loosely in his. "You're not married, you live alone. You're a realist who considers herself very practical. You find it difficult to control your temper, but you work at it. You're a very cautious woman, Miss Swan, slow to trust, careful in relationships. You're impatient because you have something to prove—to yourself and to your father."

His eyes lost their intense directness when he smiled at her. "A parlor game, Miss Swan, or telepathy?" When Pierce released her hand, Ryan pulled it from the table into her lap. She hadn't cared for his accuracy.

"A little amateur psychology," he said comfortably, enjoying her stunned expression. "A basic knowledge of Bennett Swan and an understanding of body language." He shrugged his shoulders. "No trick, Miss Swan, just educated guesswork. How close was I?"

Ryan gripped her hands together in her lap. Her right palm was still warm from his. "I didn't come here to play games, Mr. Atkins."

"No." He smiled again, charmingly. "You came to close a deal, but I do things in my own time, in my own way. My profession encourages eccentricity, Miss Swan. Humor me."

"I'm doing my best," Ryan returned, then took a deep breath and sat back. "I think it's safe to say that we're both very serious about our professions."

"Agreed."

"Then you understand that it's my job to sign you with Swan, Mr. Atkins." Perhaps a bit of flattery would work, she decided. "We want you because you're the best in your field."

"I'm aware of that," he answered without batting an eye.

"Aware that we want you or that you're the best?" she found herself demanding.

He flashed her a very appealing grin. "Of both."

Ryan took a deep breath and reminded herself that entertainers were often impossible. "Mr. Atkins," she began.

With a flutter of wings, Merlin swooped out of his cage and landed on her shoulder. Ryan gasped and froze.

"Oh, God," she murmured. This was too much, she thought numbly. Entirely too much.

Pierce frowned at the bird as it settled its wings. "Odd, he's never done that with anyone before."

"Aren't I lucky," Ryan muttered, sitting perfectly still. Did birds bite? she wondered. She decided she didn't care to wait to find out. "Do you think you could—ah, persuade him to perch somewhere else?"

A slight gesture of Pierce's hand had Merlin leaving Ryan's shoulder to land on his own.

"Mr. Atkins, please, I realize a man in your profession would have a taste for—atmosphere." Ryan took a breath to steady herself, but it didn't work. "It's very difficult to discuss business in—in a dungeon," she said with a sweep of her arm. "With a crazed raven swooping down on me and…"

Pierce's shout of laughter cut her off. On his shoulder the bird settled his wings and stared, steely-eyed, at Ryan. "Ryan Swan, I'm going to like you. I work in this dungeon," he explained good-naturedly. "It's private and quiet. Illusions take more than skill; they take a great deal of planning and preparation."

"I understand that, Mr. Atkins, but—"

"We'll discuss business more conventionally over dinner," he interrupted.

Ryan rose as he did. She hadn't planned to stay more than an hour or two. It was a good thirty-minute drive down the cliff road to her hotel.

"You'll stay the night," Pierce added, as if he had indeed read her thoughts.

"I appreciate your hospitality, Mr. Atkins," she began, following as he walked back to the stairs, the bird remaining placidly on his shoulder. "But I have a reservation at a hotel in town. Tomorrow—"

"Do you have your bags?" Pierce stopped to take her arm before he mounted the steps.

"Yes, in the car, but—"

"Link will cancel your reservation, Miss Swan. We're

in for a storm." He turned his head to glance at her. "I wouldn't like to think of you driving these roads tonight."

As if to accentuate his words, a blast of thunder greeted them as they came to the top of the stairs. Ryan murmured something. She wasn't certain she wanted to think of spending the night in this house.

"Nothing up my sleeve," Merlin announced.

She shot him a dubious look.

Chapter 2

Dinner did much to put Ryan's mind at rest. The dining room was huge, with a roaring fire at one end and a collection of antique pewter at the other. The long refectory table was set with Sèvres china and Georgian silver.

"Link's an excellent cook," Pierce told her as the big man set a Cornish hen in front of her. Ryan caught a glimpse of his huge hands before Link left the room. Cautiously, she picked up her fork.

"He's certainly quiet."

Pierce smiled and poured a pale gold wine into her glass. "Link only talks when he has something to say. Tell me, Miss Swan, do you enjoy living in Los Angeles?"

Ryan looked over at him. His eyes were friendly now, not intense and intrusive, as they had been before. She allowed herself to relax. "Yes, I suppose I do. It's convenient for my work."

"Crowded?" Pierce cut into the poultry.

"Yes, of course, but I'm used to it."

"You've always lived in L.A.?"

"Except when I was in school."

Pierce noted the slight change in tone, the faintest hint of resentment no one else might have caught. He went on eating. "Where did you go to school?"

"Switzerland."

"A beautiful country." He reached for his wine. *And she didn't care to be shipped off,* he thought. "Then you began to work for Swan Productions?"

Frowning, Ryan stared into the fire. "When my father realized I was determined, he agreed."

"And you're a very determined woman," Pierce commented.

"Yes," she admitted. "For the first year, I shuffled papers, went for coffee, and was kept away from the talent." The frown vanished. A gleam of humor lit her eyes. "One day some papers came across my desk, quite by mistake. My father was trying to sign Mildred Chase for a miniseries. She wasn't cooperating. I did a little research and went to see her." Laughing with the memory, she sent Pierce a grin. "*That* was quite an experience. She lives in this fabulous place in the hills—guards, a dozen dogs. She's very 'old Hollywood.' I think she let me in out of curiosity."

"What did you think of her?" he asked, mainly to keep her talking, to keep her smiling.

"I thought she was wonderful. A genuine *grande dame.* If my knees hadn't been shaking, I'm sure I would have curtsied." A light of triumph covered her face. "And when I left two hours later, her signature was on the contract."

"How did your father react?"

"He was furious." Ryan picked up her wine. The fire

sent a play of shadow and light over her skin. She was to think of the conversation later and wonder at her own expansiveness. "He raged at me for the better part of an hour." She drank, then set down the glass. "The next day, I had a promotion and a new office. Bennett Swan appreciates people who get things done."

"And do you," Pierce murmured, "get things done, Miss Swan?"

"Usually," she returned evenly. "I'm good at handling details."

"And people?"

Ryan hesitated. His eyes were direct again. "Most people."

He smiled, but his look remained direct. "How's your dinner?"

"My…" Ryan shook her head to break the gaze, then glanced down at her plate. She was surprised to see she had eaten a healthy portion of the hen. "It's very good. Your…" She looked back at him again, not certain what to call Link. *Servant? Slave?*

"Friend," Pierce put in mildly and sipped his wine.

Ryan struggled against the uncomfortable feeling that he saw inside her brain. "Your friend is a marvelous cook."

"Appearances are often deceiving," Pierce pointed out, amused. "We're both in professions that show an audience something that isn't real. Swan Productions deals in illusions. So do I." He reached toward her, and Ryan sat back quickly. In his hand was a long-stemmed red rose.

"Oh!" Surprised and pleased, Ryan took it from him. Its scent was strong and sweet. "I suppose that's the sort of thing you have to expect when you have dinner with a magician," she commented and smiled at him over the tip of the bud.

"Beautiful women and flowers belong together." The wariness that came into her eyes intrigued him. A very cautious woman, he thought again. He liked caution, respected it. He also enjoyed watching people react. "You're a beautiful woman, Ryan Swan."

"Thank you."

Her answer was close to prim and had his mouth twitching. "More wine?"

"No. No, thank you, I'm fine." But her pulse was throbbing lightly. Setting the flower beside her plate, she went back to her meal. "I've rarely been this far up the coast," she said conversationally. "Have you lived here long, Mr. Atkins?"

"A few years." He swirled the wine in his glass, but she noted he drank very little. "I don't like crowds," he told her.

"Except at a performance," she said with a smile.

"Naturally."

It occurred to Ryan, when Pierce rose and suggested they sit in the parlor, that they hadn't discussed the contract. She was going to have to steer him back to the subject.

"Mr. Atkins..." she began as they entered. "Oh! What a beautiful room!"

It was like stepping back to the eighteenth century. But there were no cobwebs, no signs of age. The furniture shone, and the flowers were fresh. A small upright piano stood in a corner with sheet music open. There were small, blown-glass figurines on the mantel. A menagerie, she noted on close study—unicorns, winged horses, centaurs, a three-headed hound. No conventional animals in Pierce Atkins's collection. Yet the fire in the grate was sedate, and the lamp standing on a piecrust table was certainly a Tiffany. It was a room Ryan would have expected to find in a cozy English country house.

"I'm glad you like it," Pierce said, standing beside her. "You seemed surprised."

"Yes. The outside looks like a prop from a 1945 horror movie, but…" Ryan stopped herself, horrified. "Oh, I'm sorry, I didn't mean…" But he was grinning, obviously delighted with her observation.

"It was used for just that more than once. That's why I bought it."

Ryan relaxed again as she wandered around the room. "It did occur to me that you might have chosen it for the atmosphere."

Pierce lifted a brow. "I have an—affection for things others take at face value." He stepped to a table where cups were already laid out. "I can't offer you coffee, I'm afraid. I don't use caffeine. The tea is herbal and very good." He was already pouring as Ryan stepped up to the piano.

"Tea's fine," she said absently. It wasn't printed sheet music on the piano, she noted, but staff paper. Automatically, she began to pick out the handwritten notes. The melody was hauntingly romantic. "This is beautiful." Ryan turned back to him. "Just beautiful. I didn't know you wrote music."

"I don't." Pierce set down the teapot. "Link does." He watched Ryan's eyes widen in astonishment. "Face value, Miss Swan?"

She lowered her eyes to her hands. "You make me quite ashamed."

"I've no intention of doing that." Crossing to her, Pierce took her hand again. "Most of us are drawn to beauty."

"But you're not?"

"I find surface beauty appealing, Miss Swan." Quickly, thoroughly, he scanned her face. "Then I look for more."

Something in the contact made her feel odd. Her voice wasn't as strong as it should have been. "And if you don't find it?"

"Then I discard it," he said simply. "Come, your tea will get cold."

"Mr. Atkins." Ryan allowed him to lead her to a chair. "I don't want to offend you. I can't afford to offend you, but…" She let out a frustrated breath as she sat. "I think you're a very strange man."

He smiled. She found it compelling, the way his eyes smiled a split second before his mouth. "You'd offend me, Miss Swan, if you didn't think so. I have no wish to be ordinary."

He was beginning to fascinate her. Ryan had always been careful to keep her professional objectivity when dealing with talent. It was important not to be awed. If you were awed, you'd find yourself adding clauses to contracts and making rash promises.

"Mr. Atkins, about our proposition."

"I've given it a great deal of thought." A crash of thunder shook the windows. Ryan glanced over as he lifted his cup. "The roads will be treacherous tonight." His eyes came back to Ryan's. Her hands had balled into fists at the blast. "Do storms upset you, Miss Swan?"

"No, not really." Carefully, she relaxed her fingers. "But I'm grateful for your hospitality. I don't like to drive in them." Lifting her cup, she tried to ignore the slashes of lightning. "If you have any questions about the terms, I'd be glad to go over them with you."

"I think it's clear enough." He sipped his tea. "My agent is anxious for me to accept the contract."

"Oh?" Ryan had to struggle to keep the triumph from her voice. It would be a mistake to push too soon.

"I never commit myself to anything until I'm certain it suits me. I'll tell you what I've decided tomorrow."

She nodded, accepting. He wasn't playing games, and she sensed that no agent, or anyone, would influence him beyond a certain point. He was his own man, first and last.

"Do you play chess, Miss Swan?"

"What?" Distracted, she looked up again. "I beg your pardon?"

"Do you play chess?" he repeated.

"Why, yes, I do."

"I thought so. You know when to move and when to wait. Would you like to play?"

"Yes," she agreed without hesitation. "I would."

Rising, he offered his hand and led her to a table by the windows. Outside, the rain hurled itself against the glass. But when she saw the chessboard already set up, she forgot the storm.

"They're exquisite!" Ryan lifted the white king. It was oversized and carved in marble. "Arthur," she said, then picked up the queen. "And Guinevere." She studied the other pieces. "Lancelot the knight, Merlin the bishop, and, of course, Camelot." She turned the castle over in her palm. "I've never seen anything like these."

"Take the white," he invited, seating himself behind the black. "Do you play to win, Miss Swan?"

She took the chair opposite him. "Yes, doesn't everyone?"

He gave her a long, unfathomable look. "No. Some play for the game."

After ten minutes Ryan no longer heard the rain on the windows. Pierce was a shrewd player and a silent one. She found herself watching his hands as they slid pieces over the board. They were long, narrow hands with nimble fingers. He wore a gold ring on his pinky with a scrolled symbol she didn't recognize. Ryan had heard it said those fingers could pick any lock, untie any knot. Watching them, she thought they were more suited for tuning a violin. When she glanced up, she found him watching her with his amused, knowing smile. She channeled her concentration on her strategy.

Ryan attacked, he defended. He advanced, she countered. Pierce was pleased to have a well-matched partner. She was a cautious player, given to occasional bursts of impulse. He felt her game-playing reflected who she was. She wouldn't be easily duped or easily beaten. He admired both the quick wits and the strength he sensed in her. It made her beauty all the more appealing.

Her hands were soft. As he captured her bishop, he wondered idly if her mouth would be, too, and how soon he would find out. He had already decided he would; now it was a matter of timing. Pierce understood the invaluable importance of timing.

"Checkmate," he said quietly and heard Ryan's gasp of surprise.

She studied the board a moment, then smiled over at him. "Damn, I didn't see that coming. Are you sure you don't have a few extra pieces tucked up your sleeve?"

"Nothing up my sleeve," Merlin cackled from across the room. Ryan shot him a glance and wondered when he had joined them.

"I don't use magic when skill will do," Pierce told her, ignoring his pet. "You play well, Miss Swan."

"You play better, Mr. Atkins."

"This time," he agreed. "You interest me."

"Oh?" She met his look levelly. "How?"

"In several ways." Sitting back, he ran a finger down the black queen. "You play to win, but you lose well. Is that always true?"

"No." She laughed but rose from the table. He was making her nervous again. "Do you lose well, Mr. Atkins?"

"I don't often lose."

When she looked back, he was standing at another table handling a pack of cards. Ryan hadn't heard him move. It made her uneasy.

"Do you know Tarot cards?"

"No. That is," she corrected, "I know they're for telling fortunes or something, aren't they?"

"Or something." He gave a small laugh and shuffled the cards gently. "Mumbo jumbo, Miss Swan. A device to keep someone's attention focused and to add mystery to quick thinking and observation. Most people prefer to be fooled. Explanations leave them disappointed. Even most realists."

"You don't believe in those cards." Ryan walked over to join him. "You know you can't tell the future with pasteboard and pretty colors."

"A tool, a diversion." Pierce lifted his shoulders. "A game, if you like. Games relax me." Pierce fanned the oversized cards in a quick, effective gesture, then spread them on the table.

"You do that very well," Ryan murmured. Her nerves were tight again, but she wasn't sure why.

"A basic skill," he said easily. "I could teach you quickly enough. You have competent hands." He lifted one, but it was her face he examined, not her palm. "Shall I pick a card?"

Ryan removed her hand. Her pulse was beginning to race. "It's your game."

With a fingertip, Pierce drew out a card and flipped it faceup. It was the Magician. "Confidence, creativity," Pierce murmured.

"You?" Ryan said flippantly to conceal the growing tension.

"So it might seem." Pierce laid a finger on another card and drew it out. The High Priestess. "Serenity," he said quietly. "Strength. You?"

Ryan shrugged. "Simple enough for you to draw whatever card you like after you've stacked the deck."

Pierce grinned, unoffended. "The cynic should choose the next to see where these two people will end. Pick a card, Miss Swan," he invited. "Any card."

Annoyed, Ryan plucked one and tossed it faceup on the table. After a strangled gasp, she stared at it in absolute silence. The Lovers. Her heart hammered lightly at her throat.

"Fascinating," Pierce murmured. He wasn't smiling now, but he studied the card as if he'd never seen it before.

Ryan took a step back. "I don't like your game, Mr. Atkins."

"Hmmm?" He glanced up distractedly, then focused on her. "No? Well then…" He carelessly flipped the cards together and stacked them. "I'll show you to your room."

Pierce had been as surprised by the card as Ryan had been. But he knew reality was often stranger than any illusion he could devise. He had work to do, a great deal of final planning for his engagement in Las Vegas in two weeks' time. Yet as he sat in his room, he was thinking of Ryan, not of the mechanics of his craft.

There was something about her when she laughed,

something brilliant and vital. It appealed to him the same way her low-key, practical voice had appealed to him when she spoke of contracts and clauses.

He already knew the contract backward and forward. He wasn't a man to brush aside the business end of his profession. Pierce signed his name to nothing unless he understood every nuance. If the public saw him as mysterious, flashy and odd, that was all to the good. The image was part illusion, part reality. That was the way he preferred it. He had spent the second half of his life arranging things as he preferred them.

Ryan Swan. Pierce stripped off his shirt and tossed it aside. He wasn't certain about her just yet. He had fully intended to sign the contracts until he had seen her coming down the stairs. Instinct had made him hesitate. Pierce relied heavily on his instincts. Now he had some thinking to do.

The cards didn't influence him. He could make cards stand up and dance if that's what he wanted. But coincidence influenced him. It was odd that Ryan had turned over the card symbolizing lovers when he had been thinking what she would feel like in his arms.

With a laugh, he sat down and began to doodle on a pad of paper. The plans he was forming for a new escape would have to be torn up or revised, but it relaxed him to turn it over in his mind, just as he turned Ryan over in his mind.

It might be wise to sign her papers in the morning and send her on her way. He didn't care to have a woman intrude on his thoughts. But Pierce didn't always do what was wise. If he did, he would still be playing the club field, pulling rabbits out of his hat and colored scarves out of his pocket at union scale. Now he turned a woman into a panther and walked through a brick wall.

Poof! he thought. Instant magic. And no one remembered the years of frustration and struggle and failure. That, too, was exactly as he wanted it. There were few who knew where he had come from or who he had been before he was twenty-five.

Pierce tossed aside the pencil. Ryan Swan was making him uneasy. He would go downstairs and work until his mind was clear. It was then he heard her scream.

Ryan undressed carelessly. Temper always made her careless. Parlor tricks, she thought furiously and pulled down the zipper of her skirt. Show people. She should be used to their orchestrations by now.

She remembered a meeting with a well-known comedian the month before. He had tried out a twenty-minute routine on her before he had settled down to discuss plans for a guest appearance on a Swan Production presentation. All the business with the Tarot cards had been just a show, designed to impress her, she decided and kicked off her shoes. Just another ego trip for an insecure performer.

Ryan frowned as she unbuttoned her blouse. She couldn't agree with her own conclusions. Pierce Atkins didn't strike her as an insecure man—on stage or off. And she would have sworn he had been as surprised as she when she had turned over that card. Ryan shrugged out of her blouse and tossed it over a chair. Well, he was an actor, she reminded herself. What else was a magician but a clever actor with clever hands?

She remembered the look of his hands on the black marble chess pieces, their leanness, their grace. She shook off the memory. Tomorrow she would get his name on that contract and drive away. He had made her uneasy; even before the little production with the cards, he had made her uneasy. Those eyes, Ryan thought and shivered. There's something about his eyes.

It was simply that he had a very strong personality, she decided. He was magnetic and yes, very attractive. He'd cultivated that, just as he had no doubt cultivated the mysterious air and enigmatic smile.

Lightning flashed, and Ryan jolted. She hadn't been completely honest with Pierce: storms played havoc with her nerves. Intellectually, she could brush it aside, but lightning and thunder always had her stomach tightening. She hated the weakness, a primarily feminine weakness. Pierce had been right; Bennett Swan had wanted a son. Ryan had gone through her life working hard to make up for being born female.

Go to bed, she ordered herself. Go to bed, pull the covers over your head and shut your eyes. Purposefully, she walked over to draw the drapes. She stared at the window. Something stared back. She screamed.

Ryan was across the room like a shot. Her damp palms skidded off the knob. When Pierce opened the door, she fell into his arms and held on.

"Ryan, what the hell's going on?" He would have drawn her away, but the arms around his neck were locked tight. She was very small without her heels. He could feel the shape of her body as she pressed desperately against him. Through concern and curiosity, Pierce experienced a swift and powerful wave of desire. Annoyed, he pulled her firmly away and held her arms.

"What is it?" he demanded.

"The window," she managed, and would have been back in his arms again if he hadn't held her off. "At the window by the bed."

Setting her aside, he walked to it. Ryan put both hands to her mouth and backed into the door, slamming it.

She heard Pierce's low oath as he drew up the glass and reached outside. He pulled in a very large, very wet black cat. On a moan, Ryan slumped against the door.

"Oh, God, what next?" she wondered aloud.

"Circe." Pierce set the cat on the floor. She shook herself once, then leaped onto the bed. "I didn't realize she was outside in this." He turned to look at Ryan. If he had laughed at her, she would never have forgiven him. But there was apology in his eyes, not amusement. "I'm sorry. She must have given you quite a scare. Can I get you a brandy?"

"No." Ryan let out a long breath. "Brandy doesn't do anything for acute embarrassment."

"Being frightened is nothing to be embarrassed about."

Her legs were still shaking, so she stayed propped against the door. "You might warn me if you have any more pets." Making the effort, she managed a smile. "That way, if I wake up with a wolf in bed with me, I can shrug it off and go back to sleep."

He didn't answer. As she watched, his eyes drifted slowly down her body. Ryan became aware she wore only a thin silk teddy. She straightened bolt upright against the door. But when his eyes came back to hers, she couldn't move, couldn't speak. Her breath had started to tremble before he took the first step toward her.

Tell him to go! her mind shouted, but her lips wouldn't form the words. She couldn't look away from his eyes. When he stopped in front of her, her head tilted back so that the look continued to hold. She could feel her pulse hammer at her wrists, at her throat, at her breast. Her whole body vibrated with it.

I want him. The knowledge stunned her. *I've never wanted a man the way I want him.* Her breath was audible now. His was calm and even. Slowly, Pierce took his finger to her shoulder and pushed aside the strap. It fell loosely on her arm. Ryan didn't move. He watched her intensely as he brushed aside the second strap. The bodice of the teddy fluttered to the points of her breasts and clung tenuously. A careless movement of his hand would have it falling to her feet. She stood transfixed.

Pierce lifted both hands, pushing the hair back from her face. He let his fingers dive deep into it. He leaned closer, then hesitated. Ryan's lips trembled apart. He watched her eyes shut before his mouth touched hers.

His lips were firm and gentle. At first they barely touched hers, just tasted. Then he lingered for a moment, keeping the kiss soft. A promise or a threat; Ryan wasn't certain. Her legs were about to buckle. In defense, she curled her hands around his arms. There were muscles, hard, firm muscles that she wouldn't think of until much later. Now she thought only of his mouth. He was barely kissing her at all, yet the shock of the impact winded her.

Degree by aching degree he deepened the kiss. Ryan's fingers tightened desperately on his arms. His mouth brushed over hers, then came back with more pressure. His tongue feathered lightly over hers. He only touched her hair, though her body tempted him. He drew out every ounce of pleasure with his mouth alone.

He knew what it was to be hungry—for food, for love, for a woman—but he hadn't experienced this raw, painful need in years. He wanted the taste of her, only the taste of her. It was at once sweet and pungent. As he drew it inside him, he knew there would come a time when he would take more. But for now her lips were enough.

When he knew he had reached the border between backing away and taking her Pierce lifted his head. He waited for Ryan to open her eyes.

Her green eyes were darkened, cloudy. He saw that she

was as stunned as she was aroused. He knew he could take her there, where they stood. He had only to kiss her again, had only to brush aside the brief swatch of silk she wore. But he did neither. Ryan's fingers loosened, then her hands dropped away from his arms. Saying nothing, Pierce moved around her and opened the door. The cat leaped off the bed to slip through the crack before Pierce shut it behind him.

Chapter 3

By morning the only sign of the storm was the steady drip of water from the balcony outside Ryan's bedroom window. She dressed carefully. It was important that she be perfectly poised and collected when she went downstairs. It would have been easier if she could have convinced herself that she had been dreaming—that Pierce had never come to her room, that he had never given her that strange, draining kiss. But it had been no dream.

Ryan was too much a realist to pretend otherwise or to make excuses. A great deal of what had happened had been her fault, she admitted as she folded yesterday's suit. She had acted like a fool, screaming because a cat had wanted in out of the rain. She had thrown herself into Pierce's arms wearing little more than shattered nerves. And lastly and most disturbing she had made no protest. Ryan was forced to concede that Pierce had given her ample time to object. But she had done nothing, made no struggle, voiced no indignant protest.

Maybe he had hypnotized her, she thought grimly as she brushed her hair into order. The way he had looked at her, the way her mind had gone blank... With a sound of frustration, Ryan tossed the brush into her suitcase. You couldn't be hypnotized with a look.

If she was to deal with it, she first had to admit it. She had wanted him to kiss her. And when he had, her senses had ruled her. Ryan clicked the locks on the suitcase, then set it next to the door. She would have gone to bed with him. It was a cold, hard fact, and there was no getting around it. Had he stayed, she would have made love with him—a man she had known for a matter of hours.

Ryan drew a deep breath and gave herself a moment before opening the door. It was a difficult truth to face for a woman who prided herself on acting with common sense and practicality. She had come to get Pierce Atkins's name on a contract, not to sleep with him.

You haven't done either yet, she reminded herself with a grimace. And it was morning. Time to concentrate on the first and forget the second. Ryan opened the door and started downstairs.

The house was quiet. After peeking into the parlor and finding it empty, she continued down the hall. Though her mind was set on finding Pierce and completing the business she had come for, an open door to her right tempted her to stop. The first glance drew a sound of pleasure from her.

There were walls—literally walls—of books. Ryan had never seen so many in a private collection, not even her father's. Somehow she knew these books were more than an investment, they were read. Pierce would know each one of them. She walked into the room for a closer look. There was a scent of leather and of candles.

The Unmasking of Robert-Houdin, by Houdini; *The*

Edge of the Unknown, by Arthur Conan Doyle; *Les Illusionnistes et Leurs Secrets.* These and dozens of other books on magic and magicians Ryan expected. But there was also T. H. White, Shakespeare, Chaucer, the poems of Byron and Shelley. Scattered among them were works by Fitzgerald, Mailer and Bradbury. Not all were leather bound or aged and valuable. Ryan thought of her father, who would know what each of his books cost, down to the last dollar and who had read no more than a dozen in his collection.

He has very eclectic taste, she mused as she wandered the room. On the mantelpiece were carved, painted figures she recognized as inhabitants of Tolkien's Middle Earth. There was a very modern metal sculpture on the desk.

Who is this man? Ryan wondered. Who is he really? Lyrical, fanciful, with hints of a firm realist beneath. It annoyed her to realize just how badly she wanted to discover the full man.

"Miss Swan?"

Ryan swung around to see Link filling the doorway. "Oh, good morning." She wasn't certain if his expression was disapproving or if it was simply her impression of his unfortunate face. "I'm sorry," she added. "Shouldn't I have come in here?"

Link lifted his massive shoulders in a shrug. "He would have locked it if he wanted you to stay out."

"Yes, of course," Ryan murmured, not certain if she should feel insulted or amused.

"Pierce said you can wait for him downstairs after you've had breakfast."

"Has he gone out?"

"Running," Link said shortly. "He runs five miles every day."

"Five miles?" But Link was already turning away. Ryan dashed across the room to keep up.

"I'll make your breakfast," he told her.

"Just coffee—tea," she corrected, remembering. She didn't know what to call him but realized that she would soon be too breathless from trying to keep pace with him to call him anything. "Link." Ryan touched his arm, and he stopped. "I saw your work on the piano last night." He was looking at her steadily, without any change of expression. "I hope you don't mind." He shrugged again. Ryan concluded he used the gesture often in place of words. "It's a beautiful melody," she continued. "Really lovely."

To her astonishment, he blushed. Ryan hadn't thought it possible for a man of his size to be embarrassed. "It's not finished," he mumbled, with his wide, ugly face growing pinker.

Ryan smiled at him, touched. "What is finished is beautiful. You have a wonderful gift."

He shuffled his feet, then mumbled something about getting her tea and lumbered off. Ryan smiled at his retreating back before she walked to the dining room.

Link brought her toast, with a grumble about her having to eat something. Ryan finished it off dutifully, thinking of Pierce's remark about face value. If nothing else came of her odd visit, she had learned something. Ryan didn't believe she would ever again make snap decisions about someone based on appearance.

Though she deliberately loitered over the meal, there was still no sign of Pierce when Ryan had finished. Reluctance to brave the lower floor again had her sipping at cold tea and waiting. At length, with a sigh, she rose, picked up her briefcase and headed down the stairs.

Someone had switched on the lights, and Ryan was grateful. The room wasn't brilliantly illuminated; it was too large for the light to reach all the corners. But the feeling of apprehension Ryan had experienced the day before didn't materialize. This time she knew what to expect.

Spotting Merlin standing in his cage, she walked over to him. The door of the cage was open, so she stood cautiously to the side as she studied him. She didn't want to encourage him to perch on her shoulder again, particularly since Pierce wasn't there to lure him away.

"Good morning," she said, curious as to whether he'd talk to her when she was alone.

Merlin eyed her a moment. "Buy you a drink, sweetie?"

Ryan laughed and decided Merlin's trainer had an odd sense of humor. "I don't fall for that line," she told him and bent down until they were eye to eye. "What else can you say?" she wondered out loud. "I bet he's taught you quite a bit. He'd have the patience for it." She grinned, amused that the bird seemed to be listening attentively to her conversation. "Are you a smart bird, Merlin?" she demanded.

"Alas, poor Yorick!" he said obligingly.

"Good grief, the bird quotes *Hamlet*." Shaking her head, Ryan turned toward the stage. There were two large trunks, a wicker hamper and a long, waist-high table. Curious, Ryan set down her briefcase and mounted the stairs. On the table was a deck of playing cards, a pair of empty cylinders, wine bottles and glasses and a pair of handcuffs.

Ryan picked up the playing cards and wondered fleetingly how he marked them. She could see nothing, even when she held them up to the light. Setting them aside, she examined the handcuffs. They appeared to be regulation police issue. Cold, steel, unsympathetic. She searched the table for a key and found none.

Ryan had done her research on Pierce thoroughly. She

knew there wasn't supposed to be a lock made that could hold him. He had been shackled hand and foot and stuffed into a triple-locked steamer trunk. In less than three minutes he had been out, unmanacled. Impressive, she admitted, still studying the cuffs. Where was the trick?

"Miss Swan."

Ryan dropped the handcuffs with a clatter as she spun around. Pierce stood directly behind her. But he couldn't have come down the stairs, she thought. She would have heard, or certainly seen. Obviously, there was another entrance to his workroom. And how long, she wondered, had he been standing and watching? He was doing no more than that now while the cat busied herself by winding around his ankles.

"Mr. Atkins," she managed in a calm enough voice.

"I hope you slept well." He crossed to the table to join her. "The storm didn't keep you awake?"

"No."

For a man who had just run five miles, he looked remarkably fresh. Ryan remembered the muscles in his arms. There was strength in him, and obviously stamina. His eyes were very steady, almost measuring, on hers. There was no hint of the restrained passion she had felt from him the night before.

Abruptly, Pierce smiled at her, then gestured with his hand. "What do you see here?"

Ryan glanced at the table again. "Some of your tools."

"Ah, Miss Swan, your feet are always on the ground."

"I like to think so," she returned, annoyed. "What should I see?"

He seemed pleased with her response and poured a small amount of wine into a glass. "The imagination, Miss Swan, is an incredible gift. Do you agree?"

"Yes, of course." She watched his hands carefully. "To a point."

"To a point." He laughed a little and showed her the empty cylinders. "Can there be restrictions on the imagination?" He slipped one cylinder inside the other. "Don't you find the possibilities of the power of the mind over the laws of nature interesting?" Pierce placed the cylinders over the wine bottle, watching her.

Ryan was frowning at his hands now. "As a theory," she replied.

"But only a theory." Pierce slipped one cylinder out and set it over the wineglass. Lifting the first cylinder, he showed her that the bottle remained under it. "Not in practice."

"No." Ryan kept her eyes on his hands. He could hardly pull anything off right under her nose.

"Where's the glass, Miss Swan?"

"It's there." She pointed to the second cylinder.

"Is it?" Pierce lifted the tube. The bottle stood under it. With a sound of frustration, Ryan looked at the other tube. Pierce lifted it, revealing the partially filled glass. "They seem to have found the theory more viable," he stated and dropped the cylinders back in place.

"That's very clever," she said, irritated that she had stood inches away and not seen the trick.

"Would you care for some wine, Miss Swan?"

"No, I…"

Even as she spoke, Pierce lifted the cylinder. There, where she had just seen the bottle, stood the glass. Charmed despite herself, Ryan laughed. "You're very good, Mr. Atkins."

"Thank you."

He said it so soberly, Ryan looked back at him. His

eyes were calm and thoughtful. Intrigued, she tilted her head. "I don't suppose you'd tell me how you did it."

"No."

"I didn't think so." She lifted the handcuffs. The briefcase at the foot of the stage was, for the moment, forgotten. "Are these part of your act, too? They look real."

"They're quite real," he told her. He was smiling again, pleased that she had laughed. He knew it was a sound he would be able to hear clearly whenever he thought of her.

"There's no key," Ryan pointed out.

"I don't need one."

She passed the cuffs from hand to hand as she studied him. "You're very sure of yourself."

"Yes." The hint of amusement in the word made her wonder what twist his thoughts had taken. He held out his hands, wrists close. "Go ahead," he invited. "Put them on."

Ryan hesitated only a moment. She wanted to see him do it—right there in front of her eyes. "If you can't get them off," she said as she snapped the cuffs into place, "we'll just sit down and talk about those contracts." She glanced up at him, eyes dancing. "When you've signed them, we can send for a locksmith."

"I don't think we'll need one." Pierce held up the cuffs, dangling and open.

"Oh, but how..." She trailed off and shook her head. "No, that was too quick," she insisted, taking them back from him. Pierce appreciated the way her expression changed from astonishment to doubt. It was precisely what he had expected from her. "You had them made." She was turning them over, searching closely. "There must be a button or something."

"Why don't you try it?" he suggested and had the cuffs

snapped on her wrists before she could decline. Pierce waited to see if she'd be angry. She laughed.

"I talked myself right into that one." Ryan gave him a good-humored grimace, then concentrated on the cuffs. She juggled her wrists. "They certainly feel real enough." Though she tried several different angles, the steel held firmly shut. "If there's a button," she muttered, "you'd have to dislocate your wrist to get to it." She tugged another moment, then tried to slip her hands through the opening. "All right, you win," she announced, giving up. "They're real." Ryan grinned up at him. "Can you get me out of these?"

"Maybe," he murmured, taking her wrists in his hands.

"That's a comforting answer," she returned dryly, but they both felt her pulse leap as his thumb brushed over it. He continued to stare down at her until she felt the same draining weakness she had experienced the night before. "I think," she began, her voice husky as she struggled to clear it. "I think you'd better..." The sentence trailed off as his fingers traced the vein in her wrist. "Don't," she said, not even certain what she was trying to refuse.

Silently, Pierce lifted her hands, slipping them over his head so that she was pressed against him.

She wouldn't allow it to happen twice. This time she would protest. "No." Ryan tugged once, uselessly, but his mouth was already on hers.

This time his mouth wasn't so patient or his hands so still. Pierce held her hips as his tongue urged her lips apart. Ryan fought against the helplessness—a helplessness that had more to do with her own needs than the restraints on her wrists. She was responding totally. Under the pressure of his, her lips were hungry. His were cool and firm while hers heated and softened. She heard him murmur something as he dragged her closer. An incantation, she thought dizzily. He was bewitching her; there was no other explanation.

But it was a moan of pleasure, not of protest, that slipped from her when his hands trailed up to the sides of her breasts. He drew slow, aching circles before his thumbs slipped between their bodies to stroke over her nipples. Ryan pressed closer, nipping at his bottom lip as she craved more. His hands were in her hair, pulling her head back so that his lips had complete command of hers.

Perhaps he was magic. His mouth was. No one else had ever made her ache and burn with only a kiss.

Ryan wanted to touch him, to make him hunger as desperately as she. She fretted against the restraints on her wrists, only to find her hands were free. Her fingers could caress his neck, run through his hair.

Then, as quickly as she had been captured, she was released. Pierce had his hands on her shoulders, holding her away.

Confused, still aching, Ryan stared up at him. "Why?"

Pierce didn't answer for a moment. Absently, he caressed her shoulders. "I wanted to kiss Miss Swan. Last night I kissed Ryan."

"You're being ridiculous." She started to jerk away, but his hands were suddenly firm.

"No. Miss Swan wears conservative suits and worries about contracts. Ryan wears silk and lace underneath and is frightened of storms. The combination fascinates me."

His words troubled her enough to make her voice cool and sharp. "I'm not here to fascinate you, Mr. Atkins."

"A side benefit, Miss Swan." He grinned, then kissed her fingers. Ryan jerked her hand away.

"It's time we settled our business one way or the other."

"You're right, Miss Swan." She didn't like the hint of

amusement or the way he emphasized her name. Ryan found she no longer cared whether or not he signed the papers she carried. She simply wanted to shake loose of him.

"Well, then," she began and stooped to pick up her briefcase.

Pierce laid his hand over hers on the handle. His fingers closed gently. "I'm willing to sign your contracts with a few adjustments."

Ryan schooled herself to relax. Adjustments normally meant money. She'd negotiate with him and be done with it. "I'll be glad to discuss any changes you might want."

"That's fine. I'll want to work with you directly. I want you to handle Swan's end of the production."

"Me?" Ryan's fingers tightened on the handle again. "I don't get involved with the production end. My father—"

"I'm not going to work with your father, Miss Swan, or any other producer." His hand was still gently closed over hers, with the contracts between them. "I'm going to work with you."

"Mr. Atkins, I appreciate—"

"I'll need you in Vegas in two weeks."

"In Vegas? Why?"

"I want you to watch my performances—closely. There's nothing more valuable to an illusionist than a cynic. You'll keep me sharp." He smiled. "You're very critical. I like that."

Ryan heaved a sigh. She would have thought criticism would annoy, not attract. "Mr. Atkins, I'm a businesswoman, not a producer."

"You told me you were good at details," he reminded her amiably. "If I'm going to break my own rule and perform on television, I want someone like you handling the details. More to the point," he continued, "I want *you* handling the details."

"You're not being practical, Mr. Atkins. I'm sure your agent would agree. There are any number of people at Swan Productions who are better qualified to produce your special. I don't have any experience in that end of the business."

"Miss Swan, do you want me to sign your contracts?"

"Yes, of course, but—"

"Then make the changes," he said simply. "And be at Caesar's Palace in two weeks. I have a week's run." Stooping, he lifted the cat into his arms. "I'll look forward to working with you."

Chapter 4

When she stalked into her office at Swan Productions four hours later, Ryan was still fuming. He had nerve, she decided. She would give him top of the list for nerve. He thought he had her boxed into a corner. Did he really imagine he was the only name talent she could sign for Swan Productions? What outrageous conceit! Ryan slammed her briefcase down on her desk and flopped into the chair behind it. Pierce Atkins was in for a surprise.

Leaning back in her chair, Ryan folded her hands and waited until she was calm enough to think. Pierce didn't know Bennett Swan. Swan liked to run things his own way. Advice could be considered, discussed, but he would never be swayed on a major decision. As a matter of fact, she mused, he would more than likely go in the opposite direction he was pushed. He wouldn't appreciate being told who to put in charge of a production.

Particularly, Ryan thought ruefully, when that person was his daughter.

There was going to be an explosion when she told her father of Pierce's conditions. Her only regret was that the magician wouldn't be there to feel the blast. Swan would find another hot property to sign, and Pierce could go back to making wine bottles disappear.

Ryan brooded into space. The last thing she wanted to do was worry about rehearsal calls and shooting schedules—and all the thousands of other niggling details involved in producing an hour show—not to mention the outright paranoia of it being a live telecast. What did she know about dealing with technical breakdowns and union rules and set designing? Producing was a complicated job. She had never had any desire to try her hand at that end of the business. She was perfectly content with the paperwork and preproduction details.

She leaned forward again, elbows on the desk, and cupped her chin in her hands. How foolish it is, she mused, to lie to yourself. And how fulfilling it would be to follow through on a project from beginning to end. She had ideas—so many ideas that were constantly being restricted by legal niceties.

Whenever she had tried to convince her father to give her a chance on the creative side, she had met the same unyielding wall. She didn't have the experience; she was too young. He conveniently forgot that she had been around the business all of her life and that she would be twenty-seven the following month.

One of the most talented directors in the business had done a film for Swan that had netted five Oscars. And he'd been twenty-six, Ryan remembered indignantly. How could Swan know if her ideas were gold or trash if he wouldn't listen to them? All she needed was one opportunity.

No, she had to admit that nothing would suit her better than to follow a project from signing to wrap party. But not this one. This time she would cheerfully admit failure and toss the contracts and Pierce Atkins right back in her father's lap. There was enough Swan in her to get her back up when given an ultimatum.

Change the contracts. With a snort of derision, Ryan flipped open her briefcase. He overplayed his hand, she thought, and now he'll... She stopped, staring down at the neatly stacked papers inside the case. On top of them was another long-stemmed rose.

"Now how did he..." Ryan's own laughter cut her off. Leaning back, she twirled the flower under her nose. He was clever, she mused, drawing in the scent. Very clever. But who the devil was he? What made him tick? Sitting there in her tailored, organized office, Ryan decided she very much wanted to know. Perhaps it would be worth an explosion and a bit of conniving to find out.

There were depths to a man who spoke quietly and could command with his eyes alone. Layers, she thought. How many layers would she have to peel off to get to the core of him? It would be risky, she decided, but... Shaking her head, Ryan reminded herself that she wasn't going to be given the opportunity to find out, in any case. Swan would either sign him on his own terms or forget him. She drew out the contracts, then snapped the briefcase shut. Pierce Atkins was her father's problem now. Still, she kept the rose in her hand.

The buzzer on her phone reminded her she didn't have time for daydreaming. "Yes, Barbara."

"The boss wants to see you."

Ryan grimaced at the intercom. Swan would have

known she was back the moment she passed the guard at the gate. "Right away," she agreed. Leaving the rose on her desk, Ryan took the contracts with her.

Bennett Swan smoked an expensive Cuban cigar. He liked expensive things. More, he liked knowing his money could buy them. If there were two suits of equal cut and value, Swan would choose the one with the biggest price tag. It was a matter of pride.

The awards in his office were also a matter of pride. Swan Productions was Bennett Swan. Oscars and Emmys proved he was a success. The paintings and sculptures his art broker had advised him to purchase showed the world that he knew the value of success.

He loved his daughter, would have been shocked if anyone had said otherwise. There was no doubt in his mind that he was an excellent father. He had always given Ryan everything his money could buy: the best clothes, an Irish nanny when her mother had died, an expensive education, then a comfortable job when she had insisted on working.

He had been forced to admit that the girl had more on the ball than he had expected. Ryan had a sharp brain and a way of cutting through the nonsense and getting to the heart of a matter. It proved to him that the money spent on the Swiss school had been well spent. Not that he would begrudge his daughter the finest education. Swan expected results.

He watched the smoke curl from the tip of his cigar. Ryan had paid off for him. He was very fond of his daughter.

She knocked, then entered when he called out. He watched her cross the wide space of thick carpet to his desk. A pretty girl, he thought. Looks like her mother.

"You wanted to see me?" She waited for the signal to

sit. Swan wasn't a big man but had always made up for his lack of size with expansiveness. The wide sweep of his arm told her to sit. His face was still handsome in the rugged, outdoorsy manner women found appealing. He had put on a bit of flesh in the last five years and had lost a bit of hair. Essentially, however, he looked the same as Ryan's earliest memory of him. Looking at him, she felt the familiar surge of love and frustration. Ryan knew too well the limitations of her father's affection for her.

"You're feeling better?" she asked, noting that his bout with the flu hadn't left any mark of sickness on him. His face was healthily ruddy, his eyes clear. With another sweeping gesture, he brushed the question aside. Swan was impatient with illness, particularly his own. He didn't have time for it.

"What did you think of Atkins?" he demanded the moment Ryan was settled. It was one of the small concessions Swan made to her, the asking of her opinion on another. As always, Ryan thought carefully before answering.

"He's a unique man," she began in a tone that would have made Pierce smile. "He has extraordinary talent and a very strong personality. I'm not sure that one isn't the cause for the other."

"Eccentric?"

"No, not in the sense that he does things to promote an eccentric image." Ryan frowned as she thought of his house, his life-style. *Face value.* "I think he's a very deep man and one who lives precisely as he chooses. His profession is more than a career. He's dedicated to it the way an artist is to painting."

Swan nodded and blew out a cloud of expensive smoke. "He's hot box office."

Ryan smiled and shifted the contracts. "Yes, because

he's probably the best at what he does; plus he's dynamic on stage and a bit mysterious off it. He seems to have locked up the beginnings of his life and tossed away the key. The public loves a puzzle. He gives them one."

"And the contracts?"

Here it comes, Ryan thought, bracing herself. "He's willing to sign, but with certain conditions. That is, he—"

"He told me about his conditions," Swan interrupted.

Ryan's carefully thought out dissertation was thrown to the winds. "He told you?"

"Phoned a couple of hours ago." Swan plucked the cigar from his mouth. The diamond on his finger shot light as he eyed his daughter. "He says you're cynical and dedicated to details. That's what he claims he wants."

"I simply don't believe his tricks were anything but clever staging," Ryan countered, annoyed that Pierce had spoken to Swan before she had. She felt, uncomfortably, as if she were playing chess again. He'd already outmatched her once. "He has a habit of incorporating his magic into the everyday. It's effective, but distracting at a business meeting."

"Insulting him seems to have turned the trick," Swan commented.

"I didn't insult him!" At that Ryan rose with the contracts in her hand. "I spent twenty-four hours in that house with talking birds and black cats, and I didn't insult him. I did everything I could to get his name on these except letting him saw me in half." She dropped the papers on her father's desk. "There are limits to what I'll do to humor the talent, no matter how hot they are at the box office."

Swan steepled his fingers and watched her. "He also said he didn't mind your temper. He doesn't like to be bored."

Ryan bit off the next words that sprang to mind. Carefully, she sat back down. "All right, you told me what he said to you. What did you say to him?"

Swan took his time answering. It was the first time anyone connected with the business had referred to Ryan's temper. Swan knew she had one and knew, too, that she kept it scrupulously controlled on the job. He decided to let it pass. "I told him we'd be glad to oblige him."

"You…" Ryan choked on the word and tried again. "You agreed? Why?"

"We want him. He wants you."

No explosion, she thought, not a little confused. What spell had Pierce used to manage this one? Whatever it was, she told herself grimly, she wasn't under it. She rose again. "Do I have any say in this?"

"Not as long as you work for me." Swan gave the contracts an idle glance. "You've been itching to do something along these lines for a couple of years," he reminded her. "I'm giving you your chance. And," he looked up then and met her eyes, "I'll be watching you closely. If you mess it up, I'll pull you."

"I'm not going to mess it up," she retorted, barely controlling a new wave of fury. "It'll be the best damn special Swan's ever produced."

"Just see that it is," he warned. "And that you don't go over budget. Take care of the changes and send the new contracts to his agent. I want him signed before the end of the week."

"He will be." Ryan scooped up the papers before she headed for the door.

"Atkins said you two would work well together," Swan added as she yanked the door open. "He said it was in the cards."

Ryan shot an infuriated glance over her shoulder before she marched out, slamming the door behind her.

Swan grinned a little. She certainly did favor her mother, he thought, then pushed a button to summon his secretary. He had another appointment.

If there was one thing Ryan detested, it was being manipulated. By the time her temper had cooled and she was back in her office, it dawned on her how smoothly both Pierce and her father had maneuvered her. She didn't mind it as much from Swan—he had had years to learn that to suggest she might not be able to handle something was the certain way to see that she did. Pierce was a different matter. He didn't know her at all, or shouldn't have. Yet he had handled her, subtly, expertly, in the same the-hand-is-quicker-than-the-eye fashion he had handled the empty cylinders. He had what he wanted. Ryan drafted out the new contracts and brooded.

She had gotten past that one little point, and she had what she wanted as well. She decided to look at the entire matter from a new angle. Swan Productions would have Pierce sewed up for three prime-time specials, and she would have her chance to produce.

Ryan Swan, Executive Producer. She smiled. Yes, she liked the sound of it. She said it again to herself and felt the first stirring of excitement. Pulling out her date book, Ryan began to calculate how quickly she could tie up loose ends and devote herself to the production.

Ryan had plowed through an hour's paperwork when the phone interrupted her. "Ryan Swan," she answered briskly, balancing the receiver on her shoulder as she continued to scribble.

"Miss Swan, I've interrupted you."

No one else called her *Miss Swan* in just that way. Ryan broke off the sentence she had been composing and forgot it. "That's all right, Mr. Atkins. What can I do for you?"

He laughed, annoying her instantly.

"What's so funny?"

"You've a lovely business voice, Miss Swan," he said with the trace of humor still lingering. "I thought, with your penchant for detail, you'd like to have the dates I'll need you in Vegas."

"The contracts aren't signed yet, Mr. Atkins," Ryan began primly.

"I open on the fifteenth," he told her as if she hadn't spoken. "But rehearsals begin on the twelfth. I'd like you there for them as well." Ryan frowned, marking down the dates. She could almost see him sitting in his library, holding the cat in his lap. "I close on the twenty-first." She noted idly that the twenty-first was her birthday.

"All right. We could begin outlining the production of the special the following week."

"Good." Pierce paused a moment. "I wonder if I could ask you for something, Miss Swan."

"You could ask," Ryan said cautiously.

Pierce grinned and scratched Circe's ears. "I have an engagement in L.A. on the eleventh. Would you come with me?"

"The eleventh?" Ryan shifted the phone and turned back the pages of her desk calendar. "What time?"

"Two o'clock."

"Yes, all right." She marked it down. "Where should I meet you?"

"I'll pick you up—one-thirty."

"One-thirty. Mr. Atkins…" She hesitated, then picked up the rose on her desk. "Thank you for the flower."

"You're welcome, Ryan."

Pierce hung up, then sat for a moment, lost in thought.

He imagined Ryan was holding the rose even now. Did she know that her skin was as soft as its petals? Her face, just at the jawline—he could still clearly feel its texture on his fingertips. He ran them down the cat's back. "What did you think of her, Link?"

The big man continued to push books back into place and didn't turn. "She has a nice laugh."

"Yes, I thought so, too." Pierce could remember the tone of it perfectly; it had been unexpected, a stark contrast to her serious expression of a moment before. Both her laugh and her passion had surprised him. He remembered the way her mouth had heated under his. He hadn't been able to work at all that night, thinking of her upstairs in bed with only that swatch of silk covering her.

He didn't like having his concentration disturbed, yet he was pulling her back. Instinct, he reminded himself. He was still following his instinct.

"She said she liked my music," Link murmured, still shuffling books.

Pierce glanced up, bringing his thoughts back. He knew how sensitive Link was about his music. "She did like it, very much. She thought the melody you'd left on the piano was beautiful."

Link nodded, knowing Pierce would tell him nothing but the truth. "You like her, don't you?"

"Yes." Pierce answered absently as he stroked the cat. "Yes, I believe I do."

"I guess you must want to do this TV thing."

"It's a challenge," Pierce replied.

Link turned then. "Pierce?"

"Hmmm?"

He hesitated to ask, afraid he already knew the answer. "Are you going to do the new escape in Las Vegas?"

"No." Pierce frowned, and Link felt a flood of relief. Pierce remembered that he'd been trying to work on that particular escape the night Ryan had stayed in his house in the room just down the hall from his own. "No, I haven't worked it all out yet." Link's relief was short-lived. "I'll use it for the special instead."

"I don't like it." It came out quickly, causing Pierce to look up again. "Too many things can go wrong."

"Nothing's going to go wrong, Link. It just needs some more work before I use it in the act."

"The timing's too close," Link insisted, taking an un-characteristic step by arguing. "You could make some changes or just postpone it. I don't like it, Pierce," he said again, knowing it was useless.

"You worry too much," Pierce assured him. "It's going to be fine. I just have a few more things to work out."

But he wasn't thinking of the mechanics of his escape. He was thinking of Ryan.

Chapter 5

Ryan caught herself watching the clock. *One-fifteen.* The days before the eleventh had gone quickly. She had been up to her ears in paperwork, often working ten hours a day trying to clear her desk before the trip to Las Vegas. She wanted a clear road and no lingering contractual problems hanging over her head once she began work on the special. She would make up for lack of experience by giving the project all of her time and attention.

She still had something to prove—to herself, to her father, and now, to Pierce. There was more to Ryan Swan than contracts and clauses.

Yes, the days had gone quickly, she mused, but this last hour...*one-seventeen.* With a sound of annoyance, Ryan pulled out a file folder and opened it. She was watching the clock as if she were waiting for a date rather than a business appointment. That was ridiculous. Still, when the knock came, her head shot up and she forgot the neatly typed pages in the folder. Pushing away a surge of anticipation, Ryan answered calmly.

"Yes, come in."

"Hi, Ryan."

She struggled with disappointment as Ned Ross strolled into the room. He gave her a polished smile.

"Hello, Ned."

Ned Ross—thirty-two, blond and personable with casual California chic. He let his hair curl freely and wore expensive designer slacks with quiet silk shirts. No tie, Ryan noted. It went against his image, just as the subtle whiff of breezy cologne suited it. Ned knew the effects of his charm, which he used purposefully.

Ryan chided herself half-heartedly for being critical and returned his smile, though hers was a great deal cooler.

Ned was her father's second assistant. For several months, up to a few weeks ago, he had also been Ryan's constant escort. He had wined and dined her, given her a few thrilling lessons in surfing, showed her the beauty of the beach at sunset and made her believe she was the most attractive, desirable woman he had ever met. It had been a painful disillusionment when she had discovered he was more interested in cultivating Bennett Swan's daughter than Ryan herself.

"The boss wanted me to check in with you, see how things were shaping up before you take off for Vegas." He sat on the corner of her desk, then leaned over to give her a light kiss. He still had plans for his boss's daughter. "And I wanted to say goodbye."

"All my work's cleared up," Ryan told him, casually shifting the file folder between them. It was still difficult to believe that the attractive, tanned face and amiable smile masked an ambitious liar. "I intended to bring my father up to date myself."

"He's tied up," Ned told her easily and picked up the folder to flip through it. "Just took off for New York. Something on a location shoot he wants to see to personally. He won't be back until the end of the week."

"Oh." Ryan looked down at her hands. He might have taken a moment to call her, she thought, then sighed. When had he ever? And when would she ever stop expecting him to? "Well, you can tell him everything's taken care of." She took the folder back from him and set it down again. "I've a report written out."

"Always efficient." Ned smiled at her again but made no move to leave. He knew too well he had made a misstep with Ryan and had some lost ground to cover. "So, how do you feel about moving up to producer?"

"I'm looking forward to it."

"This Atkins," Ned continued, overlooking the coolness, "he's kind of a strange guy, isn't he?"

"I don't know him well enough to say," Ryan said evasively. She found she didn't want to discuss Pierce with Ned. The day she had spent with him was hers, personally. "I have an appointment in a few minutes, Ned," she continued, rising. "So if you'd—"

"Ryan." Ned took her hands in his as he had habitually done when they had dated. The gesture had always made her smile. "I've really missed you these past weeks."

"We've seen each other several times, Ned." Ryan allowed her hands to lie limply in his.

"Ryan, you know what I mean." He massaged her wrists gently but felt no increase in her pulse. His voice softened persuasively. "You're still angry with me for making that stupid suggestion."

"About using my influence with my father to have you

head the O'Mara production?" Ryan lifted a brow. "No, Ned," she said evenly, "I'm not angry with you. I heard Bishop was given the job," she added, unable to resist the small jibe. "I hope you're not too disappointed."

"That's not important," he replied, masking his annoyance with a shrug. "Let me take you to dinner tonight." Ned drew her a fraction closer, and Ryan didn't resist. Just how far, she wondered, would he go? "That little French place you like so much. We could go for a drive up the coast and talk."

"Doesn't it occur to you that I might have a date?"

The question stopped him from lowering his mouth to hers. It hadn't occurred to him that she would be seeing anyone else. He was certain that she was still crazy about him. He had spent a lot of time and effort leading her to that end. He concluded she wanted to be persuaded.

"Break it," he murmured and kissed her softly, never noticing that her eyes stayed open and cold.

"No."

Ned hadn't expected a flat, unemotional refusal. He knew from experience that Ryan's emotions were easily tapped. He'd been prepared to disappoint a very friendly assistant director to be with Ryan again. Off guard, he raised his head to stare at her. "Come on, Ryan, don't be—"

"Excuse me." Ryan whipped her hands from Ned's and looked to the doorway. "Miss Swan," Pierce said with a nod.

"Mr. Atkins." She was flushed and furious to have been caught in a compromising situation in her own office. Why hadn't she told Ned to shut the door when he had come in? "Ned, this is Pierce Atkins. Ned Ross is my father's assistant."

"Mr. Ross." Pierce moved into the room but didn't extend his hand.

"A pleasure to meet you, Mr. Atkins." Ned flashed a smile. "I'm a big fan."

"Are you?" Pierce gave him a polite smile that made Ned feel as though he had been thrust into a very cold, very dark room.

His eyes faltered, then he turned back to Ryan. "Have a good time in Vegas, Ryan." He was already heading to the door. "Nice to have met you, Mr. Atkins."

Ryan watched Ned's hurried retreat with a frown. He had certainly lost his characteristic laid-back style. "What did you do to him?" she demanded when the door shut.

Pierce lifted a brow as he crossed to her. "What do you think I did?"

"I don't know," Ryan muttered. "But whatever you did to him don't ever do it to me."

"Your hands are cold, Ryan." He took them in his. "Why didn't you just tell him to go?"

He unnerved her when he called her Ryan. He unnerved her when he called her Miss Swan in the lightly mocking tone he used. Ryan looked down at their joined hands. "I did—that is, I was…" She caught herself, amazed that she was stammering out an explanation. "We'd better go if you're going to make your engagement, Mr. Atkins."

"Miss Swan." Pierce's eyes were full of humor as he lifted her hands to his lips. They were no longer cold. "I've missed that serious face and professional tone." Leaving her with nothing to say, Pierce took her arm and led her from the room.

Once they had settled in his car and joined the streaming traffic, Ryan tried for casual conversation. If they were going to be working closely together, she had to establish the correct relationship and quickly. *Queen's pawn to bishop two,* she thought, remembering the chess game. "What sort of engagement do you have this afternoon?"

Pierce stopped at a red light and glanced at her. His eyes met hers with brief but potent intensity. "A gig's a gig," he said enigmatically. "You're not fond of your father's assistant."

Ryan stiffened. He attacked, she defended. "He's good at his job."

"Why did you lie to him?" Pierce asked mildly when the light turned. "You could have told him you didn't want to have dinner with him instead of pretending you had a date."

"What makes you think I was pretending?" Ryan countered impulsively, hurt pride in her voice.

Pierce downshifted into second to take a corner and maneuvered his way around the point. "I simply wondered why you felt you had to."

Ryan didn't care for his calmness. "That's my affair, Mr. Atkins."

"Do you think we could drop the 'Mr. Atkins' for the afternoon?" Pierce pulled off into a lot and guided the car into a parking space. Then, turning his head, he smiled at her. He was, Ryan decided, entirely too charming when he smiled in just that way.

"Maybe," she agreed when her lips curved in response. "For the afternoon. Is Pierce your real name?"

"As far as I know." With this, he slid from the car. When Ryan climbed out her side, she noted they were in the parking lot of Los Angeles General Hospital.

"What are we doing here?"

"I have a show to do." Pierce took a black bag, not unlike one a doctor might use, from the trunk. "Tools of the trade," he told Ryan as she gave it a curious study. "No hypos or scalpels," he promised and held out a hand to her. His eyes were on hers, patient as she hesitated. Ryan accepted his hand, and together they walked through the side door.

Wherever Ryan had expected to spend the afternoon, it hadn't been in the pediatric ward of L.A. General. Whatever she had expected of Pierce Atkins, it hadn't been a communion with children. After the first five minutes, Ryan saw that he gave them much more than a show and a bagful of tricks. He gave himself.

Why, he's a beautiful man, she realized with something of a jolt. He plays in Vegas for thirty-five dollars a head, crams Covent Garden, but he comes here just to give a bunch of kids a good time. There were no reporters to note his humanitarianism and write it up in tomorrow's columns. He was giving his time and his talent for nothing more than bringing happiness. Or perhaps more accurately, she thought, relieving unhappiness.

That was the moment, though she didn't realize it, when Ryan fell in love.

She watched as he slipped a ball in and out of his fingers with continual motion. Ryan was as fascinated as the children. With a quick movement of his hand, the ball vanished, only to be plucked from the ear of a boy who squealed in delight.

His illusions were unsophisticated, flashy little bits of business an amateur could have performed. The ward was noisy with gasps and giggles and applause. It obviously meant more to Pierce than the thundering approval he heard on stage after a complicated feat of magic. His roots were there, among children. He had never forgotten it. He remembered too well the antiseptic and floral smell of a sick room and the confinement of a hospital bed. Boredom, he thought, could be the most debilitating disease there.

"You'll notice I brought along a beautiful assistant," Pierce pointed out. It took Ryan a moment to realize he meant her. Her eyes widened in astonishment, but he only smiled. "No magician travels without one. Ryan." He held out a hand, palm up. Amid giggles and applauses, she had no choice but to join him.

"What are you doing?" she demanded in a quick whisper.

"Making you a star," he said easily before turning back to the audience of children in beds and wheelchairs. "Ryan will tell you she keeps her lovely smile by drinking three glasses of milk every day. Isn't that so, Ryan?"

"Ah—yes." She glanced around at the expectant faces. "Yes, that's right." *What is he doing?* She'd never had so many large, curious eyes on her at one time.

"I'm sure everyone here knows how important it is to drink milk."

This was answered by some unenthusiastic agreements and a few muffled moans. Pierce looked surprised as he reached in his black bag and pulled out a glass already half-filled with white liquid. No one questioned why it hadn't spilled. "You do all drink milk, don't you?" He got laughter this time, along with more moans. Shaking his head, Pierce pulled out a newspaper and began to fashion it into a funnel. "This is a very tricky business. I don't know if I can make it work unless everyone promises to drink his milk tonight."

Immediately a chorus of promises sprang out. Ryan saw that he was as much Pied Piper as magician, as much psychologist as entertainer. Perhaps it was all the same. She noticed that Pierce was watching her with a lifted brow.

"Oh, I promise," she said agreeably and smiled. She was as entranced as the children.

"Let's see what happens," he suggested. "Do you suppose you could pour the milk from that glass into here?" he asked Ryan, handing her the glass. "Slowly," he warned, winking at the audience. "We wouldn't want to spill it. It's magic milk, you know. The only kind magicians drink." Pierce took her hand and guided it, holding the top of the funnel just above her eye level.

His palm was warm and firm. There hung about him some scent she couldn't place. It was of the outdoors, of the forest. Not pine, she decided, but something darker, deeper, closer to the earth. Her response to it was unexpected and unwanted. She tried to concentrate on holding the glass directly above the opening of the funnel. A few drops of milk dripped out of the bottom.

"Where do you buy magic milk?" one of the children wanted to know.

"Oh, you can't buy it," Pierce said gravely. "I have to get up very early and put a spell on a cow. There, now, that's good." Smoothly, Pierce dropped the empty glass back into his bag. "Now, if all's gone well…" He stopped, then frowned into the funnel. "This was my milk, Ryan," he said with a hint of censure. "You could have had yours later."

As she opened her mouth to speak, he whipped the funnel open. Automatically, she gasped and stepped back to keep from being splashed. But the funnel was empty.

The children shrieked in delight as she gasped at him. "She's still beautiful," he told the audience as he kissed Ryan's hand. "Even if she is greedy."

"I poured that milk myself," she stated later as they walked down the hospital corridor to the elevator. "It was dripping through the paper. I *saw* it."

Pierce nudged her into the elevator. "The way things seem and the way things are. Fascinating, isn't it, Ryan?"

She felt the elevator begin its descent and stood in silence for a moment. "You're not entirely what you seem, either, are you?"

"No. Who is?"

"You did more for those kids in an hour than a dozen doctors could have done." He looked down at her as she continued. "And I don't think it's the first time you've done this sort of thing."

"No."

"Why?"

"Hospitals are a hell of a place to be when you're a child," he said simply. It was all the answer he would give her.

"They didn't think so today."

Pierce took her hand in his again when they reached the first level. "There's no tougher audience than children. They're very literal-minded."

Ryan had to laugh. "I suppose you're right. What adult would have thought to ask you where you buy your magic milk?" She shot Pierce a look. "I thought you handled that one rather smoothly."

"I've had a bit of practice," he told her. "Kids keep you on your toes. Adults are more easily distracted by some clever patter and flash." He smiled down at her. "Even you. Though you watch me with very intriguing green eyes."

Ryan looked across the parking lot as they stepped outside. When he looked at her, it wasn't easy to focus on anything but him when he spoke. "Pierce, why did you ask me to come with you today?"

"I wanted your company."

Ryan turned back to him. "I don't think I understand."

"Do you have to?" he asked. In the sunlight her hair was the color of early wheat. Pierce ran his fingers through it, then framed her face with his hands as he had done that first night. "Always?"

Ryan's heart pounded in her throat. "Yes, I think…"

But his mouth was already on hers, and she could think no longer. It was just as it had been the first time. The gentle kiss drew everything from her. She felt a warm, fluttering ache pass through her as his fingers brushed her temple and then traveled to just under her heart. People walked by them, but she never knew. They were shadows, ghosts. The only things of substance were Pierce's mouth and hands.

Was it the wind she felt, or his fingers gliding over her skin? Did he murmur something, or had she?

Pierce drew her away. Ryan's eyes were clouded. They began to clear and focus as if she were coming out of a dream. He wasn't ready for the dream to end. Bringing her back, he took her lips again and tasted the dark, mysterious flavor of her.

He had to fight with the need to crush her against him, to savage her warm, willing mouth. She was a woman made for a gentle touch. Desire tore at him, and he suppressed it. There were times when he was locked in a dark, airless box that he had to push back the need to rush, the urge to claw his way out. Now he almost felt the same hint of panic. *What was she doing to him?* The question ran through his mind even as he brought her closer. Pierce knew only that he wanted her with a desperation he hadn't thought himself capable of.

Was there silk next to her skin again? Thin, fragile silk lightly scented with the fragrance she wore? He wanted to make love to her by candlelight or in a field with the sun pouring over her. Dear God, how he wanted her.

"Ryan, I want to be with you." The words were whispered inside her mouth and made her tremble. "I need to be with you. Come with me now." With his hands he tilted her head to another angle and kissed her again. "Now, Ryan. Let me love you."

"Pierce." She was sinking and struggling to find solid ground. She leaned against him even as she shook her head. "I don't know you."

Pierce controlled a sudden wild desire to drag her to his car, to take her back to his home. To his bed. "No." He said it as much to himself as to Ryan. Drawing her away, he held her by the shoulders and studied her. "No, you don't. And Miss Swan would need to." He didn't like the erratic beating of his heart. Calm and control were intimate parts of his work, and therefore, of him. "When you know me," he told her quietly, "we'll be lovers."

"No." Ryan's objection sprang from his matter-of-fact tone, not from the statement. "No, Pierce, we won't be lovers unless it's what I want. I make deals on contracts, not in my personal life."

Pierce smiled, more relaxed with her annoyance than he would have been with malleability. Anything that came too easily he suspected. "Miss Swan," he murmured as he took her arm. "We've already seen the cards."

Chapter 6

Ryan arrived in Las Vegas alone. She had insisted on it. Once her nerves had settled and she had been able to think practically, she had decided it would be unwise to have too much personal contact with Pierce. When a man was able to make you forget the world around you with a kiss, you kept your distance. That was Ryan Swan's new rule.

Through most of her life she had been totally dominated by her father. She had been able to do nothing without his approval. He might not have given her his time, but he had always given her his opinion. And his opinion had been law.

It was only upon reaching her early twenties that Ryan had begun to explore her own talents, her own independence. The taste of freedom had been very sweet. She wasn't about to allow herself to be dominated again, certainly not by physical needs. She knew from experience that men weren't particularly trustworthy. Why should Pierce Atkins be any different?

After paying off the cab, Ryan took a moment to look around. It was her first trip to Vegas. Even at ten in the morning it was an eye-opener. The Strip stretched long in both directions, and lining it were names like The Dunes, The Sahara, The MGM. The hotels vied for attention with gushing fountains, elaborate neon and fabulous flowers.

Billboards announced famous names in huge letters. Stars, stars, stars! The most beautiful women in the world, the most talented performers, the most colorful, the most exotic—they were all here. Everything was packed together; an adult amusement park circled by desert and ringed by mountains. The morning sun baked the streets; at night the neon would light them.

Ryan turned and looked at Caesar's Palace. It was huge and white and opulent. Above her head in enormous letters was Pierce's name and the dates of his engagements. What sort of feeling did it give a man like him, she wondered, to see his name advertised so boldly?

She lifted her bags and took the moving walkway that would transport her past the glittering fountain and Italian statues. In the morning quiet she could hear the water spurt up and splash down. She imagined that at night the streets would be noisy, filled with cars and people.

The moment she entered the hotel lobby, Ryan heard the whirl and chink of the slot machines. She had to curb a desire to walk into the casino for a look instead of going to the front desk.

"Ryan Swan." She set down her suitcases at the foot of the long counter. "I have a reservation."

"Yes, Miss Swan." The desk clerk beamed at her without checking his files. "The bellboy will take your bags." He signaled, then handed a key to the answering bellboy. "Enjoy your stay, Miss Swan. Please let us know if there's anything we can do for you."

"Thank you." Ryan accepted the clerk's deference without a thought. When people knew she was Bennett Swan's daughter, they treated her like a visiting dignitary. It was nothing new and only mildly annoying.

The elevator took her all the way to the top floor with the bellboy keeping a respectful silence. He led the way down the corridor, unlocked the door, then stepped back to let her enter.

Ryan's first surprise was that it wasn't a room but a suite. Her second was that it was already occupied. Pierce sat on the sofa working with papers he had spread out on the table in front of him.

"Ryan." He rose, then, going to the bellboy, handed him a bill. "Thank you."

"Thank *you,* Mr. Atkins."

Ryan waited until the door shut behind him. "What are you doing here?" she demanded.

"I have a rehearsal scheduled this afternoon," he reminded her. "How was your flight?"

"It was fine," she told him, annoyed with his answer and with the suspicions that were creeping into her mind.

"Can I get you a drink?"

"No, thank you." She glanced around the well-appointed room, took a brief glimpse out the window, then gestured broadly. "What the hell is this?"

Pierce lifted a brow at her tone but answered mildly. "Our suite."

"Oh, no," she said with a definite shake of her head. "*Your* suite." Picking up her bags, she headed for the door.

"Ryan." It was the calm quality of his voice that stopped her—and that snapped her temper.

"What a very small, very dirty trick!" Ryan dropped

her bags with a thud and turned on him. "Did you really think you could change my reservation and—and—"

"And what?" he prompted.

She gestured around the room again. "Set me up here with you without me making a murmur? Did you really think I'd pop cozily into your bed because you arranged it so nicely? How *dare* you! How dare you lie to me about needing me to watch you perform when all you wanted was for me to keep your bed warm!"

Her voice had changed from low accusation to high fury before Pierce grabbed her wrist. The strength in his fingers had her gasping in surprise and alarm. "I don't lie," Pierce said softly, but his eyes were darker than she had ever seen them. "And I don't need tricks to find a woman for my bed."

She didn't try to free herself. Instinct warned her against it, but she couldn't control her temper. "Then what do you call this?" she tossed back.

"A convenient arrangement." He felt her pulse racing under his fingers. Anger made his voice dangerously cool.

"For whom?" she demanded.

"We'll need to talk over a number of things in the next few days." He spoke with quiet deliberation, but his grip never slackened. "I don't intend to run down to your room every time I have something to say to you. I'm here to work," he reminded her. "And so are you."

"You should have consulted me."

"I didn't," he countered icily. "And I don't sleep with a woman unless she wants me to, Miss Swan."

"I don't appreciate you taking it upon yourself to change arrangements without discussing it with me first." Ryan stood firm on this, though her knees were threatening to tremble. His fury was all the more frightening in its restraint.

"I warned you before, I do things in my own way. If you're nervous, lock your door."

The jibe made her voice sharp. "A lot of good that would do with you. A lock would hardly keep you out."

His fingers tightened on her wrist quickly, painfully, before he tossed it aside. "Perhaps not." Pierce opened the door. "But a simple *no* would."

He was gone before Ryan could say any more. She leaned back against the door as the shudders ran through her. Until that moment she hadn't realized how badly she had been frightened. She was accustomed to dealing with histrionic bursts of temper or sulky silences from her father. But this…

There had been ice-cold violence in Pierce's eyes. Ryan would rather have faced the raging, shouting fury of any man than the look that could freeze her.

Without knowing she did so, Ryan rubbed her wrist. It throbbed lightly in each separate spot that Pierce's fingers had gripped. She had been right when she had said she didn't know him. There was more to him than she had ever guessed. Having uncovered one layer, she wasn't entirely certain she could deal with what she had discovered. For another moment she leaned against the door, waiting for the shaking to stop.

She looked around the room. Perhaps she had been wrong to have reacted so strongly to a harmless business arrangement, she finally decided. Sharing a suite was essentially the same thing as having adjoining rooms. If that had been the case, she would have thought nothing of it.

But he had been wrong, too, she reminded herself. They might have come to an easy agreement about the suite if he had only discussed it with her first. She had

promised herself when she had left Switzerland that she
would no longer be directed.

And Pierce's phrasing had worried her. *He didn't sleep
with a woman unless she wanted him to.* Ryan was too
aware that they both knew she wanted him.

A simple *no* would keep him out. Yes, she mused as
she picked up her bags. That she could depend on. He
would never force himself on any woman—very simply, he would have no need to. She wondered how long
it would be before she forgot to say no.

Ryan shook her head. The project was as important
to Pierce as it was to her. It wasn't smart to start off by
bickering over sleeping arrangements or worrying about
remote possibilities. She knew her own mind. She went
to unpack.

When Ryan went down to the theatre, the rehearsal
was already underway. Pierce held center stage. There
was a woman with him. Even though she was dressed
plainly in jeans and a bulky sweatshirt, Ryan recognized
the statuesque redhead who was Pierce's assistant. On
the tapes, Ryan recalled, she had worn brief, sparkling
costumes or floaty dresses. *No magician travels without
a beautiful assistant.*

Hold on, Ryan, she warned herself. No business of
yours. Quietly, she walked down and took a seat in the
center of the audience. Pierce never glanced in her direction. Hardly aware of what she did, Ryan began to think
of camera angles and sets.

Five cameras, she thought, and nothing too showy
in the background. Nothing glittery to pull attention
away from him. Something dark, she decided. Something to enhance the image of wizard or warlock rather
than showman.

It came as a complete surprise to her when Pierce's assistant drifted slowly backward until she was lying horizontally in thin air. Ryan stopped planning and watched. He used no patter now but only gestures—wide, sweeping gestures that brought black capes and candlelight to mind. The woman began revolving, slowly at first and then with greater speed.

Ryan had seen the illusion on tape, but seeing it in the flesh was a totally different experience. There were no props to distract from the two at stage center, no costumes, music or flashing lights to enhance the mood. Ryan discovered she was holding her breath and forced herself to let it out. The woman's cap of red curls fluttered as she spun. Her eyes were closed, her face utterly peaceful while her hands were folded neatly at her waist. Ryan watched closely, looking for wires, for gimmicks. Frustrated, she leaned forward.

She couldn't prevent a small gasp of appreciation as the woman began to roll over and over as she continued to spin. The calm expression on her face remained unchanged, as if she slept rather than whirled and circled three feet above the stage floor. With a gesture, Pierce stopped the motion, bringing her vertical again, slowly, until her feet touched the stage. When he passed his hand in front of her face, she opened her eyes and grinned.

"How was it?"

Ryan almost jolted at the commonplace words that bounced cheerfully off the theater walls.

"Good," Pierce said simply. "It'll be better with the music. I want red lights, something hot. Start soft and then build with the speed." He gave these orders to the lighting director before turning back to his assistant. "We'll work on the transportation."

For an hour Ryan watched, fascinated, frustrated and

undeniably entertained. What seemed to her flawless, Pierce repeated again and again. With each illusion, he had his own ideas of the technical effects he wanted. Ryan could see that his creativity didn't stop at magic. He knew how to use lighting and sound to enhance, accent, underline.

A perfectionist, Ryan noted. He worked quietly, without the dynamics he exuded in a performance. Nor was there the careless ease about him she had seen when he had entertained the children. He was working. It was a plain and simple fact. A wizard, perhaps, she mused with a smile, but one who pays his dues with long hours and repetition. The longer she watched, the more respect she felt.

Ryan had wondered what it would be like to work with him. Now she saw. He was relentless, tireless and as fanatical about details as she was herself. They were going to argue, she predicted and began to look forward to it. It was going to be one hell of a show.

"Ryan, would you come up, please?"

She was startled when he called her. Ryan would have sworn he hadn't known she was in the theater. Fatalistically, she rose. It was beginning to appear that there was nothing he didn't know. As Ryan came forward, Pierce said something to his assistant. She gave a quick, lusty laugh and kissed him on the cheek.

"At least I get to stay all in one piece on this run," she told him, then turned to grin at Ryan as she mounted the stage.

"Ryan Swan," Pierce said, "Bess Frye."

On closer study Ryan saw the woman wasn't a beauty. Her features were too large for classic beauty. Her hair was brilliantly red and cropped into curls around a large-boned face. Her eyes were almost round and shades darker than Ryan's green. Her make-up was as exotic as her clothes were casual, and she was nearly as tall as Pierce.

"Hi!" There was a burst of friendliness in the one word. Bess extended her hand to give Ryan's an enthusiastic shake. It was hard to believe that the woman, as solid as a redwood, had been spinning three feet above the stage. "Pierce has told me all about you."

"Oh?" Ryan glanced over at him.

"Oh, yeah." She rested an elbow on his shoulder as she spoke to Ryan. "Pierce thinks you're real smart. He likes the brainy type, but he didn't say you were so pretty. How come you didn't tell me she was so pretty, sweetie?" It didn't take Ryan long to discover that Bess habitually spoke in long, explosive bursts.

"And have you accuse me of seeing a woman only as a stage prop?" He dipped his hands into his pockets.

Bess gave another burst of lusty laughter. "He's smart, too," she confided to Ryan, giving Pierce a squeeze. "You're going to be the producer on this special?"

"Yes." A little dazed by the overflowing friendliness, Ryan smiled. "Yes, I am."

"Good. About time we had a woman running things. I'm surrounded by men in this job, sweetie. Only one woman in the road crew. We'll have a drink sometime soon and get acquainted."

Buy you a drink, sweetie? Ryan remembered. Her smile became a grin. "I'd like that."

"Well, I'm going to see what Link's up to before the boss decides to put me back to work. See you later." Bess strode off stage—six feet of towering enthusiasm. Ryan watched her all the way.

"She's wonderful," Ryan murmured.

"I've always thought so."

"She seems so cool and reserved on stage." Ryan smiled up at Pierce. "Has she been with you long?"

"Yes."

The warmth Bess had brought was rapidly fading. Clearing her throat, Ryan began again. "The rehearsal went very well. We'll have to discuss which illusions you plan to incorporate into the special and whatever new ones you intend to develop."

"All right."

"There'll have to be some adjustments, naturally, for television," she continued, trying to overlook his monosyllabic responses. "But basically I imagine you want a condensed version of your club act."

"That's right."

In the short time Ryan had known Pierce, she had come to learn he possessed a natural friendliness and humor. Now he was looking at her with his eyes guarded, obviously impatient for her to leave. The apology she had planned couldn't be made to this man.

"I'm sure you're busy," she said stiffly and turned away. It hurt, she discovered, to be shut out. He had no right to hurt her. Ryan left the stage without looking back.

Pierce watched her until the doors at the back of the theatre swung shut behind her. With his eyes still on the door, he crushed the ball he held in his hand until it was flat. He had very strong fingers, strong enough to have snapped the bones of her wrist instead of merely bruising it.

He hadn't liked seeing those bruises. He didn't like remembering how she had accused him of trying to take her by deceit. He had never had to take any woman by deceit. Ryan Swan would be no different.

He could have had her that first night with the storm raging outside and her body pressed close to his.

And why didn't I? he demanded of himself and tossed the mangled ball aside. Why hadn't he taken her to bed and done all the things he had so desperately wanted to do? Because she had looked up at him with her eyes full of panic and acceptance. She had been vulnerable. He had realized, with something like fear, that he had been vulnerable, too. And still she haunted his mind.

When she had walked into the suite that morning, Pierce had forgotten the careful notes he had been making on a new illusion. He had seen her, walking in wearing one of those damn tailored suits, and he had forgotten everything. Her hair had been windblown from the drive, like the first time he had seen her. And all he had wanted to do was hold her—to feel the small, soft body yield against his.

Perhaps his anger had started to grow even then, to fire up with her words and accusing eyes.

He shouldn't have hurt her. Pierce stared down at his empty hands and swore. He had no right to mark her skin—the ugliest thing a man could do to a woman. She was weaker than he, and he had used that—used his temper and his strength, two things he had promised himself long, long ago he would never use on a woman. In his mind no provocation could justify it. He could blame no one but himself for the lapse.

He couldn't dwell on it or on Ryan any longer and continue to work. He needed his concentration. The only thing to do was to put their relationship back where Ryan had wanted it from the beginning. They would work together successfully, and that would be all. He had learned to control his body through his mind. He could control his needs, his emotions, the same way.

With a final oath Pierce walked back to talk with his road crew about props.

Chapter 7

Las Vegas was difficult to resist. Inside the casinos it was neither day nor night. Without clocks and with the continual clinking of slots, there was a perpetual timelessness, an intriguing disorientation. Ryan saw people in evening dress continuing a night's gambling into late morning. She watched thousands of dollars change hands at the blackjack and baccarat tables. More than once she held her breath while the roulette wheel spun with a small fortune resting on the caprices of the silver ball.

She learned that the fever came in many forms—cool, dispassionate, desperate, intense. There was the woman feeding the nickel slot machine and the dedicated player tossing the dice. Smoke hung in the air over the sounds of winning and of losing. The faces would change, but the mood remained. Just one more roll of the dice, one more pull of the lever.

The years in the prim Swiss school had cooled the gambling blood Ryan had inherited from her father.

Now, for the first time, Ryan felt the excitement of the urge to test Lady Luck. She refused it, telling herself she was content to watch. There was little else for her to do.

She saw Pierce onstage at rehearsals and hardly at all otherwise. It was amazing to her that two people could share a suite and so rarely come into contact with each other. No matter how early she rose, he was already gone. Once or twice after she was long in bed, Ryan heard the quick click of the lock on the front door. When they spoke, it was only to discuss ideas on how to alter his club act for television. Their conversations were calm and technical.

He's trying to avoid me, she thought the night of his opening performance, and doing a damn good job of it. If he had wanted to prove that sharing a suite meant nothing personal, he had succeeded beautifully. That, of course, was what she wanted, but she missed the easy camaraderie. She missed seeing him smile at her.

Ryan decided to watch the show from the wings. There she would have a perfect view and be in a position to note Pierce's timing and style while getting a backstage perspective. Rehearsals had given her an insight into his work habits, and now she would watch him perform from as close to his point of view as she could manage. She wanted to see more than the audience or a camera would see.

Careful to stay out of the way of the stagehands and grips, Ryan settled herself into a corner and watched. From the first wave of applause as he was introduced, Pierce had his audience in the palm of his hand. *My God, he's beautiful!* she thought as she studied his style and flare. Dynamic, dramatic, his personality alone would have held the audience. The charisma he possessed was no illusion but as integral a part of him as the color of his hair. He dressed in black, as was his habit, needing no brilliant colors to keep eyes glued to him.

He spoke as he performed. Patter, he would have called it, but it was much more. He tuned the mood with words and cadence. He could string them along, then dazzle them completely—a shot of flame from his naked palm, a glittering silver pendulum that swung, unsupported, in thin air. He was no longer pragmatic, as he had been in rehearsals, but dark and mysterious.

Ryan watched as he was padlocked into a duffel bag, slipped into a chest and chained inside. Standing on it, Bess pulled up a curtain and counted to twenty. When the curtain dropped, Pierce himself stood on the chest in a complete costume change. And, of course, when he unlocked the chest and bag, Bess was inside. He called it transportation. Ryan called it incredible.

His escapes made her uneasy. Watching volunteers from the audience nail him into a sturdy packing crate she herself had examined had her palms dampening. She could imagine him in the dark, airless box and feel her own breath clogging in her lungs. But his freedom was accomplished in less than two minutes.

For the finale, he locked Bess in a cage, curtaining it and levitating it to the ceiling. When he brought it down moments later, there was a sleek young panther in her place. Watching him, seeing the intensity of his eyes, the mysterious hollows and shadows on his face, Ryan almost believed he had transcended the laws of nature. For that moment before the curtain came down, the panther was Bess and he was more enchanter than showman.

Ryan wanted to ask him, convince him to explain just this one illusion in terms she could understand. When he came offstage and their eyes held, she swallowed the words.

His face was damp from the lights and his own concentration. She wanted to touch him, finding, to her own astonishment, that watching him perform had aroused her. The drive was more basic and more powerful than anything she had ever experienced. She could imagine him taking her with his strong, clever hands. Then his mouth, his impossibly sensual mouth, would be on hers, taking her to that strange, weightless world he knew. If she went to him now—offered, demanded—would she find him as hungry as herself? Would he say nothing, only lead her away to show her his magic?

Pierce stopped in front of her, and Ryan stepped back, shaken by her own thoughts. Her blood was heated, churning under her skin, demanding that she make the move toward him. Aware, aroused but unwilling, she kept her distance.

"You were marvelous," she said but heard the stiffness in the compliment.

"Thank you." Pierce said nothing more as he moved past her.

Ryan felt pain in her palms and discovered she was digging her nails into her flesh. This has got to stop, she told herself and turned to go after him.

"Hey, Ryan!" She stopped as Bess poked her head out of her dressing room. "What did you think of the show?"

"It was wonderful." She glanced down the corridor; Pierce was already out of reach. Perhaps it was for the best. "I don't suppose you'd let me in on the secret of the finale?" she asked.

Bess laughed. "Not if I value my life, sweetie. Come on in; talk to me while I change."

Ryan obliged, closing the door behind her. The air tingled with the scents of greasepaint and powder. "It must be quite an experience, being turned into a panther."

"Oh, Lord, Pierce has turned me into everything imaginable that walks, crawls or flies; he's sawed me to pieces and balanced me on swords. In one gag he had me sleeping on a bed of nails ten feet above the stage." As she spoke, she stripped out of her costume with no more modesty than a five-year-old.

"You must trust him," Ryan commented as she looked around for an empty chair. Bess had a habit of strewing her things over all available space.

"Just toss something out of your way," she suggested as she plucked a peacock blue robe from the arm of a chair. "Trust Pierce?" she continued as she belted the robe. "He's the best." Sitting at the vanity, she began to cream off her stage make-up. "You saw how he is at rehearsals."

"Yes." Ryan folded a crumpled blouse and set it aside. "Exacting."

"That's not the half of it. He works out his illusions on paper, then goes over them again and again in that dungeon of his before he even thinks about showing anything to me or Link." She looked at Ryan with one eye heavily mascaraed and the other naked. "Most people don't know how hard he works because he makes it look so easy. That's the way he wants it."

"His escapes," Ryan began as she straightened Bess's clothes. "Are they dangerous?"

"I don't like some of them." Bess tissued off the last of the cream. Her exotic face was unexpectedly young and fresh. "Getting out of manacles and a straightjacket is one thing." She shrugged as she rose. "But I've never liked it when he does his version of Houdini's Water Torture or his own A Thousand Locks."

"Why does he do it, Bess?" Ryan set a pair of jeans

aside but continued to roam the room restlessly. "His illusions would be enough."

"Not for Pierce." Bess dropped the robe, then snapped on a bra. "The escapes and the danger are important to him. They always have been."

"Why?"

"Because he wants to test himself all the time. He's never satisfied with what he did yesterday."

"Test himself," Ryan murmured. She had sensed this herself but was a long way from understanding it. "Bess, how long have you been with him?"

"Since the beginning," Bess told her as she tugged on jeans. "Right from the beginning."

"Who is he?" Ryan demanded before she could stop herself. "Who is he really?"

With a shirt hanging from her fingertips, Bess gave Ryan a sudden, penetrating glance. "Why do you want to know?"

"He…" Ryan stopped, not knowing what to say. "I don't know."

"Do you care about him?"

Ryan didn't answer at once. She wanted to say no and shrug it off. She had no reason to care. "Yes, I do," she heard herself say. "I care about him."

"Let's go have a drink," Bess suggested and pulled on her shirt. "We'll talk."

"Champagne cocktails," Bess ordered when they slipped into a booth in the lounge. "I'm buying." She pulled out a cigarette and lit it. "Don't tell Pierce," she added with a wink. "He frowns on the use of tobacco. He's a fanatic about body care."

"Link told me he runs five miles every day."

"An old habit. Pierce rarely breaks old habits." Bess

drew in smoke with a sigh. "He's always been really determined, you know? You could see it, even when he was a kid."

"You knew Pierce when he was a boy?"

"We grew up together—Pierce, Link and me." Bess glanced up at the waitress when their cocktails were served. "Run a tab," she directed and looked back at Ryan. "Pierce doesn't talk about back then, not even to Link or me. He's shut it off—or tried to."

"I thought he was trying to promote an image," Ryan murmured.

"He doesn't need to."

"No." Ryan met her eyes again. "I suppose he doesn't. Did he have a difficult childhood?"

"Oh, boy." Bess took a long drink. "And then some. He was a real puny kid."

"Pierce?" Ryan thought of the hard, muscled body and stared.

"Yeah." Bess gave a muffled version of her full-throated laugh. "Hard to believe, but true. He was small for his age, skinny as a rail. The bigger kids tormented him. They needed someone to pick on, I guess. Nobody likes growing up in an orphanage."

"Orphanage?" Ryan pounced on the last word. Studying Bess's open, friendly face, she felt a flood of sympathy. "All of you?"

"Oh, hell." Bess shrugged. Ryan's eyes were full of eloquent distress. "It wasn't so bad, really. Food, a roof over your head, plenty of company. It's not like you read about in that book, that *Oliver Twist*."

"Did you lose your parents, Bess?" Ryan asked with interest rather than the sympathy she saw was unwanted.

"When I was eight. There wasn't anybody else to take me. It was the same with Link." She continued with no trace of self-pity or regret. "People want to adopt babies, mostly. Older kids aren't placed so easily."

Lifting her drink, Ryan sipped thoughtfully. It would have been twenty years ago, before the current surge of interest in adoptable children. "What about Pierce?"

"Things were different with him. He had parents. They wouldn't sign, so he was unadoptable."

Ryan's brows creased with confusion. "But if he had parents, what was he doing in an orphanage?"

"Courts took him away from them. His father…" Bess let out a long stream of smoke. She was taking a chance, talking like this. Pierce wasn't going to like it if he found out. She could only hope it paid off. "His father used to beat his mother."

"Oh, my God!" Ryan's horrified eyes clung to Bess's. "And—and Pierce?"

"Now and again," Bess answered calmly. "But mostly his mother. First he'd hit the booze, then he'd hit his wife."

A surge of raw pain spread in the pit of her stomach. Ryan lifted her drink again. Of course she knew such things happened, but her world had always been so shielded. Her own parents might have ignored her a great deal of her life, but neither had ever lifted a hand to her. True, her father's shouting had been frightening at times, but it had never gone beyond a raised voice and impatient words. She had never dealt with physical violence of any sort firsthand. Though she tried to conceive the kind of ugliness Bess was calmly relating, it was too distant.

"Tell me," she asked finally. "I want to understand him."

It was what Bess wanted to hear. She gave Ryan a silent vote of approval and continued. "Pierce was five. This time his father beat his mother badly enough to put her in the hospital. Usually, he locked Pierce in a closet before he started on one of his rages, but this time he knocked him around a little first."

Ryan controlled the need to protest what she was hearing but kept silent. Bess watched her steadily as she spoke. "That's when the social workers took over. After the usual paperwork and court hearings, his parents were judged unfit, and he was placed in the orphanage."

"Bess, his mother." Ryan shook her head, trying to think it through. "Why didn't she leave his father and take Pierce with her? What kind of woman would—"

"I'm not a psychiatrist," Bess interrupted. "As far as Pierce ever knew, she stayed with his father."

"And gave up her child," Ryan murmured. "He must have felt so completely rejected, so frightened and alone."

What sort of damage does that do to a small mind? she wondered. What sort of compensations does a child like that make? Did he escape from chains and trunks and safes because he had once been a small boy locked in a dark closet? Did he continually seek to do the impossible because he had once been so helpless?

"He was a loner," Bess continued as she ordered another round. "Maybe that's one of the reasons the other kids tormented him. At least until Link came." Bess grinned, enjoying this part of her memories. "Nobody ever touched Pierce when Link was in sight. He's always been twice as big as anyone else. And that face!"

She laughed again, but there was nothing callous in the sound. "When Link first came, none of the other kids would go near him. Except Pierce. They were both outcasts. So was I. Link's been attached to Pierce ever since. I really don't know what might have happened to him without Pierce. Or to me."

"You really love him, don't you?" Ryan asked, drawn close in spirit to the large, exuberant redhead.

"He's my best friend," Bess answered simply. "They let me into their little club when I was ten." She smiled over the rim of her glass. "I saw Link coming and climbed up a tree. He scared me to death. We called him the Missing Link."

"Children can be cruel."

"You betcha. Anyway, just as he was passing underneath, the branch broke and I fell out. He caught me." She leaned forward, cupping her chin on her hands. "I'll never forget that. One minute I'm falling a mile a minute, and the next he's holding me. I looked up at that face and got ready to scream blue blazes. Then he laughed. I fell in love on the spot."

Ryan swallowed champagne quickly. There was no mistaking the dreamy look in Bess's eyes. "You—you and Link?"

"Well, me, anyway," Bess said ruefully. "I've been nuts about the big lug for twenty years. He still thinks I'm Little Bess. All six feet of me." She grinned and winked. "But I'm working on him."

"I thought you and Pierce…" Ryan began, then trailed off.

"Me and Pierce?" Bess let loose with one of her lusty laughs, causing heads to turn. "Are you kidding? You know enough about show business to cast better than that, sweetie. Do I look like Pierce's type?"

"Well, I…" Embarrassed by Bess's outspoken humor, Ryan shrugged. "I wouldn't have any idea what his type would be."

Bess laughed into her fresh drink. "You look smarter than that," she commented. "Anyway, he was always a quiet kid, always—what's the word?" Her forehead furrowed in thought. "Intense, you know? He had a temper." Grinning again, she rolled her eyes. "He gave a black eye for every one he got in the early days. But as he got older, he'd hold back. It was pretty clear he'd made up his mind not to follow in his old man's footsteps. When Pierce makes up his mind, that's it."

Ryan remembered the cold fury, the iced-over violence, and began to understand.

"When he was about nine, I guess, he had this accident." Bess drank, then scowled. "At least that's what he called it. He went head first down a flight of stairs. Everybody knew he'd been pushed, but he'd never say who. I think he didn't want Link to do something he could have gotten in trouble for. The fall hurt his back. They didn't think he'd walk again."

"Oh, no!"

"Yeah." Bess took another long drink. "But Pierce said he was going to walk. He was going to run five miles every day of his life."

"Five miles," Ryan murmured.

"He was determined. He worked at therapy like his life depended on it. Maybe it did," she added thoughtfully. "Maybe it did. He spent six months in the hospital."

"I see." She was seeing Pierce in the pediatric ward, giving himself to children, talking to them, making them laugh. Bringing them magic.

"While he was in, one of the nurses gave him a magic set. That was it." Bess toasted with her glass. "A five-dollar magic set. It was like he'd been waiting for it, or it was waiting for him. By the time he got out, he could do things a lot of guys in the club field have trouble with." Love and pride mingled in her voice. "He was a natural."

Ryan could see him, a dark, intense boy in a white hospital bed, perfecting, practicing, discovering.

"Listen," Bess laughed again and leaned forward. Ryan's eyes were speaking volumes. "Once when I visited him in the hospital, he set the sheet on fire." She paused as Ryan's expression became one of horror. "I swear, I *saw* it burning. Then he patted it with his hand." She demonstrated with her palm on the table. "Smoothed it out, and there was nothing. No burn, no hole, not even a singe. The little creep scared me to death."

Ryan found herself laughing despite the ordeal he must have experienced. He'd beaten it. He'd won. "To Pierce," she said and lifted her glass.

"Damn right." Bess touched rims before she tossed off the champagne. "He took off when he was sixteen. I missed him like crazy. I never thought I'd see him or Link again. I guess it was the loneliest two years of my life. Then, one day I was working in this diner in Denver, and he walks in. I don't know how he found me, he never said, but he walks in and tells me to quit. I was going to go work for him."

"Just like that?" Ryan demanded.

"Just like that."

"What did you say?"

"I didn't say anything. It was Pierce." With a smile, Bess signaled the waitress again. "I quit. We went on the road. Drink up, sweetie, you're one behind."

Ryan studied her a moment, then obliged by finishing off her drink. It wasn't every man who could command that sort of unquestioning loyalty from a strong woman. "I usually stop at two," Ryan told her, indicating the cocktail.

"Not tonight," Bess announced. "I always drink champagne when I get sentimental. You wouldn't believe some of the places we played those first years," she went on. "Kids' parties, stag parties, the works. Nobody handles a rowdy crowd like Pierce. When he looks at a guy, then whips a fireball out of his pocket, the guy quiets down."

"I imagine so," Ryan agreed and laughed at the image. "I'm not even sure he'd need the fireball."

"You got it," Bess said, pleased. "Anyway, he always knew he was going to make it, and he took Link and me along. He didn't have to. That's just the kind of man he is. He doesn't let many people in close, but the ones he does, it's forever." She stirred the champagne quietly a moment. "I know Link and me could never keep up with him up here, you know?" Bess tapped her temple. "But it doesn't matter to Pierce. We're his friends."

"I think," Ryan said slowly, "he chooses his friends very well."

Bess sent her a brilliant smile. "You're a nice lady, Ryan. A real lady, too. Pierce is the kind of man who needs a lady."

Ryan became very interested in the color of her drink. "Why do you say that?"

"Because he has class, always has. He needs a classy woman and one who's warm like he is."

"Is he warm, Bess?" Ryan's eyes came back up, searching. "Sometimes he seems so…distant."

"You know where he got that stupid cat?" Ryan shook her head at the question. "Somebody'd hit it and left it on the side of the road. Pierce was driving back after a week's run in San Francisco. He stopped and took it to the vet. Two o'clock in the morning, and he's waking up the vet and making him operate on some stray cat. Cost him three hundred dollars. Link told me." She pulled out another cigarette. "How many people you know who'd do that?"

Ryan looked at her steadily. "Pierce wouldn't like it if he knew you'd told me all this, would he?"

"No."

"Why have you?"

Bess flashed her a smile again. "It's a trick I learned from him over the years. You look dead in somebody's eyes and you know if you can trust them."

Ryan met the look and spoke seriously. "Thank you."

"And," Bess added casually as she downed more champagne, "you're in love with him."

The words Ryan had begun to say jammed in her throat. She began coughing fitfully.

"Drink up, sweetie. Nothing like love to make you choke. Here's to it." She clinked her glass against Ryan's. "And good luck to both of us."

"Luck?" Ryan said weakly.

"With men like those two, we need it."

This time Ryan signaled for another round.

Chapter 8

When Ryan walked through the casino with Bess, she was laughing. The wine had lifted her mood, but more, Bess's company had cheered her. Since she had returned from school, Ryan had given herself little time to develop friendships. Finding one so quickly took her higher than the champagne.

"Celebrating?"

Both of them looked up and spotted Pierce. In unison, their faces registered the abashed guilt of children caught with one hand in the cookie jar. Pierce's brow lifted. With a laugh, Bess leaned over and kissed him enthusiastically.

"Just a little girl talk, sweetie. Ryan and I found out we have a lot in common."

"Is that so?" He watched as Ryan pressed her fingers to her mouth to stifle a giggle. It was apparent they'd had more than talk.

"Isn't he terrific when he's all serious and dry?" Bess asked Ryan. "Nobody does it better than Pierce." She kissed him again. "I didn't get your lady drunk, just maybe a little looser than she's used to. Besides, she's a big girl." Still resting her hand on his shoulder, Bess looked around. "Where's Link?"

"Watching the keno board."

"See you later." She gave Ryan a wink and was off.

"She's crazy about him, you know," Ryan said confidentially.

"Yes, I know."

She took a step closer. "Is there anything you don't know, Mr. Atkins?" She watched his lips curve at her emphasis on his surname. "I wondered if you'd ever do that for me again."

"Do what?"

"Smile. You haven't smiled at me in days."

"Haven't I?" He couldn't stop the surge of tenderness but contented himself with brushing the hair back from her face.

"No. Not once. Are you sorry?"

"Yes." Pierce steadied her with a hand on her shoulder and wished she wouldn't look at him in quite that way. He had managed to back down on needs while sharing the same set of rooms with her. Now, surrounded by noise and people and lights, he felt the force of desire building. He removed his hand. "Would you like me to take you upstairs?"

"I'm going to play blackjack," she informed him grandly. "I've wanted to for days, but I kept remembering gambling was foolish. I've just forgotten that."

Pierce held her arm as she started to walk to the table. "How much money do you have on you?"

"Oh, I don't know." Ryan rummaged in her purse. "About seventy-five dollars."

"All right." If she lost, Pierce decided, seventy-five

would put no great hole in her bank account. He went with her.

"I've been watching this for days," she whispered as she took a seat at a ten-dollar table. "I've got it all figured out."

"Doesn't everyone?" he muttered and stood beside her. "Give the lady twenty dollars worth of chips," he told the dealer.

"Fifty," Ryan corrected, counting out bills.

With a nod from Pierce, the dealer exchanged the bills for colored chips.

"Are you going to play?" Ryan asked him.

"I don't gamble."

She lifted her brows. "What do you call being nailed inside a packing crate?"

He gave her one of his slow smiles. "My profession."

She laughed and sent him a teasing grin. "Do you disapprove of gambling and other vices, Mr. Atkins?"

"No." He felt another leap of desire and controlled it. "But I like to figure my own odds." He nodded as the cards were dealt. "It's never easy to beat the house at its own game."

"I feel lucky tonight," she told him.

The man beside Ryan swirled a bourbon and signed his name on a sheet of paper. He had just dropped over two thousand dollars. Philosophically, he bought another five thousand dollars worth of chips. Ryan watched a diamond glitter on his pinky as the cards were dealt. A triple deck, she remembered and lifted the tips of her own cards carefully. She saw an eight and a five. A young blonde in a black Halston took a hit and busted on twenty-three. The man with the diamond held on eighteen. Ryan took a hit and was pleased with another five. She held, then waited patiently as two more players took cards.

The dealer turned over fourteen, flipped over his next card and hit twenty. The man with the diamond swore softly as he lost another five hundred dollars.

Ryan counted her next cards, watched the hits and lost again. Undaunted, she waited for her third deal. She drew seventeen. Before she could signal the dealer she would hold, Pierce nodded for the hit.

"Wait a minute," Ryan began.

"Take it," he said simply.

With a huff and a shrug, she did. She hit twenty. Eyes wide, she swiveled in her chair to stare at him, but he was watching the cards. The dealer held on nineteen and paid her off.

"I won!" she exclaimed, pleased with the stack of chips pushed at her. "How did you know?"

He only smiled at her and continued to watch the cards.

On the next hand she drew a ten and a six. She would have taken the hit, but Pierce touched her shoulder and shook his head. Swallowing her protest, Ryan stayed pat. The dealer broke on twenty-two.

She laughed, delighted, but looked over at him again. "How do you do that?" she demanded. "It's a triple deck. You can't possibly remember all the cards dealt or figure what's left." He said nothing, and her brow creased. "Can you?"

Pierce smiled again and shook his head simply. Then he steered Ryan to another win.

"Want to take a look at mine?" the man with the diamond demanded, pushing aside his cards in disgust.

Ryan leaned toward him. "He's a sorcerer, you know. I take him everywhere."

The young blonde tucked her hair behind her ear. "I

could use a spell or two myself." She sent Pierce a slow invitation. Ryan caught her eye as the cards were dealt.

"Mine," she said coolly and didn't see Pierce's brow go up. The blonde went back to her cards.

For the next hour Ryan's luck—or Pierce's—held. When the pile of chips in front of her had grown considerably, he opened her purse and swept them inside.

"Oh, but wait. I'm just getting started!"

"The secret of winning is knowing when to stop," Pierce told her and helped her off the stool. "Cash them in, Ryan, before you take it into your head to lose them at baccarat."

"But I did want to play," she began, casting a glance behind her.

"Not tonight."

With a heavy sigh she dumped the contents of her purse at the cashier's booth. Along with the chips was a comb, a lipstick and a penny that had been flattened by the wheel of a train.

"That's for luck," she said when Pierce picked it up to examine it.

"Superstition, Miss Swan," he murmured. "You surprise me."

"It's not superstition," she insisted, stuffing bills in her purse as the cashier counted them out. "It's for luck."

"I stand corrected."

"I like you, Pierce." Ryan linked her arm with his. "I thought I should tell you."

"Do you?"

"Yes," she said definitely. She could tell him that, she thought as they moved to the elevators. That was safe and certainly true. She wouldn't tell him what Bess had said so casually. *Love him?* No, that was far from safe, and it wasn't necessarily true. Even though...even though she was becoming more and more afraid it was.

"Do you like me?" Ryan turned to him and smiled as the elevator doors clicked shut.

"Yes, Ryan." He ran his knuckles over her cheek. "I like you."

"I wasn't sure." She stepped closer to him, and he felt a tingle race along his skin. "You've been angry with me."

"No, I haven't been angry with you."

She was staring up at him. Pierce could feel the air grow thick, as it did when the lid closed on him in a box or a trunk. His heart rate speeded up, and with sheer mental determination, he leveled it. He wasn't going to touch her again.

Ryan saw something flicker in his eyes. A hunger. Hers grew as well, but more, she felt a need to touch, to soothe. To love. She knew him now, though he was unaware of it. She wanted to give him something. She reached up to touch his cheek, but Pierce caught her fingers in his as the door opened.

"You must be tired," he said roughly and drew her into the corridor.

"No." Ryan laughed with the new sense of power. He was just a little afraid of her. She sensed it. Something shot into her—a combination of wine and winning and knowledge. And she wanted him.

"Are you tired, Pierce?" she asked when he unlocked the door to the suite.

"It's late."

"No. No, it's never late in Las Vegas." She tossed her purse aside and stretched. "There's no time here, don't you know? No clocks." Lifting her hair, she let it fall slowly through her fingers. "How can it be late when you don't know what time it is?" She spotted his papers on the table and crossed to them, kicking off her shoes as she went. "You work too much, Mr. Atkins." Laughing, she turned back to him. "Miss Swan's like that, isn't she?"

Her hair had tumbled over her shoulders, and her cheeks were flushed. Her eyes were alive, dancing, alluring. In them he saw that his thoughts were no secret to her. Desire was a hammer thrust in his stomach. Pierce said nothing.

"But you like Miss Swan," she murmured. "I don't always. Come sit down. Explain this to me." Ryan dropped to the couch and picked up one of his papers. It was covered with drawings and notes that made absolutely no sense to her.

Pierce moved then, telling himself it was only to keep her from disturbing his work. "It's too complicated." He took the sheet from her hand and set it back down.

"I've a very quick mind." Ryan pulled his arm until he sat beside her. She looked at him and smiled. "Do you know, the first time I looked into your eyes I thought my heart stopped." She put her hand to his cheek. "The first time you kissed me I knew it did."

Pierce caught her hand again, knowing he was close to the edge. Her free one ran up his shirtfront to his throat. "Ryan, you should go to bed."

She could hear the desire in his voice. Under her fingertip the pulse in his throat throbbed quickly. Her own heart began to match the rhythm. "No one's ever kissed me like that before," she murmured and slipped her fingers to the first button of his shirt. She freed it, watching his eyes. "No one's ever made me feel like that before. Was it magic, Pierce?" She loosened the second and third buttons.

"No." He reached up to stop the questing fingers that were driving him mad.

"I think it was." Ryan shifted and caught his earlobe lightly between her teeth. "I know it was." The whispering breath went straight to the pit of his stomach to stoke the flames. They flared high and threatened to explode. Catching her by the shoulders, Pierce started to draw her away, but her hands were on his naked chest. Her mouth brushed his throat. His fingers tightened as the tug of war went on inside him.

"Ryan." Though he concentrated, he couldn't steady his pulse. "What are you trying to do?"

"I'm trying to seduce you," she murmured, trailing her lips down to follow her fingers. "Is it working?"

Her hands ran down his rib cage to play lightly over his stomach. She felt the quiver of response and grew bolder.

"Yes, it's working very well."

Ryan laughed, a throaty, almost mocking sound that made his blood pound. Though he didn't touch her, he was no longer able to stop her from touching him. Her hands were soft and teasing while her tongue flicked lightly at his ear.

"Are you sure?" she whispered as she slipped his shirt from his shoulders. "Maybe I'm doing something wrong." She trailed her mouth to his chin, then let her tongue run briefly over his lips. "Maybe you don't want me to touch you like this." She ran a fingertip down the center of his chest to the waist of his jeans. "Or like this." She nipped his bottom lip, still watching his eyes.

No, she'd been wrong. They were black—black, not gray. Needs drove her until she thought she would be swallowed by them. Could it be possible to want so much? So much that your whole body ached and pounded and threatened to shatter?

"I wanted you when you walked offstage tonight,"

she said huskily. "Right then, while I still half-believed you were a wizard and not a man. And now." She ran her hands up his chest to link them behind his neck. "Now, knowing you're a man, I want you more." She let her eyes lower to his mouth, then lifted them back to his. "But maybe you don't want me. Maybe I don't…arouse you."

"Ryan." He'd lost the ability to control his pulse, his thoughts, his concentration. He'd lost the will to try to find it again. "There won't be any turning back in a moment."

She laughed, giddy with excitement, driven by desire. She let her lips hover a breath from his. "Promise?"

Ryan exulted in the power of the kiss. His mouth was on hers fiercely, painfully. She was under him with such speed, she never felt the movement, only his hard body on hers. He was pulling at her blouse, impatient with buttons. Two flew off to land somewhere on the carpet before his hand took her breast. Ryan moaned and arched against him, desperate to be touched. His tongue went deep to tangle with hers.

Desire was white-hot—flashes of heat, splashes of color. Her skin was searing wherever he touched. She was naked without knowing how she had become so, and his bare flesh was melded to hers. His teeth were on her breast, lightly at the edge of control, then his tongue swept across her nipple until she moaned and pressed closer.

Pierce could feel the hammer beat of her pulse, almost taste it as his mouth hurried to her other breast. Her moans and her urging hands were driving him beyond reason. He was trapped in a furnace, but there would be no escape this time. He knew his flesh would melt into hers until there was nothing left to keep him separate. The heat, her scent, her taste all whirled inside his head.

Excitement? No, this was more than excitement. It was obsession.

He slipped his fingers inside her. She was so soft, so warm and moist, he had no more will left.

He entered her with a wildness that stunned them both. Then she was moving with him, frantic and strong. He felt the pain of impossible pleasure, knowing he had been the enchanted, not the enchanter. He was utterly hers.

Ryan felt his ragged breath against her neck. His heart was still racing. For me, she thought dreamily as she floated on the aftermath of passion. *Mine,* she thought again and sighed. How had Bess known before she had? Ryan closed her eyes and let herself drift.

It must show on her face like a neon sign. Is it too soon to tell him? she wondered. Wait, she decided, touching his hair. She would let herself have time to get used to love before she proclaimed it. At that moment she felt she had all the time in the world.

She gave a murmured protest when Pierce took his weight from her. Slowly, she opened her eyes. He stared down at his hands. He was cursing himself steadily.

"Did I hurt you?" he demanded in a quick, rough burst.

"No," she said, surprised, then remembered Bess's story. "No, you didn't hurt me, Pierce. You couldn't. You're a very gentle man."

His eyes whipped back to hers, dark, anguished. There had been no gentleness in him when he had loved her. Only needs and desperation. "Not always," he said sharply and reached for his jeans.

"What are you doing?"

"I'll go down and get another room." He was dressing swiftly as she looked on. "I'm sorry this happened. I won't…" He stopped when he looked and saw tears welling in her eyes. Something ripped inside his stomach.

"Ryan, I am sorry." Sitting beside her again, he brushed a tear away with his thumb. "I swore I wasn't going to touch you. I shouldn't have. You'd had too much to drink. I knew that and should've—"

"Damn you!" She slapped his hand away. "I was wrong. You *can* hurt me. Well, you don't have to get another room." She reached down for her blouse. "I'll get one myself. I won't stay here after you've turned something wonderful into a mistake."

She was up and tugging on her blouse, which was inside out.

"Ryan, I—"

"Oh, shut up!" Seeing the two middle buttons were missing, she tore the blouse off again and stood facing him, haughtily naked, eyes blazing. He nearly pulled her to the floor and took her again. "I knew exactly what I was doing, do you hear? Exactly! If you think it only takes a few drinks to make me throw myself at a man, then you're wrong. I wanted you, I thought you wanted me. So if it was a mistake, it was yours."

"It wasn't a mistake for me, Ryan." His voice had softened, but when he reached out to touch her, she jerked back. He let his hand drop to his side and chose his words carefully. "I wanted you; perhaps, I thought, too much. And I wasn't as gentle with you as I wanted to be. It's difficult for me to deal with knowing I couldn't stop myself from having you."

For a moment she studied him, then brushed tears away with the back of her hand. "Did you want to stop yourself?"

"The point is, I tried and couldn't. And I've never taken a woman with less..." He hesitated. "Care," he murmured. "You're very small, very fragile."

Fragile? she thought and lifted a brow. No one had

ever called her that before. At another time she might have enjoyed it, but now she felt there was only one way to handle a man like Pierce. "Okay," she told him and took a deep breath. "You've got two choices."

Surprised, Pierce drew his brows together. "What are they?"

"You can get yourself another room or you can take me to bed and make love to me again." She took a step toward him. "Right now."

He met the challenge in her eyes and smiled. "Those are my only choices?"

"I suppose I could seduce you again if you want to be stubborn," she said with a shrug. "It's up to you."

He let his fingers dive into her hair as he drew her closer. "What if we combined two of those choices?"

She gave him a look of consideration. "Which two?"

He lowered his mouth to hers for a soft, lingering kiss. "How about I take you to bed and you seduce me?"

Ryan allowed him to lift her into his arms. "I'm a reasonable person," she agreed as he walked to the bedroom. "I'm willing to discuss a compromise as long as I get my own way."

"Miss Swan," Pierce murmured as he laid her gently on the bed, "I like your style."

Chapter 9

Ryan's body ached. Sighing, she snuggled deeper into the pillow. It was a pleasant discomfort. It reminded her of the night—the night that had lasted until dawn.

She hadn't known she had so much passion to give or so many needs to fill. Each time she had thought herself drained, body and mind, she had only to touch him again, or he her. Strength would flood back into her, and with it the unrelenting demands of desire.

Then they had slept, holding each other as the rosy tones of sunrise had slipped into the room. Drifting awake, clinging to sleep, Ryan shifted toward Pierce, wanting to hold him again.

She was alone.

Confusion had her eyes slowly opening. Sliding her hand over the sheets beside her, Ryan found them cold. *Gone?* she thought hazily. How long had she been sleeping alone? All of her dreamy pleasure died. Ryan touched the sheets again. No, she told herself and stretched, he's just in the other room. He wouldn't have left me alone.

The phone shrilled and jolted her completely awake.

"Yes, hello." She answered it on the first ring and pushed her hair from her face with her free hand. *Why was the suite so quiet?*

"Miss Swan?"

"Yes, this is Ryan Swan."

"Bennett Swan calling, please hold."

Ryan sat up, automatically pulling the sheets to her breast. Disoriented, she wondered what time it was. And where, she thought again, was Pierce?

"Ryan, give me an update."

An update? she repeated silently, hearing her father's voice. She struggled to put her thoughts into order.

"Ryan!"

"Yes, I'm sorry."

"I haven't got all day."

"I've watched Pierce's rehearsals daily," she began, wishing for a cup of coffee and a few moments to pull herself together. "I think you'll find he has the technical areas and his own crew well in hand." She glanced around the bedroom, looking for some sign of him. "He opened last night, flawlessly. We've already discussed some alterations for the special, but nothing's firmed up as yet. At this point whatever new routines he's worked out he's keeping to himself."

"I want some firm estimates on the set within two weeks," he told her. "We might have a change in the scheduling. You work it out with Atkins. I want a list of his proposed routines and the time allowance for each one."

"I've already discussed it with him," Ryan said coolly,

annoyed that her father was infringing on her territory. "I am the producer, aren't I?"

"You are," he agreed. "I'll see you in my office when you get back."

Hearing the click, Ryan hung up with a sigh of exasperation. It had been a typical Bennett Swan conversation. She pushed the phone call from her mind and scrambled from the bed. Pierce's robe lay draped over a chair, and picking it up, Ryan slipped it on.

"Pierce?" Ryan hurried out into the living area of the suite but found it empty. "Pierce?" she called again, stepping on one of the lost buttons from her blouse. Absently, Ryan picked it up and dropped it in the pocket of the robe before she walked through the suite.

Empty. The pain started in her stomach and spread. He had left her alone. Shaking her head, Ryan searched the rooms again. He must have left her a note telling her why and where he'd gone. He wouldn't just wake up and leave her, not after last night.

But there was nothing. Ryan shivered, suddenly cold.

It was the pattern of her life, she decided. Moving to the window, she stared out at unlit neon. Whoever she cared for, whoever she gave love to, always went their own way. Yet somehow, she still expected it to be different.

When she had been small, it had been her mother, a young, glamour-loving woman jetting off to follow Bennett Swan all over the world. *You're a big girl, Ryan, and so self-sufficient. I'll be back in a few days.* Or a few weeks, Ryan remembered. There had always been a housekeeper and other servants to see that she was tended to. No, she had never been neglected or abused. Just forgotten.

Later it had been her father, dashing here and there

at a moment's notice. But of course, he'd seen that she had had a solid, dependable nanny whom he had paid a very substantial salary. Then she'd been shipped off to Switzerland, the best boarding school available. *That daughter of mine has a head on her shoulders. Top ten percent of her class.*

There'd always been an expensive present on her birthday with a card from thousands of miles away telling her to keep up the good work. Of course, she had. She would never have risked disappointing him.

Nothing ever changes, Ryan thought as she turned to stare at herself in the mirror. Ryan's strong. Ryan's practical. Ryan doesn't need all the things other women do—hugs, gentleness, romance.

They're right, of course, she told herself. It's foolish to be hurt. We wanted each other. We spent the night together. Why romanticize it? I don't have any claim on Pierce. And he has none on me. She fingered the lapel of his robe, then quickly dropped her hand. Moving swiftly, Ryan stripped and went to shower.

Ryan kept the water almost unbearably hot, allowing it to beat full force against her skin. She wasn't going to think. She knew herself well. If she kept her mind a blank, when she opened it again, she'd know what she had to do.

The air in the bath was steamy and moist when she stepped out to towel herself. Her moves were brisk again. There was work to be done—notes to write on ideas and plans. Ryan Swan, Executive Producer. That's what she had to concentrate on. It was time to stop worrying about the people who couldn't—or wouldn't—give her what she wanted. She had a name to make for herself in the industry. That was all that really mattered.

As she dressed, she was perfectly calm. Dreams

were for sleeping, and she was wide awake. There were dozens of details to be seen to. She had meetings to set up, department heads to deal with. Decisions had to be made. She had been in Las Vegas long enough. She knew Pierce's style as well as she ever would. And, more important to her at the moment, she knew precisely what she wanted in the finished product. Back in Los Angeles, Ryan could start putting her ideas into motion.

It was going to be her first production, but she'd be damned if it was going to be her last. This time she had places of her own to go to.

Ryan picked up her comb and ran it through her damp hair. The door opened behind her.

"So, you're awake." Pierce smiled and started to cross to her. The look in her eyes stopped him. Angry hurt— he could feel waves of it.

"Yes, I'm awake," she said easily and continued to comb her hair. "I've been up for some time. My father called earlier. He wanted a progress report."

"Oh?" Her emotions weren't directed toward her father, Pierce decided, watching her steadily. "Have you ordered anything from room service?"

"No."

"You'll want some breakfast," he said, taking another step toward her. He went no farther, feeling the wall she had thrown up between them.

"No, actually, I don't." Ryan took out her mascara and began to apply it with great care. "I'll get some coffee at the airport. I'm going back to L.A. this morning."

The cool, matter-of-fact tone had his stomach muscles tightening. Could he have been so wrong? Had the night they had shared meant so little to her? "This morning?" he repeated, matching her tone. "Why?"

"I think I have a fairly good handle on how you work

and what you'll want for the special." She kept her eyes focused only on her own in the mirror. "I should start on the preliminary stages, then we can set up a meeting when you're back in California. I'll call your agent."

Pierce bit off the words he wanted to say. He never put chains on anyone but himself. "If that's what you want."

Ryan's fingers tightened on the tube of mascara before she set it down. "We both have our jobs to do. Mine's in L.A.; yours, for the moment, is here." She turned to go to the closet, but he laid a hand on her shoulder. Pierce dropped it immediately when she stiffened.

"Ryan, have I hurt you?"

"Hurt me?" she repeated and continued on to the closet. Her tone was like a shrug, but he couldn't see her eyes. "How could you have possibly hurt me?"

"I don't know." He spoke from directly behind her. Ryan pulled out an armful of clothes. "But I have." He turned her to face him. "I can see it in your eyes."

"Forget it," she told him. "I will." She started to walk away, but this time he kept his hands firm.

"I can't forget something unless I know what it is." Though he kept his hands light, annoyance had crept into his tone. "Ryan, tell me what's wrong."

"Drop it, Pierce."

"No."

Ryan tried to jerk away again, and again he held her still. She told herself to be calm. "You *left* me!" she exploded and tossed the clothes aside. The passion erupted from her so swiftly, it left him staring and speechless. "I woke up and you were gone, without a word. I'm not used to one-night stands."

His eyes kindled at that. "Ryan—"

"No, I don't want to hear it." She shook her head vigorously. "I expected something different from you. I was wrong. But that's all right. A woman like me doesn't need all the niceties. I'm an expert on surviving." She twisted but found herself held against him. "Don't! Let me go, I have to pack."

"Ryan." Even as she resisted, he held her closer. The hurt went deep, he thought, and hadn't started with him. "I'm sorry."

"I want you to let me go, Pierce."

"You won't listen to me if I do." He stroked a hand down her wet hair. "I need you to listen."

"There's nothing to say."

Her voice had thickened, and he felt a wicked stab of self-blame. How could he have been so stupid? How could he not have seen what would be important to her?

"Ryan, I know a lot about one-night stands." Pierce drew her away, just far enough so that he could see her eyes. "That isn't what last night was for me."

She shook her head fiercely, struggling for composure. "There's no need for you to say that."

"I told you once, I don't lie, Ryan." He slipped his hands up to her shoulders. "What we had together last night is very important to me."

"You were gone when I woke up." She swallowed and shut her eyes. "The bed was cold."

"I'm sorry. I went down to smooth out a few things before tonight's show."

"If you'd woke me—"

"I never thought to wake you, Ryan," he said quietly. "Just as I never thought how you might feel waking up alone. The sun was coming in when you fell asleep."

"You were up as long as I was." She tried to turn away again. "Pierce, *please!*" Hearing the desperation in the word, she bit her lip. "Let me go."

He lowered his hands, then watched as she gathered

her clothes again. "Ryan, I never sleep more than five or six hours. It's all I need." Was this panic he was feeling watching her fold a blouse into a suitcase? "I thought you'd still be sleeping when I got back."

"I reached for you," she said simply. "And you were gone."

"Ryan—"

"No, it doesn't matter." She pressed her hands to her temples a moment and let out a deep breath. "I'm sorry. I'm acting like a fool. You haven't done anything, Pierce. It's me. I always expect too much. I'm always floored when I don't get it." Quickly, she began to pack again. "I didn't mean to make a scene. Please forget it."

"It isn't something I want to forget," he murmured.

"I'd feel less foolish if I knew you would," she said, trying to make her voice light. "Just put it down to a lack of sleep and a bad disposition. I should be going back, though. I've a lot of work to do."

He had seen her needs from the first—her response to gentleness, her pleasure in the gift of a flower. She was an emotional, romantic woman who tried very hard not to be. Pierce cursed himself, thinking how she must have felt to find the bed empty after the night they had spent together.

"Ryan, don't go." That was difficult for him. It was something he never asked of anyone.

Her fingers hesitated at the locks of her suitcase. Clicking them shut, Ryan set it on the floor, then turned. "Pierce, I'm not angry, honestly. A little embarrassed, maybe." She managed a smile. "I really should go back and start things moving. There might be a change in the scheduling, and—"

"Stay," he interrupted, unable to stop himself. "Please."

Ryan remained silent a moment. Something she saw

in his eyes had a block lodging in her throat. It was costing him something to ask. Just as it was going to cost her something to ask. "Why?"

"I need you." He took a breath after what was for him a staggering admission. "I don't want to lose you."

Ryan took a step toward him. "Does it matter?"

"Yes. Yes, it matters."

She waited for a moment but was unable to convince herself to walk out the door. "Show me," she told him.

Going to her, he gathered her close. Ryan shut her eyes. It was exactly what she had needed—to be held, just to be held. His chest was firm against her cheek, his arms strong around her. Yet she knew she was being held as if she were something precious. Fragile, he had called her. For the first time in her life, Ryan wanted to be.

"Oh, Pierce, I'm an idiot."

"No." He lifted her chin with a finger and kissed her. "You're very sweet." He smiled then and laid his forehead on hers. "Are you going to complain when I wake you up after five hours sleep?"

"Never." Laughing, she threw her arms around his neck. "Or maybe just a little."

She smiled at him, but his eyes were suddenly serious. Pierce slid a hand up to cup the back of her neck before his mouth lowered to hers.

It was like the first time—the gentleness, the featherlight pressure that turned her blood to flame. She was utterly helpless when he kissed her like this, unable to pull him closer, unable to demand. She could only let him take in his own time.

Pierce knew that this time the power was his alone. It made his hands move tenderly as they undressed her. He let her blouse slip slowly off her shoulders, down her back, to flutter to the floor. Her skin quivered as his hands passed over it.

Unhooking her trousers, he drew them down her hips, letting his fingers toy with the tiny swatch of silk and lace that rose high at her thighs. All the while his mouth nibbled at hers. Her breath caught, then she moaned as he trailed a finger inside the silk. But he didn't remove it. Instead, he slid his hand to her breast to stroke and tease until she began to tremble.

"I want you," she said shakily. "Do you know how much I want you?"

"Yes." He brushed soft, butterfly kisses over her face. "Yes."

"Make love to me," Ryan whispered. "Pierce, make love to me."

"I am," he murmured and pressed his mouth to the frantic pulse in her neck.

"Now," she demanded, too weak to pull him to her.

He laughed, deep in his throat, and lowered her to the bed. "You drove me mad last night, Miss Swan, touching me like this." Pierce trailed a finger down the center of her body, stopping to linger at the soft mound between her legs. Slowly, lazily, he took his mouth to follow the trail.

In the night a madness had been on him. He had known impatience, desperation. He had taken her again and again, passionately, but had been unable to savor. It was as though he had been starved, and greed had driven him. Now, though he wanted her no less, he could restrain the need. He could taste and sample and enjoy.

Ryan's limbs were heavy. She couldn't move them, could only let him touch and caress and kiss wherever he wished. The strength that had driven her the night before had been replaced by a honeyed weakness. She lay steeped in it.

His mouth loitered at her waist, his tongue circling lower while he ran his hands lightly over her, tracing the shape of her breasts, stroking her neck and shoulders. He teased rather than possessed, aroused rather than fulfilled.

He caught the waistband of the silk in his teeth and took it inches lower. Ryan arched and moaned. But it was the skin of her thigh he tasted, savoring until she knew madness was only a breath away. She heard herself sighing his name, a soft, urgent sound, but he made no answer. His mouth was busy doing wonderful things to the back of her knee.

Ryan felt the heated skin of his chest brush over her leg, though she had no idea how or when he had rid himself of his shirt. She had never been more aware of her own body. She learned of the drugging, heavenly pleasure that could come from the touch of a fingertip on the skin.

He was lifting her, Ryan thought mistily, though her back was pressed into the bed. He was levitating her, making her float. He was showing her magic, but this trance was no illusion.

They were both naked now, wrapped together as his mouth journeyed back to hers. He kissed her slowly, deeply, until she was limp. His nimble fingers aroused. She hadn't known passion could pull two ways at once— into searing fire and into the clouds.

Her breath was heaving, but still he waited. He would give her everything first, every dram of pleasure, every dark delight he knew. Her skin was like water in his hands, flowing, rippling. He nibbled and sucked gently on her swollen lips and waited for her final moan of surrender.

"Now, love?" he asked, spreading light, whispering kisses over her face. "Now?"

She couldn't answer. She was beyond words and reason. That was where he wanted her. Exhilarated, he laughed and pressed his mouth to her throat. "You're mine, Ryan. Tell me. Mine."

"Yes." It came out on a husky breath, barely audible. "Yours." But his mouth swallowed the words even as she said them. "Take me." She didn't hear herself say it. She thought the demand was only in her brain, but then he was inside her. Ryan gasped and arched to meet him. And still he moved with painful slowness.

The blood was roaring in her ears as he drew the ultimate pleasure to its fullest. His lips rubbed over hers, capturing each trembling breath.

Abruptly, he crushed his mouth on hers—no more gentleness, no more teasing. She cried out as he took her with a sudden, wild fury. The fire consumed them both, fusing skin and lips until Ryan thought they both had died.

Pierce lay on her, resting his head between her breasts. Under his ear he heard the thunder of her heartbeat. She had yet to stop trembling. Her arms were twined around him, with one hand still tangled in his hair. He didn't want to move. He wanted to keep her like this—alone, naked, his. The fierce desire for possession shook him. It wasn't his way. Had never been his way before Ryan. The drive was too strong to resist.

"Tell me again," he demanded, lifting his face to watch hers.

Ryan's eyes opened slowly. She was drugged with love, sated with pleasure. "Tell you what?"

His mouth came to hers again, seeking, then lingered

to draw the last taste. When he lifted it, his eyes were dark and demanding. "Tell me that you're mine, Ryan."

"Yours," she murmured as her eyes closed again. She sighed into sleep. "For as long as you want me."

Pierce frowned at her answer and started to speak, but her breathing was slow and even. Shifting, he lay beside her and pulled her close.

This time he would wait until she woke.

Chapter 10

Ryan had never known time to pass so quickly. She should have been glad of it. When Pierce's Las Vegas engagement was over, they could begin work on the special. It was something she was eager to do, for herself and for him. She knew it could be the turning point of her career.

Yet she found herself wishing the hours wouldn't fly by. There was something fanciful about Vegas, with its lack of time synchronization, its honky-tonk streets and glittery casinos. There, with the touch of magic all around, it seemed natural to love him, to share the life he lived. Ryan wasn't certain it would be so simple once they returned to the practical world.

They were both taking each day one at a time. There was no talk of the future. Pierce's burst of possessiveness had never reoccurred, and Ryan wondered at it. She nearly believed she had dreamed those deep, insistent words—*You're mine. Tell me.*

He had never demanded again, nor had he given her any words of love. He was gentle, at times achingly so, with words or looks or gestures. But he was never completely free with her. Nor was Ryan ever completely free with him. Trusting came easily to neither of them.

On closing night Ryan dressed carefully. She wanted a special evening. Champagne, she decided as she slipped into a frothy dress in a rainbow of hues. She would order champagne to be sent up to the suite after the performance. They had one long, last night to spend together before the idyll ended.

Ryan studied herself critically in the mirror. The dress was sheer and much more daring, she noted, than her usual style. Pierce would say it was more Ryan than Miss Swan, she thought and laughed. He would be right, as always. At the moment she didn't feel at all like Miss Swan. Tomorrow would be soon enough for business suits.

She dabbed perfume on her wrists, then at the hollow between her breasts.

"Ryan, if you want dinner before the show, you'll have to hurry along. It's nearly…" Pierce broke off as he came into the room. He stopped to stare at her. The dress floated here, clung there, wisping enticingly over her breasts in colors that melded and ran like a painting left in the rain.

"You're so lovely," he murmured, feeling the familiar thrill along his skin. "Like something I might have dreamed."

When he spoke like that, he had her heart melting and her pulse racing at the same time. "A dream?" Ryan walked to him and slid her arms around his neck. "What sort of a dream would you like me to be?" She kissed one cheek, then the other. "Will you conjure a dream for me, Pierce?"

"You smell of jasmine." He buried his face in her neck. He thought he had never wanted anything—anyone—so much in his life. "It drives me mad."

"A woman's spell." Ryan tilted her head to give his mouth more freedom. "To enchant the enchanter."

"It works."

She gave a throaty laugh and pressed closer. "Wasn't it a woman's spell that was Merlin's undoing in the end?"

"Have you been researching?" he asked in her ear. "Careful, I've been in the business longer than you." Lifting his face, he touched his lips to hers. "It isn't wise to tangle with a magician, you know."

"I'm not in the least wise." She let her fingers run up the back of his neck, then through the thick mane of his hair. "Not in the least."

He felt a wave of power—and a wave of weakness. It was always the same when she was in his arms. Pierce pulled her close again just to hold her. Sensing some struggle, Ryan remained passive. He had so much to give, she thought, so much emotion he would offer or hold back. She could never be sure which he would choose to do. Yet wasn't it the same with her? she asked herself. She loved him but hadn't been able to say the words aloud. Even as the love grew, she still wasn't able to say them.

"Will you be in the wings tonight?" he asked her. "I like knowing you're there."

"Yes." Ryan tilted back her head and smiled. It was so rare for him to ask anything of her. "One of these days I'm going to spot something. Even *your* hand isn't always quicker than the eye."

"No?" He grinned, amused at her continued determination to catch him. "About dinner," he began and toyed with the zipper at the back of her dress. He was beginning to wonder what she wore under it. If he chose, he could have the dress on the floor at her feet before she could draw a breath.

"What about it?" she asked with a gleam of mischief in her eyes.

The knock at the door had him swearing.

"Why don't you turn whoever it is into a toad?" Ryan suggested. Then, sighing, she rested her head on his shoulder. "No, that would be rude, I suppose."

"I rather like the idea."

She laughed and drew back. "I'll answer it. I can't have that on my conscience." Toying with his top button, she lifted a brow. "You won't forget what you were thinking about while I'm sending them away?"

He smiled. "I have a very good memory." Pierce let her go and watched her walk away. Miss Swan hadn't picked out that dress, he decided, echoing Ryan's earlier thoughts.

"Package for you, Miss Swan."

Ryan accepted the small plainly wrapped box and the card from the messenger. "Thank you." After closing the door, she set down the package and opened the envelope. The note was brief and typewritten.

Ryan,
Your report in good order. Expect a thorough briefing on Atkins project on your return. First full meeting scheduled one week from today. Happy birthday.
Your Father

Ryan read it over twice, then glanced briefly at the package. He wouldn't miss my birthday, she thought as she scanned the typed words a third time. Bennett Swan always did his duty. Ryan felt a surge of disappointment, of anger, of futility. All the familiar emotions of Swan's only child.

Why? she demanded of herself. Why hadn't he waited and given her something in person? Why had he sent an impersonal note that read like a telegram and a proper token his secretary no doubt selected? Why couldn't he have just sent his love?

"Ryan?" Pierce watched her from the doorway of the bedroom. He had seen her read the note. He had seen the look of emptiness in her eyes. "Bad news?"

"No." Quickly, Ryan shook her head and slipped the note into her purse. "No, it's nothing. Let's go to dinner, Pierce. I'm starving."

She was smiling, reaching out her hand for his, but the hurt in her eyes was unmistakable. Saying nothing, Pierce took her hand. As they left the suite, he glanced at the package she had never opened.

As Pierce had requested, Ryan watched the show from the wings. She had blocked all thoughts of her father from her mind. It was her last night of complete freedom, and Ryan was determined to let nothing spoil it.

It's my birthday, she reminded herself. I'm going to have my own private celebration. She had said nothing to Pierce, initially because she had forgotten her birthday entirely until her father's note had arrived. Now, she decided, it would be foolish to mention it. She was twenty-seven, after all, too old to be sentimental about the passing of a year.

"You were wonderful, as always," she told Pierce as he walked offstage, applause thundering after him. "When are you going to tell me how you do that last illusion?"

"Magic, Miss Swan, has no explanation."

She narrowed her eyes at him. "I happen to know that Bess is in her dressing room right now, and that the panther—"

"Explanations disappoint," he interrupted. He took her hand to lead her into his own dressing room. "The mind's a paradox, Miss Swan."

"Do tell," she said dryly, knowing full well he was going to explain nothing.

He managed to keep his face seriously composed as he stripped off his shirt. "The mind wants to believe the impossible," he continued as he went into the bath to wash. "Yet it doesn't. Therein lies the fascination. If the impossible is *not* possible, then how was it done before your eyes and under your nose?"

"That's what I want to know," Ryan complained over the sound of running water. When he came back in, a towel slung over his shoulder, she shot him a straight, uncompromising look. "As your producer in this special, I should—"

"Produce," he finished and pulled on a fresh shirt. "I'll do the impossible."

"It's maddening not to know," she said darkly but did up the buttons of his shirt herself.

"Yes." Pierce only smiled when she glared at him.

"It's just a trick," Ryan said with a shrug, hoping to annoy him.

"Is it?" His smile remained infuriatingly amiable.

Knowing defeat when faced with it, Ryan sighed. "I suppose you'd suffer all sorts of torture and never breathe a word."

"Did you have some in mind?"

She laughed then and pressed her mouth to his. "That's just the beginning," she promised dangerously. "I'm going to take you upstairs and drive you crazy until you talk."

"Interesting." Pierce slipped an arm around her shoulders and led her into the corridor. "It could take quite a bit of time."

"I'm in no hurry," she said blithely.

They rode to the top floor, but when Pierce started to slip the key into the lock of the suite, Ryan laid her hand on his. "This is your last chance before I get tough," she warned. "I'm going to make you talk."

He only smiled at her and pushed the door open.

"Happy birthday!"

Ryan's eyes widened in surprise. Bess, still in costume, opened a bottle of champagne while Link did his best to catch the spurt of wine in a glass. Speechless, Ryan stared at them.

"Happy birthday, Ryan." Pierce kissed her lightly.

"But how…" She broke off to look up at him. "How did you know?"

"Here you go." Bess stuck a glass of champagne in Ryan's hand, then gave her a quick squeeze. "Drink up, sweetie. You only get one birthday a year. Thank God. The champagne's from me—a bottle for now and one for later." She winked at Pierce.

"Thank you." Ryan looked helplessly into her glass. "I don't know what to say."

"Link's got something for you, too," Bess told her.

The big man shifted uncomfortably as all eyes turned to him. "I got you a cake," he mumbled, then cleared his throat. "You have to have a birthday cake."

Ryan walked over to see a sheet cake decorated in delicate pinks and yellows. "Oh, Link! It's lovely."

"You have to cut the first piece," he instructed.

"Yes, I will in a minute." Reaching up, Ryan drew his head down until she could reach it on tiptoe. She pressed a kiss on his mouth. "Thank you, Link."

He turned pink, grinned, then sent Bess an agonized look. "Welcome."

"I have something for you." Still smiling, Ryan turned to Pierce. "Will you kiss me, too?" he demanded.

"After I get my present."

"Greedy," he decided and handed her a small wooden box.

It was old and carved. Ryan ran her finger over it to feel the places that had worn smooth with age and handling. "It's beautiful," she murmured. She opened it and saw a tiny silver symbol on a chain. "Oh!"

"An ankh," Pierce told her, slipping it out to fasten it around her neck. "An Egyptian symbol of life. Not a superstition," he said gravely. "It's for luck."

"Pierce." Remembering her flattened penny, Ryan laughed and threw her arms around him. "Don't you ever forget anything?"

"No. Now you owe me a kiss."

Ryan complied, then forgot there were eyes on them.

"Hey, look, we want some of this cake. Don't we, Link?" Bess slipped an arm around his thick waist and grinned as Ryan surfaced.

"Will it taste as good as it looks?" Ryan wondered aloud as she picked up the knife and sliced through it. "I don't know how long it's been since I've eaten birthday cake. Here, Link, you have the first piece." Ryan licked icing from her finger as he took it. "Terrific," she judged, then began to cut another slice. "I don't know how you found out. I'd forgotten myself until…" Ryan stopped cutting and straightened. "You read my note!" she accused Pierce. He looked convincingly blank.

"What note?"

She let out an impatient breath, not noticing that Bess

had taken the knife and was slicing the cake herself. "You went in my purse and read that note."

"Went in your purse?" Pierce repeated, lifting a brow. "Really, Ryan, would I do something so crude?"

She thought about that for a moment. "Yes, you would."

Bess snickered, but he only sent her a mild glance. He accepted a piece of cake. "A magician doesn't need to stoop to picking pockets to gather information."

Link laughed, a deep rumbling sound that caught Ryan by surprise. "Like the time you lifted that guy's keys in Detroit?" he reminded Pierce.

"Or the earrings from the lady in Flatbush," Bess put in. "Nobody's got a smoother touch than you, Pierce."

"Really?" Ryan drew out the word as she looked back at him. Pierce bit into a piece of cake and said nothing.

"He always gives them back at the end of the show," Bess went on. "Good thing Pierce didn't decide on a life of crime. Think of what would happen if he started cracking safes from the outside instead of the inside."

"Fascinating," Ryan agreed, narrowing her eyes at him. "I'd love to hear more about it."

"How about the time you broke out of that little jail in Wichita, Pierce?" Bess continued obligingly. "You know when they locked you up for—"

"Have some more champagne, Bess," Pierce suggested, lifting the bottle and tilting it into her glass.

Link let out another rumbling laugh. "Sure would liked to've seen that sheriff's face when he looked in and saw an empty cell, all locked up and tidy."

"Jail-breaking," Ryan mused, fascinated.

"Houdini did it routinely." Pierce handed her a glass of champagne.

"Yeah, but he worked it out with the cops first." Bess

chuckled at the look Pierce sent her and cut Link another piece of cake.

"Picking pockets, breaking jail." Ryan enjoyed the faint discomfort she saw in Pierce's eyes. It wasn't often she had him at a disadvantage. "Are there any other things I should know about?"

"It would seem you know too much already," he commented.

"Yes." She kissed him soundly. "And it's the best birthday present I've ever had."

"Come on, Link." Bess lifted the half-empty bottle of champagne. "Let's go finish this and your cake. We'll leave Pierce to work his way out of this one. You ought to tell her the one about that salesman in Salt Lake City."

"Good night, Bess," Pierce said blandly and earned another chuckle.

"Happy birthday, Ryan." Bess gave Pierce a flashing grin as she pulled Link out of the room.

"Thank you, Bess. Thank you, Link." Ryan waited until the door shut before she looked back at Pierce. "Before we discuss the salesman in Salt Lake City, why were you in a little cell in Wichita?" Her eyes laughed at him over the rim of her glass.

"A misunderstanding."

"That's what they all say." Her brow arched. "A jealous husband, perhaps?"

"No, an annoyed deputy who found himself locked to a bar stool with his own handcuffs." Pierce shrugged. "He wasn't appreciative when I let him go."

Ryan smothered a laugh. "No, I imagine he wasn't."

"A small wager," Pierce added. "He lost."

"Then instead of paying off," Ryan concluded, "he tossed you in jail."

"Something like that."

"A desperate criminal." Ryan heaved a sigh. "I suppose I'm at your mercy." Setting down her glass, she went to him. "It was very sweet of you to do this for me. Thank you."

Pierce brushed back her hair. "Such a serious face," he murmured and kissed her eyes shut. He thought of the hurt he had seen in them when she had read her father's letter. "Aren't you going to open the present from your father, Ryan?"

She shook her head, then laid her cheek on his shoulder. "No, not tonight. Tomorrow. I've been given the presents that matter already."

"He didn't forget you, Ryan."

"No, he wouldn't forget. It would be marked on his calendar. Oh, I'm sorry." She shook her head again, drawing away. "That was petty. I've always wanted too much. He does love me—in his own way."

Pierce took her hands in his. "He only knows his own way."

Ryan looked back up at him. Her frown cleared into an expression of understanding. "Yes, you're right. I've never thought about it that way. I keep struggling to please him so he'll turn to me one day and say, 'Ryan, I love you. I'm proud to be your father.' It's silly." She sighed. "I'm a grown woman, but I keep waiting."

"We don't ever stop wanting that from our parents." Pierce drew her close again.

Ryan thought of his childhood while he wondered about hers.

"We'd be different people, wouldn't we, if our parents had acted differently?"

"Yes," he answered. "We would."

Ryan tilted her head back. "I wouldn't want you to be any different, Pierce. You're exactly what I want." Hungrily, she pressed her mouth to his. "Take me to bed," she whispered. "Tell me what you were thinking all those hours ago before we were interrupted."

Pierce swept her up, and she clung, delighting in the strength of his arms. "Actually," he began, crossing to the bedroom, "I was wondering what you had on under that dress."

Ryan laughed and pressed her mouth to his throat. "Well, there's hardly anything there to wonder about at all."

The bedroom was dark and quiet as Ryan lay curled up at Pierce's side. His fingers played absently with her hair. He thought she was sleeping; she was very still. He didn't mind his own wakefulness. It allowed him to enjoy the feel of her skin against his, the silken texture of her hair. While she slept, he could touch her without arousing her, only to comfort himself that she was there. He didn't like knowing she wouldn't be in his bed the following night.

"What are you thinking about?" she murmured and startled him.

"About you." He drew her closer. "I thought you were sleeping."

"No." He felt the brush of her lashes on his shoulder as she opened her eyes. "I was thinking about you." Lifting her finger, she traced it along his jawline. "Where did you get this scar?"

He didn't answer immediately. Ryan realized she'd unwittingly probed into his past. "I suppose it was in a battle with a sorceress," she said lightly, wishing she could take the question back.

"Not quite so romantic. I fell down some stairs when I was a kid."

She held her breath a moment. She hadn't expected him to volunteer anything on his past, even so small a detail. Shifting, she rested her head on his chest. "I tripped over a stool once and loosened a tooth. My father was furious when he found out. I was terrified it would fall out and he'd disown me."

"Did he frighten you so much?"

"His disapproval, yes. I suppose it was foolish."

"No." Staring up at the dark ceiling, Pierce continued to stroke her hair. "We're all afraid of something."

"Even you?" she asked with a half-laugh. "I don't believe you're afraid of anything."

"Of not being able to get out once I'm in," he murmured.

Surprised, Ryan looked up and caught the gleam of his eyes in the darkness. "Do you mean in one of your escapes?"

"What?" He brought his thoughts back to her. He hadn't realized he had spoken aloud.

"Why do you do the escapes if you feel that way?"

"Do you think that if you ignore a fear it goes away?" he asked her. "When I was small," he said calmly, "it was a closet, and I couldn't get out. Now it's a steamer trunk or a vault, and I can escape."

"Oh, Pierce." Ryan turned her face into his chest. "I'm sorry. You don't have to talk about it."

But he was compelled to. For the first time since his childhood, Pierce heard himself speak of it. "Do you know, I think that the memory of scent stays with you longer than anything else. I could always remember the scent of my father so clearly. It wasn't until ten years after I last saw him that I learned what it was. He smelled of gin. I couldn't have told you what he looked like, but I remembered that smell."

He continued to stare up at the ceiling as he spoke. Ryan knew he had forgotten her as he went back into his own past. "One night when I was about fifteen, I was down in the cellar. I used to like to explore down there when everyone was in bed. I came across the janitor passed out in a corner with a bottle of gin. That smell— I remember being terrified for a moment without having any idea why. But I went over and picked up the bottle, and then I knew. I stopped being afraid."

Pierce was silent for a long time, and Ryan said nothing. She waited, wanting him to continue yet knowing she couldn't ask him to. The room was quiet but for the sound of his heart beating under her ear.

"He was a very cruel, very sick man," Pierce murmured, and she knew he spoke again of his father. "For years I was certain that meant I had the same sickness."

Gripping him tighter, Ryan shook her head. "There's nothing cruel in you," she whispered. "Nothing."

"Would you think so if I told you where I came from?" he wondered. "Would you be willing to let me touch you then?"

Ryan lifted her head and swallowed tears. "Bess told me a week ago," she said steadily. "And I'm here." He said nothing, but she felt his hand fall away from her hair. "You have no right to be angry with her. She's the most loyal, the most loving woman I've ever met. She told me because she knew I cared, knew I needed to understand you."

He was very still. "When?"

"The night…" Ryan hesitated and took a breath. "Opening night." She wished she could see his expression, but the darkness cloaked it. "You said we'd be lovers when I knew you," she reminded him. "You were

right." Because her voice trembled, she swallowed. "Are you sorry?"

It seemed to her an eternity before he answered. "No." Pierce drew her down to him again. "No." He kissed her temple. "How could I be sorry to be your lover?"

"Then don't be sorry that I know you. You're the most magnificent man I've ever met."

He laughed at that, half amused, half moved. And relieved, he discovered. The relief was tremendous. It made him laugh again. "Ryan, what an incredible thing to say."

She tilted up her chin. There would be no tears for him. "It's very true, but I won't tell you again. You'll get conceited." She lifted her palm to his cheek. "But just for tonight I'll let you enjoy it. And besides," she added, pulling his ear, "I like the way your eyebrows sweep up at the ends." She kissed his mouth, then let her lips roam his face. "And the way you write your name."

"The way I what?" he asked.

"On the contracts," Ryan elaborated, still planting light kisses all over his face. "It's very dashing." She felt the smile move his cheeks. "What do you like about me?" she demanded.

"Your taste," he said instantly. "It's impeccable."

Ryan bit his bottom lip, but he only rolled her over and turned the punishment into a very satisfying kiss. "I knew it would make you conceited," she said disgustedly. "I'm going to sleep."

"I don't think so," Pierce corrected, then lowered his mouth.

He was right again.

Chapter 11

Saying goodbye to Pierce was one of the most difficult things Ryan had ever done. She had been tempted to forget every obligation, all of her ambitions, and ask him to take her with him. What were ambitions but empty goals if she was without him? She would tell him that she loved him, that nothing mattered but that they be together.

But when they had parted at the airport, she made herself smile, kiss him goodbye, and let go. She had to drive into Los Angeles, and he had to drive up the coast. The work that had brought them together would also keep them apart.

There had still been no talk of the future. Ryan had come to learn that Pierce didn't speak of tomorrows. That he had spoken to her of his past, however briefly, reassured her. It was a step, perhaps a bigger one than either of them realized.

Time, Ryan thought, would tell if what had been between them in Las Vegas would strengthen or fade. This was the period of waiting. She knew that if he had regrets they would surface now while they were apart. Absence didn't always make the heart grow fonder. It also allowed the blood and the brain to cool. Doubts had a habit of forming when there was time to think. When he came to L.A. for the first meetings, she would have her answer.

When Ryan entered her office, she glanced at her watch and ruefully realized that time and schedules were part of her world again. She had left Pierce only an hour before and missed him unbearably already. Was he thinking of her—right now, at this moment? If she concentrated hard enough, would he know that she thought of him? With a sigh Ryan sat behind her desk. Since she had become involved with Pierce, she'd become freer with her imagination. There were times, she had to admit, that she believed in magic.

What's happened to you, Miss Swan? she asked herself. Your feet aren't on the ground, where they belong. Love, she mused and cupped her chin on her hands. When you're in love, nothing's impossible.

Who could say why her father had taken ill and sent her to Pierce? What force had guided her hand to choose that fateful card from the Tarot deck? Why had the cat picked her window in the storm? Certainly there were logical explanations for each step that had taken her closer to where she was at that moment. But a woman in love doesn't want logic.

It *had* been magic, Ryan thought with a smile. From the first moment their eyes had met, she had felt it. It had simply taken her time to accept it. Now that she did, her only choice was to wait and see if it lasted. No, she corrected, this wasn't a time for choices. She was going to make it last. If it took patience, then she'd be patient. If it took action, then she would act. But she was going to make it work, even if it meant trying her own hand at enchantment.

Shaking her head, she sat back in her chair. Nothing could be done until he was back in her life again. That would take a week. For now, there was still work to do. She couldn't wave a wand and brush the days away until he came back. She had to fill them. Flipping open her notes on Pierce Atkins, Ryan began to transcribe them. Less than thirty minutes later her buzzer sounded.

"Yes, Barbara."

"The boss wants you."

Ryan frowned at the litter of papers on her desk. "Now?"

"Now."

"All right, thanks." Swearing under her breath, Ryan stacked her papers, then separated what was in order to take with her. He might have given her a few hours to get organized, she thought. But the fact remained that he was going to be looking over her shoulder on this project. She was a long way from proving her worth to Bennett Swan. Knowing this, Ryan slipped papers into a folder and went to see her father.

"Good morning, Miss Swan." Bennett Swan's secretary glanced up as Ryan entered. "How was your trip?"

"It went very well, thank you." Ryan watched the woman's eyes shift briefly to the discreet, expensive pearl clusters at her ears. Ryan had worn her father's birthday gift knowing he would want to see them to assure himself they were correct and appreciated.

"Mr. Swan had to step out for a moment, but he'll be right with you. He'd like you to wait in his office. Mr. Ross is already inside."

"Welcome back, Ryan." Ned rose as she shut the door behind her. The coffee he held in his hand was steaming.

"Hello, Ned. Are you in on this meeting?"

"Mr. Swan wants me to work with you on this." He gave her a charming, half-apologetic smile. "Hope you don't mind."

"Of course not," she said flatly. Setting down the folder, she accepted the coffee Ned offered her. "In what capacity?"

"I'll be production coordinator," he told her. "It's still your baby, Ryan."

"Yes." With you as my proctor, she thought bitterly. Swan would still be calling the shots.

"How was Vegas?"

"Unique," Ryan told him as she wandered to the window.

"I hope you found some time to try your luck. You work too hard, Ryan."

She fingered the ankh at her neck and smiled. "I played some blackjack. I won."

"No kidding! Good for you."

After sipping at the coffee, she set the cup aside. "I think I have a firm basis for what will suit Pierce, Swan Productions and the network," she went on. "He doesn't need names to draw ratings. I think more than one guest star would crowd him. As for the set, I'll need to talk to the designers, but I have something fairly definite in mind already. As to the sponsors—"

"We can talk shop later," Ned interrupted. He moved to her and twined the ends of her hair around his fingers. Ryan stayed still and stared out of the window. "I've missed you, Ryan," Ned said softly. "It seemed as though you were gone for months."

"Strange," she murmured watching a plane cruise across the sky. "I've never known a week to pass so quickly."

"Darling, how long are you going to punish me?" He

kissed the top of her head. Ryan felt no resentment. She felt nothing at all. Oddly, Ned had found himself more attracted to her since she had rejected him. There was something different about her now, which he couldn't quite put his finger on. "If you'd just give me a chance, I could make it up to you."

"I'm not punishing you, Ned." Ryan turned to face him. "I'm sorry if it seems that way."

"You're still angry with me."

"No, I told you before that I wasn't." She sighed, deciding it would be better to clear the air between them. "I was angry and hurt, but it didn't last. I was never in love with you, Ned."

He didn't like the faint apology in her voice. It put him on the defensive. "We were just getting to know each other." When he started to take her hands, she shook her head.

"No, I don't think you know me at all. And," she added without rancor, "if we're going to be honest, that wasn't what you were after."

"Ryan, how many times do I have to apologize for that stupid suggestion?" There was a combination of hurt and regret in his voice.

"I'm not asking for an apology, Ned, I'm trying to make myself clear. You made a mistake assuming I could influence my father. You have more influence with him than I have."

"Ryan—"

"No, hear me out," she insisted. "You thought because I'm Bennett Swan's daughter I have his ear. That's just not true and never has been. His business associates have more input with him than I do. You wasted your time cultivating me to get to him. And, leaving that aside," she continued, "I'm not interested in a man who wants to use

me as a springboard. I'm sure we'll work together very
well, but I have no desire to see you outside of the office."

They both jolted when they heard the office door shut.

"Ryan...Ross." Bennett Swan walked over to his desk
and sat down.

"Good morning." Ryan fumbled a bit over the greeting before she took a chair. How much had he heard? she
wondered. His face revealed nothing, so Ryan reached
for the folder. "I've outlined my thoughts and ideas on
Atkins," she began, "though I haven't had time to complete a full report."

"Give me what you have." He waved Ned to a chair,
then lit a cigar.

"He has a very tight club act." Ryan laced her fingers
together to keep them still. "You've seen the tapes yourself, so you know that his act ranges from sleight of hand
to large, complicated illusions to escapes that take two
or three minutes. The escapes will keep him off camera
for that amount of time, but the public expects that." She
paused to cross her legs. "Of course, we know there'll
have to be modifications for television, but I see no problem. He's an extraordinarily creative man."

Swan gave a grunt that might have been agreement
and held out his hand for Ryan's report. Rising, she
handed it to him, then took her seat again. He wasn't in
one of his better moods, she noted. Someone had dis-
pleased him. She could only be grateful she hadn't been
that someone.

"This is pretty slim," he commented, scowling at the
folder.

"It won't be by the end of the day."

"I'll talk to Atkins myself next week," Swan stated
as he skimmed through the papers. "Coogar's going to
direct."

"Good, I'd like to work with him. I want Bloomfield on the set design," she said casually, then held her breath.

Swan glanced up and stared at her. Bloomfield had been his own choice. He'd decided on him less than an hour before. Ryan met the hard look unwaveringly. Swan wasn't altogether certain if he was pleased or annoyed that his daughter was one step ahead of him. "I'll consider it," he said and went back to her report. Quietly, Ryan let out her breath.

"He'll bring his own music director," she went on, thinking of Link. "And his own crew and gimmicks. If we have a problem, I'd say it'll be getting him to cooperate with our people in preproduction and on the set. He has his own way of doing things."

"That can be dealt with," Swan muttered. "Ross will be your production coordinator." Lifting his eyes, he met Ryan's.

"So I understand." Ryan met the look equally. "I can't argue with your choice, but I do feel that if I'm the producer on this project, I should pick my own team."

"You don't want to work with Ross?" Swan demanded as if Ned hadn't been sitting beside her.

"I think Ned and I will deal very well together," she said mildly. "And I'm sure Coogar knows the camera people he wants. It would be ridiculous to interfere with him. However," she added with a hint of steel in her voice, "I also know who *I* want working on this project."

Swan sat back and puffed for a moment on his cigar. The flush of color in his cheeks warned of temper. "What the hell do you know about producing?" he demanded.

"Enough to produce this special and make it a success," she replied. "Just as you told me to do a few weeks ago."

Swan had had time to regret the impulse that had made

him agree to Pierce's terms. "You're the producer on record," he told her shortly. "Your name will be on the credits. Just do as you're told."

Ryan felt the tremor in her stomach but kept her eyes level. "If you feel that way, pull me now." She rose slowly. "But if I stay, I'm going to do more than watch my name roll on the credits. I know how this man works, and I know television. If that isn't enough for you, get someone else."

"Sit down!" he shouted at her. Ned sank a bit deeper in his own chair, but Ryan remained standing. "Don't give me ultimatums. I've been in this business for forty years." He banged his palm on the desk. "*Forty years!* So you know television," he said scornfully. "Pulling off a live show isn't like changing a damn contract. I can't have some hysterical little girl come running to me five minutes before air time telling me there's an equipment failure."

Ryan swallowed raw rage and answered coldly. "I'm not an hysterical little girl, and I've never come running to you for anything."

Completely stunned, he stared at her. The twinge of guilt made his anger all the more explosive. "You're just getting your feet wet," he snapped as he flipped the folder shut. "And you're getting them wet because I say so. You're going to take my advice when I give it to you."

"Your advice?" Ryan countered. Her eyes glistened with conflicting emotions, but her voice was very firm. "I've always respected your advice, but I haven't heard any here today. Just orders. I don't want any favors from you." She turned and headed for the door.

"Ryan!" There was absolute fury in the word. No one but no one walked out on Bennett Swan. "Come back here and sit down. *Young lady!*" he bellowed when she ignored the command.

"I'm not your young lady," she returned, spinning back. "I'm your employee."

Taken aback, he stared at her. What answer could he make to that? He waved his hand at a chair impatiently. "Sit down," he said again, but she stayed at the door. "Sit, sit," he repeated with more exasperation than temper.

Ryan came back and calmly took her place.

"Take Ryan's notes and start working on a budget," he told Ned.

"Yes, sir." Grateful for the dismissal, Ned took the folder and retreated. Swan waited for the door to close before he looked back at his daughter.

"What do you want?" he asked her for the first time in his life. The fact occurred to them both at the same moment.

Ryan took time to separate her personal and professional feelings. "The same respect you'd show any other producer."

"You haven't got any track record," he pointed out.

"No," she agreed. "And I never will if you tie my hands."

Swan let out a sigh, saw his cigar was dead and dropped it into an ashtray. "The network has a tentative slot, the third Sunday in May, nine to ten east coast time."

"That only gives us two months."

He nodded. "They want it before the summer season. How fast can you work?"

Ryan lifted a brow and smiled. "Fast enough. I want Elaine Fisher to guest star."

Swan narrowed his eyes at her. "Is that all?" he asked dryly.

"No, but it's a start. She's talented, beautiful and as

popular with women as she is with men. Plus, she's had experience at working clubs and live theater," she pointed out as Swan frowned and said nothing. "That guileless, wide-eyed look of hers is the perfect contrast for Pierce."

"She's shooting in Chicago."

"That film wraps next week." Ryan sent him a calm smile. "And she's under contract with Swan. If the film goes a week or two over schedule, it won't matter," she added as he remained silent. "We won't need her in California for more than a few days. Pierce carries the show."

"She has other commitments," Swan pointed out.

"She'll fit it in."

"Call her agent."

"I will." Ryan rose again. "I'll set up a meeting with Coogar and get back to you." She paused a moment, then on impulse walked around his desk to stand beside his chair. "I've watched you work for years," she began. "I don't expect you to have the confidence in me you have in yourself or someone with experience. And if I make mistakes, I wouldn't want them to be overlooked. But if I do a good job, and I'm going to, I want to be sure *I* did it, not that I just got the credit for it."

"Your show," he said simply.

"Yes." Ryan nodded. "Exactly. There are a lot of reasons why this project is particularly important to me. I can't promise not to make mistakes, but I can promise you there's no one else who'll work harder on it."

"Don't let Coogar push you around," he muttered after a moment. "He likes to drive producers crazy."

Ryan smiled. "I've heard the stories, don't worry." She started to leave again, then remembered. After a brief hesitation, she leaned down to brush his cheek with her lips. "Thank you for the earrings. They're lovely."

Swan glanced at them. The jeweler had assured his

secretary they were an appropriate gift and a good investment. What had he said in the note he had sent with them? he wondered. Chagrined that he couldn't remember, he decided to ask his secretary for a copy of it.

"Ryan." Swan took her hand. Seeing her blink in surprise at the gesture, he stared down at his own fingers. He had heard all of her conversation with Ned before he had come into the office. It had angered him, disturbed him, and now, when he saw his daughter stunned that he took her hand, it left him frustrated.

"Did you have a good time in Vegas?" he asked, not knowing what else to say.

"Yes." Uncertain what to do next, Ryan went back to business. "I think it was a smart move. Watching Pierce work up close gave me a good perspective. It's a much more overall view than a tape. And I got to know the people who work with him. That won't hurt when they have to work with me." She gave their joined hands another confused look. Could he be ill? she wondered and glanced quickly at his face. "I'll—I'll have a much more concise report for you by tomorrow."

Swan waited until she was finished. "Ryan, how old were you yesterday?" He watched her closely. Her eyes went from bewildered to bleak.

"Twenty-seven," she told him flatly.

Twenty-seven! On a long breath, Swan released her hand. "I've lost some years somewhere," he mumbled. "Go set up with Coogar," he told her and shuffled through the papers on his desk. "Send me a memo after you contact Fisher's agent."

"All right."

Over the top of the papers, Swan watched her walk to the door. When she had left him, he sat back in his chair. He found it staggering to realize he was getting old.

Chapter 12

Producing, Ryan found, kept her as effectively buried in paperwork as contracts had. She spent her days behind her desk, on the phone or in someone else's office. It was hard, grueling work with little glamour. The hours were long, the problems endless. Yet she found she had a taste for it. She was, after all, her father's daughter.

Swan hadn't given her a free hand, but their confrontation on the morning of her return to L.A. had had its benefits. He was listening to her. For the most part she found him surprisingly agreeable to her proposals. He didn't veto arbitrarily as she had feared he would but altered from time to time. Swan knew the business from every angle. Ryan listened and learned.

Her days were full and chaotic. Her nights were empty. Ryan had known Pierce wouldn't phone her. It wasn't his way. He would be down in his workroom, planning, practicing, perfecting. She doubted he would even notice the passing of time.

Of course, she could phone him, Ryan thought as she wandered around her empty apartment. She could invent any number of viable excuses for calling him. There was the change in the taping schedule. That was a valid reason, though she knew he'd already been informed through his agent. And there were at least a dozen minor points they could go over before the meeting the following week.

Ryan glanced thoughtfully at the phone, then shook her head. It wasn't business that she wanted to discuss with him, and she wouldn't use it as a smoke screen. Going into the kitchen, she began to prepare herself a light supper.

Pierce ran through the water illusion for a third time. It was nearly perfect. But nearly was never good enough. He thought, not for the first time, that the camera's eye would be infinitely sharper than the human eye. Every time he had watched himself on tape, he had found flaws. It didn't matter to Pierce that only he knew where to look for them. It only mattered that they were there. He ran through the illusion again.

His workroom was quiet. Though he knew Link was upstairs at the piano, the sound didn't carry down to him. But he wouldn't have heard it if they had been in the same room. Critically, he watched himself in a long mirror as water seemed to shimmer in an unsupported tube. The mirror showed him holding it, top and bottom, while it flowed from palm to palm. Water. It was only one of the four elements he intended to command for Ryan's special.

He thought of the special as hers more than his own. He thought of her when he should have been thinking of his work. With a graceful movement of his hands, Pierce had the water pouring back into a glass pitcher.

He had almost phoned her a dozen times. Once, at three o'clock in the morning, his hand had been on the dial. Just her voice—he had only wanted to hear her voice. He hadn't completed the call, reminding himself of his vow never to put obligations on anyone. If he phoned, it meant he expected her to be there to answer. Ryan was free to do as she pleased; he had no claim on her. Or on anyone. Even the bird he kept had its cage door open at all times.

There had been no one in his life whom he had belonged to. Social workers had brought rules and compassion, but ultimately he had been just one more name in the file. The law had seen to it that he was properly placed and properly cared for. And the law had kept him bound to two people who didn't want him but wouldn't set him free.

Even when he loved—as with Link and Bess—he accepted but demanded no bonds. Perhaps that was why he continued to devise more complicated escapes. Each time he succeeded, it proved no one could be held forever.

Yet he thought of Ryan when he should have been working.

Picking up the handcuffs, Pierce studied them. They had fit cleanly over her wrist. He had held her then. Idly, he snapped one half over his right wrist and toyed with the other, imagining Ryan's hand locked to his.

Was that what he wanted? he wondered. To lock her to him? He remembered how warm she was, how steeped in her he would become after one touch. Who would be locked to whom? Annoyed, Pierce released himself as swiftly as he had snapped on the cuff.

"Double, double, toil and trouble," Merlin croaked from his perch.

Amused, Pierce glanced over. "I think you're quite

right," he murmured, jiggling the cuffs in his hand a moment. "But then, you couldn't resist her either, could you?"

"Abracadabra."

"Abracadabra indeed," Pierce agreed absently. "But who's bewitched whom?"

Ryan was just about to step into the tub when she heard the knock on the door. "Damn!" Irritated by the interruption, she slipped back into her robe and went to answer. Even as she pulled the door open, she was calculating how to get rid of the visitor before her bath water chilled.

"Pierce!"

He saw her eyes widen in surprise. Then, with a mixture of relief and pleasure, he saw the joy. Ryan launched herself into his arms.

"Are you real?" she demanded before her mouth fastened on his. Her hunger shot through him, matching his own. "Five days," Ryan murmured and clung to him. "Do you know how many hours there are in five days?"

"A hundred and twenty." Pierce drew her away to smile at her. "We'd better go inside. Your neighbors are finding this very entertaining."

Ryan pulled him in and shut the door by pressing him back against it. "Kiss me," she demanded. "Hard. Hard enough for a hundred and twenty hours."

His mouth came down on hers. She felt the scrape of his teeth against her lips as he groaned and crushed her to him. Pierce struggled to remember his strength and her fragility, but her tongue was probing, her hands were seeking. She was laughing that husky, aroused laugh that drove him wild.

"Oh, you're real." Ryan sighed and rested her head on his shoulder. "You're real."

But are you? he wondered, a little dazed by the kiss.

After one last hug she pulled out of his arms. "What are you doing here, Pierce? I didn't expect you until Monday or Tuesday."

"I wanted to see you," he said simply and lifted his palm to her cheek. "To touch you."

Ryan caught his hand and pressed the palm to her lips. A fire kindled in the pit of his stomach. "I've missed you," she murmured as her eyes clung to his. "So much. If I had known wishing you here would bring you, I'd have wished harder."

"I wasn't certain you'd be free."

"Pierce," she said softly and laid her hands on his chest. "Do you really think I want to be with anyone else?"

He stared down at her without speaking, but she felt the increased rate of his heartbeat under her hand. "You interfere with my work," he said at length.

Puzzled, Ryan tilted her head. "I do? How?"

"You're in my mind when you shouldn't be."

"I'm sorry." But she smiled, clearly showing she wasn't. "I've been breaking your concentration?"

"Yes."

She slid her hands up to his neck. "That's too bad." Her voice was mocking and seductive. "What are you going to do about it?"

For an answer, Pierce dragged her to the floor. The movement was so swift, so unexpected, Ryan gasped but the sound was swallowed by his mouth. The robe was whipped from her before she could draw a breath. Pierce took her to the summit so quickly, she was powerless to do anything but answer the desperate mutual need.

His clothes were gone with more speed than was reasonable, but he gave her no time to explore him. In one move Pierce rolled her on top of him, then, lifting her as though she were weightless, he set her down to plunge fully inside her.

Ryan cried out, stunned, exhilarated. The speed had her mind spinning. The heat had her skin drenched. Her eyes grew wide as pleasure went beyond all possibilities. She could see Pierce's face, damp with passion, eyes closed. She could hear each tearing breath as he dug his long fingers into her hips to keep her moving with him. Then a film was over her eyes—a white, misty film that hazed her vision. She pressed her hands to his chest to keep from falling. But she was falling, slowly, slowly, drained of everything.

When the mist cleared, Ryan found she was in his arms with his face buried in her hair. Their damp bodies were fused together.

"Now I know you're real, too," Pierce murmured and helped himself to her mouth. "How do you feel?"

"Dazed," Ryan answered breathlessly. "Wonderful."

Pierce laughed. Rising, he lifted her into his arms. "I'm going to take you to bed and love you again before you recover."

"*Mmm,* yes." Ryan nuzzled his neck. "I should let the water out of the tub first."

Pierce lifted a brow, then smiled. With Ryan half-dozing in his arms, he wandered the apartment until he found the bath. "Were you in the tub when I knocked?"

"Almost." Ryan sighed and snuggled against him. "I was going to get rid of whoever had interrupted me. I was very annoyed."

With a flick of his wrist, Pierce turned the hot water on full. "I didn't notice."

"Couldn't you see how I was trying to get rid of you?"

"I have very thick skin at times," he confessed. "I suppose the water's cooled off a bit by now."

"Probably," she agreed.

"You use a free hand with the bubbles."

"*Mmm-hmm.* Oh!" Ryan's eyes shot open as she found herself lowered into the tub.

"Cold?" He grinned at her.

"No." Ryan reached up and turned off the water that steamed hot into the tub. For a moment she allowed her eyes to feast on him—the long, lean body, the wiry muscles and narrow hips. She tilted her head and twirled a finger in the bubbles. "Would you like to join me?" she invited politely.

"The thought had crossed my mind."

"Please." She gestured with her hand. "Be my guest. I've been very rude. I didn't even offer you a drink." She gave him a sassy grin.

The water rose when Pierce lowered himself into it. He sat at the foot of the tub, facing her. "I don't often drink," he reminded her.

"Yes, I know." She gave him a sober nod. "You don't smoke, rarely drink, hardly ever swear. You're a paragon of virtue, Mr. Atkins."

He threw a handful of bubbles at her.

"In any case," Ryan continued, brushing them from her cheek, "I did want to discuss the sketches for the set design with you. Would you like the soap?"

"Thank you, Miss Swan." He took it from her. "You were going to tell me about the set?"

"Oh, yes, I think you'll approve the sketches, though you might want some minor changes." She shifted, sighing a little as her legs brushed against his. "I told Bloomfield I wanted something a little fanciful, medieval, but not too cluttered."

"No suits of armor?"

"No, just atmosphere. Something moody, like…" She broke off when he took her foot in his hand and began to soap it.

"Yes?" he prompted.

"A tone," she said as gentle pulses of pleasure ran up her leg. "Muted colors. The sort you have in your parlor."

Pierce began to massage her calf. "Only one set?"

Ryan trembled in the steamy water as he slid soapy fingers up her leg. "Yes, I thought—*mmm*—I thought the basic mood…" He moved his hands slowly up and down her legs as he watched her face.

"What mood?" He lifted a hand to soap her breast in circles while using his other to massage the top of her thigh.

"Sex," Ryan breathed. "You're very sexy onstage."

"Am I?" Through drugging ripples of sensation, she heard the amusement in the question.

"Yes, dramatic and rather coolly sexy. When I watch you perform…" She trailed off, struggling for breath. The heady scent of the bath salts rose around her. She felt the water lap under her breasts, just below Pierce's clever hand. "Your hands," she managed, steeped in hot, tortured pleasure.

"What about them?" he asked as he slipped a finger inside her.

"Magic." The word trembled out. "Pierce, I can't talk when you're doing things to me."

"Shall I stop?" She was no longer looking at him. Her eyes were closed, but he watched her face, using fingertips only to arouse her.

"No." Ryan found his hand under the water and pressed it against herself.

"You're so beautiful, Ryan." The water swayed as he moved to nibble at her breast, then at her mouth. "So soft. I could see you when I was alone in the middle of the night. I could imagine touching you like this. I couldn't stay away."

"Don't." Her hands were in his hair, pulling his mouth more firmly to hers. "Don't stay away. I've waited so long already."

"Five days," he murmured as he urged her legs apart.

"All my life."

At her words something coursed through him which passion wouldn't permit him to explore. He had to have her, that was all.

"Pierce," Ryan murmured hazily. "We're going to sink."

"Hold your breath," he suggested and took her.

"I'm sure my father will want to see you," Ryan told Pierce the next morning as he pulled into her space in the parking complex of Swan Productions. "And I imagine you'd like to see Coogar."

"Since I'm here," Pierce agreed and shut off the ignition. "But I came to see you."

With a smile Ryan leaned over and kissed him. "I'm so glad you did. Can you stay over the weekend, or do you have to get back?"

He tucked a lock of hair behind her ear. "We'll see."

She slid from the car. She could hope for no better answer. "Of course, the first full meeting isn't scheduled until next week, but I imagine they'll accommodate you." They walked into the building. "I can make the calls from my office."

Ryan led him down the corridors briskly, nodding or answering now and again when someone greeted her. She was all business, he noted, the moment she stepped through the front doors.

"I don't know where Bloomfield is today," she continued as she pushed the button in the elevator for her floor. "But if he's unavailable, I can get the sketches and go over them with you myself." They stepped inside as she began to outline her day's schedule, balancing and altering to allow for Pierce's presence. "You and I might go over the timing, too," she continued. "We have fifty-two minutes to fill. And…"

"Will you have dinner with me tonight, Miss Swan?"

Ryan broke off what she was saying and found him smiling at her. The look in his eyes made it difficult for her to recall her plans for the day. She could only remember what had passed in the night. "I think I might fit that into my schedule, Mr. Atkins," she murmured as the elevator doors opened.

"You'll check your calendar?" he asked and kissed her hand.

"Yes." Ryan had to stop the doors from closing again. "And don't look at me like that today," she said breathlessly. "I'll never be able to function."

"Is that so?" Pierce let her pull him into the corridor. "I might consider it suitable revenge for all the times you've made it impossible for me to do my work."

Unnerved, Ryan led him into her office. "If we're going to manage to pull off this show…" she began.

"Oh, I have complete faith in the very organized, very dependable Miss Swan," Pierce said easily. He took a chair and waited for her to sit behind her desk.

"You're going to be difficult to work with, aren't you?" she asked.

"Most likely."

Wrinkling her nose at him, Ryan picked up the phone and pushed a series of buttons. "Ryan Swan," she announced, deliberately keeping her eyes away from Pierce. "Is he free?"

"Please hold, Miss Swan."

In a moment she heard her father's voice answer impatiently. "Make it fast, I'm busy."

"I'm sorry to disturb you," she said automatically. "I have Pierce Atkins in my office. I thought you might like to see him."

"What's he doing here?" Swan demanded, then continued before Ryan could answer. "Bring him up." He hung up without waiting for her agreement.

"He'd like to see you now," Ryan said as she replaced the receiver.

Pierce nodded, rising as she did. The brevity of the phone conversation had told him a great deal. Minutes later, after entering Swan's office, he learned a great deal more.

"Mr. Atkins." Swan rose to come around his massive desk with his hand extended. "What a pleasant surprise. I didn't expect to meet you personally until next week."

"Mr. Swan." Pierce accepted the offered hand and noted Swan had no greeting for his daughter.

"Please sit down," he suggested with a wide sweep of his hand. "What can I get for you? Coffee?"

"No, nothing."

"Swan Productions is very pleased to have your talents, Mr. Atkins." Swan settled behind his desk again. "We're going to put a lot of energy into this special. Promotion and press have already been set into motion."

"So I understand. Ryan keeps me informed."

"Of course." Swan sent her a quick nod. "We'll shoot

in studio twenty-five. Ryan can arrange for you to see it today if you'd like. And anything else you'd like to see while you're here." He sent her another look.

"Yes, of course," she answered. "I thought Mr. Atkins might like to see Coogar and Bloomfield if they're available."

"Set it up," he ordered, dismissing her. "Now, Mr. Atkins, I have a letter from your representative. There are a few points we might go over before you meet the more artistic members of the company."

Pierce waited until Ryan had shut the door behind her. "I intend to work with Ryan, Mr. Swan. I contracted with you with that stipulation."

"Naturally," Swan answered, thrown off balance. As a rule talent was flattered to receive his personal attention. "I can assure you she's been hard at work on your behalf."

"I don't doubt it."

Swan met the measuring gray eyes levelly. "Ryan is producing your special at your request."

"Your daughter is a very interesting woman, Mr. Swan." Pierce waited a moment, watching Swan's eyes narrow. "On a professional level," he continued smoothly. "I have complete faith in her abilities. She's sharp and observant and very serious about her business."

"I'm delighted you're satisfied with her," Swan replied, not certain what lay beyond Pierce's words.

"It would be a remarkably stupid man who wasn't satisfied with her," Pierce countered, then continued before Swan could react. "Don't you find talent and professionalism pleasing, Mr. Swan?"

Swan studied Pierce a moment, then leaned back in his chair. "I wouldn't be the head of Swan Productions if I didn't," he said wryly.

"Then we understand each other," Pierce said mildly. "Just what are the points you would like to clear up?"

It was five-fifteen before Ryan was able to wind up the meeting with Bloomfield and Pierce. She'd been on the run all day, arranging spur-of-the-moment conferences and covering her scheduled work. There had been no moment to spare for a *tête-à-tête* with Pierce. Now, as they walked down the corridor together from Bloomfield's office, she let out a long breath.

"Well, that seems to be about it. Nothing like the unexpected appearance of a magician to throw everybody into a dither. As seasoned as Bloomfield is, I think he was just waiting for you to pull a rabbit out of your hat."

"I didn't have a hat," Pierce pointed out.

"Would that stop you?" Ryan laughed and checked her watch. "I'll have to stop by my office and clear up a couple of things, touch base with my father and let him know the talent was properly fussed over, then…"

"No."

"No?" Ryan looked up in surprise. "Is there something else you wanted to see? Was there something wrong with the sketches?"

"No," Pierce said again. "You're not going back to your office to clear up a couple of things or to touch base with your father."

Ryan laughed again and continued to walk. "It won't take long, twenty minutes."

"You agreed to have dinner with me, Miss Swan," he reminded her.

"As soon as I clear my desk."

"You can clear your desk Monday morning. Is there something urgent?"

"Well, no, but…" She trailed off when she felt something on her wrist, then stared down at the handcuff. "Pierce, what are you doing?" Ryan tugged her arm but found it firmly chained to his.

"Taking you to dinner."

"Pierce, take this thing off," she ordered with amused exasperation. "It's ridiculous."

"Later," he promised before he pulled her to the elevator. He waited calmly for it to reach their floor as two secretaries eyed him, the cuffs and Ryan.

"Pierce," she said in undertones. "Take these off right now. They're staring at us."

"Who?"

"Pierce, I mean it!" She let out a frustrated moan as the doors opened and revealed several other members of Swan Productions' staff. Pierce stepped inside the car, leaving her no choice but to follow. "You're going to pay for this," she muttered, trying to ignore speculative stares.

"Tell me, Miss Swan," Pierce said in a friendly, carrying voice, "is it always so difficult to persuade you to keep a dinner engagement?"

After an unintelligible mutter, Ryan stared straight ahead.

Still handcuffed to Pierce, Ryan walked across the parking lot. "All right, joke's over," she insisted. "Take these off. I've never been so embarrassed in my life! Do you have any idea how—"

But her heated lecture was cut off by his mouth. "I've wanted to do that all day," Pierce told her, then kissed her again before she could retort.

Ryan tried her best to hang on to her annoyance. His mouth was so soft. His hand, as it pressed into the small of her back, was so gentle. She drew closer to him, but when she started to lift her arms around his neck, the handcuff prevented her. "No," she said firmly, re-membering. "You're not going to sneak out of this one." Ryan pulled away, ready to rage at him. He smiled at her. "Damn you, Pierce," she said on a sigh. "Kiss me again."

He kissed her softly. "You're very exciting when you're angry, Miss Swan," he whispered.

"I *was* angry," she muttered, kissing him back. "I *am* angry."

"And exciting." He drew her over to the car.

"Well?" Holding their joined wrists aloft, she sent him an inquiring glance. Pierce opened the car door and ges-tured her inside. "Pierce!" Exasperated, Ryan jiggled her arm. "Take these off. You can't drive this way."

"Of course I can. You'll have to climb over," he in-structed, nudging her into the car.

Ryan sat in the driver's seat a moment and glared at him. "This is absurd."

"Yes," he agreed. "And I'm enjoying it. Move over."

Ryan considered refusing but decided he would simply lift her into the passenger seat bodily. With little trouble and less grace, she managed it. Pierce gave her another smile as he switched on the ignition.

"Put your hand on the gearshift and we'll do very well."

Ryan obeyed. His palm rested on the back of her hand as he put the car in reverse. "Just how long are you going to leave these on?"

"Interesting question. I haven't decided." He pulled out of the parking lot and headed north.

Ryan shook her head, then laughed in spite of herself. "If you'd told me you were this hungry, I'd have come along peacefully."

"I'm not hungry," he said easily. "I thought we'd stop and eat on the way."

"On the way?" Ryan repeated. "On the way where?"

"Home."

"Home?" A glance out the window showed her he was heading out of L.A. in the opposite direction of her apartment. "*Your* home?" she asked incredulously. "Pierce, that's a hundred and fifty miles from here."

"More or less," he agreed. "You're not needed in L.A. until Monday."

"Monday! Do you mean we're going there for the weekend? But I can't." She hadn't thought she could be any more exasperated than she already was. "I can't just pop in the car and go off for a weekend."

"Why not?"

"Well, I..." He made it sound so reasonable, she had to search for the flaw. "Because I can't. I don't have any clothes, for one thing, and—"

"You won't need them."

That stopped her. Ryan stared at him while a strange mixture of excitement and panic ran through her. "I think you're kidnapping me."

"Exactly."

"Oh."

"Any objections?" he asked, giving her a brief glance.

"I'll let you know Monday," she told him and settled back in the seat, prepared to enjoy her abduction.

Chapter 13

Ryan awoke in Pierce's bed. She opened her eyes to streaming sunlight. It had barely been dawn when Pierce had awakened her to murmur that he was going down to work. Ryan reached for his pillow, drew it closer and lingered a few minutes longer in bed.

What a surprising man he was, she mused. She would never have thought he would do anything as outrageous as handcuffing her to him and bundling her off for a weekend with nothing more than the clothes on her back. She should have been angry, indignant.

Ryan buried her face in his pillow. How could she be? Could you be angry with a man for showing you—with a look, with a touch—that you were needed and desired? Could you be indignant when a man wanted you enough to spirit you off to make love to you as though you were the most precious creature on earth?

Ryan stretched luxuriously, then picked up her watch

from the nightstand. Nine-thirty! she thought with a jolt. How could it be so late? It seemed only moments ago that Pierce had left her. Jumping from the bed, she raced to the shower. They only had two days together; she wasn't going to waste them sleeping.

When she came back into the bedroom with a towel wrapped around her, Ryan studied her clothes dubiously. There was something to be said for being kidnapped by a dashing magician, she admitted, but it was really too bad he hadn't let her pack something first. Philosophically, she began to dress in the suit she had worn the day before. He'd simply have to find her something else to wear, she decided, but for now she'd make do.

With some consternation Ryan realized she didn't even have her purse with her. It was still in the bottom drawer of her desk. She wrinkled her nose at the reflection in the mirror. Her hair was tumbled, her face naked of cosmetics. Not even a comb and a lipstick, she thought and sighed. Pierce was going to have to conjure up something. With this in mind she went downstairs to look for him.

When she came to the foot of the stairs, she saw Link getting ready to leave. "Good morning." Ryan hesitated, unsure what to say to him. He'd been nowhere to be seen when they had arrived the night before.

"Hi." He grinned at her. "Pierce said you were here."

"Yes, I—he invited me for the weekend." It seemed the simplest way to put it.

"I'm glad you came. He missed you."

Her eyes lit up at that. "I missed him, too. Is he here?"

"In the library. He's on the phone." He hesitated, and Ryan saw the faint pink flush in his cheeks.

Smiling, she came down the last step. "What is it, Link?"

"I—uh—I finished writing that song you liked."

"That's wonderful. I'd love to hear it."

"It's on the piano." Excruciatingly embarrassed, he lowered his eyes to his shoes. "You can play it later if you want to."

"Won't you be here?" She wanted to take his hand as she would a little boy's but felt it would only embarrass him more. "I've never heard you play."

"No, I'm…" His color deepened, and he sent her a quick look. "Bess and I…well, she wanted to drive to San Francisco." He cleared his throat. "She likes to ride the streetcars."

"That's nice, Link." On impulse, Ryan decided to see if she could give Bess a hand. "She's a very special lady, isn't she?"

"Oh, sure. There's nobody else like Bess," he agreed readily, then stared at his shoes again.

"She feels just the same way about you."

His eyes darted to her face, then over her shoulder. "You think so?"

"Oh, yes." Though she wanted badly to smile, Ryan kept her voice serious. "She told me how she first met you. I thought it was terribly romantic."

Link gave a nervous little laugh. "She was awful pretty. Lots of guys hang around her when we go on the road."

"I imagine so," Ryan agreed and gave him a mental shove. "But I think she has a taste for musicians. Piano players," she added when he looked back at her. "The kind who know how to write beautifully romantic songs. Time's wasting, don't you think?"

Link was staring at her as though trying to sort out her words. "Huh? Oh, yeah." He wrinkled his brow, then nodded. "Yeah, I guess so. I should go get her now."

"I think that's a very good idea." She did take his hand now, giving it a quick squeeze. "Have a good time."

"Okay." He smiled and turned for the door. With his hand on the knob, he stopped to look over his shoulder. "Ryan, does she really like piano players?"

"Yes, Link, she really does."

He grinned again and opened the door. "Bye."

"Goodbye, Link. Give Bess my love."

When the door shut, Ryan remained where she was a moment. What a sweet man, she thought, then crossed her fingers for Bess. They would be wonderful together if they could just get over the obstacle of his shyness. Well, Ryan thought with a pleased smile, she had certainly done all she could in her first attempt at matchmaking. The rest was up to the two of them.

Turning down the hall, she went to the library. The door was open, and she could hear Pierce's low-pitched voice as it carried to her. Even the sound of it had something stirring inside her. He was here with her, and they were alone. When she stood in the doorway, his eyes met hers.

Pierce smiled, and continued his conversation, gestured her inside. "I'll send you the exact specifications in writing," he said, watching Ryan enter and wander to a bookshelf. Why was it, he wondered, that the sight of her in one of those prim business suits never failed to excite him? "No, I'll need it completed in three weeks. I can't give you any more time than that," he continued with his eyes fixed on Ryan's back. "I need time to work with it before I can be sure I can use it."

Ryan turned around, then, perching on the arm of a chair, she watched him. He wore jeans with a short-sleeved sweatshirt, and his hair was disheveled, as though he had run his hands through it. She thought he had never looked more attractive, sunk back in an overstuffed chair, more relaxed than usual. The energy was still there, the live-wire energy that seemed to spark from him onstage or off. But it was on hold, she mused. He was more at ease in this house than he was anywhere else.

He continued to give instructions to whomever it was he spoke to, but Ryan watched his eyes skim her briefly. Something impish shot through her. Perhaps she could ruffle that calm of his.

Rising idly, she began to wander the room again, stepping out of her shoes as she did so. She took a book from the shelf, skimmed through it, then replaced it.

"I'll need the entire list delivered here," Pierce stated and watched Ryan slip out of her suit jacket. She draped it over the back of a chair. "Yes, that's exactly what I want. If you'll—" He broke off as she began to unbutton her blouse. She looked up when he stopped speaking and smiled at him. "If you'll contact me when you have…" The blouse slid to the floor before she casually unzipped her skirt. "When you have…" Pierce went on, struggling to remember what he had been saying, "the—ah—all the items, I'll arrange for the freight."

Bending over after she stepped out of her skirt, Ryan began to unhook her stockings. "No, that won't—it won't be necessary." She tossed her hair behind her shoulder and sent Pierce another smile. The look held for several pulsing seconds. "Yes," Pierce mumbled into the phone. "Yes, that's fine."

Leaving the pool of nylons on the discarded skirt, she straightened. Her chemise laced up the front. With one finger Ryan pulled at the small bow between her breasts until it loosened. She kept her eyes on his, smiling again when she watched them lower to where her fingers worked slowly with the laces.

"What?" Pierce shook his head. The man's voice had been nothing but an unintelligible buzz in his ear. "What?" he said again as the silk parted. Very slowly, Ryan drew it off. "I'll get back to you." Pierce dropped the receiver back on the hook.

"All finished?" she asked as she walked to him. "I wanted to talk to you about my wardrobe."

"I like what you have on." He pulled her into the chair with him and found her mouth. Tasting the wild need, she let herself go limp.

"Was that an important call?" she asked when his lips moved to her neck. "I didn't want to disturb you."

"The hell you didn't." He reached for her breast, groaning when he took possession. "God, you drive me crazy! Ryan..." His voice was rough with urgency as he slid her to the floor. "Now."

"Yes," she murmured even as he entered her.

He trembled as he lay on top of her. His breath was ragged. No one, he thought, no one had ever been able to destroy his control this way. It was terrifying. Part of him wanted to stand up and walk away—to prove he could still walk away. But he stayed where he was.

"Dangerous," he murmured in her ear just before he let the tip of his tongue trace it. He heard her sigh. "You're a dangerous woman."

"*Mmm,* how so?"

"You know my weaknesses, Ryan Swan. Maybe you are my weakness."

"Is that bad?" she murmured.

"I don't know." He lifted his head and stared down at her. "I don't know."

Ryan lifted a hand to tenderly brush the hair from his forehead. "It doesn't matter today. Today there's only the two of us."

The look he gave her was long and deep, as intense as the first time their eyes had met. "The more I'm with you, the more there are only the two of us."

She smiled, then pulled him back to cradle him in her arms. "The first time you kissed me, the whole world dropped away. I tried to tell myself you had hypnotized me."

Pierce laughed and reached up to fondle her breast. The nipple was still taut, and she quivered at his touch. "Do you have any idea how badly I wanted to take you to bed that night?" He ran his thumb lazily back and forth over the point of her breast, listening to her quickening breathing as he spoke. "I couldn't work, I couldn't sleep. I lay there thinking about how you'd looked in that little bit of silk and lace."

"I wanted you," Ryan said huskily as fresh passion kindled. "I was shocked that I'd only known you for a few hours and I wanted you."

"I would have made love to you like this that night." Pierce touched his mouth to hers. He kissed her, using his lips only until hers were hot and soft and hungry. Both of his hands were in her hair now, drawing it back from her face as his tongue gently plundered.

It seemed he would kiss her endlessly. There were soft, murmuring sounds as their lips parted and met again, then again. Hot, heady, unbearably sweet. He stroked her shoulders, lingering at the slope while the kiss went on and on. She knew the world centered on his lips.

No matter where else he touched, his mouth remained on hers. He might run his hands wherever he chose, but his kiss alone kept her prisoner. He seemed to crave her taste more than he craved breath. She gripped his shoulders, digging her nails into his flesh and totally unaware of it. Her only thought was that the kiss go on forever.

He knew her body was totally his and touched where it gave them both the most pleasure. At the slightest urging, her legs parted for him. He traced a fingertip up and down the inside of her thigh, delighting in its silken texture and in her trembling response. He passed over the center of her only briefly on the journey to her other thigh, all the while toying with her lips.

He used his teeth and his tongue, then his lips only. Her delirious murmuring of his name sent fresh thrills racing along his skin. There was the subtle sweep of her hips to trace, the curve of her waist. Her arms were satin smooth. He could find endless delight in touching only them. She was his—he thought it again and had to control an explosive urge to take her quickly. Instead, he let the kiss speak for him. It spoke of dark, driving needs and infinite tenderness.

Even when he slipped inside her, Pierce continued to savor the taste of her mouth. He took her slowly, waiting for her needs to build, forcing back his own passion until it was no longer possible to deny it.

His mouth was still crushed to hers when she cried out with the final flash of pleasure.

No one but her, he thought dizzily as he breathed in the scent of her hair. No one but her. Ryan's arms came around him to keep him close. He knew he was trapped.

Hours later Ryan slid two steaks under the broiler. She was dressed now in a pair of Pierce's jeans, cinched at the waist with a belt, with the legs rolled up several times to adjust for their difference in height. The sweatshirt bagged over her hips. Ryan pushed the sleeves up past the elbow while she helped him prepare dinner.

"Do you cook as well as Link?" she demanded, turning to watch him add croutons to the salad he was making.

"No. When you're kidnapped, Miss Swan, you can't expect gourmet meals."

Ryan went to stand behind him, then slipped her arms around his waist. "Are you going to demand a ransom?" With a sigh she rested her cheek on his back. She had never been happier in her life.

"Perhaps. When I'm through with you."

She pinched him hard, but he didn't even flinch. "Louse," she said lovingly, then slipped her hands under his shirt to trail her fingers up his chest. This time she felt him quiver.

"You distract me, Ryan."

"I was hoping to. It isn't the simplest thing to do, you know."

"You've been having a remarkable streak of success," he commented as she ran her hands over his shoulders.

"Can you really dislocate your shoulders to get out of a straightjacket?" she wondered aloud as she felt the strength of their solidity.

Amused, he continued to cube cheese for the salad. "Where did you hear that?"

"Oh, somewhere," she said vaguely, not willing to admit she had devoured every write-up she could find on him. "I also heard you have complete control over your muscles." They rippled under her curious fingers. She pressed into his back, enjoying the faint forest scent that clung to him.

"Do you also hear that I only eat certain herbs and roots that I gather under a full moon?" He popped a morsel of cheese in his mouth before he turned to gather her into his arms. "Or that I studied the magic arts in Tibet when I was twelve?"

"I read that you were tutored by Houdini's ghost," she countered.

"Really? I must have missed that one. Very flattering."

"You really enjoy the ridiculous things they print about you, don't you?"

"Of course." He kissed her nose. "I'd have a sorry sense of humor if I didn't."

"And of course," she added, "if the fact and fantasy are so mixed, nobody ever knows which is which or who you are."

"There's that, too." He twined a lock of her hair around his finger. "The more they print about me, Ryan, the more actual privacy I have."

"And your privacy is important to you."

"When you grow up the way I did, you learn to value it."

Pressing her face to his chest, Ryan clung to him. Pierce put his hand under her chin and lifted it. Her eyes were already glistening with tears.

"Ryan," he said carefully, "there's no need for you to feel sorry for me."

"No." She shook her head, understanding his reluctance to accept sympathy. It had been the same with Bess. "I know that, but it's difficult not to feel sorry for a small boy."

He smiled, brushing a finger over her lips. "He was very resilient." He set her away from him. "You'd better turn those steaks."

Ryan busied herself with the steaks, knowing he wanted the subject dropped. How could she explain she was hungry for any detail of his life, anything that would bring him closer to her? And perhaps she was wrong, she thought, to touch on the past when she was afraid to touch on the future.

"How do you like them cooked?" she asked as she bent down to the broiler.

"*Mmm,* medium rare." He was more interested in the

view she provided as she leaned over. "Link has his own dressing made up for the salad. It's quite good."

"Where did he learn to cook?" she asked as she turned the second steak.

"It was a matter of necessity," Pierce told her. "He likes to eat. Things were lean in the early days when we were on the road. It turned out he was a lot more handy with a can of soup than Bess or me."

Ryan turned and sent him a smile. "You know, they were going to San Francisco today."

"Yes." He quirked a brow. "So?"

"He's just as crazy about her as she is about him."

"I know that, too."

"You might have done something to move things along after all these years," she stated, gesturing with the kitchen fork. "After all, they're your friends."

"Which is exactly why I don't interfere," he said mildly. "What did you do?"

"Well, I didn't interfere," she said with a sniff. "I merely gave him a very gentle shove in the right direction. I mentioned that Bess has a preference for piano players."

"I see."

"He's so shy," she said in exasperation. "He'll be ready for social security before he works up the nerve to—to…"

"To what?" Pierce asked, grinning.

"To anything," Ryan stated. "And stop leering at me."

"Was I?"

"You know very well you were. And anyway—" She gasped and dropped the kitchen fork with a clatter when something brushed past her ankles.

"It's just Circe," Pierce pointed out, then grinned as Ryan sighed. "She smells the meat." He picked up the fork to rinse it off while the cat rubbed against Ryan's legs and purred lovingly. "She'll do her best to convince you she deserves some for herself."

"Your pets have a habit of catching me off guard."

"Sorry." But he smiled, not looking sorry at all.

Ryan put her hands on her hips. "You like to see me rattled, don't you?"

"I like to see you," he answered simply. He laughed and caught her up in his arms. "Though I have to admit, there's something appealing about seeing you wear my clothes while you putter around the kitchen in your bare feet."

"Oh," she said knowingly. "The caveman syndrome."

"Oh, no, Miss Swan." He nuzzled her neck. "I'm your slave."

"Really?" Ryan considered the interesting possibilities of the statement. "Then set the table," she told him. "I'm starving."

They ate by candlelight. Ryan never tasted a mouthful of the meal. She was too full of Pierce. There was wine—something smooth and mellow, but it might have been water, for all it mattered. In the baggy sweatshirt and jeans, she had never felt more like a woman. His eyes told her constantly that she was beautiful, interesting, desirable. It seemed as though they had never been lovers, never been intimate. He was wooing her.

He made her glow with a look, with a soft word or the touch of his hand on hers. It never ceased to please her, even overwhelm her, that he had so much romance in him. He had to know that she would be with him under any circumstances, yet he courted her. Flowers and candlelight and the words of a man captivated. Ryan fell in love again.

Long after both of them had lost any interest in the meal, they lingered. The wine grew warm, the candles low. He was content to watch her in the flickering light, to let her quiet voice flow over him. Whatever needs built inside him could be soothed by merely running his fingers over the back of her hand. He wanted nothing more than to be with her.

Passion would come later, he knew. In the night, in the dark when she lay beside him. But for now it was enough to see her smile.

"Will you wait for me in the parlor?" he murmured and kissed her fingers one at a time. Shivery delight shot up her arm.

"I'll help with the dishes." But her thoughts were far, far away from practical matters.

"No, I'll see to it." Pierce turned her hand over and pressed his lips to her palm. "Wait for me."

Her knees trembled, but she rose when he drew her to her feet. She couldn't take her eyes from his. "You won't be long?"

"No." He slid his hands down her arms. "I won't be long, love." Gently, he kissed her.

Ryan walked to the parlor in a daze. It hadn't been the kiss but the one simple word of endearment that had her heart pounding. It seemed impossible, after what they had been to each other, that a casual word would send her pulses racing. But Pierce was careful with words.

And it was a night for enchantment, she thought as she entered the parlor. A night made for love and romance. She walked to the window to look out at the sky. Even the moon was full, as if it knew it had to be. It was quiet enough that she could just hear the sound of waves against rock.

They were on an island, Ryan imagined. It was a small, windswept island in some dark sea. And the nights were long. There was no phone, no electricity. On impulse, she turned from the window and began to light the candles that were scattered around the room. The fire was laid, and she set a match to the kindling. The dry wood caught with a crackle.

Rising, she looked around the room. The light was just as she wanted it—insubstantial with shadows shifting. It added just a touch of mystery and seemed to reflect her own feelings toward Pierce.

Ryan glanced down at herself and brushed at the sweatshirt. If only she had something lovely to wear, something white and filmy. But perhaps Pierce's imagination would be as active as hers.

Music, she thought suddenly and looked around. Surely he had a stereo, but she wouldn't have any idea where to look for it. Inspired, she went to the piano.

Link's staff paper was waiting. Between the glow from the fire behind her and the candles on the piano, Ryan could see the notes clearly enough. Sitting down, she began to play. It took only moments for her to be caught up in the melody.

Pierce stood in the doorway and watched her. Although her eyes were fixed on the paper in front of her, they seemed to be dreaming. He'd never seen her quite like this—so caught up in her own thoughts. Unwilling to break her mood, he stood where he was. He could have watched her forever.

In the candlelight her hair was only a mist falling over her shoulders. Her skin was pale. Only her eyes were dark, moved by the music she played. He caught the faint whiff of wood smoke and melting wax. It was a moment he knew he would remember for the rest of his life. Years and years could pass, and he would be able to close his eyes and see her just like this, hear the music drifting, smell the candles burning.

"Ryan." He hadn't meant to speak aloud, indeed had only whispered her name, but her eyes lifted to his.

She smiled, but the flickering light caught the glistening tears. "It's so beautiful."

"Yes." Pierce could hardly trust himself to speak. A word, a wrong move might shatter the mood. What he saw, what he felt might be an illusion after all. "Please, play it again."

Even after she had begun, he came no closer. He wanted the picture to remain exactly as it was. Her lips were just parted. He could taste them as he stood there. He knew how her cheek would feel if he laid his hand on it. She would look up at him and smile with that special warmth in her eyes. But he wouldn't touch her, only absorb all she was in this one special moment out of time.

The flames of the candles burned straight. A log shifted quietly in the grate. And then she was finished.

Her eyes lifted to his. Pierce went to her.

"I've never wanted you more," he said in a low, almost whispering voice. "Or been more afraid to touch you."

"Afraid?" Her fingers stayed lightly on the keys. "Why?"

"If I were to touch you, my hand might pass through you. You might only be a dream after all."

Ryan took his hand and pressed it to her cheek. "It's no dream," she murmured. "Not for either of us."

Her skin was warm and real under his fingers. He was struck by a wave of incredible tenderness. Pierce lifted her other hand, holding it as though it were made of porcelain. "If you had one wish, Ryan, only one, what would it be?"

"That tonight, just tonight, you'd think of nothing and no one but me."

Her eyes were brilliant in the dim, shifting light.

Pierce drew her to her feet, then cupped her face in his hand. "You waste your wishes, Ryan, asking for something that already is." He kissed her temples, then her cheeks, leaving her mouth trembling for the taste of his.

"I want to fill your mind," she told him, her voice wavering, "so there's no room for anything else. Tonight I want there to be only me. And tomorrow—"

"Shh." He kissed her mouth to silence her, but so lightly she was left with only a promise of what was to come. "There's no one but you, Ryan." Her eyes were closed, and he brushed his lips delicately over the lids. "Come to bed," he murmured. "Let me show you."

Taking her hand, he walked through the room, putting out the candles. He lifted one, letting its quivering light show them the way.

Chapter 14

They had to be separated again. Ryan knew it was necessary in the course of preparing the special. When she was lonely for him, she had only to remember that last magic night they had spent together. It would be enough to hold her until she could see him again.

Though she saw him off and on during the next weeks, it was only professionally. He came to her for meetings or to oversee certain points of his own business. He kept to himself on these. Ryan still knew nothing about the construction of the props and gags he would use. He would give her a detailed list of the illusions he would perform, their time sequence and only the barest explanation of their mechanics.

Ryan found this frustrating, but she had little else to complain about. The set was forming along the lines she, Bloomfield and Pierce had ultimately agreed on. Elaine Fisher was signed for a guest appearance. Ryan had managed to hold her own through the series of tough, emotional meetings. And so, she recalled with amusement, had Pierce.

He could say more with his long silences and one or two calm words than a dozen frantic, bickering department heads. He sat through their demands and complaints with complete amiability and always came out on top.

He wouldn't agree to use a professional script for the show. It was as simple as that. He said no. And he had stuck to it—because he knew he was right. He had his own music, his own director, his own prop crew. Nothing would sway him from using his own people on key posts. He turned down six costume sketches with a careless shake of the head.

Pierce did things his own way and bent only when it suited him to bend. Yet Ryan saw that the creative staff, as temperamental as they came, offered little complaint about him. He charmed them, she noted. He had a way with people. He would warm you or freeze you—it only took a look.

Bess was to have the final say on her own wardrobe. Pierce simply stated that she knew best what suited her. He refused to rehearse unless the set was closed. Then he entertained the stagehands with sleight of hand and card tricks. He knew how to keep control without rippling the waters.

Ryan, however, found it difficult to function around the restrictions he put on her and her staff. She tried reasoning, arguing, pleading. She got nowhere.

"Pierce." Ryan cornered him on the set during a break in rehearsal. "I have to talk to you."

"Hmm?" He watched his crew set up the torches for the next segment. "Exactly eight inches apart," he told them.

"Pierce, this is important."

"Yes, I'm listening."

"You can't bar Ned from the set during rehearsal," she said and tugged on his arm to get his full attention.

"Yes, I can. I did. Didn't he tell you?"

"Yes, he told me." She let out a sigh of exasperation. "Pierce, as production coordinator, he has a perfectly legitimate reason to be here."

"He gets in the way. Make sure there's a foot between the rows, please."

"Pierce!"

"What?" he said pleasantly and turned back to her. "Have I told you that you look lovely today, Miss Swan?" He ran the lapel of her jacket between his thumb and forefinger. "That's a very nice suit."

"Listen, Pierce, you've got to give my people a little more room." She tried to ignore the smile in his eyes and continued. "Your crew is very efficient, but on a production of this size we need more hands. Your people know your work, but they don't know television."

"I can't have your people poking into my props, Ryan. Or wandering around when I'm setting up."

"Good grief, do you want them to sign a blood oath not to reveal your secrets?" she demanded, waving her clipboard. "We could set it up for the next full moon."

"A good idea, but I don't know how many of your people would go along with it. Not your production coordinator, at any rate," he added with a grin. "I don't think he'd care for the sight of his own blood."

Ryan lifted a brow. "Are you jealous?"

He laughed with such great enjoyment she wanted to hit him. "Don't be absurd. He's hardly a threat."

"That's not the point," she muttered, miffed. "He's

very good at his job, but he can hardly do it if you won't be reasonable."

"Ryan," he said, looking convincingly surprised, "I'm always reasonable. What would you like me to do?"

"I'd like you to let Ned do what he has to do. And I'd like you to let my people in the studio."

"Certainly," he agreed. "But not when I'm rehearsing."

"Pierce," she said dangerously. "You're tying my hands. You have to make certain concessions for television."

"I'm aware of that, Ryan, and I will." He kissed her brow. "When I'm ready. No," he continued before she could speak again, "you have to let me work with my own crew until I'm sure it's smooth."

"And how long is that going to take?" She knew he was winning her over as he had everyone from Coogar down.

"A few more days." He took her free hand. "Your key people are here, in any case."

"All right," she said with a sigh. "But by the end of the week the lighting crew will have to be in on rehearsals. That's essential."

"Agreed." He gave her hand a solemn shake. "Anything else?"

"Yes." Ryan straightened her shoulders and shot him a level look. "The time for the first segment runs over by ten seconds. You're going to have to alter it to fit the scheduled run of the commercials."

"No, you'll have to alter the scheduled run of commercials." He gave her a light kiss before he walked away.

Before she could shout at him, Ryan found there was a rosebud pinned to her lapel. Pleasure mixed with fury until it was too late to act.

"He's something, isn't he?"

Ryan turned her head to see Elaine Fisher. "Something," she agreed. "I hope you're satisfied with everything, Miss Fisher," she continued, then smiled at the petite, kittenlike blonde. "Your dressing room's agreeable?"

"It's fine." Elaine flashed her winning, toothy smile. "There's a bulb burned out on my mirror, though."

"I'll see to it."

Elaine watched Pierce and gave her quick, bubbling laugh. "I've got to tell you, I wouldn't mind finding him in my dressing room."

"I don't think I can arrange that for you, Miss Fisher," Ryan returned primly.

"Oh, honey, I could arrange it for myself if it weren't for the way he looks at you." She sent Ryan a friendly wink. "Of course, if you're not interested, I could try to console him."

The actress's charm wasn't easy to resist. "That won't be necessary," Ryan told her with a smile. "It's a producer's job to keep the talent happy, you know."

"Why don't you see if you could come up with a clone for me?" Leaving Ryan, she walked to Pierce. "Ready for me?"

Watching them work together, Ryan saw that her instincts had been on the mark. They were perfectly suited. Elaine's frothy blond beauty and ingenue charm masked a sharp talent and flair for comedy. It was the exact balance Ryan had hoped for.

Ryan waited, holding her breath as the torches were lit. It was the first time she had seen the illusion all the way through. The flames burned high for a moment, sending out an almost blinding light before Pierce spread his hands and calmed them. Then he turned to Elaine.

"Don't burn the dress," she cracked. "It's rented."

Ryan scribbled down a note to keep in the ad lib even

as he began to levitate Elaine. In moments she was floating just above the flames.

"It's going well."

Glancing up, Ryan smiled at Bess. "Yes, for all the problems he causes, Pierce makes it impossible for it to go otherwise. He's relentless."

"Tell me about it." They watched him in silence a moment, then Bess squeezed Ryan's arm. "I can't stand it," she said in undertones to keep from disturbing the rehearsal. "I have to tell you."

"Tell me what?"

"I wanted to tell Pierce first, but..." She grinned from ear to ear. "Link and I—"

"Oh, congratulations!" Ryan interrupted and hugged her.

Bess laughed. "You didn't let me finish."

"You were going to tell me you're getting married."

"Well, yeah, but—"

"Congratulations," Ryan said again. "When did it happen?"

"Just now, practically." Looking a little dazed, Bess scratched her head. "I was in my dressing room getting ready when he knocked on the door. He wouldn't come in, he just stood there in the doorway sort of shuffling his feet, you know? Then all of a sudden he asked me if I wanted to get married." Bess shook her head and laughed again. "I was so surprised, I asked him to whom."

"Oh, Bess, you didn't!"

"Yeah, I did. Well, you just don't expect that sort of question after twenty years."

"Poor Link," Ryan murmured with a smile. "What did he say?"

"He just stood there for a minute, staring at me and

turning colors, then he said, 'Well, to me, I guess.'" She gave a low chuckle. "It was real romantic."

"I think it was lovely," Ryan told her. "I'm so happy for you."

"Thanks." After a breathy sigh, she looked over at Pierce again. "Don't say anything to Pierce, okay? I think I'll let Link tell him."

"I won't say anything," she promised. "Will you be married soon?"

Bess sent her a lopsided grin. "Sweetie, you better believe it. As far as I can see, we've already been engaged for twenty years, and that's long enough." She pleated the hem of her sweatshirt between her fingers. "I guess we'll just wait until after the special airs, then make the jump."

"Will you stay with Pierce?"

"Sure." She looked at Ryan quizzically. "We're a team. 'Course, Link and I will live at my place, but we wouldn't break up the act."

"Bess," Ryan began slowly. "There's something I've been wanting to ask you. It's about the final illusion." She sent Pierce a worried frown as he continued to work with Elaine. "He's so secretive about it. All he'll say so far is that it's an escape and he'll need four minutes and ten seconds from intro to finish. What do you know about it?"

Bess shrugged restlessly. "He's keeping that one close because he hasn't worked out all the bugs."

"What sort of bugs?" Ryan persisted.

"I don't know, really, except…" She hesitated, torn between her own doubts and her loyalty. "Except Link doesn't like it."

"Why?" Ryan put a hand on Bess's arm. "Is it dangerous? Really dangerous?"

"Look, Ryan, all the escapes can be dangerous, unless you're talking a straightjacket and handcuffs. But he's the best." She watched Pierce lower Elaine to the floor. "He's going to need me in a minute."

"Bess." She kept her hand firm on the redhead's arm. "Tell me what you know."

"Ryan." Bess sighed as she looked down at her. "I know how you feel about him, but I can't. Pierce's work is Pierce's work."

"I'm not asking you to break the magician's code of ethics," Ryan said impatiently. "He'll have to tell me what the illusion is, anyway."

"Then he'll tell you." Bess patted her hand but moved away.

The rehearsals ran over, as Pierce's rehearsals had a habit of doing. After attending a late-afternoon production meeting, Ryan decided to wait for him in his dressing room. The problem of the final illusion had nagged at her throughout the day. She hadn't liked the worried look in Bess's eyes.

Pierce's dressing room was spacious and plush. The carpeting was thick, the sofa plump and wide enough to double as a bed. There was a large-screen television, a complex stereo system and a fully stocked bar that she knew Pierce never used. On the wall were a pair of very good lithographs. It was the sort of dressing room Swan reserved for their special performers. Ryan doubted that Pierce spent more than thirty minutes a day within its walls when he was in L.A.

Ryan poked in the refrigerator, found a quart of orange juice and fixed herself a cold drink before sinking down on the sofa. Idly, she picked up a book from the table. It was one of Pierce's, she noted, another work on Houdini. With absent interest she thumbed through the pages.

When Pierce entered, he found her curled up on the sofa, halfway through the volume.

"Research?"

Ryan's head shot up. "Could he really do all these things?" she demanded. "I mean this business about swallowing needles and a ball of thread, then pulling them out threaded. He didn't really do that, did he?"

"Yes." He stripped out of his shirt.

Ryan gave him a narrowed look. "Can you?"

He only smiled. "I don't make a habit of copying illusions. How was your day?"

"Fine. It says in here that some people thought he had a pocket in his skin."

This time he laughed. "Don't you think you'd have found mine by now if I had one?"

Ryan set the book aside and rose. "I want to talk to you."

"All right." Pierce pulled her into his arms and began to roam her face with kisses. "In a few minutes. It's been a long three days without you."

"You were the one who went away," she reminded him, then halted his wandering mouth with her own.

"I had a few details to smooth out. I can't work seriously here."

"That's what your dungeon's for," she murmured and found his mouth again.

"Exactly. We'll go to dinner tonight. Some place with candles and dark corners."

"My apartment has candles and dark corners," she said against his lips. "We can be alone there."

"You'll try to seduce me again."

Ryan laughed and forgot what she had wanted to talk to him about. "I *will* seduce you again."

"You've gotten cocky, Miss Swan." He drew her away. "I'm not always so easy."

"I like challenges."

He rubbed his nose against hers. "Did you like your flower?"

"Yes, thank you." She circled his neck with her arms. "It kept me from harassing you."

"I know. You find me difficult to work with, don't you?"

"Extremely. And if you let anyone else produce your next special, I'll sabotage every one of your illusions."

"Well, then, I'll have to keep you and protect myself."

He touched his lips to hers gently, and the wave of love hit her with such force, such suddenness, Ryan clutched at him.

"Pierce." She wanted to speak quickly before the old fear prevented her. "Pierce, read my mind." With her eyes tightly shut, she buried her face against his shoulder. "Can you read my mind?"

Puzzled by the urgency in her tone, he drew her away to study her. She opened her eyes wide, and in them he saw that she was a little frightened, a little dazed. And he saw something else that had his heart taking an erratic beat.

"Ryan?" Pierce lifted a hand to her cheek, afraid he was seeing something only he needed to see. Afraid, too, that it was real.

"I'm terrified," she whispered. "The words won't come. Can you see them?" Her voice was jerky. She bit her lip to steady it. "If you can't, I'll understand. It doesn't have to change anything."

Yes, he saw them, but she was wrong. Once they were said, they changed everything. He hadn't wanted it to happen, yet he had known, somehow, they would come to this. He had known the moment he had seen her walk down the steps to his workroom. She was the woman who would change everything. Whatever power he had would become partially hers once he said three words. It was the only real incantation in a world of illusion.

"Ryan." He hesitated a moment but knew there was no stopping what already was. "I love you."

Her breath came out in a rush of relief. "Oh, Pierce, I was so afraid you wouldn't want to see." They drew together and clung. "I love you so much. So very much." Her sigh was shaky. "It's good, isn't it?"

"Yes." He felt her heartbeat match his own. "Yes, it's good."

"I didn't know I could be so happy. I wanted to tell you before," she murmured against his throat. "But I was so afraid. It seems silly now."

"We were both afraid." He drew her closer, but it still wasn't enough. "We've wasted time."

"But you love me," she whispered, only wanting to hear the words again.

"Yes, Ryan, I love you."

"Let's go home, Pierce." She ran her lips along his jaw. "Let's go home. I want you."

"Uh-uh. Now."

Ryan threw her head back and laughed. "Now? Here?"

"Here and now," he agreed, enjoying the flash of devilment in her eyes.

"Somebody might come in," she said and drew away from him.

Saying nothing, Pierce turned to the door and flicked the lock. "I don't think so."

"Oh." Ryan bit her lip, trying not to smile. "It looks like I'm going to be ravished."

"You could call for help," he suggested as he pushed the jacket from her shoulders.

"Help," she said quietly while he unbuttoned her blouse. "I don't think anyone heard me."

"Then it looks like you're going to be ravished."

"Oh, good," Ryan whispered. Her blouse slid to the floor.

They touched each other and laughed with the sheer joy of being in love. They kissed and clung as though there were no tomorrow. They murmured soft words and sighed with pleasure. Even when the lovemaking intensified and passion began to rule, there was an underlying joy that remained innocent.

He loves me, Ryan thought and ran her hands up his strong back. *He belongs to me.* She answered his kiss with fervor.

She loves me, Pierce thought and felt her skin heat under his fingers. *She belongs to me.* He sought her mouth and savored it.

They gave to each other, took from each other until they were more one than two. There was rising passion, an infinite tenderness and a new freedom. When the loving was over, they could still laugh, dizzy with the knowledge that for them it was only the beginning.

"You know," Ryan murmured, "I thought it was the producer who lured the talent to the couch."

"Didn't you?" Pierce let her hair run through his fingers.

With a chuckle Ryan kissed him between the eyes. "You were supposed to think it was all your idea." Sitting up, she reached for her blouse.

Pierce sat up behind her and ran a fingertip up her spine. "Going somewhere?"

"Look, Atkins, you'll get your screen test." She squealed when he bit her shoulder. "Don't try to change my mind," she said before she slipped out of reach. "I'm finished with you."

"Oh?" Pierce leaned back on his elbow to watch her dress.

"Until we get home." Ryan wriggled into her teddy, then began to hook her stockings. She eyed his nakedness. "You'd better get dressed before I change my mind. We'll end up locked in the building for the night."

"I could get us out when we wanted to go."

"There are alarms."

He laughed. "Ryan, really."

She shot him a look. "I suppose it is a good thing you decided not to be a criminal."

"It's simpler to charge for picking locks. People will always find a fascination in paying to see if it can be done." He grinned as he sat up. "They don't appreciate it if you do it for free."

Curious, she tilted her head. "Have you ever come across a lock you can't beat?"

"Given enough time," Pierce said as he reached for his clothes, "any lock can be opened."

"Without tools?"

He lifted a brow. "There are tools, and there are tools."

Ryan frowned at him. "I'm going to have to check for that pocket in your skin again."

"Anytime," he agreed obligingly.

"You could be nice and teach me just one thing, like how to get out of those handcuffs."

"Uh-uh." He shook his head as he slipped into his jeans. "They might come in handy again."

Ryan shrugged as if she didn't care anyway and began to button her blouse. "Oh, I forgot. I wanted to talk to you about the finale."

Pierce pulled a fresh shirt out of the closet. "What about it?"

"That's precisely what I want to know," Ryan told him. "What exactly do you have planned?"

"It's an escape, I told you." He drew on the shirt.

"I need more than that, Pierce. The show goes on in ten days."

"I'm working it out."

Recognizing the tone, Ryan stepped to him. "No, this isn't a solo production. I'm the producer, Pierce; you wanted it that way. Now, I can go along with some of your oddities about the staff." She ignored his indignant expression. "But I have to know exactly what's going to be aired. You can't keep me in the dark with less than two weeks to go until taping."

"I'm going to break out of a safe," he said simply and handed Ryan her shoe.

"Break out of a safe." She took it, watching him. "There's more to it than that, Pierce. I'm not a fool."

"I'll have my hands and feet manacled first."

Ryan stooped to retrieve her other shoe. His continued reluctance to elaborate brought on a very real fear. Wanting her voice to be steady, she waited a moment. "What else, Pierce?"

He said nothing until he had buttoned his shirt. "It's a play on a box within a box within a box. An old gimmick."

The fear grew. "Three safes? One within the other?"

"That's right. Each one's larger than the last."

"Are the safes airtight?"

"Yes."

Ryan's skin grew cold. "I don't like it."

He gave her a calm measuring look. "You don't have to like it, Ryan, but you don't have to worry, either."

She swallowed, knowing it was important to keep her

head. "There's more, too, isn't there? I know there is, tell me."

"The last safe has a time lock," he said flatly. "I've done it before."

"A time lock?" Ice ran down her back. "No, you can't. It's just foolish."

"Hardly foolish," Pierce returned. "It's taken me months to work out the mechanics and timing."

"Timing?"

"I have three minutes of air."

Three minutes! she thought and struggled not to lose control. "And how long does the escape take?"

"At the moment, just over three minutes."

"Just over," Ryan repeated numbly. "Just over. What if something goes wrong?"

"I don't intend for anything to go wrong. I've been over and over it, Ryan."

She spun away, then whirled back to him. "I'm not going to allow this. It's out of the question. Use the panther business for the finale, but not this."

"I'm using the escape, Ryan." His voice was very calm and very final.

"No!" Panicked, she grabbed his arms. "I'm cutting it. It's out, Pierce. You can use one of your other illusions or come up with a new one, but this is out."

"You can't cut it." His tone never altered as he looked down at her. "I have final say; read the contract."

She paled and stepped back from him. "Damn you, I don't care about the contract. I know what it says. I wrote it!"

"Then you know you can't cut the escape," he said quietly.

"I won't let you do this." Tears had sprung to her eyes, but she blinked them away. "You can't do it."

"I'm sorry, Ryan."

"I'll find a way to scrub the show." Her breath was heaving with anger and fear and hopelessness. "I can find a way to break the contract."

"Maybe." He laid his hands on her shoulders. "I'll still do the escape, Ryan, next month in New York."

"Pierce, God!" Desperately, she clung to his arms. "You could die in there. It's not worth it. Why do you have to try something like this?"

"Because I can do it. Ryan, understand that this is my work."

"I understand that I love you. Doesn't that matter?"

"You know that it does," he said roughly. "You know how much."

"No, I don't know how much." Frantically, she pushed away from him. "I only know that you're going to do this no matter how much I beg you not to. You'll expect me to stand by and watch you risk your life for some applause and a write-up."

"It has nothing to do with applause or write-ups." The first hint of anger shot into his eyes. "You should know me better than that."

"No, no, I don't know you," she said desperately. "How can I understand why you insist on doing something like this? It's not necessary to the show, to your career!"

He struggled to hold his temper in check and answered calmly. "It's necessary to me."

"Why?" she demanded furiously. "Why is it necessary to risk your life?"

"That's your viewpoint, Ryan, not mine. This is part of my work and part of what I am." He paused but didn't go to her. "You'll have to accept that if you accept me."

"That's not fair."

"Maybe not," he agreed. "I'm sorry."

Ryan swallowed, fighting back tears. "Where does that leave us?"

He kept his eyes on hers. "That's up to you."

"I won't watch." She backed to the door. "I won't! I won't spend my life waiting for the time you go too far. I can't." She fumbled for the lock with trembling fingers. "Damn your magic," she sobbed as she darted through the door.

Chapter 15

After leaving Pierce, Ryan went straight to her father's office. For the first time in her life she entered without knocking. Annoyed at the interruption, Swan bit off what he was saying into the phone and scowled up at her. For a moment he stared at her. He'd never seen Ryan like this: pale, trembling, her eyes wide and brilliant with suppressed tears.

"I'll get back to you," he muttered and hung up. She still stood by the door, and Swan found himself in the unusual position of not knowing what to say. "What is it?" he demanded, then cleared his throat.

Ryan supported herself against the door until she was sure her legs were steady enough to walk. Struggling for composure, she crossed to her father's desk. "I need—I want you to cancel the Atkins special."

"What!" He sprang to his feet and glared at her. "What the hell is this? If you've decided to fall apart under the pressure, I'll get a replacement. Ross can take over. Damn it!" He slammed his hand on the desk. "I should have known better than to put you in charge in the first place." He was already reaching for the phone.

"Please." Ryan's quiet voice stopped him. "I'm asking you to pay off the contract and scrub the show."

Swan started to swear at her again, took another careful study of her face, then walked to the bar. Saying nothing, he poured a healthy dose of French brandy into a snifter. Blast the girl for making him feel like a clumsy ox. "Here," he said gruffly as he pushed the snifter into her hands. "Sit down and drink this." Not certain what to do with a daughter who looked shattered and helpless, he awkwardly patted her shoulder before he went back behind his desk.

"Now." Settled again, he felt more in control of the situation. "Tell me what this is all about. Trouble at rehearsals?" He gave her what he hoped was an understanding smile. "Now, you've been around the business long enough to know that's part of the game."

Ryan took a deep breath, then swallowed the brandy. She let it burn through the layers of fear and misery. Her next breath was steadier. She looked at her father again. "Pierce is planning an escape for the finale."

"I know that," he said impatiently. "I've seen the script."

"It's too dangerous."

"Dangerous?" Swan folded his hands on the desk. This he could handle, he decided. "Ryan, the man's a pro. He knows what he's doing." Swan tilted his wrist slightly so he could see his watch. He could give her about five minutes.

"This is different," she insisted. To keep from screaming, she gripped the bowl of the snifter tightly. Swan would never listen to hysterics. "Even his own people don't like it."

"All right, what's he planning?"

Unable to form the words, Ryan took another swallow of brandy. "Three safes," she began. "One within the other. The last one…" She paused for a moment to keep her voice even. "The last one has a time lock. He'll only have three minutes of air once he's closed inside the first safe. He's just—he's just told me that the routine takes more time than that."

"Three safes," Swan mused, pursing his lips. "A real show-stopper."

Ryan slammed down her glass. "Especially if he suffocates. Think what that will do for the ratings! They can give him his Emmy posthumously."

Swan lowered his brows dangerously. "Calm down, Ryan."

"I will not calm down." She sprang up from her chair. "He can't be allowed to do this. We have to cancel the contract."

"Can't do it." Swan lifted his shoulders to brush off the notion.

"Won't do it," Ryan corrected furiously.

"Won't do it," Swan agreed, matching her tone. "There's too much at stake."

"*Everything's* at stake!" Ryan shouted at him. "I'm in love with him."

He had started to stand and shout back at her, but her words took him by surprise. Swan stared at her. There were tears of desperation in her eyes now. Again he was at a loss. "Ryan." He sighed and reached for a cigar. "Sit down."

"No!" She snatched the cigar from his fingers and flung it across the room. "I will not sit down, I will not calm down. I'm asking for your help. Why won't you look at me?" she demanded in angry despair. "Really look at me!"

"I am looking at you!" he bellowed in defense. "And I can tell you I'm not pleased. Now you sit down and listen to me."

"No, I'm through listening to you, trying to please you. I've done everything you've ever wanted me to do, but it's never been enough. I can't be your son, I can't change that." She covered her face with her hands and broke down completely. "I'm only your daughter, and I need you to help me."

The words left him speechless. The tears unmanned him. He couldn't remember if he had ever seen her cry before; certainly she'd never done it this passionately. Getting awkwardly to his feet, he fumbled for his handkerchief. "Here, here now." He pushed the handkerchief into her hands and wondered what to do next. "I've always…" He cleared his throat and looked helplessly around the room. "I've always been proud of you, Ryan." When she responded by weeping more desperately, he stuck his hands in his pockets and lapsed into silence.

"It doesn't matter." Her voice was muffled behind the handkerchief. She felt a wave of shame for the words and the tears. "It doesn't matter anymore."

"I'd help you if I could," he muttered at length. "I can't stop him. Even if I could scrub the show and deal with the suits the network and Atkins would bring against Swan Productions, he'd do the damn thing anyway."

Faced with the bald truth, Ryan turned away from him. "There must be something…"

Swan shifted uncomfortably. "Is he in love with you?"

Ryan let out an unsteady breath and dashed the tears

away. "It doesn't matter how he feels about me. I can't stop him."

"I'll talk to him."

Wearily, she shook her head. "No, it wouldn't do any good. I'm sorry." She turned back to her father. "I shouldn't have come here like this. I wasn't thinking straight." Looking down, she crumpled the handkerchief into a ball. "I'm sorry I made a scene."

"Ryan, I'm your father."

She looked up at him then, but her eyes were expressionless. "Yes."

He cleared his throat and found he didn't know what to do with his hands. "I don't want you to apologize for coming to see me." She only continued to look at him with eyes devoid of emotion. Tentatively, he reached out to touch her arm. "I'll do what I can to persuade Atkins to drop the routine, if that's what you want."

Ryan let out a long sigh before she sat down. "Thank you, but you were right. He'll do it another time, anyway. He told me so himself. I'm just not able to deal with it."

"Do you want Ross to take over?"

She pressed her fingers to her eyes. "No," she said with a shake of her head. "No, I'll finish what I started. Hiding won't change anything, either."

"Good girl," he said with a pleased nod. "Now, ah…" He hesitated while he sought the correct words. "About you and the magician." He coughed and fiddled with his tie. "Are you planning—that is, should I talk to him about his intentions?"

Ryan hadn't thought she could smile. "No, that won't be necessary." She saw relief in Swan's eyes and rose. "I'd appreciate some time off after the taping."

"Of course, you've earned it."

"I won't keep you any longer." She started to turn

away, but he put a hand on her shoulder. Ryan glanced at him in surprise.

"Ryan…" He couldn't get a clear hold on what he wanted to say to her. Instead, he squeezed her shoulder. "Come on, I'll take you to dinner."

Ryan stared at him. When was the last time, she wondered, she had gone to dinner with her father? An awards banquet? A business party? "Dinner?" she said blankly.

"Yes." Swan's voice sharpened as his thoughts followed the same path Ryan's had. "A man can take his daughter to dinner, can't he?" He slipped his arm around her waist and led her to the door. How small she was! he realized with a jolt. "Go wash your face," he muttered. "I'll wait for you."

At ten o'clock the next morning Swan finished reading the Atkins contract a second time. A tricky business, he thought. It wouldn't be easy to break. But he had no intention of breaking it. That would not only be poor business sense but a useless gesture. He'd just have to deal with Atkins himself. When his buzzer sounded, he turned the contract facedown.

"Mr. Atkins is here, Mr. Swan."

"Send him in."

Swan rose as Pierce entered, and as he had done the first time, he walked across the room with his hand extended. "Pierce," he said jovially. "Thanks for coming up."

"Mr. Swan."

"Bennett, please," he said as he drew Pierce to a chair.

"Bennett," Pierce agreed, taking a seat.

Swan sat in the chair opposite him and leaned back. "Well, now, are you satisfied with how everything's going?"

Pierce lifted a brow. "Yes."

Swan took out a cigar. The man's too cool, he thought grudgingly. He doesn't give anything away. Swan decided to approach the subject from the side door. "Coogar tells me the rehearsals are smooth as silk. Worries him." Swan grinned. "He's a superstitious bastard, likes plenty of trouble before a taping. He tells me you could almost run the show yourself."

"He's a fine director," Pierce said easily, watching Swan light his cigar.

"The best," Swan agreed heartily. "We are a bit concerned about your plans for the finale."

"Oh?"

"This is television, you know," Swan reminded him with an expansive smile. "Four-ten is a bit long for one routine."

"It's necessary." Pierce let his hands rest on the arms of the chair. "I'm sure Ryan's told you."

Swan's eyes met the direct stare. "Yes, Ryan's told me. She came up here last night. She was frantic."

Pierce's fingers tensed slightly, but he kept his eyes level. "I know. I'm sorry."

"Look, Pierce, we're reasonable men." Swan leaned toward him, poking with his cigar. "This routine of yours sounds like a beauty. The time lock business is a real inspiration, but with a little modification—"

"I don't modify my illusions."

The cool dismissal had Swan blustering. "No contract's carved in stone," he said dangerously.

"You can try to break it," Pierce agreed. "It'll be a great deal more trouble for you than for me. And in the end it won't change anything."

"Damn it, man, the girl's beside herself!" Banging his

thigh with his fist, Swan flopped back in the chair. "She says she's in love with you."

"She is in love with me," Pierce returned quietly and ignored the twist in his stomach.

"What the hell do you mean to do about it?"

"Are you asking me as her father or as Swan Productions?"

Swan drew his brows together and muttered for a moment. "As her father," he decided.

"I'm in love with Ryan." Pierce met Swan's stare calmly. "If she's willing to have me, I'll spend my life with her."

"And if she's not?" Swan retorted.

Pierce's eyes darkened, something flickered, but he said nothing. That was something he'd yet to deal with. In the brief passage of seconds Swan saw what he wanted to know. He pressed his advantage.

"A woman in love isn't always reasonable," he said with an avuncular smile. "A man has to make certain adjustments."

"There's very little I wouldn't do for Ryan," Pierce returned. "But it isn't possible for me to change what I am."

"We're talking about a routine," Swan tossed back, losing patience.

"No, we're talking about my way of life. I could drop this escape," he continued while Swan frowned at him, "but there'd be another one and still another. If Ryan can't accept this one now, how can she accept one later?"

"You'll lose her," Swan warned.

Pierce rose at that, unable to sit any longer. "Perhaps I've never had her." He could deal with the pain, he told himself. He knew how to deal with pain. His voice was even when he continued. "Ryan has to make her own choices. I have to accept them."

Swan rose to his feet and glared. "Damn if you sound like a man in love to me."

Pierce gave him a long, cold stare that had Swan swallowing. "In a lifetime of illusions," he said roughly, "she's the only thing that's real." Turning, he strode from the room.

Chapter 16

They would tape at six o'clock west coast time. By 4:00 p.m. Ryan had dealt with everything from an irate property manager to a frazzled hairstylist. There was nothing like a live broadcast to throw even the most seasoned veterans into a state of madness. As it was put to her by a fatalistic stagehand, "Whatever could go wrong, would." It wasn't what Ryan wanted to hear.

But the problems, the demands, the touch of insanity kept her from crawling into a convenient corner to weep. She was needed and had no choice but to be dependable. If her career was all she was going to have left, Ryan knew she had to give it her best shot.

She had avoided Pierce for ten days by keeping an emotional distance. They had no choice but to come together time and again, but only as producer and star. He made no attempt to close the gap between them.

Ryan hurt. At times it still amazed her how much.

Still, she welcomed it. The hurt helped smother the fear. The three safes had been delivered. When she had forced herself to examine them, she had seen that the smallest was no more than three feet high and two feet across. The thought of Pierce folding himself into the small black box had her stomach rolling.

She had stood studying the largest safe with its thick door and complex time lock when she had sensed him behind her. When she had turned, they had looked at each other in silence. Ryan had felt the need, the love, the hopelessness before she had walked away from him. Neither by word nor gesture had he asked her to stay.

From then on Ryan had kept away from the safes, concentrating instead on the checking and rechecking of all the minute details of production.

Wardrobe had to be supervised. A broken spotlight needed repair at the eleventh hour. A sick technician had to be replaced. And timing, the most crucial element of all, had to be worked out to the last second.

There seemed to be no end to the last-minute problems, and she could only be grateful when each new one cropped up. There was no time for thinking, right up to the moment when the studio audience began to file in.

With her stomach in knots, her face composed, Ryan waited in the control booth as the floor director gave the final countdown.

It began.

Pierce was onstage, cool and competent. The set was perfect: clean, uncluttered and faintly mysterious with the understated lighting. In unrelieved black, he was a twentieth-century sorcerer with no need for magic wands or pointed hats.

Water flowed between his palms, fire shot from his fingertips. Ryan watched as he balanced Bess on the point of a saber, making her spin like a top, then drawing the sword out with a flourish until she spun on nothing at all.

Elaine floated on the torch flames while the audience held their breath. Pierce enclosed her in a clear glass bubble, covered it with red silk and sent it floating ten feet above the stage. It swayed gently to Link's music. When Pierce brought it down and whipped off the silk, Elaine was a white swan.

He varied his illusions—dashing, spectacular and simply beautiful. He controlled the elements, defied nature and baffled all.

"Going like a dream," Ryan heard someone say excitedly. "See if we don't cop a couple of Emmys for this one. Thirty seconds, camera two. God, is this guy good!"

Ryan left the control booth and went down to the wings. She told herself she was cold because the air-conditioning in the booth was turned up so high. It would be warmer near the stage. The lights there shone hotly, but her skin stayed chilled. She watched while he did a variation on the transportation illusion he had used in Vegas.

He never glanced in her direction, but Ryan sensed he knew she was there. He had to know, because her thoughts were so completely centered on him.

"It's going good, isn't it?"

Looking up, Ryan saw Link beside her. "Yes, perfect so far."

"I liked the swan. It's pretty."

"Yes."

"Maybe you should go into Bess's dressing room and sit down," he suggested, wishing she didn't look so pale and cold. "You could watch on the TV in there."

"No. No, I'll stay."

Pierce had a tiger onstage, a lean, pacing cat in a gilt cage. He covered it with the same silk he had used on the bubble. When he removed it, Elaine was caged and the tiger had vanished. Knowing it was the last illusion before the final escape, Ryan took a deep breath.

"Link." She reached for his hand, needing something to hold on to.

"He'll be all right, Ryan." He gave her fingers a squeeze. "Pierce is the best."

The smallest safe was brought out, its door open wide as it was turned around and around to show its solidity. Ryan tasted the iron tang of fear. She didn't hear Pierce's explanation to the audience as he was manacled hand and foot by a captain of the Los Angeles Police Department. Her eyes were glued to his face. She knew the deepest part of his mind was already locked inside the vault. Already, he was working his way out. That's what she held on to as firmly as Link's hand.

He barely fit inside the first safe. His shoulders brushed the sides.

He won't be able to move in there, she thought on a stab of panic. As the door was shut, she took a step toward the stage. Link held her by the shoulders.

"You can't, Ryan."

"But, God, he can't move. He can't breathe!" She watched with mounting horror as the second safe was brought out.

"He's already out of the cuffs," Link said soothingly, though he didn't like watching the safe that held Pierce lifted and locked inside the second one. "He'll be opening the first door now," he said to comfort himself as much as Ryan. "He works fast. You know, you've seen him."

"Oh, no." The third safe had the fear rocketing almost beyond her control. She felt a bright dizziness and would have swayed if Link's hands hadn't held her upright. The largest safe swallowed the two others and the man inside.

It was shut, bolted. The time lock was set for midnight. There was no way in from the outside now.

"How long?" she whispered. Her eyes were glued to the safe, on the shiny, complicated timer. "How long since he's been in?"

"Two and a half minutes." Link felt a bead of sweat run down his back. "He's got plenty of time."

He knew the safes fit together so snugly that the doors could only be pushed open far enough for a child to crawl through. He never understood how Pierce could twist and fold his body the way he did. But he'd seen him do it. Unlike Ryan, Link had watched Pierce rehearse the escape countless times. The sweat continued to roll down his back.

The air was thin, Ryan could barely draw it into her lungs. That was how it was inside the safe, she thought numbly. No air, no light. "Time, Link!" She was shaking like a leaf now. The big man stopped praying to answer.

"Two-fifty. It's almost over. He's working on the last one now."

Gripping her hands together, Ryan began to count off the seconds in her head. The roaring in her ears had her biting down hard on her lip. She had never fainted in her life, but she knew she was perilously close to doing so now. When her vision blurred, she squeezed her eyes tight to clear it. But she couldn't breathe. Pierce had no air now and neither did she. On a bubble of hysteria, she thought she would suffocate standing there as surely as Pierce would inside the trio of safes.

Then she saw the door opening, heard the unified gasp of relief from the audience before the burst of applause. He stood on the stage, damp with sweat and drawing in air.

Ryan swooned back against Link as darkness blocked

out the spotlights. She lost consciousness for no more than seconds, coming back when she heard Link calling her.

"Ryan, Ryan, it's all right. He's out. He's okay."

Bracing herself against Link, she shook her head to clear it. "Yes, he's out." For one last second she watched him, then turning, she walked away.

The moment the cameras shut off, Pierce walked offstage. "Where's Ryan?" he demanded of Link.

"She left." He watched a trickle of sweat run down Pierce's face. "She was pretty upset." He offered Pierce the towel he'd been holding for him. "I think maybe she fainted for a minute."

Pierce didn't brush away the sweat, he didn't grin as he always did when an escape was completed. "Where did she go?"

"I don't know. She just left."

Without a word, Pierce went to look for her.

Ryan lay baking in the strong sun. There was an itch in the center of her back, but she didn't move to scratch it. She lay still and let the heat soak into her skin.

She had spent a week on board her father's yacht off the coast of St. Croix. Swan had let her go alone, as she requested, asking no questions when she had arrived at his house and asked for the favor. He'd made the arrangements for her and had taken her to the airport himself. Ryan was to think later that it was the first time he hadn't put her in a limo with a driver and sent her off to catch a plane by herself.

For days now she had lain in the sun, swam and kept her mind a blank. She hadn't even gone back to her apartment after the taping. She had arrived in St. Croix with the clothes on her back. Whatever she needed she bought on the island. She spoke to no one but the crew and sent no messages back to the States. For a week she simply slipped off the face of the earth.

Ryan rolled over on her back and dropped the sunglasses over her eyes. She knew that if she didn't force herself to think, the answer she needed would come to her in time. When it came, it would be right, and she would act on it. Until then, she waited.

In his workroom, Pierce shuffled and cut the Tarot cards. He needed to relax. The tension was eating at him.

After the taping he had searched the entire building for Ryan. When she was nowhere to be found, he had broken one of his own cardinal rules and had picked the lock on her apartment. He had waited for her through the next morning. She had never come home. It had driven him wild, furious. He'd let the rage take him, blocking out the pain. Anger, the undisciplined anger he never allowed himself, came in full force. Link had borne the brunt of his temper in silence.

It had taken Pierce days to regain his control. Ryan was gone, and he had to accept it. His own set of rules left him no choice. Even if he'd known where to find her, he couldn't bring her back.

In the week that had passed he had done no work. He had no power. Whenever he tried to focus his concentration, he saw only Ryan—felt her, tasted her. It was all he could conjure. He had to work his way back. Pierce knew if he didn't find his rhythm again soon he would be finished.

He was alone now, with Link and Bess honeymooning in the mountains. When he had regained some of his control, he had insisted they keep to their plans. He had sent them on their way, struggling to give them happiness while his own life loomed empty ahead of him.

It was time to go back to the only thing he had left. And even that brought a small trickle of fear. He was no longer sure he had any magic.

Setting the cards aside, Pierce rose to set up one of his more complicated illusions. He wouldn't test himself on anything simplistic. Even as he began to train his concentration, flex his hands, he looked up and saw her.

Pierce stared hard at the image. She had never come this clearly to him before. He could even hear her footsteps as she crossed the room to the stage. Her scent reached him first and had his blood humming. He wondered, almost dispassionately, if he were going mad.

"Hello, Pierce."

Ryan saw him jolt as if she had startled him out of a dream. "Ryan?" Her name on his lips was soft, questioning.

"Your front door wasn't locked, so I came in. I hope you don't mind."

He continued to stare at her and said nothing. She mounted the steps of the stage.

"I've interrupted your work."

Following her gaze, Pierce looked down at the glass vial in his hand and the colored cubes on the table.

"Work? It—no, it's all right." He set the vial down. He couldn't have managed the most basic illusion.

"This won't take long," Ryan told him with a smile. She had never seen him rattled and was all but certain she would never see him so again. "There's a new contract we need to discuss."

"Contract?" he repeated, unable to take his eyes from hers.

"Yes, that's why I've come."

"I see." He wanted to touch her but kept his hands on the table. He wouldn't touch what was no longer his. "You look well," he managed and started to offer her a chair. "Where have you been?" It was out before he could stop it; it was perilously close to an accusation. Ryan only smiled again.

"I've been away," she said simply, then took a step closer. "Have you thought of me?"

It was he who stepped back. "Yes, I've thought of you."

"Often?" The word was quiet as she moved toward him again.

"Don't, Ryan!" His voice was defensively sharp as he moved back.

"I've thought of you often," she continued as if he hadn't spoken. "Constantly, though I tried not to. Do you dabble in love potions, Pierce? Is that what you did to me?" She took another step toward him. "I tried very hard to hate you and harder still to forget you. Your magic's too strong."

Her scent whirled through his senses until they were all clouded with her. "Ryan, I'm only a man, and you're my weakness. Don't do this." Pierce shook his head and called on the last of his control. "I have work to do."

Ryan glanced at the table, then toyed with one of the colored cubes. "It'll have to wait. Do you know how many hours there are in a week?" she asked and smiled at him.

"No. Stop this, Ryan." The blood was pounding in his head. The need was growing unmanageable.

"A hundred and sixty-eight," she whispered. "A lot to make up for."

"If I touch you, I won't let you go again."

"And if I touch you?" She laid her hand on his chest.

"Don't," he warned quickly. "You should leave while you still can."

"You'll do that escape again, won't you?"

"Yes. Yes, damn it." His fingertips were tingling, demanding that he reach for her. "Ryan, for God's sake, go."

"You'll do it again," she went on. "And others, probably more dangerous, or at least more frightening, because that's who you are. Isn't that what you told me?"

"Ryan—"

"That's who I fell in love with," she said calmly. "I don't know why I thought I could or should try to change that. I told you once you were exactly what I wanted, that was the truth. But I suppose I had to learn what that meant. Do you still want me, Pierce?"

He didn't answer, but she saw his eyes darken, felt his heart speed under her hand. "I can leave and have a very calm, undemanding life." Ryan took the last step to him. "Is that what you want for me? Have I hurt you so much you wish me a life of unbearable boredom? Please, Pierce," she murmured, "won't you forgive me?"

"There's nothing to forgive." He was drowning in her eyes no matter how he struggled not to. "Ryan, for the love of God!" Desperate, he pushed her hand from his chest. "Can't you see what you're doing to me?"

"Yes, and I'm so glad. I was afraid you could really shut me out." She let out a quiet sigh of relief. "I'm staying, Pierce. There's nothing you can do about it." She had her arms around his neck and her mouth a breath away from his. "Tell me again that you want me to go."

"No." He dragged her against him. "I can't." His mouth was devouring hers. Power flowed into him again, hot and painful. He pressed her closer and felt her mouth respond to the savageness of his. "It's too late," he murmured. "Much too late." Excitement was burning through him. He couldn't hold her near enough. "I won't be able to leave the door open for you now, Ryan. Do you understand?"

"Yes. Yes, I understand." She drew her head back, wanting to see his eyes. "But it'll be closed for you, too. I'm going to see to it this is one lock you can't beat."

"No escape, Ryan. For either of us." And his mouth was on hers again, hot, desperate. He felt her give against him as he crushed her to him, but her hands were strong and sure on his body. "I love you, Ryan," he told her again as he roamed her face and neck with kisses. "I love you. I lost everything when you left me."

"I won't leave you again." She took his face in her hands to stop his wandering lips. "I was wrong to ask you what I did. I was wrong to run away. I didn't trust enough."

"And now?"

"I love you, Pierce, exactly as you are."

He pulled her close again and pressed his mouth to her throat. "Beautiful Ryan, so small, so soft. God, how I want you. Come upstairs, come to bed. Let me love you properly."

Her pulses hammered at the quiet, rough words he spoke against her throat. Ryan took a deep breath, then, putting her hands on his shoulders, she pulled away. "There's the matter of a contract."

"The hell with contracts," he mumbled and tried to pull her back.

"Oh, no." Ryan stepped away from him. "I want this settled."

"I've already signed your contract," he reminded her impatiently. "Come here."

"This is a new one," she stated, ignoring him. "An exclusive life term."

He frowned. "Ryan, I'm not going to tie myself to Swan Productions for the rest of my life."

"Not Swan Productions," she countered. "Ryan Swan."

The annoyed retort on the tip of his tongue never materialized. She saw his eyes change, become intense. "What sort of contract?"

"A one-to-one, with an exclusivity clause and a lifetime term." Ryan swallowed, losing some of the confidence that had carried her this far.

"Go on."

"It's to begin immediately, with the provision of a legally binding ceremony to follow at the first reasonable opportunity." She laced her fingers together. "With a proviso for the probability of offspring." She saw Pierce's brow lift, but he said nothing. "The number of which is negotiable."

"I see," he said after a moment. "Is there a penalty clause?"

"Yes. If you try to break the terms, I'm allowed to murder you."

"Very reasonable. Your contract's very tempting, Miss Swan. What are my benefits?"

"Me."

"Where do I sign?" he asked, taking her in his arms again.

"Right here." She let out a sigh as she lifted her mouth. The kiss was gentle, promising. With a moan, Ryan drew closer.

"This ceremony, Miss Swan." Pierce nibbled at her lip as his hands began to roam. "What do you consider the first reasonable opportunity?"

"Tomorrow afternoon." She laughed and again pulled out of his arms. "You don't think I'm going to give you time to find an escape hatch, do you?"

"I've met my match, I see."

"Absolutely," she agreed with a nod. "I have a few tricks up my sleeve." Lifting the Tarot cards, she surprised Pierce by fanning them with some success. She'd been practicing for months.

"Very good." He grinned and went to her. "I'm impressed."

"You haven't seen anything yet," she promised. "Pick a card," she told him, her eyes laughing. "Any card."

* * * * *

SEARCH FOR LOVE

Chapter 1

The train ride seemed endless, and Serenity was tired. The argument the night before with Tony had not helped her disposition, plus the long flight from Washington to Paris, and now the arduous hours in the stuffy train had her gritting her teeth to hold back the groan. All in all, she decided miserably, she was a poor traveler.

The trip had been the excuse for the last, terminal battle between Serenity and Tony, their relationship having been strained and uneven for weeks. Her continued refusal to be pressured into marriage had provoked several minor tiffs, but Tony had wanted her, and his patience seemed inexhaustible. Not until her announcement of the intended trip had his forebearance cracked, and the war had begun.

"You can't go rushing off this way to France to see some supposed grandmother you never knew existed until a couple of weeks ago." Tony had paced, his agitation obvious by the way he allowed his hand to disturb his well-styled fair hair.

"Brittany," Serenity had elaborated. "And it doesn't matter when I found out she existed; I know now."

"This old lady writes you a letter, tells you she's your grandmother and wants to see you, and off you go, just like that." He had been totally exasperated. She knew his logical mind was unable to comprehend her impulse, and she had hung on to the threads of her own temper and had attempted to speak calmly.

"She's my mother's mother, Tony, the only family I have left, and I intend to see her. You know I've been making plans to go since her letter arrived."

"The old girl lets twenty-four years go by without a word, and now suddenly, this big summons." He had continued to pace the large, high-ceilinged room before whirling back to her. "Why in heaven's name did your parents never speak of her? Why did she wait until they were dead to contact you?"

Serenity had known he had not meant to be cruel; it was not in Tony's nature to be cruel, merely logical, his lawyer's mind dealing constantly in facts and figures. Even he could not know the slow, deadly ache that remained, lingering after two months, the time since her parents' sudden, unexpected deaths. Knowing that his words had not been intended to hurt did not prevent her from lashing out, and the argument had grown in proportion until Tony had stomped out and left her alone, seething and resentful.

Now, as the train chugged its way across Brittany, Serenity was forced to admit that she, too, had doubts. Why had her grandmother, this unknown Comtesse Françoise de Kergallen, remained silent for nearly a quarter of a century? Why had her mother, her lovely, fragile, fascinatingly different mother, never mentioned a relative in far-off Brittany? Not even her father, as volatile, outspoken, and direct as he had been, had ever spoken of ties across the Atlantic.

They had been so close, Serenity mused with a sigh of memory. The three of them had done so much together. Even when she had been a child, her parents had included her when they visited senators, congressmen, and ambassadors.

Jonathan Smith had been a much-sought-after artist; a portrait created by his talented hand, a prized possession. Those in Washington society had clamored for his commissions for more than twenty years. He had been well liked and respected as a man as well as an artist, and the gentle charm and grace of Gaelle, his wife, had made the couple a highly esteemed addition to the capital set.

When Serenity had grown older, and her natural artistic abilities became apparent, her father's pride had known no bounds. They had sketched and painted together, first as tutor and pupil, then as man and woman, and they drew even closer with the shared joy of art.

The small family had shared an idyllic existence in the elegant rowhouse in Georgetown, a life full of love and laughter, until Serenity's world had crashed in around her, along with the plane which had been carrying her parents to California. It had been impossible to believe they were dead, and she still lived on. The high-ceilinged rooms would no longer echo with her father's booming voice or her mother's gentle laughter. The house was empty but for memories that lay like shadows in each corner.

For the first two weeks, Serenity could not bear the sight of a canvas or brush, or the thought of entering the third-floor studio where she and her father had spent so many hours, where her mother would enter and remind them that even artists had to eat.

When she had finally gathered up the courage to climb the stairs and enter the sun-filled room, she found, rather than unbearable grief, a strange, healing peace. The skylight showered the room with the sun's warmth, and the walls retained the love and laughter which had once existed there. She had begun to live again, paint again, and Tony had been kind and gentle, helping to fill the hollowness left by loss. Then, the letter had come.

Now she had left Georgetown and Tony behind in a quest for the part of her that belonged to Brittany and an unknown grandmother. The strange, formal letter which had brought her from the familiarity of Washington's crowded streets to the unaccustomed Breton countryside lay safely tucked in the smooth leather bag at her side. There had been no affection in the missive, merely facts and an invitation, more like a royal command, Serenity mused, half-annoyed, half-amused. But if her pride would have scoffed at the command, her curiosity, her desire to know more of her mother's family, had accepted. With her innate impulsiveness and organization, she had arranged her trip, closed up the beloved house in Georgetown, and burned her bridges with Tony.

The train groaned and screeched in protest as it dragged into the station at Lannion. Tingling excitement warred with jet lag as Serenity gathered her hand luggage and stepped onto the platform, taking her first attentive look at her mother's native country. She stared around her with an artist's eyes, lost for a moment in the simple beauty and soft, melding colors that were Brittany.

The man watched her concentration, the small smile playing on her parted lips, and his dark brow rose slightly in surprise. He took his time surveying her, a tall, willow-slim figure in a powder-blue traveling suit, the soft skirt floating around long, shapely legs. The soft breeze ran easy fingers through her sunlit hair, feathering it back to frame the delicate-boned, oval face. The eyes, he noted, were large and wide, the color of brandy, surrounded by thick lashes shades darker than her pale hair. Her skin looked incredibly soft, smooth like alabaster, and the combination lent an ethereal appearance: a delicate, fragile orchid. He would all too soon discover that appearances are often deceptive.

He approached her slowly, almost reluctantly. "You are Mademoiselle Serenity Smith?" he inquired in lightly accented English.

Serenity started at the sound of his voice, so absorbed in the countryside she had not noted his nearness. Brushing back a lock of hair, she turned her head and found herself looking up, much higher than was her habit, into dark, heavy-lidded brown eyes.

"Yes," she answered, wondering why those eyes made her feel so strange. "Are you from the Château Kergallen?"

The slow lifting of one dark brow was the only change in his expression. "*Oui,* I am Chrístophe de Kergallen. I have come to take you to the countess."

"De Kergallen?" she repeated with some surprise. "Not another mysterious relative?"

The brow remained lifted, and full, sensuous lips curved so slightly as to be imperceptible. "One could say, Mademoiselle, that we are, in an obscure manner, cousins."

"Cousins," she murmured as they studied each other, rather like two prizefighters sizing each other up before a bout.

Rich black hair fell thick and straight to his collar, and

the dark eyes which continued to remain steady seemed nearly as black against his deep bronze skin. His features were sharp, hawklike, somewhat piratical, and he exuded a basic masculine aura which both attracted and repelled her. She immediately wished for her sketch pad, wondering if she could possibly capture his aristocratic virility with pencil and paper.

Her lengthy scrutiny left him unperturbed, and he held her gaze, his eyes cool and aloof. "Your trunks will be delivered to the château." He bent down, picking up the bags she had set on the platform. "If you will come with me, the countess is anxious to see you."

He led her to a gleaming black sedan, assisted her into the passenger's side, and stowed her bags in the back, his manner so cold and impersonal that Serenity felt both annoyed and curious. He began to drive in silence, and she turned in her seat and examined him with open boldness.

"And how," she demanded, "are we cousins?" *What do I call him?* she wondered. *Monsieur? Christophe? Hey, you?*

"The countess's husband, your mother's father, died when your mother was a child." He began his explanation in polite, faintly bored tones, and she was tempted to tell him not to strain himself. "Several years later, the countess married my grandfather, the Comte de Kergallen, whose wife had died and left him with a son, my father." He turned his head and spared her a brief glance. "Your mother and my father were raised as brother and sister in the château. My grandfather died, my father married, lived long enough to see me born, and then promptly killed himself in a hunting accident. My mother pined for him for three years, then joined him in the family crypt."

The story had been recited in remote, unemotional tones, and the sympathy Serenity would have normally felt for the child left orphaned never materialized. She watched his hawk-like profile for another moment.

"So, that makes you the present Comte de Kergallen and my cousin through marriage."

Again, a brief, negligent glance. *"Oui."*

"I can't tell you how both facts thrill me," she stated, a definite edge of sarcasm in her tone. His brow rose once more as he turned to her, and she thought for an instant that she had detected laughter lighting the cool, dark eyes. She decided against it, positive that the man sitting next to her never laughed. "Did you know my mother?" she inquired when the silence grew.

"Oui. I was eight when she left the château."

"Why did she leave?" Serenity demanded, turning to him with direct amber eyes. He twisted his head and met them with equal directness, and she was assaulted by their power before he turned his attention back to the road.

"The countess will tell you what she wishes you to know."

"What she wishes?" Serenity sputtered, angered by the deliberate rebuff. "Let's understand each other, Cousin. I fully intend to find out exactly why my mother left Brittany, and why I've spent my life ignorant of my grandmother."

With slow, casual movements, Christophe lit a cheroot, expelling smoke lazily. "There is nothing I can tell you."

"You mean," she corrected, narrowing her eyes, "there is nothing you *will* tell me."

His broad shoulders moved in a purely Gallic shrug, and Serenity turned to stare out the front window, copying his movement with the American version, missing the slight smile which played on his mouth at her gesture.

They continued to drive in sporadic silence, with Serenity occasionally inquiring about the scenery, Christophe answering in polite monosyllables, making no effort to expand the conversation. Golden sun and pure sky might have been sufficient to soothe the disposition ruffled by the journey, but his continued coolness outbalanced nature's gift.

"For a count from Brittany," she observed with deceptive sweetness after being spared another two syllables, "you speak remarkably fine English."

Sarcasm rolled off him like a summer's breeze, and his response was lightly patronizing. "The countess also speaks English quite well, Mademoiselle. The servants, however, speak only French or Breton. If you find yourself in difficulty, you have only to ask the countess or myself for assistance."

Serenity tilted her chin and turned her rich golden eyes on him with haughty disdain. *"Ce n'est pas nécessaire,* Monsieur le Comte. *Je parle bien le français."*

One dark brow lifted in harmony with his lips. *"Bon,"* he replied in the same language. "That will make your visit less complicated."

"Is it much farther to the château?" she inquired, continuing to speak in French. She felt hot, crumpled, and tired. Due to the long trip and the time change, it seemed as if she had been in some kind of vehicle for days, and she longed for a stationary tub filled with hot, soapy water.

"We have been on Kergallen land for some time, Mademoiselle," he replied, his eyes remaining on the winding road. "The château is not much farther."

The car had been climbing slowly to a higher elevation. Serenity closed her eyes on the headache which had begun to throb in her left temple, and wished fervently that her mysterious grandmother lived in a less complicated place, like Idaho or New Jersey. When she opened her eyes again, all aches, fatigue, and complaints vanished like a mist in the hot sun.

"Stop!" she cried, reverting to English, unconsciously laying a hand on Christophe's arm.

The château stood high, proud, and solitary: an immense stone edifice from another century with drum towers and crenellated walls and a tiled conical roof glowing warm and gray against a cerulean-blue sky. The windows were many, high and narrow, reflecting the diminishing sunlight with a myriad of colors. It was ancient, arrogant, confident, and Serenity fell immediately in love.

Christophe watched the surprise and pleasure register on her unguarded face, her hand still warm and light on his arm. A stray curl had fallen loose onto her forehead, and he reached out to brush it back, catching himself before he reached her and staring at his own hand in annoyance.

Serenity was too absorbed with the château to notice his movement, already planning what angles she would use for sketches, imagining the moat that might have encircled the château at one time in the past.

"It's fabulous," she said at last, turning to her companion. Hastily, she removed her hand from his arm, wondering how it could have gotten there. "It's like something out of a fairy tale. I can almost hear the sound of trumpets, see the knights in armor, and ladies in full, floating dresses and high, pointed hats. Is there a neighborhood dragon?" She smiled at him, her face illuminated and incredibly lovely.

"Not unless one counts Marie, the cook," he answered, lowering the cool, polite wall for a moment and allowing her a quick glimpse of the wide, disarming smile which made him seem younger and approachable.

So, *he's human, after all,* she concluded. But as her

pulse leaped in response to the sudden smile, she realized
that when human, he was infinitely more dangerous. As
their eyes met and held, she had the strange sensation of
being totally alone with him, the rest of the world only a
backdrop as they sat alone in private, enchanted solitude,
and Georgetown seemed a lifetime away.

The stiffly polite stranger soon replaced the charming
escort, and Christophe resumed the drive in silence, all
the more thick and cold after the brief friendly interlude.

Watch it, Serenity, she cautioned herself. *Your imagination's running rampant again. This man is most definitely not for you. For some unknown reason, he doesn't
even like you, and one quick smile doesn't change him
from a cold, condescending aristocrat.*

Christophe pulled the car to a halt in a large, circular
drive bordered by a flagstone courtyard, its low stone
walls spilling over with phlox. He alighted from the car
with swift, agile grace, and Serenity copied him before
he had rounded the hood to assist her, so enchanted by the
storybook atmosphere that she failed to note the frown
which creased his brow at her action.

Taking her arm, he led her up stone steps to a massive
oaken door, and, pulling a gleaming brass handle, inclined his head in a slight bow and motioned her to enter.

The entrance hall was huge. The floors were buffed
to a mirrorlike shine and scattered with exquisite hand-
hooked rugs. The walls were paneled, hung with tapestries, wide and colorful and incredibly old. A large hall
rack and hunt table, both oak and glowing with the patina
of age, oaken chairs with hand-worked seats, and the scent
of fresh flowers graced the room, which seemed oddly
familiar to her. It was as if she had known what to expect when she had crossed the threshold into the château,
and the room seemed to recognize her, and welcome her.

"Something is wrong?" Christophe asked, noting her expression of confusion.

She shook her head with a slight shiver. *"Déjà vu,"* she murmured, and turned to him. "It's very strange; I feel as though I've stood right here before." She caught herself with a jolt of shock before she added, "with you." Letting out a deep breath, she made a restless movement with her shoulders. "It's very odd."

"So, you have brought her, Christophe."

Serenity turned away from suddenly intense brown eyes to watch her grandmother approach.

La Comtesse de Kergallen was tall and nearly as slender as Serenity. Her hair was a pure, brilliant white, lying like clouds around a sharp, angular face that defied the network of wrinkles age had bestowed on it. The eyes were clear, a piercing blue under well-arched brows, and she carried herself regally, as one who knows that more than six decades had not dimmed her beauty.

No Mother Hubbard, this, Serenity thought quickly. *This lady is a countess right down to her fingertips.*

The eyes surveyed Serenity slowly, completely, and she observed a flicker of emotion cross the angular face before it once again became impassive and guarded. The countess extended a well-shaped, ringed hand.

"Welcome to the Château Kergallen, Serenity Smith. I am Madame la Comtesse Françoise de Kergallen."

Serenity accepted the offered hand in her own, wondering whimsically if she should kiss it and curtsy. The clasp was brief and formal—no affectionate embrace, no smile of welcome. She swallowed disappointment and spoke with equal formality.

"Thank you, Madame. I am pleased to be here."

"You must be tired after your journey," the countess stated. "I will show you to your room myself. You will wish to rest before you change for dinner."

She moved to a large, curving staircase, and Serenity followed. Pausing on the landing, she glanced back to find Christophe watching her, his face creased in a brooding frown. He made no effort to smooth it away or remove his eyes from hers, and Serenity found herself turning swiftly and hurrying after the countess's retreating back.

They walked down a long, narrow corridor with brass lights set at intervals into the walls, replacing, she imagined, what would have once been torches. When the countess stopped at a door, she turned once more to Serenity, and after giving her another quick study, she opened the door and motioned her to enter.

The room was large and open, yet somehow retained an air of delicate grace. The furniture was glossy cherry, and a large four-poster canopied bed dominated the room, its silk coverlet embroidered with time-consuming stitches. A stone fireplace was set in the wall opposite the foot of the bed, its mantle carved and ornate, a collection of Dresden figures reflecting in the large framed mirror over it. One end of the room was curved and glassed, an upholstered windowseat inviting one to sit and ponder the breathtaking view.

Serenity felt the uncontrollable pull of the room, an aura of love and happiness, the gentle elegance well remembered. "This was my mother's room."

Again, the quick play of emotion flickered, like a candle caught in a draft. "*Oui.* Gaelle decorated it herself when she was sixteen."

"Thank you for giving it to me, Madame." Even the cool reply could not dispel the warmth the room brought her, and she smiled. "I shall feel very close to her during my stay."

The countess merely nodded and pressed a small button next to the bed. "Bridget will draw your bath. Your trunks will arrive shortly, and she will see to your unpacking. We dine at eight, unless you would care for some refreshment now."

"No, thank you, Countess," Serenity replied, beginning to feel like a boarder in a very well-run hotel. "Eight will be fine."

The countess moved to the doorway. "Bridget will show you to the drawing room after you have rested. We have cocktails at seven-thirty. If there is anything you require, you have only to ring."

The door closed behind her, and Serenity took a deep breath and sat heavily on the bed.

Why did I come? she asked herself, closing her eyes on a sudden surge of loneliness. *I should have stayed in Georgetown, stayed with Tony, stayed with what I could understand. What am I searching for here?* Taking a long breath, she fought the encompassing depression and surveyed her room again. *My mother's room,* she reminded herself and felt the soothing hands of comfort. *This is something I can understand.*

Moving to the window, Serenity watched day soften into twilight, the sun flashing with final, brilliant fire before surrendering to slumber. A breeze stirred the air, and the few scattered clouds moved with it, rolling lazily across the darkening sky.

A château on a hill in Brittany. Shaking her head at the thought, she knelt on the windowseat and watched evening's nativity. *Where does Serenity Smith fit into this?* Somewhere. She frowned at the knowledge which sprang from her heart. *Somehow I belong here, or a part of me does. I felt it the moment I saw those incredible stone walls, and again when I walked into the hall.* Pushing the feeling to the depths of her brain, she concentrated on her grandmother.

She certainly wasn't overwhelmed by the reunion, Serenity decided with a rueful smile. Or perhaps it was just the European formality that made her seem so cold and distant. It hardly seems reasonable that she would ask me to come if she hadn't wanted to see me. I suppose I expected more because I wanted more. Lifting her shoulders, she allowed them to fall slowly. *Patience has never been one of my virtues, but I suppose I'd better develop it. Perhaps if my greeting at the station had been a bit more welcoming...* Her frown appeared again as she replayed Christophe's attitude.

I could swear he would have liked to bundle me back on the train the minute he set eyes on me. Then, that infuriating conversation in the car. Frown deepened into scowl, and she ceased to focus on the quiet dimness of dusk. *That is a very frustrating man,* and she added, her scowl softening into thoughtfulness, *the very epitome of a Breton count. Perhaps that's why he affected me so strongly.* Resting her chin on her palm, she recalled the awareness which had shimmered between them as they had sat alone in the lengthening shadow of the château. *He's unlike any man I've ever known: elegant and vital at the same time. There's a potency there, a virility wrapped inside the sophistication.* Power. The word flashed into her brain, drawing her brows close. *Yes,* she admitted with a reluctance she could not quite understand, *there's power there, and an essence of self-assurance.*

From an artist's standpoint, he's a remarkable study. He attracts me as an artist, she told herself, *certainly not as a woman. A woman would have to be mad to get tangled up with a man like that. Absolutely mad,* she repeated to herself firmly.

Chapter 2

The oval, free-standing gilt-framed mirror reflected a slim, fair-haired woman. The flowing, high-necked gown in a muted "ashes of roses" shade lent a glow to the creamy skin, leaving arms and shoulders bare. Serenity met the reflection's amber eyes, held them, and sighed. It was nearly time to go down and again meet her grandmother—the regal, reserved countess—and her cousin, the formal, oddly hostile count.

Her trunks had arrived while she was enjoying the bath drawn by the small, dark Breton maid. Bridget had unpacked and put away her clothes, shyly at first, then chattering and exclaiming over the articles as she hung them in the large wardrobe or folded them in the antique bureau. The simple friendliness had been a marked contrast to the attitude of those who were her family.

Serenity's attempts to rest between the cool linen sheets of the great canopied bed had been futile, all her emotions in turmoil. The strange awareness she had experienced upon entering the château, the stiff, formal welcome of her grandmother, and the strong, physical response to the remote count had all banded together to make her unaccustomedly nervous and unsure of herself. She found herself wishing again she had allowed Tony to sway her, and had remained among the things and people she knew and understood.

Letting out a deep breath, she straightened her shoulders and lifted her chin. She was not a naïve schoolgirl to be awed by castles and overdone formality, she reminded herself. She was Serenity Smith, Jonathan and Gaelle Smith's daughter, and she would hold her head up and deal with counts and countesses.

Bridget knocked softly at her door, and Serenity followed her down the narrow corridor and began her descent down the curved staircase, cloaked in confidence.

"*Bonsoir,* Mademoiselle Smith." Christophe greeted her with his usual formality as she reached the bottom landing, and Bridget made a quick, unobtrusive exit.

"*Bonsoir,* Monsieur le Comte," Serenity returned, equally ritualistic, as they once more surveyed each other closely.

The black dinner suit lent a certain Satanic appearance to his aquiline features, the dark eyes glistening to near jet-black, the skin against the black and stark white of his shirt gleaming dusky-bronze. If there were pirates in his lineage, Serenity decided, they were elegant ones—and, she concluded further, as his eyes lingered on her, probably highly successful in all aspects of piratical pursuits.

"The countess awaits us in the drawing room," he announced when he had looked his fill, and with unexpected charm, he offered her his arm.

The countess watched as they entered the room, the

tall, haughty man and the slim, golden-haired woman, a perfect foil at his side. A remarkably handsome couple, she reflected, one that would cause heads to turn wherever they went. "*Bonsoir,* Serenity, Christophe." She greeted them, regally resplendent in a gown of sapphire-blue, diamonds shooting fire from her throat. "*Mon apéritif,* Christophe, *s'il te plaît.* And for you, Serenity?"

"Vermouth, thank you, Madame," she replied, the practiced social smile on her lips.

"You rested well, I hope," the older woman inquired as Christophe handed her the small crystal glass.

"Yes, very well, Madame." She turned to accept the offered wine. "I…" The inane words she was about to utter stuck in her throat as the portrait caught her eye, and she turned around fully and faced it.

A cream-skinned, pale-haired woman looked back at her, the face the mirror image of her own. But for the length of the light gold mist of hair, falling to the shoulders, and the eyes that shone deep blue rather than amber, the portrait was Serenity: the oval face, delicate, with interesting hollows, the full, shapely mouth, the fragile, elusive beauty of her mother, reproduced in oil a quarter of a century earlier.

Her father's work—Serenity knew this immediately and unmistakably. The brush strokes, the use of color, the individual technique that shouted Jonathan Smith as surely as if she had read the small signature in the bottom corner. Her eyes filled, and she blinked back the threatening mist. Seeing the portrait had brought her parents close for a moment, and she was saturated with a deep sense of warmth and belonging that she had just been learning to live without.

She continued to study the painting, allowing herself to take in the details of her father's work, the folds of the oyster-white gown which seemed to float on a hidden breeze, the rubies at her mother's ears, a sharp contrast of color, the stone repeated in the ring on her finger. During the survey, something nagged at the back of her mind, some small detail out of place which refused to bring itself out of her consciousness, and she let it fade and merely experienced.

"Your mother was a very beautiful woman," the countess remarked after a time, and Serenity answered absently, still absorbed by the glowing look of love and happiness in her mother's eyes.

"Yes, she was. It's amazing how little she changed since my father painted this. How old was she?"

"Barely twenty," the countess replied, cultured tones edging with curtness. "You recognized your father's work quickly."

"Of course," Serenity agreed, not noticing the tones, and turning, she smiled with honest warmth. "As his daughter and a fellow artist, I recognize his work as quickly as his handwriting." Facing the portrait again, she gestured with a slim, long-fingered hand. "That was painted twenty-five years ago, and it still breathes with life, almost as if they were both right here in this room."

"Your resemblance to her is very strong," Christophe observed as he sipped his wine from his place by the mantel, capturing her attention as completely as if he had put his hands on her. "I was quite struck by it when you stepped from the train."

"But for the eyes," the countess pronounced before Serenity could form a suitable comment. "The eyes are his."

There was no mistaking the bitterness which vibrated in her voice, and narrowing the eyes under discussion, Serenity spun around, the skirt of her gown following lazily. "Yes, Madame, I have my father's eyes. Does that displease you?"

Elegant shoulders moved in dismissal, and the countess lifted her glass and sipped.

"Did my parents meet here, in the château?" Serenity demanded, patience straining. "Why did they leave and never come back? Why did they never speak to me of you?" Glancing from her grandmother to Christophe, she met two cool, expressionless faces. The countess had lifted a shield, and Serenity knew Christophe would help her maintain it. He would tell her nothing; any answers must come from the woman. She opened her mouth to speak again when she was cut off with a wave of a ringed hand.

"We will speak of it soon enough." The words were spoken like a royal decree as the countess rose from her chair. "Now, we will go in to dinner."

The dining room was massive, but Serenity had decided everything was massive in the château. High-beamed ceilings towered like those in a cathedral, and the dark wainscotted walls were broken by high windows framed with rich velvet drapes, the color of blood. A fireplace large enough to stand in commanded an entire wall, and she thought, when lit, it must be an awesome sight. A heavy chandelier gave the room its lights, its crystals trembling in a glistening rainbow of colors on the suite of dark majestic oak.

The meal began with an onion soup, thick, rich, and very French, and the trio maintained a polite conversation throughout the course. Serenity glanced at Christophe, intrigued against her will by his darkly handsome looks and haughty bearing.

He certainly doesn't like me, she concluded with a puzzled frown. *He didn't like me the moment he set eyes on me. I wonder why.* With a mental shrug, she began to eat her creamed salmon. *Perhaps he doesn't like women in general.* Looking over, his eyes met hers with a force that rivaled an electric storm, and her heart leaped suddenly, as if seeking to escape from behind her ribs. *No,* she amended quickly, tearing her eyes from his and studying the clear white wine in her glass, *he's no woman hater; those eyes are full of knowledge and experience. Tony never made me react like this.* Lifting her glass, she sipped with determination. *No one ever made me react like this.*

"Stevan," the countess commanded, "*du vin pour* Mademoiselle."

The countess's order to the hovering servant brought Serenity back from her contemplations. *"Mais non, merci. C'est bien."*

"You speak French very well for an American, Serenity," the dowager observed. "I am grateful your education was complete, even in that barbarous country."

The disdain in the last few words was so blatant that Serenity was unsure whether to be insulted or amused by the slight on her nationality. "That 'barbarous' country, Madame," she said dryly, "is called America, and it's nearly civilized these days. Why, we go virtually weeks between Indian attacks."

The proud head lifted imperiously. "There is no need for impudence, young woman."

"Really?" Serenity asked with a guileless smile. "Strange, I was sure there was." Lifting her wineglass, she saw, to her surprise, Christophe's teeth flash white against his dark skin in a wide, quick grin.

"You may have your mother's gentle looks," the countess observed, "but you have your father's tongue."

"Thank you." She met the clear blue eyes with an acknowledging nod. "On both counts."

The meal concluded, the conversation was allowed to drift back into generalities. And if the interlude took on the aspect of a truce, Serenity was still floundering as to the reason for the war. They adjourned once more to the main drawing room, Christophe lounging idly in an overstuffed chair swirling his after-dinner brandy while the countess and Serenity sipped coffee from fragile china cups.

"Jean-Paul le Goff, Gaelle's fiancé, met Jonathan Smith in Paris." The countess began to speak without preamble, and Serenity's cup halted on its journey to her lips, her eyes flying to the angular face. "He was quite taken with your father's talent and commissioned him to paint Gaelle's portrait as a wedding gift."

"My mother was engaged to another man before she married my father?" Serenity asked, setting down her cup with a great deal of care.

"*Oui.* The betrothal had been understood between the families for years; Gaelle was content with the arrangement. Jean-Paul was a good man, of good background."

"It was to be an arranged marriage, then?"

The countess waved away Serenity's sense of distaste with a gesture of her hand. "It is an old custom, and as I said, Gaelle was content. Jonathan Smith's arrival at the château changed everything. Had I been more alert, I would have recognized the danger, the looks which passed between them, the blushes which rose to Gaelle's cheeks when his name was spoken."

Françoise de Kergallen sighed deeply and gazed up at the portrait of her daughter. "Never did I imagine Gaelle would break her word, disgrace the family honor. Always she was a sweet, obedient child, but your father blinded her to her duty." The blue eyes shifted from the portrait to the living image. "I had no knowledge of what had passed between them. She did not, as she had always done before, confide in me, seek my advice. The day the portrait was completed, Gaelle fainted in the garden. When I insisted on summoning a doctor, she told me there was no need—she was not ill, but with child."

The countess stopped speaking, and the silence spread like a heavy cloak through the room. "Madame," Serenity said, breaking the silence in clear, even tones, "if you are attempting to shock my sensibilities by telling me I was conceived before my parents were married, I must disappoint you. I find it irrelevant. The days of stone-throwing and branding have passed, in my country at least. My parents loved each other; whether they expressed that love before or after they exchanged vows does not concern me."

The countess sat back in her chair, laced her fingers, and studied Serenity intently. "You are very outspoken, *n'est-ce pas?*"

"Yes, I am." She gave the woman a level look. "However, I try to prevent my honesty from causing injury."

"Touché," Christophe murmured, and the arched white brows rose fractionally before the countess gave her attention back to Serenity.

"Your mother had been married a month before you were conceived." The statement was given without a change of expression. "They were married in secret in a small chapel in another village, intending to keep the knowledge to themselves until your father was able to take Gaelle to America with him."

"I see." Serenity sat back with a slight smile. "My existence brought matters into the open a bit sooner than expected. And what did you do, Madame, when you discovered your daughter married and carrying the child of an obscure artist?"

"I disowned her, told them both to leave my home. From that day, I had no daughter." The words were spoken quickly, as if to throw off a burden no longer tolerable.

A small sound of anguish escaped Serenity, and her eyes flew to Christophe only to meet a blank, brooding wall. She rose slowly, a deep ache assailing her, and turning her back on her grandmother, she faced the gentle smile in her mother's portrait.

"I'm not surprised they put you out of their lives and kept you out of mine." Whirling back, she confronted the countess, whose face remained impassive, the pallor of her cheeks the only evidence of emotion. "I'm sorry for you, Madame. You robbed yourself of great happiness. It is you who have been isolated and alone. My parents shared a deep, encompassing love, and you cloistered yourself with pride and bruised honor. She would have forgiven you; if you knew her at all, then you know that. My father would have forgiven you for her sake, for he could deny her nothing."

"Forgive me?" High color replaced the pallor, and rage shook the cultured voice. "What need I with the forgiveness of a common thief and a daughter who betrayed her heritage?"

Amber eyes grew hot, like golden flames against flushed cheeks, and Serenity shrouded her fury in frigidity. "Thief? Madame, do you say my father stole from you?"

"*Oui,* he stole from me." The answering voice was hard and steady, matching the eyes. "He was not content to steal my child, a daughter I loved more than life. He added to his loot the Raphael Madonna which had belonged to my family for generations. Both priceless, both irreplaceable, both lost to a man I foolishly welcomed into my home and trusted."

"A Raphael?" Serenity repeated, lifting a hand to her temple in confusion. "You're implying my father stole a Raphael? You must be mad."

"I imply nothing," the countess corrected, lifting her head like a queen about to pronounce sentence. "I am stating that Jonathan Smith took both Gaelle and the Madonna. He was very clever. He knew it was my intention to donate the painting to the Louvre and he offered to clean it. I trusted him." The angular face was once more a grim mask of composure. "He exploited my trust, blinded my daughter to her duty, and left the château with both my treasures."

"It's a lie!" Serenity raged, anger welling up inside her with a force of a tidal wave. "My father would never steal—never! If you lost your daughter, it was because of your own pride, your own blindness."

"And the Raphael?" The question was spoken softly, but it rang in the room and echoed from the walls.

"I have no idea what became of your Raphael." She looked from the rigid woman to the impassive man and felt very much alone. "My father didn't take it; he was not a thief. He never did one dishonest thing in his life." She began to pace the room, battling the urge to shout and shatter their wall of composure. "If you were so sure he had your precious painting, why didn't you have him arrested? Why didn't you prove it?"

"As I said, your father was very clever," the countess rejoined. "He knew I would not involve Gaelle in such a scandal, no matter how she had betrayed me. With or without my consent, he was her husband, the father of the child she carried. He was secure."

Stopping her furious pacing, Serenity turned, her face incredulous. "Do you think he married her for security? You have no conception of what they had. He loved her more than his life, more than a hundred Raphaels."

"When I found the Raphael missing," the dowager continued, as if Serenity had not spoken, "I went to your father and demanded an explanation. They were already preparing to leave. When I accused him of taking the Raphael, I saw the look which passed between them— this man I had trusted, and my own daughter. I saw that he had taken the painting, and Gaelle knew him to be a thief but would stand with him against me. She betrayed herself, her family, and her country." The speech ended on a weary whisper, a brief spasm of pain appearing on the tightly controlled face.

"You have talked of it enough tonight," Christophe stated and rose to pour a brandy from a decanter, bringing the countess the glass with a murmur in Breton.

"They did not take it." Serenity took a step closer to the countess, only to be intercepted by Christophe's hand on her arm.

"We will speak of it no more at this time."

Jerking her arm away from his hold, she emptied her fury on him. "You won't tell me when I will speak! I will not tolerate my father being branded a thief! Tell me, Monsieur le Comte, if he had taken it, where is it? What did he do with it?"

Christophe's brow lifted, and his eyes held hers, the meaning in his look all too clear. Serenity's color ebbed, then flowed back in a rush, her mouth opening helplessly, before she swallowed and spoke in calm, distinct tones.

"If I were a man, you would pay for insulting both my parents and me."

"*Alors,* Mademoiselle," he returned with a small nod, "it is my good fortune you are not."

Serenity turned from the mockery in his tone and addressed the countess, who sat watching their exchange in silence. "Madame, if you sent for me because you believed I might know of the whereabouts of your Raphael, you will be disappointed. I know nothing. In turn, I have my own disappointment, because I came to you thinking to find a family tie, another bond with my mother. We must both learn to live with our disappointments."

Turning, she left the room without so much as a backward glance.

Giving the door to her bedroom a satisfactory slam, Serenity dragged her cases from the wardrobe and dropped them onto the bed. Mind whirling in near-incoherent fury, she began pulling neatly hung clothing from its sanctuary and tossing it into the mouth of the open suitcases in a colorful jumble of confusion.

"Go away!" she called out with distinct rudeness as a knock sounded on her door, then turned and spared Christophe a lethal glare as he ignored the command.

He gave her packing technique a raised-brow study before closing the door quietly behind him. "So, Mademoiselle, you are leaving."

"Perfect deduction." She tossed a pale pink blouse atop the vivid mountain on her bed and proceeded to ignore him.

"A wise decision," he stated as she pointedly kept her back to him. "It would have been better if you had not come."

"Better?" she repeated, turning to face him as the slow, simmering rage began to boil. "Better for whom?"

"For the countess."

She advanced on him slowly, eyes narrowing as one

prepared for battle, giving one brief mental oath on his advantage of height. "The countess invited me to come. Summoned," she corrected, allowing her tone to edge. "Summoned is more accurate. How dare you stand there and speak to me as if I had trampled on sacred ground! I never even knew the woman existed until her letter came, and I was blissfully happy in my ignorance."

"It would have been more prudent if the countess had left you to your bliss."

"That, Monsieur le Comte, is a brilliant example of understatement. I'm glad you understand I could have struggled through life without ever knowing any of my Breton connections." Turning in dismissal, Serenity vented her anger on innocent clothing.

"Perhaps you will find the struggle remains simple since the acquaintance will be brief."

"You want me out, don't you?" Spinning, she felt the last thread of dignity snap. "The quicker the better. Let me tell you something, Monsieur le Comte de Kergallen, I'd rather camp on the side of the road than accept your gracious hospitality. Here." She tossed a flowing flowered skirt in his general direction. "Why don't you help me pack?"

Stooping, he retrieved the skirt and laid it on a graceful upholstered chair, his cool, composed manner infuriating Serenity all the more. "I will send Bridget to you." The astringent politeness of his tone caused Serenity to glance quickly for something more solid to hurl at him. "You do seem to require assistance."

"Don't you dare send anyone!" she shouted as he turned for the door, and he faced her again, inclining his head at the order.

"As you wish, Mademoiselle. The state of your attire is your own concern."

Detesting his unblemished formality, Serenity found herself forced to provoke him. "I'll see to my own packing, Cousin, when I decide to leave." Deliberately, she turned and lifted a garment from the heap. "Perhaps I'll change my mind and stay for a day or two, after all. I've heard the Breton countryside has much charm."

"It is your privilege to remain, Mademoiselle." Catching the faint tint of annoyance in his tone, Serenity found it imperative to smile in victory. "I would, however, not recommend it under the circumstances."

"Wouldn't you?" Her shoulders moved in a small, elegant shrug, and she tilted her face to his in provocation. "That is yet another inducement for remaining." She saw both her words and actions had touched a chord of response as his eyes darkened with anger. His expression, however, remained calm and composed, and she wondered what form his temper would take when and if he unleashed it.

"You must do as you wish, Mademoiselle." He surprised her by closing the distance between them and capturing the back of her neck with strong fingers. At the touch, she realized his temper was not as far below the surface as she had imagined. "You may, however, find your visit not as comfortable as you might like."

"I'm well able to deal with discomfort." Attempting to pull away, she found the hand held her stationary with little effort.

"Perhaps, but discomfort is not something sought by a person of intelligence." The politeness of Christophe's smile was more arrogant than a sneer, and Serenity stiffened and endeavored to draw away again. "I would have said you possessed intelligence, Mademoiselle, if not wisdom."

Determined not to surrender to slowly growing fear,

Serenity kept both eyes and voice level. "My decision to go or stay is not something I need to discuss with you. I will sleep on it and make the suitable arrangements in the morning. Of course, you can always chain me to a wall in the dungeon."

"An interesting alternative." His smile became both mocking and amused, his fingers squeezing lightly before they finally released her. "I will sleep on it." He moved to the door, giving her a brief bow as he turned the knob. "And make the suitable arrangements in the morning."

Frustrated by being outmaneuvered, Serenity hurled a shoe at the panel which closed behind him.

Chapter 3

The quiet awoke Serenity. Opening her eyes, she stared without comprehension at the sun-filled room before she remembered where she was. She sat up in bed and listened. Silence, the deep, rich quality of silence, broken only by the occasional music of a bird. A quiet lacking the bustling, throbbing city noises she had known all of her life, and she decided she liked it.

The small, ornate clock on the cherry writing desk told her it was barely six, so she lay back for a moment in the luxury of elegant pillows and sheets and wallowed in laziness. Though her mind had been crowded with the facts and accusations her grandmother had disclosed, the fatigue from the long journey had taken precedence, and she had slept instantly and deeply, oddly at peace in the bed which had once been her mother's. Now, she stared up at the ceiling and ran through the previous evening again in her mind.

The countess was bitter. All the layers of practiced

composure could not disguise the bitterness, or, Serenity admitted, the pain. Even through her own anger she had glimpsed the pain. Though she had banished the daughter, she had kept the portrait, and perhaps, Serenity concluded, the contradiction meant the heart was not as hard as the pride.

Christophe's attitude, however, still left her simmering. It seemed he had stood towering over her like a biased judge, ready to condemn without trial. *Well*, she determined, *I have my own share of pride, and I won't cower and shrink while my father's name is muddied, and my head put on the block. I can play the game of cold politeness, as well. I'm not running home like a wounded puppy; I'm going to stay right here.*

Gazing at the streaming sunlight, she gave a deep sigh. "*C'est un nouveau jour,* Maman," she said aloud. And, slipping from the bed, she walked over to the window. The garden spread out below her like a precious gift. "I'll go for a walk in your garden, Maman, and later I'll sketch your home." Sighing, she reached for her robe. "Then perhaps the countess and I can come to terms."

She washed and dressed quickly, choosing a pastel-printed sundress which left her arms and shoulders bare. The château remained in tranquil silence as she made her way to the main floor and stepped out into the warmth of the summer morning.

Strange, she mused, turning in a large circle. How strange not to see another building or cars or even another human being. The air was fresh and mildly scented, and she took a deep breath, consuming it before she began to circle the château on her way to the garden.

It was even more astonishing at close range than it had been from her window. Lush blooms exploded in an incredible profusion of colors, scents mixing and mingling

into one exotic fragrance, at once tangy and sweet. There
were a variety of paths cutting through the well-tended
arrangements, smooth flagstones catching the morning
sun and holding it glistening on their surface. Choosing
one path at random, she strolled in idle contentment, enjoying the solitude, the artist in her reveling in the riot
of hues and shapes.

"*Bonjour,* Mademoiselle." A deep voice broke the
quiet, and Serenity whirled around, startled at the intrusion on her solitary contemplations. Christophe
approached her slowly, tall and lean, his movements reminding her of an arrogant Russian dancer she had met at
a Washington party. Graceful, confident, and very male.

"*Bonjour,* Monsieur le Comte." She did not waste a
smile, but greeted him with careful cordiality. He was
casually dressed in a buff-colored shirt and sleek-fitting
brown jeans, and if she had felt the breeze of the buccaneer before, she was now caught in the storm.

He reached her and stared down with his habitual
thorough survey. "You are an early riser. I trust you slept
well."

"Very well, thank you," she returned, angry at having
to battle not only animosity, but also attraction. "Your
gardens are beautiful and very appealing."

"I have a fondness for what is beautiful and appealing." His eyes were direct, the dark brown smothering
the amber, until she felt unable to breathe, dropping her
eyes from the power of his.

"Oh, well, hello." They had been speaking in French,
but at the sight of the dog at Christophe's heels, Serenity reverted back to English. "What's his name?" She
crouched down to ruffle the thick, soft fur.

"Korrigan," he told her, looking down at her bent head
as the sun streamed down, making a halo of pale curls.

"Korrigan," she repeated, enchanted by the dog and forgetting her annoyance with his master. "What breed is he?"

"Brittany spaniel."

Korrigan began to reciprocate her affection with tender licks on smooth cheeks. Before Christophe could command the dog to stop, Serenity laughed and buried her face against the animal's soft neck.

"I should have known. I had a dog once; it followed me home." Glancing up, she grinned as Korrigan continued to love her with a moist tongue. "Actually, I gave him a great deal of encouragement. I named him Leonardo, but my father called him Horrible, and that's the name that stuck. No amount of washing or brushing ever improved his inherent scruffiness."

As she went to rise, Christophe extended his hand to assist her to her feet, his grasp firm and disturbing. Checking the urge to jerk away from him, she disengaged herself casually and continued her walk. Both master and dog fell into step beside her.

"Your temper has cooled, I see. I found it surprising that such a dangerous temper exists inside such a fragile shell."

"I'm afraid you're mistaken." She twisted her head, giving him a brief but level glance. "Not about the temper, but the fragility. I'm really quite sturdy and not easily dented."

"Perhaps you have not yet been dropped," he countered, and she gave her attention to a bush pregnant with roses. "You have decided to stay for a time?"

"Yes, I have," she admitted and turned to face him directly, "although I get the distinct impression you'd rather I didn't."

His shoulders moved in an eloquent shrug. "*Mais, non,*

Mademoiselle. You are welcome to remain as long as it pleases you to do so."

"Your enthusiasm overwhelms me," muttered Serenity.
"Pardon?"

"Nothing." Letting out a quick breath, she tilted her head and gave him a bold stare. "Tell me, Monsieur, do you dislike me because you think my father was a thief, or is it just me personally?"

The cool, set expression did not alter as he met her stare. "I regret to have given you such an impression. Mademoiselle, my manners must be at fault. I will attempt to be more polite."

"You're so infernally polite at times it borders on rudeness," she snapped, losing control and stomping her foot in exasperation.

"Perhaps you would find rudeness more to your taste?" His brow lifted as he regarded her temper with total nonchalance.

"Oh!" Turning away, she reached out angrily to pluck a rose. "You infuriate me! Darn!" she swore as a thorn pricked her thumb. "Now look what you made me do." Lifting her thumb to her mouth, she glared.

"My apologies," Christophe returned, a mocking light in his eyes. "That was most unkind of me."

"You are arrogant, patronizing, and stuffy," Serenity accused, tossing her curls.

"And you are bad-tempered, spoiled, and stubborn," he rejoined, narrowing his gaze and folding his arms across his chest. They stared at each other for a moment, his polite veneer slipping, allowing her a glimpse of the ruthless and exciting man beneath the coolly detached covering.

"Well, we seem to hold high opinions of each other after so short an acquaintance," she observed, smoothing back displaced curls. "If we know each other much longer, we'll be madly in love."

"An interesting conclusion, Mademoiselle." With a slight bow, he turned and headed back toward the château. Serenity felt an unexpected but tangible loss.

"Christophe," she called on impulse, wanting inexplicably to clear the air between them. He turned back, brow lifted in question, and she took a step toward him. "Can't we just be friends?"

He held her eyes for a long moment, so deep and intense a look that she felt he stripped her to the soul. "No, Serenity, I am afraid we will never just be friends."

She watched his tall, lithe figure stride away, the spaniel once more at his heels.

An hour later, Serenity joined her grandmother and Christophe at breakfast, with the countess making the usual inquiries as to how she had spent her night. The conversation was correct, if uninspired, and Serenity felt the older woman was making an effort to ease the tension brought on by the previous evening's confrontation. Perhaps, Serenity decided, it was not considered proper to squabble over croissants. *How amazingly civilized we are!* Suppressing an ironical smile, she mirrored the attitude of her companions.

"You will wish to explore the château, Serenity, *n'est-ce pas?*" Lifting her eyes as she set down the creamer, the countess stirred her coffee with a perfectly manicured hand.

"Yes, Madame, I would enjoy that," Serenity agreed with the expected smile. "I should like to make some sketches from the outside later, but I would love to see the inside first."

"*Mais, oui.* Christophe," she said, addressing the dark

man who was idly sipping his coffee, "we must escort Serenity through the château this morning."

"Nothing would give me greater pleasure, Grand-mère," he agreed, placing his cup back in its china saucer. "But I regret I shall be occupied this morning. The new bull we imported is due to arrive, and I must supervise its transport."

"Ah, the cattle," the countess sighed and moved her shoulders. "You think too much about the cattle."

It was the first spontaneous statement Serenity had noted, and she picked it up automatically. "Do you raise cattle, then?"

"Yes," Christophe confirmed, meeting her inquiring gaze. "The raising of cattle is the château's business."

"Really?" she countered with exaggerated surprise. "I didn't think the de Kergallens bothered with such mundane matters. I imagined they just sat back and counted their serfs."

His lips curved slightly and he gave a small nod. "Only once a month. Serfs do tend to be highly prolific."

She found herself laughing into his eyes. Then as his quick, answering grin pounded a warning in her brain, she gave her attention to her own coffee.

In the end, the countess herself escorted Serenity on her tour of the rambling château, explaining some of its history as they moved from one astonishing room to another.

The château had been built in the late seventeenth century, and being in existence for just slightly less than three hundred years, it was not considered old by Breton standards. The château itself and the estates which belonged to it had been handed down from generation to generation to the oldest son, and although some modernizations had been made, it remained basically the same as it had been when the first Comte de Kergallen brought his bride over the drawbridge. To Serenity it was the essence of a lost and timeless charm, and the immediate affection and enchantment she had felt at first sight only grew with the explorations.

In the portrait gallery, she saw Christophe's dark fascination reproduced over the centuries. Though varied from generation to generation, the inveterate pride remained, the aristocratic bearing, the elusive air of mystery. She paused in front of one eighteenth-century ancestor whose resemblance was so striking that she took a step nearer to make a closer study.

"You find Jean-Claud interesting, Serenity?" the countess questioned, following her gaze. "Christophe is much like him in looks, *n'est-ce pas?*"

"Yes, it's remarkable." The eyes, she decided, were much too assured, and much too alive, and unless she were very much mistaken, the mouth had known a great many women.

"He is reputed to have been a bit, uh, *sauvage*," she continued with a hint of admiration. "It is said smuggling was his pastime; he was a man of the sea. The story is told that once when in England, he fell enamored of a woman of that country, and not having the patience for a long, formal, old-fashioned courtship, he kidnapped her and brought her to the château. He married her, of course; she is there." She pointed to a portrait of a rose-and-cream-fleshed English girl of about twenty. "She does not look unhappy."

With this comment, she strolled down the corridor, leaving Serenity staring up at the smiling face of a kidnapped bride.

The ballroom was huge, the far wall being opened with lead-paned windows adding to the space. Another wall was entirely mirrored, reflecting the brilliant prisms of the trio of chandeliers which would throw their sparkling light like silent stars from the high-beamed ceiling. Stiff-backed Regency chairs with elegant tapestry seats were strategically arranged for those who merely wished to look on as couples whirled across the highly polished floor. She wondered if Jean-Claud had given a wedding ball for his Sabine wife, and decided he undoubtedly had.

The countess led Serenity down another narrow corridor to a set of steep stone steps, winding spiral-like to the topmost tower. Although the room they entered was bare, Serenity immediately gave a cry of pleasure, moving to its center and gazing about as though it had been filled with treasures. It was large and airy and completely circular, and the high windows which encompassed it allowed the streaming sunlight to kiss every inch of space. Without effort, she pictured herself painting here for hours in blissful solitude.

"Your father used this room as his studio," the countess informed her, the stiffness returning to her voice, and Serenity broke off her fantasies and turned to confront her grandmother.

"Madame, if it is your wish that I remain here for a time, we must come to an understanding. If we cannot, I will have no choice but to leave." She kept her voice firm and controlled and astringently polite, but the eyes betrayed the struggle with temper. "I loved my father very much, as I did my mother. I will not tolerate the tone you use when you speak of him."

"Is it customary in your country for a young woman to address her elders in such a manner?" The regal head was held high, temper equally apparent.

"I can speak only for myself, Madame," she returned, standing straight and tall in the glow of sunlight. "And I am not of the opinion that age always equates with wisdom. Nor am I hypocrite enough to pay you lip service while you insult a man I loved and respected above all others."

"Perhaps it would be wiser if we refrained from discussing your father while you are with us." The request was an unmistakable command, and Serenity bristled with anger.

"I intend to mention him, Madame. I intend to discover precisely what became of the Raphael Madonna and clear the black mark you have put on his name."

"And how do you intend to accomplish this?"

"I don't know," she tossed back, "but I will." Pacing the room, she spread her hands unconsciously in a completely French gesture. "Maybe it's hidden in the château; maybe someone else took it." She whirled on the other woman with sudden fury. "Maybe you sold it and placed the blame on my father."

"You are insulting!" the countess returned, blue eyes leaping with fire.

"You brand my father a thief, and you say that *I* am insulting?" Serenity retorted, meeting her fire for fire. "I knew Jonathan Smith, Countess, and he was no thief, but I do not know you."

The countess regarded the furious young woman silently for several moments, blue flames dying, replaced by consideration. "That is true," she acknowledged with a nod. "You do not know me, and I do not know you. And if we are strangers, I cannot place the blame on your head. Nor can I blame you for what happened before you were born."

Moving to a window, she stared out silently. "I have not changed my opinion of your father," she said at length, and turning, she held up a hand to silence Serenity's automatic retort. "But I have not been just where his daughter is concerned. You come to my home, a stranger, at my request, and I have greeted you badly. For this much, I apologize." Her lips curved in a small smile. "If you are agreeable, we will not speak of the past until we know each other."

"Very well, Madame," Serenity agreed, sensing both request and apology were an olive branch of sorts.

"You have a soft heart to go with a strong spirit," the dowager observed, a faint hint of approval in her tone. "It is a good match. But you also have a swift temper, *n'est-ce pas?*"

"Évidemment," Serenity acknowledged.

"Christophe is also given to quick outbursts of temper and black moods," the countess informed her in a sudden change of topic. "He is strong and stubborn and requires a wife of equal strength, but with a heart that is soft."

Serenity stared in confusion at her grandmother's ambiguous statement. "She has my sympathy," she began, then narrowed her eyes as a small seed of doubt began to sprout. "Madame, what have Christophe's needs to do with me?"

"He has reached the age when a man requires a wife," the countess stated simply. "And you are past the age when most Breton women are well married and raising a family."

"I am only half-Breton," she asserted, distracted for a moment. Her eyes widened in amazement. "Surely you don't…you aren't thinking that Christophe and I…? Oh, how beautifully ridiculous!" She laughed outright, a full, rich sound that echoed in the empty room. "Madame, I am sorry to disappoint you, but the count does not care for me. He didn't like me the moment he set eyes on me, and I'm forced to admit that I'm not overly fond of him, either."

"What has liking to do with it?" the countess demanded, her hands waving the words away.

Serenity's laughter stilled, and she shook her head in disbelief even as realization seeped through. "You've spoken to him of this already?"

"Oui, d'accord," the countess agreed easily.

Serenity shut her eyes, nearly swamped with humiliation and fury. "No wonder he resented me on sight—between this and thinking what he does of my father!" She turned away from her grandmother, then back again full of righteous indignation. "You overreach your bounds, Comtesse. The time of arranged marriages has long since passed."

"Poof!" It was a dismissive exclamation. "Christophe is too much his own man to agree to anything arranged by another, and I see you are too headstrong to do so. But—" a slow smile creased the angular face as Serenity looked on with wide, incredulous eyes—"you are very lovely, and Christophe is an attractive and virile man. Perhaps nature will—what is it? Take its course."

Serenity could only gape open-mouthed into the calm, inscrutable face.

"Come." The countess moved easily toward the door. "There is more for you to see."

Chapter 4

The afternoon was warm, and Serenity was simmering. Indignation had spread from her grandmother to encompass Christophe, and the more she simmered, the more it became directed at him.

Insufferable, conceited aristocrat! she fumed. Her pencil ran violently across her pad as she sketched the drum towers of the château. *I'd rather marry Attila the Hun than be bound to that stiff-necked boor!* She broke the midday hush with a short burst of laughter. *Madame is probably picturing dozens of miniature counts and countesses playing formal little games in the courtyard and growing up to carry on the imperial line in the best Breton style!*

What a lovely place to raise children, she thought, pencil pausing, and eyes softening. *It's so clean and quiet and beautiful.* A deep sigh filled the air, and she started. Then realizing that it had emitted from her own lips, she frowned furiously. *La Comtesse Serenity de Kergallen,* she said silently and frowned with more feeling. *That'll be the day!*

A movement caught her attention, and she twisted her head, squinting against the sun to watch Christophe approach. His strides were long and sure, and he crossed the lawn with an effortless rhythm of limbs and muscles. *He walks as if he owns the world,* she observed, part in admiration, part in resentment. By the time he reached her, resentment had emerged victorious.

"You!" she spat without preamble, rising from the soft tuft of grass and standing like a slender, avenging angel, gold and glowing.

His gaze narrowed at her tone, but his voice remained cool and controlled. "Something disturbs you, Mademoiselle?"

The ice in his voice only fanned the fire of anger, and dignity was abandoned. "Yes, I'm disturbed! You know very well I'm disturbed! Why in heaven's name didn't you tell me about this ludicrous idea of the countess's?"

"Ah." Brows rose, and lips curved in a sardonic smile. "*Alors,* Grandmère has informed you of the plans for our marital bliss. And when, my beloved, shall we have the banns announced?"

"You conceited…" she sputtered, unable to dream up an appropriately insulting term. "You know what you can do with your banns! I wouldn't have you on a bet!"

"*Bon,*" he replied with a nod. "Then we are at last in full agreement. I have no desire to tie myself to a wasp-tongued brat. Whoever christened you Serenity had very little foresight."

"You're the most detestable man I have ever met!" she raged, her temper a direct contrast to his cool composure. "I can't abide the sight of you."

"Then you have decided to cut your visit short and return to America?"

She tilted her chin and shook her head slowly. "Oh, no, Monsieur le Comte, I shall remain right here. I have inducements for staying which outweigh my feelings for you."

The dark eyes narrowed into slits as he studied her face. "It would appear the countess has added a few francs to make you more agreeable."

Serenity stared at him in puzzlement until his meaning slowly seeped through, draining her color and darkening her eyes. Her hand swung out and struck him with full force in a loud, stinging slap, and then she spun on her heel and began to run toward the château. Hard hands dug into her shoulders and whirled her around, crushing her against the firm length of his body as his lips descended on hers in a brutal, punishing kiss.

The shock was electric, like a brilliant light flashed on, then extinguished. For a moment, she was limp against him, unable to surface from a darkness teeming with heat and demand. Her breath was no longer her own; she realized suddenly he was stealing even that, and she began to push at his chest, then pound with helpless, impotent fists, terrified she would be captured forever in the swirling, simmering darkness.

His arms banded around her, molding her soft slenderness to the hard, unyielding lines of his body, merging them into one passionate form. His hand slid up to cup the back of her neck with firm fingers, forcing her head to remain still, his other arm encircling her waist, maintaining absolute possession.

Her struggles slipped off him as though they were not taking place, emphasizing his superior strength and the violence which bubbled just beneath the surface. Her lips were forced apart as his mouth continued its assault, exploring hers with an intimacy without mercy or compassion. The musky scent of his maleness was assailing her senses, numbing both brain and will, and dimly she heard her grandmother describing the long-dead count with Christophe's face. *Sauvage,* she had said. *Sauvage.*

He gave her mouth its freedom, his grip returning to her shoulders as he looked down into clouded, confused eyes. For a moment, the silence hung like a shimmering wall of heat.

"Who gave you permission to do that?" she demanded unevenly, a hand reaching to her head to halt its spinning.

"It was either that or return your slap, Mademoiselle," he informed her, and from his tone and expression, she could see he had not yet completed the transformation from pirate to aristocrat. "Unfortunately, I have a reluctance to strike a woman, no matter how richly she may deserve it."

Serenity jerked away from his restraint, feeling the treacherous tears stinging, demanding release. "Next time, slap me. I'd prefer it."

"If you ever raise your hand to me again, my dear cousin, rest assured I will bruise more than your pride," he promised.

"You had it coming," she tossed back, but the temerity of her words was spoiled by wide eyes shimmering like golden pools of light. "How dare you accuse me of accepting money to stay here? Did it ever occur to you that I might *want* to know the grandmother I was denied all my life? Did you ever think that I might *want* to know the place where my parents met and fell in love? That I need to stay and prove my father's innocence?" Tears escaped and rolled down smooth cheeks, and Serenity despised each separate drop of weakness. "I only wish I could have hit you harder. What would you have done if someone had accused *you* of being bought like a side of beef?"

He watched the journey of a tear as it spilled from her eye and clung to satin skin, and a small smile tilted one corner of his mouth. "I would have beat them soundly, but I believe your tears are a more effective punishment than fists."

"I don't use tears as a weapon." She wiped at them with the back of her hand, wishing she could have stemmed the flow.

"No; they are therefore all the more potent." A long bronzed finger brushed a drop from ivory skin, the contrast of colors lending her a delicate, vulnerable appearance, and he removed his hand quickly, addressing her in a casual tone. "My words were unjust, and I apologize. We have both received our punishment, so now we are—how do you say?—quits."

He gave her his rare, charming smile, and she stared at him, drawn by its power and enchanted by the positive change it lent to his appearance. Her own smile answered, the sudden shining of the sun through a veil of rain. He made a small, impatient sound, as though he regretted the momentary lapse, and nodding, he turned on his heel and strode away, leaving Serenity staring after him.

During the evening meal, the conversation was once more strictly conventional, as if the astonishing conversation in the tower room and the tempestuous encounter on the château grounds had not taken place. Serenity marveled at the composure of her companions as they carried on a light umbrella of table talk over *langoustes à la crème*. If it had not been for the fact that her lips still felt the imprint, she would have sworn she had imagined the stormy, breathtaking kiss Christophe had planted there. It had been a kiss which had stirred some deep inner feeling of response and had jolted her cool detachment more than she cared to admit.

It meant nothing, she insisted silently and applied herself to the succulent lobster on her plate. She'd been kissed before and she would be kissed again. She would not allow any moody tyrant to give her one more moment's concern. Deciding to resume her role in the game of casual formality, she sipped from her glass and made a comment on the character of the wine.

"You find it agreeable?" Christophe picked up the trend of conversation in an equally light tone. "It is the château's own Muscadet. We produce a small quantity each year for our own enjoyment and for the immediate vicinity."

"I find it very agreeable," Serenity commented. "How exciting to enjoy wine made from your own vineyards. I've never tasted anything quite like it."

"The Muscadet is the only wine produced in Brittany," the countess informed Serenity with a smile. "We are primarily a province of the sea and lace."

Serenity ran a finger over the snowy-white cloth that adorned the oak table. "Brittany lace, it's exquisite. It looks so fragile, yet years only increase the beauty."

"Like a woman," Christophe murmured, and Serenity lifted her eyes to meet his dark regard.

"But then, there are also the cattle." She grabbed at the topic to cover momentary confusion.

"Ah, the cattle." His lips curved, and Serenity had the uncomfortable impression that he was well aware of his effect on her.

"Having lived in the city all my life, I'm totally ignorant when it comes to cattle." She floundered on, more and more disconcerted by the directness of his eyes. "I'm sure they make quite a picture grazing in the fields."

"We must introduce you to the Breton countryside," the countess declared, drawing Serenity's attention. "Perhaps you would care to ride out tomorrow and view the estate?"

"I would enjoy that, Madame. I'm sure it will be a pleasant change from sidewalks and government buildings."

"I would be pleased to escort you, Serenity," Christophe offered, surprising her. Turning back to him, her expression mirrored her thoughts. He smiled and inclined his head. "Do you have the suitable attire?"

"Suitable attire?" she repeated, surprise melting into confusion.

"But yes." He appeared to be enjoying her changing expressions, and his smile spread. "Your taste in clothing is impeccable, but you would find it difficult to ride a horse in a gown like that."

Her gaze lowered to the gently flowing lines of her willow-green dress before rising to his amused glance. "Horse?" she said, frowning.

"You cannot tour the estate in an automobile, *ma petite*. The horse is more adaptable."

At his laughing eyes, she straightened and drew out her dignity. "I'm afraid I don't ride."

"C'est impossible!" the countess exclaimed in disbelief. "Gaelle was a marvelous horsewoman."

"Perhaps equestrian abilities are not genetic, Madame," Serenity suggested, amused by her grandmother's incredulous expression. "I am no horsewoman at all. I can't control a merry-go-round pony."

"I will teach you." Christophe's words were a statement rather than a request, and she turned to him, amusement fading into hauteur.

"How kind of you to offer, Monsieur, but I have no desire to learn. Do not trouble yourself."

"Nevertheless," he stated and lifted his wineglass, "you shall. You will be ready at nine o'clock, *n'est-ce pas?* You will have your first lesson."

She glared at him, astonished by his arbitrary dismissal of her refusal. "I just told you…"

"Try to be punctual, *chérie,*" he warned with deceptive laziness as he rose from the table. "You will find it more comfortable to walk to the stables than to be dragged by your golden hair." He smiled as if the latter prospect held great appeal for him. "*Bonne nuit,* Grandmère," he added with affection before he disappeared from the room, leaving Serenity fuming, and his grandmother unashamedly pleased.

"Of all the insufferable nerve!" she sputtered when she located her voice. Turning angry eyes on the other woman, she added defiantly, "If he thinks I'm going to meekly obey and…"

"You would be wise to obey, meekly or otherwise," the dowager interrupted. "Once Christophe has set his mind…" With a small, meaningful shrug, she left the rest of the sentence to Serenity's imagination. "You have slacks, I presume. Bridget will bring you a pair of your mother's riding boots in the morning."

"Madame," Serenity began slowly, as if attempting to make each word understood, "I have no intention of getting on a horse in the morning."

"Do not be foolish, child." A slender, ringed hand reached negligently for a wineglass. "He is more than capable of carrying out his threat. Christophe is a very stubborn man." She smiled, and for the first time Serenity felt genuine warmth. "Perhaps even more stubborn than you."

* * *

Muttering strong oaths, Serenity pulled on the sturdy boots that had been her mother's. They had been cleaned and polished to a glossy black shine and fit her small feet as if custom-made for them.

It seems even you are conspiring against me, Maman, she silently chided her mother in despair. Then she called out a casual *"Entrez"* as a knock sounded on her door. It was not the little maid, Bridget, who opened the door, however, but Christophe, dressed with insouciant elegance in fawn riding breeches and a white linen shirt.

"What do you want?" she asked with a scowl, pulling on the second boot with a firm tug.

"Merely to see if you are indeed punctual, Serenity," he returned with an easy smile, his eyes roaming over her mutinous face and the slim, supple body clad in a silkscreen-printed T-shirt and French tailored jeans.

Wishing he would not always look at her as if memorizing each feature, she rose in defense. "I'm ready, Captain Bligh, but I'm afraid you won't find me a very apt pupil."

"That remains to be seen, *ma chérie.*" His eyes swept over her again, as if considering. "You seem to be quite capable of following a few simple instructions."

Her eyes narrowed into jeweled slits, and she struggled with the temper he had a habit of provoking. "I am reasonably intelligent, thank you, but I don't like being bulldozed."

"Pardon?" His blank expression brought out a smug smile.

"I shall have to recall a great many colloquialisms, Cousin. Perhaps I can slowly drive you mad."

Serenity accompanied Christophe to the stables in haughty silence, determinedly lengthening her strides to match his gait and preventing the necessity of trailing after him like an obedient puppy. When they reached the outbuilding, a groom emerged leading two horses, bridled and saddled in anticipation. One was full black and gleaming, the other a creamy buckskin, and to Serenity's apprehensive eyes, both were impossibly large.

She halted suddenly and eyed the pair with a dubious frown. *He wouldn't really drag me by the hair,* she thought carefully. "If I just turned around and walked away, what would you do about it?" Serenity inquired aloud.

"I would only bring you back, *ma petite.*" The dark brow rose at her deepening frown, revealing he had already anticipated her question.

"The black is obviously yours, Comte," she concluded in a light voice, struggling to control a mounting panic. "I can already picture you galloping over the countryside in the light of a full moon, the gleam of a saber at your hip."

"You are very astute, Mademoiselle." He nodded, and taking the buckskin's reins from the groom, he walked the mount toward her. She took an involuntary step back and swallowed.

"I suppose you want me to get on him."

"Her," he corrected, mouth curving.

She flashed at him, angry and nervous and disgusted with her own apprehension. "I'm not really concerned about its sex." Looking over the quiet horse, she swallowed again. "She's...she's very large." Her voice was fathoms weaker than she had hoped.

"Babette is as gentle as Korrigan," Christophe assured her in unexpectedly patient tones. "You like dogs, *n'est-ce pas?*"

"Yes, but..."

"She is soft, no?" He took her hand and lifted it to Babette's smooth cheek. "She has a good heart and wishes only to please."

Her hand was captured between the smooth flesh of the horse and the hard insistence of Christophe's palm, and she found the combination oddly enjoyable. Relaxing, she allowed him to guide her hand over the mare and twisted her head, smiling over her shoulder.

"She feels nice," she began, but as the mare blew from wide nostrils, she jumped nervously and stumbled back against Christophe's chest.

"Relax, *chérie.*" He chuckled softly, his arms encircling her waist to steady her. "She is only telling you that she likes you."

"It just startled me," Serenity returned in defense, disgusted with herself, and decided it was now or never. She turned to tell him she was ready to begin, but found herself staring wordlessly into dark, enigmatic eyes as his arms remained around her.

She felt her heart stop its steady rhythm, remaining motionless for a stifling moment, then race sporadically at a wild pace. For an instant, she believed he would kiss her again, and to her own astonishment and confusion, she realized she wanted to feel his lips on hers above all else. A frown creased his brow suddenly, and he released her in a sharp gesture.

"We will begin." Cool and controlled, he stepped effortlessly into the role of instructor.

Pride took over, and Serenity became determined to be a star pupil. Swallowing her anxiety, she allowed Christophe to assist her in mounting. With some surprise, she noted that the ground was not as far away as she had anticipated, and she gave her full attention to Christophe's instructions. She did as he bade, concentrating on following his directions precisely, determined not to make a fool of herself again.

Serenity watched Christophe mount his stallion with a fluid grace and economy of movement she envied. The spirited black suited the dark, haughty man to perfection, and she reflected, with some distress, that not even Tony at his most ardent had ever affected her the way this strange, remote man did with his enveloping stares.

She couldn't be attracted to him, she argued fiercely. He was much too unpredictable, and she realized, with a flash of insight, that he could hurt her as no man had been able to hurt her before. *Besides,* she thought, frowning at the buckskin's mane, *I don't like his superior, dominating attitude.*

"Have you decided to take a short nap, Serenity?" Christophe's mocking voice brought her back with a snap, and meeting his laughing eyes, she felt herself flush to her undying consternation. *"Allons-y, chérie."* Her deepening color was noted with a curve of his lips, as he directed his horse away from the stables and proceeded at a slow walk.

They moved side by side, and after several moments Serenity found herself relaxing in the saddle. She passed Christophe's instructions on to the mare, which responded with smooth obedience. Confidence grew, and she allowed herself to view the scenery, enjoying the caress of the sun on her face and the gentle rhythm of the horse under her.

"Maintenant, we trot," Christophe commanded suddenly, and Serenity twisted her head to regard him seriously.

"Perhaps my French is not as good as I supposed. Did you say trot?"

"Your French is fine, Serenity."

"I'm quite content to amble along," she returned with a careless shrug. "I'm in no hurry at all."

"You must move with the jogging of the horse," he instructed, ignoring her statement. "Rise with every other jog. Press gently with your heels."

"Now, listen…"

"Afraid?" he taunted, his brow lifting high in mockery. Before common sense could overtake pride, Serenity tossed her head and pressed her heels against the horse's side.

This must be what it feels like to operate one of those damnable jackhammers they're forever tearing up the streets with, she thought breathlessly, bouncing without grace on the trotting mare.

"Rise with every other jog," Christophe reminded her, and she was too preoccupied with her own predicament to observe the wide grin which accompanied his words. After a few more awkward moments, she caught onto the timing.

"Comment ça va?" he inquired as they moved side by side along the dirt path.

"Well, now that my bones have stopped rattling, it's not so bad. Actually"—she turned and smiled at him—"it's fun."

"Bon. Now we canter," he said simply, and she sent him a withering glance.

"Really, Christophe, if you want to murder me, why not try something simpler like poison, or a nice clean stab in the back?"

He threw back his head and laughed, a full, rich sound that filled the quiet morning, echoing on the breeze. When he turned his head and smiled at her, Serenity felt the world tilt, and her heart, ignoring the warnings of her brain, was lost.

"Allons, ma brave." His voice was light, carefree, and contagious. "Press in your heels, and I will teach you to fly."

Her feet obeyed automatically, and the mare responded, quickening her gate to a smooth, easy canter. The wind played with Serenity's hair and brushed her cheeks with cool fingers. She felt as though she were riding on a cloud, unsure whether the lightness was a result of the rush of wind or the dizziness of love. Enthralled with the novelty of both, she did not care.

At Christophe's command, she drew back on the reins, slowing the mare from a canter to a trot to a walk before finally coming to a halt. Lifting her face to the sky, she gave a deep sigh of pleasure before turning to her companion. The wind and excitement had whipped a rose blush onto her cheeks, her eyes were wide, golden, and bright, and her hair was tousled, an unruly halo around her happiness.

"You enjoyed yourself, Mademoiselle?"

She flashed him a brilliant smile, still intoxicated with love's potent wine. "Go ahead; say 'I told you so.' It's perfectly all right."

"Mais non, chérie, it is merely a pleasure to see one's pupil progress with such speed and ability." He returned her smile, the invisible barrier between them vanishing. "You move naturally in the saddle; perhaps the talent is genetic, after all."

"Oh, Monsieur." She fluttered her lashes over a gleam of mischief. "I must give the credit to my teacher."

"Your French blood is showing, Serenity, but your technique needs practice."

"Not so good, huh?" Pushing back disheveled hair, she gave a deep sigh. "I suppose I'll never get it right. Too much American Puritan from my father's ancestors."

"Puritan?" Christophe's full laugh once more disturbed the quiet morning. "*Chérie,* no Puritan was ever so full of fire."

"I shall take that as a compliment, though I sincerely doubt it was intended as one." Turning her head, she looked down from the hilltop to the spreading valley below. "Oh, how beautiful."

A scene from a postcard slumbered in the distance, gentle hills dotted with grazing cattle against a backdrop of neat cottages. Farther in the distance, she observed a tiny village, a small toy town set down by a giant hand, dominated by a white church, its spire reaching heavenward.

"It's perfect," she decided. "Like slipping back in time." Her eyes roamed back to the grazing cattle. "Those are yours?" she asked, gesturing with her hand.

"*Oui,*" he asserted.

"This is all your property, then?" she asked again, feeling a sudden sinking sensation.

"This is part of the estates." He answered with a careless movement of his shoulders.

We've been riding for so long, she thought with a frown, *and we're still on his land. Lord knows how far it spreads in other directions. Why can't he be an ordinary man?* Turning her head, she studied his hawklike profile. *But he is not an ordinary man,* she reminded herself. *He is the Comte de Kergallen, master of all he surveys, and I must remember that.* Her gaze moved back to the valley, her frown deepening. *I don't want to be in love with him.* Swallowing the sudden dryness of her throat, she used her words as a defense against her heart.

"How wonderful to possess so much beauty."

He turned to her, brow raising at her tone. "One cannot possess beauty, Serenity, merely care for and cherish it."

She fought against the warmth his soft words aroused, keeping her eyes glued to the valley. "Really? I was under the impression that young aristocrats took such things for granted." She made a wide, sweeping gesture. "After all, this is only your due."

"You have no liking for aristocracy, Serenity, but you have aristocratic blood, as well." Her blank look brought a slow smile to his chiseled features, and his tone was cool. "Yes, your mother's father was a count, though his estates were ravaged during the war. The Raphael was one of the few treasures your grandmother salvaged when she escaped."

The damnable Raphael again! Serenity thought dismally. He was angry; she determined this from the hard light in his eyes, and she found herself oddly pleased. It would be easier to control her feelings for him if they remained at odds with each other.

"So, that makes me half-peasant, half-aristocrat," she retorted, moving her slim shoulders in dismissal. "Well, *mon cher cousin,* I much prefer the peasant half myself. I'll leave the blue blood in the family to you."

"You would do well to remember there is no blood between us, Mademoiselle." Christophe's voice was low, and meeting his narrowed eyes, Serenity felt a trickle of fear. "The de Kergallens are notorious for taking what they want, and I am no exception. Take care how you use your brandy eyes."

"The warning is unnecessary, Monsieur. I can take care of myself."

He smiled, a slow, confident smile, more unnerving than a furious retort, and turned his mount back toward the château.

The return ride was accomplished in silence, broken only by Christophe's occasional instructions. They had crossed swords again, and Serenity was forced to admit he had parried her thrust easily.

When they reached the stables, Christophe dismounted with his usual grace, handing the reins to a groom and moving to assist her before she could copy his action.

Defiantly, she ignored the stiffness in her limbs as she eased herself from the mare's back and Christophe's hands encircled her waist. They remained around her for a moment, and he brooded down at her before releasing the hold that seemed to burn through the light material of her shirt.

"Go have a hot bath," he ordered. "It will ease the stiffness you are undoubtedly feeling."

"You have an amazing capacity for issuing orders, Monsieur."

His eyes narrowed before his arm went around her with incredible speed, pulling her close and crushing her lips in a hard, thorough kiss that left no time for struggle or protest, but drew a response as easily as a hand turning a water tap.

For an eternity he kept her the prisoner of his will, plunging her deeper and deeper into the kiss. Its bruising intensity released a new and primitive need in her, and abandoning pride for love, she surrendered to demands she could not conquer. The world evaporated, the soft Breton landscape melting like a watercolor left out in the rain, leaving nothing but warm flesh and lips which sought her surrender. His hand ran over the slim curve of her hip, then up her spine with sure authority, crushing her against him with a force which would have cracked her bones had they not already dissolved in the heat.

Love. Her mind whirled with the word. Love was walks in soft rain, a quiet evening beside a crackling fire. How could it be a throbbing, turbulent storm which left you weak and breathless and vulnerable? How could it be that one would crave the weakness as much as life itself? Was this how it had been for Maman? Was this what put the dreamy mists of knowledge in her eyes? *Will he never set me free?* she wondered desperately, and her arms encircled his neck, body contradicting will.

"Mademoiselle," he murmured with soft mockery, keeping his mouth a breath from hers, his fingers teasing the nape of her neck, "you have an amazing capacity for provoking punishment. I find the need to discipline you imperative."

Releasing her, he turned and strode carelessly away, stopping to acknowledge the greeting of Korrigan, who trotted faithfully at his heels.

Chapter 5

Serenity and the countess shared their lunch on the terrace, surrounded by sweet-smelling blossoms. Refusing the offered wine, Serenity requested coffee instead, enduring the raised white brow with tranquil indifference.

I suppose this makes me an undoubted Philistine, she concluded, suppressing a smile as she enjoyed the strong black liquid along with the elegant shrimp bisque.

"I trust you found your ride enjoyable," the countess stated after they had exchanged comments on the food and weather.

"To my utter amazement, Madame," Serenity admitted, "I did. I only wished I had learned long ago. Your Breton scenery is magnificent."

"Christophe is justifiably proud of his land," the countess asserted, studying the pale wine in her glass. "He loves it as a man loves a woman, an intense sort of passion. And though the land is eternal, a man needs a wife. The earth is a cold lover."

Serenity's brows rose at her grandmother's frankness, the sudden abandonment of formality. Her shoulders moved in a faintly Gallic gesture. "I'm sure Christophe has little trouble finding warm ones." *He probably merely snaps his fingers and dozens tumble into his arms,* she added silently, almost wincing at the fierce stab of jealousy.

"Naturellement," the countess agreed, a glimmer of amusement lighting up her eyes. "How could it be otherwise?" Serenity digested this with a scowl, and the dowager lifted her wineglass. "But men like Christophe require constancy rather than variety after a time. Ah, but he is so like his grandfather." Looking over quickly, Serenity saw the soft expression transform the angular face. "They are wild, these Kergallen men, dominant and arrogantly masculine. The women who are given their love are blessed with both heaven and hell." Blue eyes focused on amber once more and smiled. "Their women must be strong or be trampled beneath them, and they must be wise enough to know when to be weak."

Serenity had been listening to her grandmother's words as if under a spell. Shaking herself, she pushed back the plate of shrimp for which her appetite had fled. "Madame," she began, determined to make her position clear, "I have no intention of entering into the competition for the present count. As I see it, we are incredibly ill matched." She recalled suddenly the feel of his lips against hers, the demanding pressure of his hard body, and she trembled. Raising her eyes to her grandmother's, she shook her head in fierce denial. "No." She did not stop to reason if she was speaking to her heart or the woman across from her, but stood and hurried back into the château.

* * *

The full moon had risen high in the star-studded sky, its silver light streaming through the high windows as Serenity awoke, miserable, sore, and disgusted. Though she had retired early, latching onto the inspiration of a fictitious headache to separate herself from the man who clouded her thoughts, sleep had not come easily. Now, just a few short hours since she had captured it, it had escaped. Turning in the oversized bed, she moaned aloud at her body's revolt.

I'm paying the price for this morning's little adventure. She winced and sat up with a deep sigh. *Perhaps I need another hot bath,* she decided with dim hope. *Lord knows it couldn't make me any stiffer.* She eased herself from the mattress, legs and shoulders protesting violently. Ignoring the robe at the foot of the bed, she made her way across the dimly lit room toward the adjoining bath, banging her shin smartly against an elegant Louis XVI chair.

She swore, torn between anger and pain. Still muttering, she nursed her leg, pulling the chair back into position and leaning on it. "What?" she called out rudely as a knock sounded on her door.

It swung open, and Christophe, dressed casually in a robe of royal-blue silk, stood observing her. "Have you injured yourself, Serenity?" It was not necessary to see his expression to be aware of his mockery.

"Just a broken leg," she snapped. "Pray, don't trouble yourself."

"May one inquire as to why you are groping about in the dark?" He leaned against the doorframe, cool, calm, and in total command, his arrogance all the catalyst Serenity's mercurial temper required.

"I'll tell you why I'm groping about in the dark, you

smug, self-assured beast!" she began, her voice a furious whisper. "I was going to drown myself in the tub to put myself out of the misery you inflicted on me today!"

"I?" he said innocently, his eyes roaming over her, slim and golden in the shimmering moonlight, her long, shapely legs and pure alabaster-toned skin exposed by the briefness of her flimsy nightdress. She was too angry to be aware of her dishabille or his appreciation, oblivious to the moonlight which seeped through the sheerness of her gown and left her curves delectably shadowed.

"Yes, you!" she shot back at him. "It was you who got me up on that horse this morning, wasn't it? And now each individual muscle in my body despises me." Groaning, she rubbed her palm against the small of her back. "I may never walk properly again."

"Ah."

"Oh, what a wealth of meaning in a single syllable." She glared at him, doing her best to stand with some dignity. "Could you do it again?"

"Ma pauvre petite," he murmured in exaggerated sympathy. *"Je suis désolé."* He straightened and began to move toward her. Then, suddenly recalling her state of dress, her eyes grew wide.

"Christophe, I…" she began as his hands descended on her bare shoulders, but the words ended in a sigh as his fingers massaged the strain.

"You have discovered new muscles, yes? And they are not being agreeable. It will not be so difficult the next time." He led her to the bed and pressed her shoulders so that she sat, unresisting, savoring the firm movements on her neck and shoulders. Easing down behind her, his long fingers continued down her back, kneading away the ache as if by magic.

She sighed again, unconsciously moving against him.

"You have wonderful hands," she murmured, a blessed lethargy seeping into her as the soreness disappeared and a warm contentment took its place. "Marvelous strong fingers; I'll be purring any minute."

She was not aware when the transition occurred, when the gentle relaxation became a slow kindling in her stomach, his objective massage an insistent caress, but she felt her head suddenly spinning with the heat.

"That's better, much better," she faltered and made to move away, but his hands went quickly to her waist, holding her immobile as his lips sought the soft vulnerability of her neck in a gentle feather of a kiss. She trembled, then started like a frightened doe, but before she could escape, he had twisted her to face him, his lips descending in possession on hers, stilling all protests.

Struggle died before it became a reality, the kindling erupting into a burst of flame, and her arms encircled his neck as she was pressed against the mattress. His mouth seemed to devour hers, hard and assured, and his hands followed the curves of her body as if he had made love to her countless times. Impatiently, he pushed aside the thin strap on her shoulder, seeking and finding the satin smoothness of her breast, his touch inciting a tempest of desire, and she began to move under him. His demands became more urgent, his hands more insistent as they moved down the whisper of silk, his lips leaving hers to assault her neck with an insatiable hunger.

"Christophe," she moaned, knowing she was incapable of combating both him and her own weakness. "Christophe, please, I can't fight you here. I could never win."

"Do not fight me, *ma belle*," he whispered into her neck. "And we shall both win."

His mouth took hers again, soft and lingering, causing desire to swell, then soar. Slowly, his lips explored her face, brushing along the hollows of her cheeks, teasing the vulnerability of parted lips before moving on to other conquests. A hand cupped her breast in lazy possession, fingers tracing its curve, tarrying over the nipple until a dull, throbbing ache spread through her. The sweet, weakening pain brought a moan, and her hands began to seek the rippling muscles of his back, as if to accentuate his power over her.

His lazy explorations altered to urgency once more, as if her submission had fanned the fires of his own passions. Hands bruised soft flesh, and her mouth was savaged by his, the teeth which had nibbled along her bottom lip replaced by a mouth which ravaged her senses, and demanded more than surrender, but equal passion.

The hand left her breast to run down her side, pausing over her hip before he continued on, claiming the smooth, fresh skin of her thigh, and her breath came only in shuddering sighs as his lips moved lower along her throat to taste the warm hollow between her breasts.

With one final flash of lucidity, she knew she stood on the edge of a precipice, and one more step would plunge her into an everlasting void.

"Christophe, please." She began to tremble, though nearly suffocating with the heat. "Please, you frighten me, I frighten me. I've never…I've never been with a man before."

His movements stopped, and the silence became thick as he lifted his face and stared down at her. Slivers of moonlight slept on her pale hair, tousled on the snowy pillow, her eyes smoky with awakened passion and fear.

With a short, harsh sound, he lifted his weight from her. "Your timing, Serenity, is incredible."

"I'm sorry," she began, sitting up.

"For what do you apologize?" he demanded, anger

just below the surface of icy calm. "For your innocence, or for allowing me to come very close to claiming it?"

"That's a rotten thing to say!" she snapped, fighting to steady her breathing. "This happened so quickly, I couldn't think. If I had been prepared, you would never have come so close."

"You think not?" He dragged her up until she was kneeling on the surface of the bed, once more molded against him. "You are prepared now. Do you think I could not take you this minute with you more than willing to allow it?"

He glared down at her, the air around him tingling with assurance and fury, and she could say nothing, knowing she was helpless against his authority and her own surging need. Her eyes were huge in her pale face, fear and innocence shining like beacons, and he swore and pushed her away.

"*Nom de Dieu!* You look at me with the eyes of a child. Your body disguises your innocence well; it is a dangerous masquerade." Moving to the door, he turned back to survey the lightly clad form made small by the vastness of the bed. "Sleep well, *mignonne,*" he said with a touch of mockery. "The next time you choose to run into the furniture, it would be wise if you lock your door; I will not walk away again."

Serenity's cool greeting to Christophe over breakfast was returned in kind, his eyes meeting hers briefly, showing no trace of the passion or anger they had held the previous night. Perversely, she was annoyed at his lack of reaction as he chatted with the countess, addressing Serenity only when necessary, and then with a strict politeness which could be detected only by the most sensitive ear.

"You have not forgotten Geneviève and Yves are dining with us this evening?" the countess asked Christophe.

"*Mais non,* Grandmère," he assured her, replacing his cup in its saucer. "It is always a pleasure to see them."

"I believe you will find them pleasant company, Serenity." The countess turned her clear blue eyes on her granddaughter. "Geneviève is very close to your age, perhaps a year younger, a very sweet, well-mannered young woman. Her brother, Yves, is very charming and quite attractive." A smile was born on her lips. "You will find his company, uh, *diverting.* Do you not agree, Christophe?"

"I am sure Serenity will find Yves highly entertaining."

Serenity glanced over quickly at Christophe. Was there a touch of briskness to his tone? He was sipping his coffee calmly, and she decided she had been mistaken.

"The Dejots are old family friends," the countess went on, drawing Serenity's attention back to her. "I am sure you will find it pleasant to have company near your own age, *n'est-ce pas?* Geneviève is often a visitor to the château. As a child she trotted after Christophe like a faithful puppy. *Bien sûr,* she is not a child any longer." She threw a meaningful glance at the man at the head of the long oak table, and Serenity used great willpower not to wrinkle her nose in disdain.

"Geneviève grew from an awkward pigtailed child into an elegant, lovely woman," Christophe replied, and the affection in his voice was unmistakable.

Good for her, Serenity thought, struggling to keep an interested smile in place.

"She will make a marvelous wife," the countess predicted. "She has a quiet beauty and natural grace. We must persuade her to play for you, Serenity. She is a highly skilled pianist."

Chalk up one more for the paragon of virtue, Serenity brooded to herself silently, miserably jealous of the absent Geneviève's relationship with Christophe. Aloud, she said, "I shall look forward to meeting your friends, Madame." Silently, she assured herself that she would dislike the perfect Geneviève on sight.

The golden morning passed quietly, a lazy mid-morning hush falling over the garden as Serenity sketched. She had exchanged a few words with the gardener before they had both settled down to their respective tasks. Finding him an interesting study, she sketched him as he bent over the bushes, trimming the overblown blossoms and chattering, scolding and praising his colorful, scented friends.

His face was timeless, weathered and lined with character, unexpectedly bright blue eyes shining against a ruddy complexion. The hat covering his shock of steel-gray hair was black, a wide, flat-brimmed cap with velvet ribbons streaming down the back. He wore a sleeveless vest and aged knickers, and she marveled at his agility in the wooden *sabots.*

So deep was her concentration on capturing his Old World aura with her pencil that she failed to hear the footsteps on the flagstones behind her. Christophe watched her for some moments as she bent over her work, the graceful curve of her neck calling to his mind an image of a proud white swan floating on a cool, clear lake. Only when she tucked her pencil behind her ear and brushed an absent hand through her hair did he make his presence known.

"You have captured Jacques admirably, Serenity." His brow rose in amusement at the startled jump she made and the hand that flew to her heart.

"I didn't know you were there," she said, cursing the breathlessness of her voice and the pounding of her pulse.

"You were deep in your work," he explained, casually sitting next to her on the white marble bench. "I did not wish to disturb you."

Ho, she amended silently, *you'd disturb me if you were a thousand miles away.* Aloud, she spoke politely: "*Merci.* You are most considerate." In defense, she turned her attention to the spaniel at their feet. "Ah, Korrigan, *comment ça va?*" She scratched behind his ear, and he licked her hand with loving kisses.

"Korrigan is quite taken with you," Christophe remarked, watching the long, tapering fingers being bathed. "He is normally much more reserved, but it appears you have captured his heart." Korrigan collapsed in an adoring heap over her feet.

"A very sloppy lover," she remarked, holding out her hand.

"A small price to pay, *ma belle,* for such devotion."

He drew a handkerchief from his pocket, captured her hand, and began to dry it. The effect on Serenity was violent. Sharp currents vibrated from the tips of her fingers and up her arm, spreading a tingling heat through her body.

"That's not necessary. I have a rag right here." She indicated her case of chalks and pencils and attempted to pull her hand away from his.

His eyes narrowed, his grip increasing, and she found herself outmatched in the short, silent struggle. With a sigh of angry exasperation, she allowed her hand to lay limp in his.

"Do you always get your own way?" she demanded, eyes darkening with suppressed fury.

"*Bien sûr,*" he replied with irritating confidence, releasing her now-dry hand and giving her a long, measuring look. "I feel you are also used to having your own way, Serenity Smith. Will it not be interesting to see who, how do you say, 'comes out on top' during your visit?"

"Perhaps we should put up a scoreboard," she suggested, retreating behind the armor of frigidity. "Then there would be no doubt as to who comes out on top."

He gave her a slow, lazy smile. "There will be no doubt, *cousine*."

Her retort was cut off by the appearance of the countess, and Serenity automatically smoothed her features into relaxed lines to avoid the other woman's speculation.

"Good morning, my children." The countess greeted them with a maternal smile that surprised her granddaughter. "You are enjoying the beauty of the garden. I find it at its most peaceful at this time of day."

"It's lovely, Madame," Serenity concurred. "One feels there is no other world beyond the colors and scents of this one solitary spot."

"I have often felt that way." The angular lines softened. "The hours I have spent here over the years are uncountable." She seated herself on a bench across from the dark man and fair-skinned woman and sighed. "What have you drawn?" Serenity offered her pad, and the countess studied the drawing before raising her eyes to study the woman in turn. "You have your father's talent." At the grudging admission, Serenity's eyes sharpened, and her mouth opened to retort. "Your father was a very talented artist," the countess continued. "And I begin to see he had some quality of goodness to have earned Gaelle's love and your loyalty."

"Yes, Madame," Serenity replied, realizing she had been awarded a difficult concession. "He was a very good man, both a constant loving father and husband."

She resisted the urge to bring up the Raphael, unwilling to break the tenuous threads of understanding being woven. The countess nodded. Then, turning to Christophe, she made a comment about the evening's dinner party.

Picking up drawing paper and chalks Serenity began idly to draw her grandmother. The voices hummed around her, soothing, peaceful sounds suited to the garden's atmosphere. She did not attempt to follow the conversation, merely allowing the murmuring voices to wash over her as she began to concentrate on her work with more intensity.

In duplicating the fine-boned face and the surprisingly vulnerable mouth, she saw more clearly the countess's resemblance to her mother, and so, in fact, to herself. The countess's expression was relaxed, an ageless beauty that instinctively held itself proud. But somehow now, Serenity saw a glimpse of her mother's softness and fragility, the face of a woman who would love deeply—and therefore be hurt deeply. For the first time since she had received the formal letter from her unknown grandmother, Serenity felt a stirring of kinship, the first trickle of love for the woman who had borne her mother, and so had been responsible for her own existence.

Serenity was unaware of the variety of expressions flitting across her face, or of the man who sat beside her, observing the metamorphosis while he carried on his conversation. When she had finished, she lay down her chalks and wiped her hands absently, starting when she turned her head and encountered Christophe's direct stare. His eyes dropped to the portrait in her lap before coming back to her bemused eyes.

"You have a rare gift, *ma chérie*," he murmured. And she frowned in puzzlement, unsure from his tone whether he was speaking of her work or something entirely different.

"What have you drawn?" the countess inquired. Serenity tore her eyes from his compelling regard and handed her grandmother the portrait.

The countess studied it for several moments, the first expression of surprise fading into something Serenity could not comprehend. When the eyes rose and rested on her, the face altered with a smile.

"I am honored and flattered. If you would permit me, I would like to purchase this." The smile increased. "Partly for my vanity, but also because I would like a sample of your work."

Serenity watched her for a moment, hovering on the line between pride and love. "I'm sorry, Madame." She shook her head and took the drawing. "I cannot sell it." She glanced down at the paper in her hand before handing it back and meeting the blue eyes. "It is a gift for you, Grandmère." She watched the play of emotion move both mouth and eyes before speaking again. "Do you accept?"

"Oui." The word came on a sigh. "I shall treasure your gift, and this"—she looked down once more at the chalk portrait— "shall be my reminder that one should never allow pride to stand in the way of love." She rose and touched her lips to Serenity's cheeks before she moved down the flagstone path toward the château.

Standing, Serenity moved away from the bench. "You have a natural ability to invite love," Christophe observed, and she rounded on him, her emotions highly tuned.

"She's my grandmother, too."

He noted the veil of tears shimmering in her eyes and rose to his feet in an easy movement. "My statement was a compliment."

"Really? I thought it a condemnation." Despising the mist in her eyes, she wanted both to be alone and to lean against his broad shoulder.

"You are always on the defensive with me, are you not, Serenity?" His eyes narrowed as they did when he was angry, but she was too involved with battling her own emotions to care.

"You've given me plenty of cause," she tossed back. "From the moment I stepped off the train, you made your feelings clear. You'd condemned both my father and me. You're cold and autocratic and without a bit of compassion or understanding. I wish you'd go away and leave me alone. Go flog some peasants or something; it suits you."

He moved so quickly that she had no chance to back away, his arms nearly splitting her in two as they banded around her. "Are you afraid?" he demanded, and his lips crushed hers before she could answer, and all reason was blotted out.

She moaned against the pain and pleasure his mouth inflicted, going limp as his hold increased, conquering even her breath.

How is it possible to hate and love at the same time? her heart demanded of her numbed brain, but the answer was lost in a flood of turbulent, triumphant passion. Fingers tangled ruthlessly in her hair, pulling her head back to expose the creamy length of her neck, and he claimed the vulnerable skin with a mouth hot and hungry. The thinness of her blouse was no defense against the sultry heat of his body, but he disposed of the brief barrier, his hand sliding under, then up along her flesh to claim the swell of her breast with a consummate and absolute possession.

His mouth returned to ravage hers, bruising softness with a demand she could not deny. No longer did she question the complexity of her love, but yielded like a willow in a storm to the entreatment of her own needs.

He lifted his face, and his eyes were dark, the fires of anger and passion burning them to black. He wanted her, and her eyes grew wide and terrified at the knowledge. No one had ever wanted her this intensely, and no one had ever possessed the power to take her this effortlessly. For even without his love, she knew she would submit, and even without her submission, he would take.

He read the fear in her eyes, and his voice was low and dangerous. "*Oui, petite cousine,* you have cause to be afraid, for you know what will be. You are safe for the moment, but take care how and where you provoke me again."

Releasing her, he walked easily up the path his grandmother had chosen, and Korrigan bounded up, sent Serenity an apologetic glance, and then followed close on his master's heels.

Chapter 6

Serenity dressed with great care for dinner that evening, using the time to put her feelings in order and decide on a plan of action. No amount of arguments or reasoning could alter the fact that she had plunged headlong into love with a man she had known only a few days, a man who was as terrifying as he was exciting.

An arrogant, domineering, audaciously stubborn man, she added, pulling up the zipper at the back of her dress. And one who had condemned her father as a thief. *How could I let this happen?* she berated herself. *How could I have prevented it?* she reflected with a sigh. *My heart may have deserted me, but my head is still on my shoulders, and I'm going to have to use it. I refuse to allow Christophe to see that I've fallen in love with him and subject myself to his mockery.*

Seated at the cherrywood vanity, she ran a brush through soft curls and touched up her light application of makeup. War paint, she decided, and grinned at the reflection. *It fits; I'd rather be at war with him than in love. Besides*—the grin turned into a frown—*there is also Mademoiselle Dejot to contend with tonight.*

Standing, she surveyed her full reflection in the free-standing mirror. The amber silk echoed the color of her eyes and added a warm glow to her creamy skin. Thin straps revealed smooth shoulders, and the low, rounded bodice teased the subtle curve of breast. The knife-pleated skirt floated gently to her ankles, the filminess and muted color adding to her fragile, ethereal beauty.

She frowned at the effect, seeing fragility when she had desired poise and sophistication. The clock informed her that there was no time to alter gowns, so slipping on shoes and spraying a cloud of scent around her, she hurried from the room.

The murmur of voices emitting from the main drawing room made Serenity realize, to her irritation, that the dinner guests had already arrived. Her artist's eye immediately sketched the tableau which greeted her as she entered the room: the gleaming floor and warm polished paneling, the high, lead-paned windows, the immense stone fireplace with the carved mantel—all set the perfect backdrop for the elegant inhabitants of the château's drawing room, with the countess the undisputed queen in regal red silk.

The severe black of Christophe's dinner suit threw the snow-white of his shirt into relief and accented the tawny color of his skin. Yves Dejot was also in black, his skin more gold than bronze, his hair an unexpected chestnut. But it was the woman between the two dark men who caught both Serenity's eye and reluctant admiration. If her grandmother was the queen, here was the crown princess. Jet-black hair framed a small, elfin face of poignant beauty. Almond-shaped eyes of pansy-brown dominated the engaging face, and the gown of forest-green glowed against the rich golden skin.

Both men rose as she entered the room, and Serenity gave her attention to the stranger, all too aware of Christophe's habitual all-encompassing survey. As introductions were made, she found herself looking into chestnut eyes, the same shade as his hair, which held undeniable masculine approval and an unmistakable light of mischief.

"You did not tell me, *mon ami,* that your cousin was a golden goddess." He bent over Serenity's fingers, brushing them with his lips. "I shall have to visit the château more often, Mademoiselle, during your stay."

She smiled with honest enjoyment, summing up Yves Dejot as both charming and harmless. "I am sure my stay will be all the more enjoyable with that prospect in mind, Monsieur," she responded, matching his tone, and she was rewarded with a flashing smile.

Christophe continued his introductions, and Serenity's hand was clasped in a small, hesitant grip. "I am so happy to meet you at last, Mademoiselle Smith." Geneviève greeted her with a warm smile. "You are so like your mother's portrait, it is like seeing the painting come to life."

The voice was sincere, and Serenity concluded that no matter how hard she tried, it would be impossible to dislike the pixielike woman who gazed at her with the liquid eyes of a cocker spaniel.

The conversation continued light and pleasant throughout *apéritifs* and dinner, delectable oysters in champagne setting the mood for an elegantly prepared and served meal. The Dejots were curious about America and Serenity's life in its capital, and she attempted to describe the city of contrasts as the small group enjoyed *le ris de veau au Chablis.*

She began to draw a picture with words of stately old government buildings, the graceful lines and columns of the White House. "Unfortunately, there has been a great deal of modernization, with huge steel and glass monstrosities replacing some of the old buildings. Neat, vast, and charmless. But there are dozens of theatres, from Ford's, where Lincoln was assassinated, to the Kennedy Center."

Continuing, she took them from the stunning elegance of Embassy Row to the slums and tenements outside the federal enclave, through museums and galleries and the bustle of Capitol Hill.

"But we lived in Georgetown, and this is a world apart from the rest of Washington. Most of the homes are row houses or semi-detached, two or three stories, with small bricked-in yards edged with azaleas and flowerbeds. Some of the side streets are still cobblestoned, and it still retains a rather old-fashioned charm."

"Such an exciting city," Geneviève commented. "You must find our life here very quiet. Do you miss the animation, the activity of your home?"

Serenity frowned into her wineglass, then shook her head, "No," she answered, somewhat surprised by her own admission. "That's strange, I suppose." She met the brown eyes across from her. "I spent my entire life there, and I was very happy, but I don't miss it at all. I had the strangest feeling of affinity when I first walked into the château, a feeling of recognition. I've been very content here."

Glancing over, she found Christophe's eyes on her, brooding and penetrating, and she felt a quick surge of panic. "Of course, it's a relief not to enter into the daily contest for a parking space," she added with a smile, attempting to shake off the mood of seriousness. "Parking spaces are more precious than gold in Washington, and behind the wheel even the most mild-mannered person would commit murder and mayhem to obtain one."

"Have you resorted to such tactics, *ma chérie?*" Christophe asked. Raising his wineglass, he kept his eyes on her.

"I shudder to think of my crimes," she answered, relieved by the light turn of topic. "I dare not confess what lengths I've gone to in order to secure a few feet of empty space. I can be terribly aggressive."

"It is not possible to believe that aggression is a quality of such a delicate willow," Yves declared, blanketing her in his charming smile.

"You would be surprised, *mon ami,*" Christophe commented with an inclination of his head. "The willow has many unexpected qualities."

Serenity continued to frown at him as the countess skillfully changed the subject.

The drawing room was gently lit, lending an air of intimacy to the vast room. As the group enjoyed after-dinner coffee and brandy, Yves seated himself next to Serenity and began dispensing his abundant supply of Gallic charm. She noted, with a great deal of discomfort around her heart, which she was forced to recognize as pure, honest jealousy, that Christophe devoted himself to entertaining Geneviève. They spoke of her parents, who were touring the Greek islands, of mutual acquaintances and old friends. He listened attentively as Geneviève related an anecdote, flattered, laughed, teased, his attitude being one of overall gentleness, a softness Serenity had not seen in him before. Their relationship was so obviously special, so close and long standing, that Serenity felt a swift pang of despair.

He treats her as though she were made of fine, delicate crystal, small and precious, and he treats me as though I were made of stone, sturdy, strong, and dull.

It would have been infinitely easier if Serenity could have disliked the other woman, but natural friendliness overcame jealousy, and as time went by, she found herself liking both Dejots more and more.

Geneviève consented, after some gentle prompting by the countess, to play a few selections on the piano. The music floated through the room as sweet and fragile as its mistress.

I suppose she's perfect for him, Serenity concluded dismally. *They have so much in common, and she brings out a tenderness in him that will keep him from hurting her.* She glanced over to where Christophe sat, relaxed against the cushions of the sofa, his dark, fascinating eyes fixed on the woman at the piano. A swift variety of emotions ran through her—longing, despair, resentment, settling into a hopeless fog of depression as she realized no matter how perfect Geneviève might be for him, she could never happily watch Christophe court another woman.

"As an artist, Mademoiselle," Yves began as the music ended and conversation resumed, "you require inspiration, *n'est-ce pas?*"

"Of one kind or another," she agreed and smiled at him.

"The gardens of the château are immensely inspirational in the moonlight," he pointed out with an answering smile.

"I am in the mood for inspiration," she decided on

quick impulse. "Perhaps I could impose on you to escort me."

"Mademoiselle," he answered happily, "I would be honored."

Yves informed the rest of the party of their intention, and Serenity accepted his proffered arm without seeing the dark look thrown at her by the remaining male member.

The garden was indeed an inspiration, the brilliance of colors muted in the silver shimmer of moonlight. The scents intertwined into a heady perfume, mellowing the warm summer evening into a night for lovers. She sighed as her thoughts strayed back to the man in the château's drawing room.

"You sigh from pleasure, Mademoiselle?" Yves questioned as they strolled down a winding path.

"Bien sûr," she answered lightly, shaking off her somber mood and granting her escort one of her best smiles. "I'm overcome by the overwhelming beauty."

"Ah, Mademoiselle." He lifted her hand to his lips and kissed it with much feeling. "The beauty of each blossom pales before yours. What rose could compare with such lips, or gardenia with such skin?"

"How do French men learn to make love with words?"

"It is taught from the cradle, Mademoiselle," he informed her with suspicious sobriety.

"How difficult for a woman to resist such a setting." Serenity took a deep, consuming breath. "A moonlit garden outside a Breton château, the air filled with perfume, a handsome man with poetry on his lips."

"Hélas!" Yves gave a heavy sigh. "I fear you will find the strength to do so."

She shook her head with mock sorrow. "I am unfortunately extremely strong, and you," she added with a grin, "are a charming Breton wolf."

His laughter broke the night's stillness. "Ah, already you know me too well. If it were not for the feeling I had when we met that we were destined to be friends and not lovers, I would pursue my campaign with more feeling. But, we Bretons are great believers in destiny."

"And it is so difficult to be both friends and lovers."

"Mais, oui."

"Then friends it shall be," Serenity stated, extending her hand. "I shall call you Yves, and you shall call me Serenity."

He accepted her hand and held it a moment. *"C'est extraordinaire* that I should be content with friendship with one like you. You possess an elusive beauty that locks into a man's mind and keeps him constantly aware of you." His shoulders moved in a Gallic shrug which said more than a three-hour speech. "Well, such is life," he remarked fatalistically. Serenity was still laughing when they re-entered the château.

The following morning, Serenity accompanied her grandmother and Christophe to Mass in the village she had viewed from the hilltop. A light, insistent rain had begun during the pre-dawn hours, its soft hissing against her window awakening her until its steady rhythm had lulled her back to sleep.

The rain continued as they drove to the village, drenching leaves and causing flowers in the cottage's neat garden to droop heavy-headed, lending them an air of a colorful congregation at prayer. She had noticed, with some puzzlement, that Christophe had maintained a strange silence since the previous evening. The Dejots had departed soon after Serenity and Yves had rejoined the group in the drawing room, and though Christophe's farewells to his guests were faultlessly charming, he had avoided addressing Serenity directly. The only communication between them had been a brief—and, she had imagined—forbidding glance, quickly veiled.

Now, he spoke almost exclusively to the countess, with occasional comments or replies made directly to Serenity, polite, with a barely discernible hostility which she decided to ignore.

The focal point of the small village was the chapel, a tiny white structure with its neatly trimmed grounds an almost humorous contrast to its slightly apologetic, crumbling state. The roof had had more than one recent repair, and the single oak door at the entrance was weathered and battered from age and constant use.

"Christophe has offered to have a new chapel built," the countess commented. "But the villagers will not have it. This is where their fathers and grandfathers have worshipped for centuries, and they will continue to worship here until it crumbles about their ears."

"It's charming," Serenity decided, for somehow the tiny chapel's faintly dilapidated air gave it a certain steadfast dignity, a sense of pride at having witnessed generations of christenings, weddings, and funerals.

The door groaned in apology as Christophe opened it, allowing the two women to precede him. The interior was dark and quiet, the high-beamed ceiling adding an illusion of space. The countess glided to the front pew, taking her place in the seats which had been reserved for the Château Kergallen for nearly three centuries. Spying Yves and Geneviève across the narrow aisle, Serenity threw them both a full smile and was rewarded with an answering one from Geneviève and a barely discernible wink from Yves.

"This is hardly the proper setting for your flirtations, Serenity," Christophe whispered in her ear as he assisted her out of her damp trenchcoat.

Her color rose, making her feel like a child caught giggling in the sacristy, and she turned her head to retort as the priest, who seemed as old as the chapel, approached the altar, and the service began.

A feeling of peace drifted over her like a soft, down-filled quilt. The rain insulated the congregation from the outside, its soft whispering on the roof adding to the quiet rather than detracting from it. The low drone of Breton from the ancient priest, and the light rumble of response, an occasional whimper from an infant, a muffled cough, the dark stained glass with rivulets of rain running down its surface—all combined into a quiet timelessness. Sitting in the well-worn pew, Serenity felt the chapel's magic and understood the villagers' refusal to give up the crumbling building for a more substantial structure, for here was peace, and the serenity for which she had been named. A continuity with the past, and a link with the future.

As the service ended, so did the rain, and a vague beam of sunlight filtered through the stained glass, introducing a subtle, elusive glow. When they emerged outside, the air was fresh, sparkling from the clean scent of rain. Drops still clung to the newly washed leaves, glistening like tears against the bright green surfaces.

Yves greeted Serenity with a courtly bow and a lingering kiss on the fingers. "You have brought out the sun, Serenity."

"Mais, oui," she agreed, smiling into his eyes. "I have ordered all my days in Brittany to be bright and sunny."

Removing her hand, she smiled at Geneviève, who resembled a dainty primrose in a cool yellow dress and narrow-brimmed hat. Greetings were exchanged, and Yves leaned down toward Serenity like a conspirator.

"Perhaps you would care to take advantage of the sunshine, *chérie,* and come for a drive with me. The countryside is exquisite after a rain."

"I'm afraid Serenity will be occupied today," Christophe answered before she could accept or decline, and she glared at him. "Your second lesson," he said smoothly, ignoring the battle lights in her amber eyes.

"Lesson?" Yves repeated with a crooked smile. "What are you teaching your lovely cousin, Christophe?"

"Horsemanship," he responded with a like smile, "at the moment."

"Ah, you could not find a finer instructor," Geneviève observed with a light touch on Christophe's arm. "Christophe taught me to ride when Yves and my father had given me up as hopelessly inadequate. You are so patient." Her cocker spaniel eyes gazed up at the lean man, and Serenity stifled an incredulous laugh.

Patient was the last word she would use to describe Christophe. Arrogant, demanding, autocratic, overconfident—she began silently listing qualities she attributed to the man at her side. Cynical and overbearing, also. Her attention wandered from the conversation, her gaze lighting on a small girl sitting on a patch of grass with a frisky black puppy. The dog was alternately bathing the child's face with enthusiastic kisses and running in frantic circles around her as the child's high, sweet laughter floated on the air. It was such a relaxing, innocent picture that it took Serenity a few extra seconds to react to what happened next.

The dog suddenly darted across the grass toward the road, and the child scrambled up, dashing after it, calling the dog's name in stern disapproval. Serenity watched without reaction as a car approached. Then a cold draft of fear overtook her as she observed the child's continuing flight toward the road.

Without thought, she streaked in pursuit, frantically calling in Breton for the child to stop, but the girl's attention was riveted on her pet, and she rushed over the grass, stepping out in the path of the oncoming car.

Serenity heard the squeal of brakes as her arms wrapped around the child, and she felt the rush of wind and slight bump of the fender against her side as she hurled both herself and the girl across the road, landing in a tangled heap on its surface. There was absolute silence for a split-second, and then pandemonium broke loose as the puppy, which Serenity was now sitting on rather heavily, yelped in rude objection, and the child's loud wails for her mother joined the animal's indignation.

Suddenly, excited voices in a mixture of languages joined the wailing and yelping, adding to Serenity's dazed, befuddled state. She could find no strength to remove her weight from the errant puppy, and the girl struggled from her now-limp grasp and ran into the arms of her pale, tearful mother.

Strong, hard arms lifted Serenity to her feet, holding her shoulders and tilting back her head so that she met Christophe's dark, stormy eyes. "Are you hurt?" When she shook her head, he continued in a tight, angry voice: "*Nom de Dieu!* You must be mad!" He shook her slightly, increasing the dizziness. "You could have been killed! How you missed being struck is a miracle."

"They were playing so sweetly," she recalled in a vague voice. "Then that silly dog goes tearing off into the street. Oh, I wonder if I hurt it; I sat right on it. I don't think the poor animal liked it."

"Serenity." Christophe's furious voice and the vigorous shaking brought her attention back to him. "*Mon Dieu!* I begin to believe you really are mad!"

"Sorry," she murmured, feeling empty and light-headed. "Silly to think of the dog first and the child later. Is she all right?"

He let out a soft stream of curses on a long breath. "*Oui,* she is with her mother. You moved like a cheetah; otherwise, both of you would not be standing up babbling now."

"Adrenaline," she muttered and swayed. "It's gone now."

His grip increased on her shoulders as he surveyed her face. "You are going to faint?" The question was accompanied by a deep frown.

"Certainly not," she replied, attempting to sound firm and dignified, but succeeding in a rather wavering denial.

"Serenity." Geneviève reached her, taking her hand and abandoning formality. "That was so brave." Tears swam in the brown eyes, and she kissed both of Serenity's pale cheeks.

"Are you hurt?" Yves echoed Christophe's question, his eyes concerned rather than angry.

"No, no, I'm fine," she assured him, unconsciously leaning on Christophe for support. "The puppy got the worst of it when I landed on it." *I just want to sit down,* she thought wearily, *until the world stops spinning.*

Suddenly, she found herself being addressed in rapid, tearful Breton by the child's mother. The words were slurred with emotion, and the dialect was so thick she had difficulty following the stream of conversation. The woman continually wiped brimming eyes with a wrinkled ball of handkerchief, and Serenity made what she hoped were the correct responses, feeling incredibly tired and faintly embarrassed as the mother's hands grabbed and kissed with fervent gratitude. At a low order from Christophe, they were relinquished, and she retreated, gathering up her child and melting away into the crowd.

"Come." He slipped an arm around Serenity's waist, and the mass of people parted like the waves of the Red Sea as he led her back toward the chapel. "I think both you and the mongrel should be put on a short leash."

"How kind of you to lump us together," she muttered, then caught sight of her grandmother sitting on a small stone bench, looking pale and suddenly old.

"I thought you would be killed," the countess stated in a thick voice, and Serenity knelt in front of her.

"I'm quite indestructible, Grandmère," she claimed with a confident smile. "I inherited it from both sides of my family."

The thin, bony hand gripped Serenity's tightly. "You are very impudent and stubborn," the countess declared in a firmer voice. "And I love you very much."

"I love you, too," Serenity said simply.

Chapter 7

Serenity insisted on receiving her riding lesson after the midday meal, vetoing both the suggested prescription of a long rest and the prospect of summoning a doctor.

"I don't need a doctor, Grandmère, and I don't need a rest. I'm perfectly all right." She shrugged aside the morning's incident. "A few bumps and bruises; I told you I'm indestructible."

"You are stubborn," the countess corrected, and Serenity merely smiled and shrugged again.

"You have had a frightening experience," Christophe inserted, studying her with critical eyes. "A less strenuous activity would be more suitable."

"For heaven's sake, not you, too!" She pushed away her coffee impatiently. "I'm not some mid-Victorian weakling who subsides into fits of vapors and needs to be coddled. If you don't want to take me riding, I'll call Yves and accept his invitation for the drive which you refused for me." Her fine-boned face was set, and her chin lifted. "I am not going to go to bed in the middle of the day like a child."

"Very well." Christophe's eyes darkened. "You will have your ride, though perhaps your lesson will not be as stimulating as what Yves intended."

She stared at him for a moment in bewilderment before color seeped into her cheeks. "Oh, really, what a ridiculous thing to say."

"I will meet you at the stables in half an hour." He interrupted her protestations, rose from the table, and strode from the room before she could formulate a suitable rebuttal.

Turning to her grandmother, her face was a picture of indignation. "Why is he so insufferably rude to me?"

The countess's slim shoulders moved expressively, and she looked wise. "Men are complicated creatures, *chérie*."

"One day," Serenity predicted with an ominous frown, "one day he's not going to walk away until I've had my say."

Serenity met Christophe at the appointed time, determined to focus every ounce of energy into developing the proper riding technique. She mounted the mare with concentrated confidence, then followed her silent instructor as he pointed his horse in the opposite direction from that which they had taken on their last outing. When he broke into a light canter, she copied his action, and she experienced the same intoxicating freedom as she had before. There was, however, no sudden, exciting flash of smile on his features, no laughter or teasing words, and she told herself she was better off without them. He called out an occasional instruction, and she obeyed immediately, needing to prove both to him and herself that she was capable. So, she contented herself with the task of riding and an infrequent glance at his dark, hawklike profile.

Lord help me, she sighed in defeat, taking her eyes from him and staring straight ahead. *He's going to haunt me for the rest of my life. I'll end up a crotchety old maid, comparing every man I see to the one I couldn't have. I wish to God I'd never laid eyes on him.*

"Pardon?" Christophe's voice broke into her silent meditations, and she started, realizing she must have muttered something aloud.

"Nothing," she stammered, "it was nothing." Taking a deep breath, she frowned. "I could swear I smell the sea." He slowed his mount to a walk, and she reined in beside him as a faint rumble broke the silence. "Is that thunder?" She gazed up into a clear blue sky, but the rumble continued. "It *is* the sea!" she exclaimed, all animosity forgotten. "Are we near it? Will I be able to see it?" He merely halted his horse and dismounted. "Christophe, for heaven's sake!" She watched in exasperation as he tied his mount's reins to a tree. "Christophe!" she repeated, struggling from the saddle with more speed than grace. He took her arm as she landed awkwardly and tied her mount beside his before leading her farther down the path. "Choose whatever language you like," she invited magnanimously, "but talk to me before I go crazy!"

He stopped, turned, and drew her close, covering her mouth with a brief, distracting kiss. "You talk too much," he stated simply and continued on his way.

"Really," she began, but subsided when he turned and looked down at her again. Satisfied with her silence, he led her on, the distant rumbling growing nearer and more 'insistent. When he stopped again, Serenity caught her breath at the scene below.

The sea stretched as far as she could see, the sun's rays dancing on its deep green surface. The surf rolled in to caress the rocks, its foam resembling frothy lace on a deep velvet gown. Teasingly, it flowed back from the shore, only to roll back like a coquettish lover.

"It's marvelous," she sighed, reveling in the sharp salt-sprayed air and the breeze which ruffled her hair. "I suppose you must be used to this by now; I doubt I ever could be."

"I always enjoy looking at the sea," he answered, his eyes focused on the distant horizon, where the clear blue sky kissed the deep green. "It has many moods; perhaps that is why the fishermen call it a woman. Today she is calm and gentle, but when she is angry, her temper is a magnificent thing to see."

His hand slid down her arm to clasp her in a simple, intimate gesture she had not expected from him, and her heart did a series of somersaults. "When I was a boy, I thought to run away to the sea, live my life on the water, and sail with her moods." His thumb rubbed against the tender skin of her palm, and she swallowed before she could speak.

"Why didn't you?"

His shoulders moved, and she wondered for a moment if he remembered she was there. "I discovered that the land has its own magic—vivid-colored grass, rich soil, purple grapes, and grazing cattle. Riding a horse over the long stretches of land is as exciting as sailing over the waves of the sea. The land is my duty, my pleasure, and my destiny."

He looked down into the amber eyes, fixed wide and open on his face, and something passed between them, shimmering and expanding until Serenity felt submerged by its power. Then, she was crushed against him, the wind swirling around them like ribbons to bind them closer as his mouth demanded an absolute surrender. She clung to him as the roar of the sea swelled to a deafening pitch, and suddenly she was straining against him and demanding more.

If the mood of the sea was calm and gentle, his did not mirror it. Helpless against her own need, she reveled in the savage possession of his mouth, the urgent insistence of the hands which claimed her, as if by right. Trembling, not with fear, but with the longing to give, she pressed yet closer, willing him to take what she offered.

His mouth lifted once, briefly, and she shook her head against the liberation, pulling his face back to hers, lips begging for the merging. Her fingers dug into the flesh of his shoulders at the force of the new embrace, his mouth seeking hers with a new hunger, as if he would taste her or starve. His hand slipped under the silk of her blouse to claim the breast which ached for his touch, the warmth of his fingers searing like glowing embers against her skin, and though her mouth was conquered, his tongue demanding the intimacy of velvet moisture, her mind murmured his name over and over until there was nothing else.

Arms banded around her again, hands abandoning their explorations, and breath flew away and was forgotten in the new, crushing power. Soft breasts pressed against the hard leanness of his chest, thigh straining against thigh, heart pounding against heart, and Serenity knew she had taken the step from the precipice and would never return to the solidity of earth.

He released her so abruptly, she would have stumbled had his hand not gripped her arm to steady her. "We must go back," he stated as if the moment had never been. "It grows late."

Her hands reached up to push the tumbled curls from her face, her eyes lifting to his, wide and full of confused pleading. "Christophe." She said his name on a whisper, unable to form any other sound, and he stared down at her, the brooding look familiar and, as always, unfathomable.

"It grows late, Serenity," he repeated, and the underlying anger in his tone brought only more bewilderment.

Suddenly cold, her arms wrapped around her body to ward off the chill. "Christophe, why are you angry with me? I haven't done anything wrong."

"Haven't you?" His eyes narrowed and darkened with familiar temper, and through the ache of rejection, her own rose to meet it.

"No. What could I do to you? You're so infuriatingly superior, up there on your little golden throne. A partial aristocrat like myself could hardly climb up to your level to cause any damage."

"Your tongue will cause you endless trouble, Serenity, unless you learn to control it." His voice was precise and much too controlled, but Serenity found discretion buried under a growing mountain of fury.

"Well, until I choose to do so, perhaps I'll use it to tell you precisely what I think about your arrogant, autocratic, domineering, and infuriating attitude toward life in general, and myself in particular."

"A woman," he began, in a voice she noted was entirely too soft and too silky, "with your temperament, *ma petite cousine,* must be continually shown there is only one master." He took her arm in a firm hold and turned away from the sea. "I said we will go."

"*You,* Monsieur," she returned, holding her ground

and sending him a look of smoldering amber, "can go whenever you want."

Her exit of furious dignity took her three feet before her shoulders were captured in a viselike grip, then whirled around to face a fury which made her own temper seem tranquil. "You cause me to think again about the wisdom of beating a woman." His mouth took hers swiftly, hard and more punishing than a fist, and Serenity felt a quick surge of pain, tasting only anger on his lips, and no desire. Fingers dug into her shoulders, but she allowed herself neither struggle nor response, remaining passive in his arms as courage fled into hopelessness.

Set free, she stared up at him, detesting the veil of moistness which clouded her eyes. "You have the advantage, Christophe, and will always win a physical battle." Her voice was calm and carefully toned, and she watched his brows draw close, as if her reaction puzzled him. His hand lifted to brush at a drop which had escaped to flow down her cheek, and she jerked away, wiping it away herself and blinking the rest back.

"I've had my quota of humiliations for one day, and I will not dissolve into a pool of tears for your benefit." Her voice became firmer as she gained control, and her shoulders straightened as Christophe watched the transformation in silence. "As you said, it's getting late." Turning, she walked back up the path to where the horses waited.

The days passed quietly, soft summer days filled with the sun and the sweet perfume of flowers. Serenity devoted most of the daylight hours to painting, reproducing the proud, indomitable lines of the château on canvas. She had noted, at first with despair and then with increasing anger, Christophe's calculated avoidance of her. Since the afternoon when they had stood on the cliff above the sea, he had barely spoken to her, and then only with astringent politeness. Pride soon covered her hurt like a bandage over an open wound, and painting became a refuge against longing.

The countess never mentioned the Raphael, and Serenity was content for the time to drift, wanting to strengthen the bond between them before delving further into its disappearance and the accusation against her father.

She was immersed in her work, clad in faded jeans and a paint-splattered smock, her hair disheveled by her own hand, when she spotted Geneviève approaching across the smooth carpet of lawn. A beautiful Breton fairy, Serenity imagined, small and lovely in a buff-colored riding jacket and dark brown breeches.

"*Bonjour,* Serenity," she called out when Serenity raised a slim hand in greeting. "I hope I am not disturbing you."

"Of course not. It's good to see you." The words came easily because she meant them, and she smiled and put down her brush.

"Oh, but I have made you stop," Geneviève began in apology.

"You've given me a marvelous excuse to stop," she corrected.

"May I see?" Geneviève requested. "Or do you not like your work viewed before it is finished?"

"Of course you may see. Tell me what you think."

She moved around to stand beside Serenity. The background was completed: the azure sky, lamb's-wool clouds, vivid green grass, and stately trees. The château itself was taking shape gradually: the gray walls glowing pearly in the sunlight, high glistening windows, the drum towers. There was much left to complete, but even in its infancy, the painting captured the fairy-tale aura Serenity had envisioned.

"I have always loved the château," Geneviève stated, her eyes still on the canvas. "Now I see you do, as well." Pansy eyes lifted from the half-completed painting and sought Serenity's. "You have captured its warmth, as well as its arrogance. I am glad to know you see it as I do."

"I fell in love with it the first moment I saw it," Serenity admitted. "The longer I stay, the more hopelessly I'm lost." She sighed, knowing her words described the man, as well as his home.

"You are lucky to have such a gift. I hope you will not think less of me if I confess something."

"No, of course not," Serenity assured her, both surprised and intrigued.

"I am terribly envious of you," she blurted out quickly, as if courage might fail her.

Serenity stared down at the lovely face incredulously. "You, envious of me?"

"Oui." Geneviève hesitated for a moment, and then began to speak in a rush. "Not only of your talent as an artist, but of your confidence, your independence." Serenity continued to gape, her mouth wide open in astonishment. "There is something about you which draws people to you—an openness, a warmth in your eyes that makes one want to confide, feeling somehow you will understand."

"How extraordinary," Serenity murmured, astonished. "But, Geneviève," she began in a lighter tone, "you're so lovely and warm, how could you envy anyone, least of all me? You make me feel like a veritable Amazon."

"Men treat you as a woman," she explained, her voice faintly desperate. "They admire you not only for the way you look, but for what you are." She turned away, then back again quickly, a hand brushing at her hair. "What would you do if you loved a man, had loved him all of your life, loved with a woman's heart, but he saw you only as an amusing child?"

Serenity felt a cloud of despair envelop her heart. *Christophe,* she concluded. *Dear Lord, she wants my advice about Christophe.* She stifled the urge to give a shout of hysterical laughter. *I'm supposed to give her pointers on the man I love. Would she seek me out if she knew what he thinks of me...of my father?* Her eyes met Geneviève's dark ones, filled with hope and trust. She sighed.

"If I were in love with such a man, I would take great pains to let him know I was a woman, and that was how I wanted him to see me."

"But how?" Geneviève's hand spread in a helpless gesture. "I am such a coward. Perhaps I would lose even his friendship."

"If you really love him, you'll have to risk it or face the rest of your life as only his friend. You must tell...your man, the next time he treats you as a child, that you are a woman. You must tell him so that there is no doubt in his mind what you mean. Then, the move is his."

Geneviève took a deep breath and squared her shoulders. "I will think about what you have said." She turned her warm eyes on Serenity's amber ones once more. "Thank you for listening, for being a friend."

Serenity watched the small, graceful figure retreat across the grass. *You're a real martyr,* Serenity, she told herself. *I thought self-sacrifice was supposed to make one glow with inner warmth; I just feel cold and miserable.* She began packing up her paints, no longer finding pleasure in the sunshine. *I think I'll give up martyrdom and take up foreclosing on widows and orphans; it couldn't make me feel any worse.*

Depressed, Serenity wandered up to her room to store her canvas and paints. With what she considered a herculean effort, she managed to produce a smile for the maid, who was busily folding freshly laundered lingerie into the bureau drawer.

"*Bonjour,* Mademoiselle." Bridget greeted Serenity with a dazzling smile of her own, and amber eyes blinked at the power.

"*Bonjour,* Bridget. You seem in remarkably good spirits." Glancing at the shafts of sunlight which flowed triumphantly through the windows, Serenity sighed and shrugged. "I suppose it is a beautiful day."

"*Oui,* Mademoiselle. *Quel jour!*" She gestured toward the sky with a hand filled with filmy silk. "I think I have never seen the sun smile more sweetly."

Unable to cling to depression under the attack of blatant good humor, Serenity plopped into a chair and grinned at the small maid's glowing face. "Unless I read the signs incorrectly, I would say it's love which is smiling sweetly."

Heightened color only added more appeal to the young face as Bridget paused in her duties to beam yet another smile over Serenity. "*Oui,* Mademoiselle, I am very much in love."

"And I gather from the look of you"—Serenity continued battling a sweet surge of envy of the youthful confidence—"that you are very much loved."

"*Oui,* Mademoiselle." Sunlight and happiness formed an aura around her. "On Saturday, Jean-Paul and I will be married."

"Married?" Serenity repeated, faintly astonished as

she studied the tiny form facing her. "How old are you, Bridget?"

"Seventeen," she stated with a sage nod for her vast collection of years.

Seventeen, Serenity mused with an unconscious sigh. "Suddenly, I feel ninety-two."

"We will be married in the village," Bridget continued, warming to Serenity's interest. "Then everyone will come back to the château, and there will be singing and dancing in the garden. The count is very kind and very generous. He says we will have champagne." Serenity watched as joy turned to awe.

"Kind," she murmured, turning the adjective over in her mind. *Kindness is not a quality I would have attributed to Christophe.* Letting out a long breath, she recalled his gentle attitude toward Geneviève. *Obviously, I simply don't bring it out in him.*

"Mademoiselle has so many lovely things." Glancing up, Serenity saw Bridget fondling a flowing white negligée, her eyes soft and dreamy.

"Do you like it?" Rising, she fingered the hem, remembering the silky texture against her skin, then let it drift like a pure fall of snow to the floor.

"It's yours," Serenity declared impulsively, and the maid turned back, soft eyes now as wide as dark saucers.

"*Pardon,* Mademoiselle?"

"It's yours," she repeated, smiling into astonishment. "A wedding present."

"Oh, *mais non,* I could not…it is too lovely." Her voice faltered to a whisper as she gazed at the gown with wistful desire, then turned back to Serenity. "Mademoiselle could not bear to part with it."

"Of course I can," Serenity corrected. "It's a gift, and it would please me to know you were enjoying it." Studying the simple white silk which Bridget clutched to her breast, she sighed with a mixture of envy and hopelessness. "It was made for a bride, and you will look beautiful in it for your Jean-Paul."

"Oh, Mademoiselle!" Bridget breathed, blinking back tears of gratitude. "I will treasure it always." She followed this declaration with a joyful stream of Breton thanks, the simple words lifting Serenity's spirits. She left the future bride gazing into the mirror, negligée spread over apron as she dreamed of her wedding night.

The sun again smiled sweetly on Bridget's wedding day, the sky a cerulean-blue touched with a few friendly white wisps of clouds.

As the days had passed, Serenity's depression had altered to a frigid resentment. Christophe's aloof demeanor fanned the fires of temper, but determinedly, she had buried them under equally haughty ice. As a result, their conversations had been limited to a few stony, formally polite sentences.

She stood, flanked by him and the countess on the tiny lawn of the village church awaiting the bridal procession. The raw-silk suit she had chosen deliberately for its cool, untouchable appearance had been categorically dismissed by a wave of her grandmother's regal hand. Instead, she had been presented with an outfit of her mother's, the scent of lavender still clinging, as fresh as yesterday. Instead of appearing sophisticated and distant, she now appeared like a young girl awaiting a party.

The full gathered skirt just brushed bare calves, its brilliant vertical stripes of red and white topped with a short white apron. The peasant scoop-necked blouse was tucked into the tiny waist, its short puffed sleeves leaving arms bare to the sun. A black sleeveless vest fitted trimly over the subtle curve of breast, her pale halo of curls topped with a beribboned straw hat.

Christophe had made no comment on her appearance, merely inclining his head when she had descended the stairs, and now Serenity continued the silent war by addressing all her conversation exclusively to her grandmother.

"They will come from the house of the bride," the countess informed her, and though Serenity was uncomfortably aware of the dark man who stood behind her, she gave the appearance of polite attentiveness. "All of her family will walk with her on her last journey as a maiden. Then, she will meet the groom and enter the chapel to become a wife."

"She's so young," Serenity murmured in a sigh, "hardly more than a child."

"*Alors,* she is old enough to be a woman, my aged one." With a light laugh, the countess patted Serenity's hand. "I was little more when I married your grandfather. Age has little to do with love. Do you not agree, Christophe?"

Serenity felt, rather than saw, his shrug. "So it would seem, Grandmère. Before she is twenty, our Bridget will have a little one tugging on her apron and another under it."

"*Hélas!*" the countess sighed with suspicious wistfulness, and Serenity turned to regard her with careful curiosity. "It appears neither of my grandchildren see fit to provide me with little ones to spoil." She gave Serenity a sad, guileless smile. "It is difficult to be patient when one grows old."

"But it becomes simpler to be shrewd," Christophe commented in a dry voice, and Serenity could not prevent herself from glancing up at him. He gave her a brief, raised-brow look, and she met it steadily, determined not to falter under its spell.

"To be wise, Christophe," the countess corrected, unperturbed and faintly smug. "This is a truer statement. *Voilà!*" she announced before any comment could be made. "They come!"

Soft new flower petals floated and danced to earth as small children tossed them from wicker baskets. They laid a carpet of love for the bride's feet. Innocent petals, wild from the meadow and forest, and the children danced in circles as they offered them to the air. Surrounded by her family, the bride walked like a small, exquisite doll. Her dress was traditional, and obviously old, and Serenity knew she had never seen a bride more radiant or a dress more perfect.

Aged white, the full, pleated skirt flowed from the waist to dance an inch from the petal-strewn road. The neck was high and trimmed with lace, and the bodice was fitted and snug, touched with delicate embroidery. She wore no veil, but instead had on a round white cap topped with a stiff lace headdress which lent the tiny dark form an exotic and ageless beauty.

The groom joined her, and Serenity noted, with a near-maternal relief, that Jean-Paul looked both kind and nearly as innocent as Bridget herself. He, too, was attired traditionally: white knickers tucked into soft boots, and a deep blue double-breasted jacket over an embroidered white shirt. The narrow-brimmed Breton cap with its velvet ribbons accentuated his youth, and Serenity surmised he was little older than his bride.

Shining young love glowed around them, pure and sweet as the morning sky, and the sudden, unexpected pang of longing caused Serenity to draw in her breath, then clutch her hands together tightly to combat a convulsive shudder. *Just once,* she thought, and swallowed against the dryness of her throat, *just once I would have*

*Christophe look at me that way, and I could live on it for
the rest of my life.*

Starting as a hand touched her arm, she looked up
to find his eyes on her, faintly mocking and altogether
cool. Tilting her chin, she allowed him to lead her inside the chapel.

The château's garden was a perfect world in which
to celebrate a new marriage, vivid and fresh and alive
with scents and hues. The terrace was laden with white-
clothed tables brimming over with food and drink. The
château had laid on its finest for the village wedding,
silver and crystal gleaming with the pride of age in the
glory of sunlight. And the village, Serenity observed, accepted it as their due. As they belonged to the château,
so it belonged to them. Music rose over the mixture of
voices and laughter: the sweet, lilting strain of violins
and the softly nasal call of bagpipes.

Serenity watched from the terrace as bride and groom
performed their first dance as man and wife, a folk dance,
full of charm and saucy movements, and Bridget flirted
with her husband with tossing head and teasing eyes,
much to the approval of the audience. Dancing continued, growing livelier, and Serenity found herself being
pulled into the crowd by a charmingly determined Yves.

"But I don't know how," she protested, unable to prevent the laugh his persistence provoked.

"I will teach you," he returned simply, taking both
her hands in his. "Christophe is not the only one with
the ability to instruct." He inclined his head in acknowledgment of her frown. "Ah-ha! I thought as much." Her
frown deepened at the ambiguity, but he merely smiled,
lifted one hand to his lips briefly, and continued. "*Maintenant,* first we step to the right."

Caught up first in her lesson, then in the pleasure of the simple music and movements, Serenity found the tensions of the past days drifting away. Yves was attentive and charming, taking her through the steps of the dances and bringing her glasses of champagne. Once seeing Christophe dancing with a small, graceful Geneviève, a cloud of despair threatened her sun, and she turned away quickly, unwilling to fall back into the well of depression.

"You see, *chérie,* you take to the dance naturally." Yves smiled down at her as the music paused.

"Assuredly, my Breton genes have come to the fore to sustain me."

"So," he said in mock censure, "will you not give credit to your instructor?"

"Mais, oui." She gave him a teasing smile and a small curtsy. "My instructor is both charming and brilliant."

"True," he agreed, chestnut eyes twinkling against the gravity of his tone. "And my student is both beautiful and enchanting."

"True," she agreed in turn, and laughing, she linked her arm through his.

"Ah, Christophe." Her laughter froze as she saw Yves's gaze travel above her head. "I have usurped your role as tutor."

"It appears you are both enjoying the transition." Hearing the icy politeness in his voice, Serenity turned to him warily. He looked entirely too much like the seafaring count in the portrait gallery for her comfort. The white silk shirt opened carelessly to reveal the strong, dark column of throat, the sleeveless black vest a startling contrast. The matching black pants were mated to soft leather boots, and Serenity decided he looked more dangerous than elegant.

"A delightful student, *mon ami,* as I am sure you agree." Yves's hand rested lightly on Serenity's shoulder as he smiled into the set, impassive face. "Perhaps you would care to test the quality of my instructions for yourself."

"Bien sûr." Christophe acknowledged the offer with a slight inclination of his head. Then, with a graceful, rather old-fashioned gesture, he held out his hand, palm up for Serenity's acquiescence.

She hesitated, both fearing and longing for the contact of flesh. Then seeing the challenge in his dark eyes, she placed her palm in his with aristocratic grace.

Serenity moved with the music, the steps of the old, flirting dance coming easily. Swaying, circling, joining briefly, the dance began as a confrontation, a formalized contest between man and woman. Their eyes held, his bold and confident, hers defiant, and they moved in alternating circles, palms touching. As his arm slipped lightly around her waist, she tossed her head back to keep the gaze unbroken, ignoring the sudden thrill as their hips brushed.

Steps quickened with the music, the melody growing more demanding, the ancient choreography growing more enticing, the contact of bodies lengthening. She kept her chin tilted insolently, her eyes challenging, but she felt the heat begin its insistent rise as his arm became more possessive of her waist, drawing her closer with each turn. What had begun as a duel was now a seduction, and she felt his silent power taking command of her will as surely as if his lips had claimed hers. Drawing on one last shred of control, she stepped back, seeking the safety of distance. His arm pulled her against him, and helplessly, her eyes sought the mouth which hovered dangerously over hers. Her lips parted, half in protest, half in invitation, and his lowered until she could taste his breath on her tongue.

The silence when the music ended was like a thunderclap, and she watched wide-eyed as he drew the promise of his mouth away with a smile of pure triumph.

"Your teacher is to be commended, Mademoiselle." His hands dropped from her waist, and with a small bow, he turned and left her.

The more remote and taciturn Christophe became, the more open and expansive became the countess, as though sensing his mood and seeking to provoke him.

"You seem preoccupied, Christophe," the countess stated artlessly as they dined at the large oak table. "Are your cattle giving you trouble, or perhaps an *affaire de coeur?*"

Determinedly, Serenity kept her eyes on the wine she swirled in her glass, patently fascinated by the gently moving color.

"I am merely enjoying the excellent meal, Grand-mère," Christophe returned, not rising to the bait. "Neither cattle nor women disturb me at the moment."

"Ah." The countess breathed life into the syllable. "Perhaps you group both together."

Broad shoulders moved in a typical gesture. "They both demand attention and a strong hand, *n'est-ce pas?*"

Serenity swallowed a bit of *canard à l'orange* before it choked her.

"Have you left many broken hearts behind in America, Serenity?" The countess spoke before Serenity could voice the murderous thoughts forming in her brain.

"Dozens," she returned, aiming a deadly glance at Christophe. "I have found that some men lack the intelligence of cattle, more often having the arms, if not the brains, of an octopus."

"Perhaps you have been dealing with the wrong men," Christophe suggested, his voice cool.

This time it was Serenity's shoulders which moved. "Men are men," she said in dismissal, seeking to annoy him with her own generalization. "They either want a warm body for groping in corners, or a piece of Dresden to sit on a shelf."

"And how, in your opinion, does a woman wish to be treated?" he demanded as the countess sat back and enjoyed the fruits of her instigation.

"As a human being with intellect, emotions, rights, needs." Her hands moved expressively. "Not as a happy convenience for a man's pleasure to be tucked away until the mood strikes him, or a child to be petted and amused."

"You seem to have a low opinion of men, *ma chérie*," Christophe intimated, neither of them aware they were speaking more in this conversation than they had in days.

"Only of antiquated ideas and prejudice," she contradicted. "My father always treated my mother as a partner; they shared everything."

"Do you look for your father in the men you meet, Serenity?" he asked suddenly, and her eyes widened, surprised and disconcerted.

"Why, no, at least I don't think so," she faltered, trying to see into her own heart. "Perhaps I look for his strength and his kindness, but not a replica. I think I look for a man who could love me as completely as he loved my mother—someone who could take me with all my faults and imperfections and love me for what I am, not what he might want me to be."

"And when you find such a man," Christophe asked, giving her an unfathomable stare, "what will you do?"

"Be content," she murmured, and made an effort to give her attention to the food on her plate.

Serenity continued her painting the following day. She had slept poorly, disturbed by the admission she had made to Christophe's unexpected question. She had spoken spontaneously, the words the fruit of a feeling she had not been aware of possessing. Now with the warmth of the sun at her back and brush and pallet in hand, she endeavored to lose her discomfort in the love of painting.

She found it difficult to concentrate, Christophe's lean features invading her mind and blurring the sharp lines of the château. Rubbing her forehead, she finally threw down her brush in disgust and began to pack her equipment, mentally cursing the man who insisted on interfering with both her work and her life. The sound of a car cut into her eloquent swearing, and she turned, her hand shading her eyes from the sun, to watch the approaching vehicle wind down the long drive.

It halted a few yards from where she stood, and her mouth dropped open in amazement as a tall, fair man got out and began walking toward her.

"Tony!" she cried in surprise and pleasure, rushing across the grass to meet him.

His arms gripped her waist, and his lips covered hers in a brief but thorough kiss.

"What are you doing here?"

"I could say I was just in the neighborhood." He grinned down at her. "But I don't think you'd buy that." He paused and studied her face. "You look terrific," he decided, and bent to kiss her again, but she eluded him.

"Tony, you haven't answered me."

"The firm had some business to conduct in Paris," he explained. "So I flew over, and when I set things straight, I drove out here to see you."

"Two birds with one stone," she concluded wryly, feeling a vague disappointment. *It would have been nice,* she reflected, *if he had dropped his business and charged across the Atlantic because he couldn't bear to be parted from me.* But not Tony! She studied his good-looking, clear-cut features. *Tony's much too methodical for impulses, and that's been part of the problem.*

He brushed her brow with a casual kiss. "I missed you."

"Did you?"

He looked slightly taken aback. "Well, of course I did, Serenity." His arm slipped around her shoulders as he began walking toward her painting apparatus. "I'm hoping you'll come back with me."

"I'm not ready to go yet, Tony. I have commitments here. There are things I have to clear up before I can even think about going back."

"What things?" he asked with a frown.

"I can't explain, Tony," she evaded, unwilling to take him into her confidence. "But I've barely had time to know my grandmother; there are so many lost years to make up for."

"You can't expect to stay here for twenty-five years and make up for lost time." His voice was filled with exasperation. "You have friends back in Washington, a home, a career." He stopped and took her by the shoulders. "You know I want to marry you, Serenity. You've been putting me off for months."

"Tony, I never made any promises to you."

"Don't I know it." Releasing her, he stared around

in abstraction. With a pang of guilt, she tried harder to make him understand.

"I've found part of myself here. My mother grew up here; her mother still lives here." She turned and faced the château, making a wide, sweeping gesture. "Just look at it, Tony. Have you ever seen anything to compare with it?"

He followed her gaze and studied the large stone structure with another frown. "Very impressive," he stated without enthusiasm. "It's also huge, rambling, and, more than likely, drafty. Give me a brick house on P Street any day."

She sighed, deflated, then turning to her companion, smiled with affection. "Yes, you're right, you don't belong here."

"And you do?" The frown deepened.

"I don't know," she murmured, her eyes roaming over the conical roof and down to the courtyard. "I just don't know."

He studied her profile a moment, then strategically changed the subject. "Old Barkley had some papers for you." He referred to the attorney who had handled her parents' affairs and for whom he worked as a junior partner. "So instead of trusting them to the mail, I'm delivering them in person."

"Papers?"

"Yes, very confidential." He grinned in his familiar way. "Wouldn't give me a clue as to what they were about; just said it was important that you get them as soon as possible."

"I'll look at them later," she said in dismissal, having had enough of papers and technical forms since her parents' death. "You must come inside and meet my grandmother."

If Tony had been unimpressed with the château, he was overwhelmed by the countess. Serenity hid her smile as she introduced Tony to her grandmother, noting the widening of his eyes as he accepted the offered hand. She was, Serenity thought with silent satisfaction, magnificent. Leading Tony into the main drawing room, the countess ordered refreshments and proceeded to pump Tony in the most charming way for every ounce of information about himself. Serenity sat back and observed the maneuver, proud of her straight face.

He doesn't stand a chance, she decided as she poured tea from the elegant silver pot. Handing the dainty china cup to her grandmother, their eyes met. The unexpected mischief in the blue eyes almost caused a burst of laughter to escape, so she busied herself with the pouring of more tea with intense concentration.

The old schemer! she thought, surprised that she was not offended. *She's determining if Tony's a worthy candidate for her granddaughter's hand, and poor Tony is so awed by her magnificence, he doesn't see what's going on.*

At the end of an hour's conversation, the countess had learned Tony's life history: his family background, education, hobbies, career, politics, many details of which Serenity had been ignorant herself. The inquisition had been skillful, so subtly accomplished that Serenity suppressed the urge to stand and applaud when it was completed.

"When do you have to get back?" she asked, feeling she should save Tony from disclosing his bank balance.

"I have to leave first thing in the morning," he told her, relaxed and totally oblivious to the gentle third degree to which he had been subjected. "I wish I could stay longer, but…" He shrugged.

"*Bien sûr,* your work comes first," the countess finished for him, looking understanding. "You must dine with us tonight, Monsieur Rollins, and stay with us until morning."

"I couldn't impose on your hospitality, Madame," he objected, perhaps halfheartedly.

"Impose? Nonsense!" His objection was dismissed with a regal wave of the hand. "A friend of Serenity's from so far away—I would be deeply offended if you would refuse to stay with us."

"You are very kind. I'm grateful."

"It is my pleasure," the countess stated as she rose. "You must show your friend around the grounds, and I will see that a room is prepared for him." Turning to Tony, she extended her hand once more. "We have cocktails at seven-thirty, Monsieur Rollins. I will look forward to seeing you then."

Chapter 8

Serenity stood in front of the full-length mirror without seeing the reflection. The tall, slender woman in the amethyst gown, soft waves of crepe flowing like a jeweled breeze, might not have stared back from the highly polished glass. Serenity's mind was playing back the afternoon's events, her emotions running from pleasure, irritation, and disappointment to amusement.

After the countess had left them alone, Serenity had conducted Tony on a brief tour of the grounds. He had been vaguely complimentary about the garden, taking in its surface beauty, his logical, matter-of-fact mind unable to see beyond the roses and geraniums to the romance of hues and textures and scents. He was lightly amused by the appearance of the ancient gardener and slightly uncomfortable with the overwhelming spaciousness of the view from the terrace. He preferred, in his words, a few houses or at least a traffic light. Serenity had shaken her head at this in indulgent affection, but had realized how little she had in common with the man with whom she had spent so many months.

He was, however, completely overawed by the château's châtelaine. Anyone less like a grandmother, he had stated with great respect, he had never encountered. She was incredible, he had said, to which Serenity silently agreed, though perhaps for different reasons. She looked as if she belonged on a throne, indulgently granting audiences, and she had been so gracious, so interested in everything he had said. *Oh, yes,* Serenity had concurred silently, trying and failing to be indignant. *Oh yes, dear, gullible Tony, she had been vastly interested.* But what was the purpose of the game she was playing?

When Tony was settled in his room, strategically placed, Serenity noted, at the farthest end of the hall from herself, she had sought out her grandmother with the excuse of thanking her for inviting Tony to stay.

Seated in her room at an elegant Regency writing desk penning correspondence on heavy-crested stationery, the countess had greeted Serenity with an innocent smile, which somehow resembled the cat who swallowed the canary.

"Alors." She had put down her pen and gestured to a low brocade divan. "I hope your friend has found his room agreeable."

"Oui, Grandmère, I am very grateful to you for inviting Tony to stay for the night."

"Pas de quoi, ma chérie." The slender hand had gestured vaguely. "You must think of the château as your home, as well as mine."

"Merci, Grandmère," Serenity had said demurely, leaving the next move to the older woman.

"A very polite young man."

"*Oui,* Madame."

"Quite attractive…"—a slight pause—"…in an ordinary sort of way."

"*Oui,* Madame," Serenity had agreed conversationally, tossing the ball into her grandmother's court. The ball was received and returned.

"I have always preferred more unusual looks in a man, more strength and vitality. Perhaps"—a slight teasing curve of the lips—"more of the buccaneer, if you know what I mean."

"Ah, *oui,* Grandmère." Serenity had nodded, keeping a guileless open gaze on the countess. "I understand very well."

"*Bien.*" The slim shoulders had moved. "Some prefer a tamer male."

"So it would seem."

"Monsieur Rollins is a very intelligent, well-mannered man, very logical and earnest."

And dull. Serenity had added the unspoken remark before speaking aloud in annoyance. "He helps little old ladies across the street twice a day."

"Ah, a credit to his parents, I am sure," the countess had decided, either unaware or unperturbed by Serenity's mockery. "I am sure Christophe will be most pleased to meet him."

A faint glimmer of uneasiness had been born in Serenity's brain. "I'm sure he will."

"*Mais, oui.*" The countess smiled. "Christophe will be very interested to meet such a close friend of yours." The emphasis on "close" had been unmistakable, and Serenity's senses had sharpened as her uneasiness had grown.

"I fail to see why Christophe should be overly interested in Tony, Grandmère."

"Ah, *ma chérie,* I am sure Christophe will be fascinated by your Monsieur Rollins."

"Tony is not *my* Monsieur Rollins," Serenity had corrected, rising from the divan and advancing on her grandmother. "And I really don't see anything they have in common."

"No?" the countess asked with such irritating innocence that Serenity fought with amusement.

"You are a devious minx, Grandmère. What are you up to?"

Blue eyes met amber with the innocence of sweet childhood. "Serenity, *ma chérie,* I have no idea what you are talking about." As Serenity had opened her mouth to retort, the countess once more cloaked herself in her royalty. "I must finish my correspondence. I will see you this evening."

The command had been crystal clear, and Serenity had been forced to leave the room unsatisfied. The closing of the door with undue force had been her only concession to her rising temper.

Serenity's thoughts returned to the present. Slowly, her slim form, draped in amethyst, came into focus in the mirror. She smoothed her blond curls absently and erased the frown from her face. *We're going to play this very cool,* she informed herself as she fastened on pearl earrings. *Unless I am very much mistaken, my aristocratic grandmother would like to stir up some fireworks this evening, but she won't set off any sparks in this corner.*

She knocked on the door of Tony's room. "It's Serenity, Tony. If you're ready, I'll walk down with you." Tony's call bade her to enter, and she opened the door to see the tall, fair man struggling with a cufflink. "Having trouble?" she inquired with a wide grin.

"Very funny." He looked up from his task with a scowl. "I can't do anything lefthanded."

"Neither could my father," she stated with a quick, warm feeling of remembrance. "But he used to curse beautifully. It's amazing how many adjectives he used to describe a small pair of cufflinks." She moved to him and took his wrist in her hand. "Here, let me do it." She began to work the small object through his cuff. "Though what you would have done if I hadn't come along, I don't know." She shook her head and bent over his hand.

"I would have spent the evening with one hand thrust in my pocket," he answered smoothly. "Sort of a suave and continental stance."

"Oh, Tony." She looked up with a bright smile and shining eyes. "Sometimes you're positively cute."

A sound outside the door caught her attention, and she turned her head as Christophe walked by, paused for a moment to take in the intimate picture of the laughing woman fastening the man's cufflink, two fair heads close together. One dark brow raised fractionally, and with a small bow, Christophe continued on his way, leaving Serenity flushed and disconcerted.

"Who was that?" Tony asked with blatant curiosity, and she bent her head over his wrist to hide her burning cheeks.

"Le Comte de Kergallen," she answered with studied nonchalance.

"Not your grandmother's husband?" His voice was incredulous, and the question elicited a bright peal of laughter from Serenity, doing much to erase her tension.

"Oh, Tony, you are cute." She patted his wrist, the errant cufflink at last secured, and she looked up at him with sparkling eyes. "Christophe is the present count, and he's her grandson."

"Oh." Tony's brow creased in thought. "He's your cousin, then."

"Well…" She drew the word out slowly. "Not precisely." She explained the rather complicated family history and the resulting relationship between herself and the Breton count. "So, you see," she concluded, taking Tony's arm and walking from the room, "in a roundabout sort of way, we could be considered cousins."

"Kissing cousins," Tony observed with a definite frown.

"Don't be silly," she protested too quickly, unnerved by the memories of hard, demanding lips on hers.

If Tony noted the rushed denial and flushed cheeks, he made no comment.

They entered the drawing room arm in arm, and Serenity felt her flush deepen at Christophe's brief but encompassing appraisal. His face was smooth and unreadable, and she wished with sudden fervor that she could see the thoughts that lived behind his cool exterior.

Serenity watched his gaze shift to the man at her side, but his gaze remained impassive and correct.

"Ah, Serenity, Monsieur Rollins." The countess sat in the high-backed, richly brocaded chair framed by the massive stone fireplace, the image of a monarch receiving her subjects. Serenity wondered whether this placement had been deliberate or accidental. "Christophe, allow me to present Monsieur Anthony Rollins from America, Serenity's guest." The countess, Serenity noted with irony, had neatly categorized Tony as her personal property.

"Monsieur Rollins," she continued without breaking her rhythm, "allow me to present your host, Monsieur le Comte de Kergallen."

The title was emphasized delicately, and Christophe's

position as master of the château was established. Serenity shot her grandmother a knowing glance.

The two men exchanged formalities, and Serenity was observant enough to note the age-old routine of sizing up, like two male dogs gauging the adversary before entering into combat.

Christophe served his grandmother an *apéritif,* then inquired as to Serenity's pleasure before continuing with his duties with Tony. He echoed Serenity's request for vermouth, and she stifled a smile, knowing Tony's taste ran strictly to dry vodka martinis or an occasional brandy.

The conversation flowed smoothly, the countess inserting several of the facts pertaining to Tony's background he had so conveniently provided her with that afternoon.

"It is so comforting to know that Serenity is in such capable hands in America," she stated with a gracious smile, and continued, ignoring the scowl Serenity threw at her. "You have been friends for some time, *non?*" The faint hesitation, barely perceptible, on the words "friends" caused Serenity's scowl to deepen.

"Yes," Tony agreed, patting Serenity's hand with affection. "We met about a year ago at a dinner party. Remember, darling?" He turned to smile at her, and she erased her scowl quickly.

"Of course. The Carsons' party."

"Now you have traveled so far just for a short visit." The countess smiled with fond indulgence. "Was that not considerate, Christophe?"

"Most considerate." With a nod, he lifted his glass.

Why, you artful minx, Serenity thought irreverently. *You know very well Tony came on business. What are you up to?*

"Such a pity you cannot remain longer, Monsieur Rollins. It is pleasant for Serenity to have company from America. Do you ride?"

"Ride?" he repeated, baffled for a moment. "No, I'm afraid not."

"*C'est dommage.* Christophe has been teaching Serenity. How is your pupil progressing, Christophe?"

"*Très bien,* Grandmère," he answered easily, his gaze moving from his grandmother to Serenity. "She has a natural ability, and now that the initial stiffness has passed"—a fleeting smile appeared, and her color rose in memory—"we are progressing nicely, eh, *mignonne?*"

"Yes," she agreed, thrown off balance by the casual endearment after days of cool politeness. "I'm glad you persuaded me to learn."

"It has been my pleasure." His enigmatic smile only served to increase her confusion.

"Perhaps you in turn will teach Monsieur Rollins, Serenity, when you have the opportunity." The countess drew her attention, and amber eyes narrowed at the innocence of the tone.

The meddler! she fumed inwardly. *She's playing the two against each other, dangling me in the middle like a meaty bone.* Irritation transformed into reluctant amusement as the clear eyes met hers, a devil of mischief dancing in their depths.

"Perhaps, Grandmère, though I doubt I shall be able to make the jump from student to instructor for some time. Two brief lessons hardly make me an expert."

"But you shall have others, *n'est-ce pas?*" She tossed off Serenity's counterploy and rose with fluid grace. "Monsieur Rollins, would you be so kind as to escort me to dinner?"

Tony smiled, greatly flattered, and took the countess's

arm, though who was leading whom from the room was painfully obvious to the woman left behind.

"Alors, chérie." Christophe advanced on Serenity and held out his hand to assist her to her feet. "It seems you must make do with me."

"I guess I can just about bear it," she retorted, ignoring the furious thumping of her heart as his hand closed over hers.

"Your American must be very slow," he began conversationally, retaining her hand and towering over her in a distracting manner. "He has known you for nearly a year, and still he is not your lover."

Her face flamed, and she glared up at him, grasping at her dignity. "Really, Christophe, you surprise me. What an incredibly rude observation."

"But a true one," he returned, unperturbed.

"Not all men think exclusively of sex. Tony is a very warm and considerate person, not overbearing like some others I could name."

He only smiled with maddening confidence. "Does your Tony make your pulse race as it does now?" His thumb caressed her wrist. "Or your heart beat like this?" His hand covered the heart that galloped like a mad horse, and his lips brushed hers in a gentle, lingering kiss so unlike any of the others he had given her that she could only stand swaying with dazed sensations.

Lips feathered over her face, teasing the corners of her mouth, withholding the promise with the experience of seduction. Teeth nibbled at the lobe of her ear, and she sighed as the small spark of pain shot inestimable currents of pleasure along her skin, drugging her with delight and slow, smoldering desire. Lightly, his fingers traced the length of her spine, then moved with devastating laziness along the bare flesh of her back until she was pliant and yielding in his arms, her mouth seeking his for fulfillment. He gave her only a brief taste of his lips before they roamed to the hollow of her throat, and his hands moved slowly from curve to curve, fingers teasing but not taking the fullness of breast before they began a circling, gentle massage at her hips.

Murmuring his name, she went limp against him, unable to demand what she craved, starving for the mouth he denied her. Wanting only to be possessed, needing what only he could give, her arms pulled him closer in silent supplication.

"Tell me," Christophe murmured, and through mists of languor, she heard the light mockery of his tone. "Has Tony heard you sigh his name, or felt your bones melt against him as he held you so?"

Stunned, she jerked back convulsively from his embrace, anger and humiliation warring with desire. "You are overconfident, Monsieur," she choked. "It's none of your business how Tony makes me feel."

"You think not?" he asked in a politely inquiring tone. "We must discuss that later, *ma belle cousine*. Now I think we had best join Grandmère and our guest." He gave her an engaging and exasperating grin. "They may well wonder what has become of us."

They need not have concerned themselves, Serenity noted as she entered the dining room on Christophe's arm. The countess was entertaining Tony beautifully, currently discussing the collection of antique Fabergé boxes displayed on a large mirrored buffet.

The meal commenced with vichyssoise, cold and refreshing, the conversation continuing in English for Tony's benefit. Talk was general and impersonal, and Serenity felt herself relaxing, commanding her muscles to uncoil as the soup course was cleared and the *homard*

grillé was served. The lobster was nothing less than perfection, and she mused idly that, if the cook was indeed
a dragon, as Christophe had joked on that first day, she
was indeed a very skilled one.

"I imagine your mother made the transition from the
château to your house in Georgetown very easily, Serenity," Tony stated suddenly, and she regarded him with a
puzzled frown.

"I'm not sure I understand what you mean."

"There are so many basic similarities," he observed,
and as she continued to look blank, he elaborated. "Of
course, everything's on a much larger scale here, but there
are the high ceilings, the fireplaces in every room, the
style of furniture. Why, even the banisters on the stairs
are similar. Surely you noticed?"

"Why, yes, I suppose I did," she answered slowly,
"though I didn't realize it until now." Perhaps, she rea-
soned, her father had chosen the Georgetown house because he, too, had noted the similarities, and her mother
had selected the furnishings from the memories of her
childhood. The thought was somehow comforting. "Yes,
even the banisters," she continued aloud with a smile.
"I used to slide down them constantly, down from the
third-floor studio, smack into the newel post, then slide
to the ground floor and smack into the next one." The
smile turned into a laugh. "Maman used to say that another part of my anatomy must be as hard as my head to
take such punishment."

"She used to say the same to me," Christophe stated
suddenly, and Serenity's eyes flew to him in surprise.
"Mais oui, petite." He answered her look of surprise with
one of his rare, full smiles. "What is the sense of walking if one can slide?"

A picture of a small, dark boy flying down the smooth

rail, and her mother, young and lovely, watching and laughing, filled her mind. Her startled look faded slowly into a smile which mirrored Christophe's.

She helped herself to the raisin soufflé, light as a cloud, accompanied by a dry and sparkling champagne. She felt herself drifting through dinner in a warm, contented glow, happy to let the easy conversation flow around her.

When they moved to the drawing room after dinner, she decided to refuse the offer of a liqueur or brandy. The glow persisted, and she suspected that at least part of it (she was determined not to think about the other part and the quick, tantalizing embrace before dinner) was due to the wine served with each course. No one appeared to notice her bemused state, her flushed cheeks, and her almost mechanical answers. She found her senses almost unbearably sharpened as she listened to the music of the voices, the deep hum of the men's mingling with the lighter tones of her grandmother. She inhaled with sensuous pleasure the tangy smoke of Christophe's cheroot drifting toward her, and she breathed deeply of the women's mingled subtle perfumes overpowered by the sweet scent of the roses spilling from every porcelain vase. A pleasing balance, she decided, the artist in her responding to and enjoying the harmony, the fluid continuity of the scene. The soft lights, the night breeze gently lifting the curtains, the quiet clink of glasses being set on the table—all merged into an impressionistic canvas to be registered and stored in her mind's eye.

The dowager countess, magnificent on her brocade throne, presided, sipping crème de menthe from an exquisite gold-rimmed glass. Tony and Christophe were seated across from each other, like day and night, angel and devil. The last comparison brought Serenity up short.

Angel and Devil? she repeated silently, surveying the two men.

Tony—sweet, reliable, predictable Tony, who applied the gentlest pressure. Tony of the infinite patience and carefully thought-out plans. What did she feel for him? Affection, loyalty, gratitude for being there when she needed him. A mild, comfortable love.

Her eyes moved to Christophe. Arrogant, dominating, exasperating, exciting. Demanding what he wanted, and taking it, bestowing his sudden, unexpected smile and stealing her heart like a thief in the night. He was moody, whereas Tony was constant; imperious, whereas Tony was persuasive. But if Tony's kisses had been pleasant and stirring, Christophe's had been wildly intoxicating, turning her blood to fire and lifting her into an unknown world of sensation and desire. And the love she felt for him was neither mild nor comfortable, but tempestuous and inescapable.

"Such a pity you do not play the piano, Serenity." The countess's voice brought her back with a guilty jerk.

"Oh, Serenity plays, Madame," Tony informed her with a wide grin. "Dreadfully, but she plays."

"Traitor!" Serenity gave him a cheerful grin.

"You do not play well?" the countess was clearly incredulous.

"I'm sorry to bring disgrace to the family once again, Grandmère," Serenity apologized. "But not only do I not play well, I play quite miserably. I even offend Tony, who is absolutely tone deaf."

"You'd offend a corpse with your playing, darling." He brushed a lock of hair from her face in a gesture of casual intimacy.

"Quite true." She smiled at him before glancing at her grandmother. "Poor Grandmère, don't look so stricken."

Her smile faded somewhat as she met Christophe's frigid stare.

"But Gaelle played so beautifully," her grandmother countered with a gesture of her hand.

Serenity brought her attention back, attempting to shake off the chill of Christophe's eyes. "She could never understand the way I slaughtered music, either, but even with her abundant patience, she finally gave in and left me to my paints and easel."

"Extraordinaire!" The countess shook her head, and Serenity shrugged and sipped her coffee. "Since you cannot play for us, *ma petite,*" she began in a change of mood, "perhaps Monsieur Rollins would enjoy a tour of the garden." She smiled wickedly. "Serenity enjoys the garden in the moonlight, *n'est-ce pas?*"

"That sounds tempting," Tony agreed before Serenity could respond. Sending her grandmother a telling look, Serenity allowed herself to be led outside.

Chapter 9

For the second time Serenity strolled in the moonlit garden with a tall, handsome man, and for the second time she wished dismally that it was Christophe by her side. They walked in companionable silence, enjoying the fresh night air and the pleasure of familiar linked hands.

"You're in love with him, aren't you?"

Tony's question broke the stillness like a rock being hurled through glass, and Serenity stopped and stared up at him with wide eyes.

"Serenity." He sighed and brushed a finger down her cheek. "I can read you like a book. You're doing your best to hide it, but you're crazy about him."

"Tony, I…" she stammered, feeling guilty and miserable. "I never meant to. I don't even like him, really."

"Lord." He gave a soft laugh and a grimace. "I wish you didn't like me that way. But then," he added, cupping her chin, "you never have."

"Oh, Tony."

"You were never anything but honest, darling," he assured her. "You've nothing to feel guilty about. I thought that with constant, persistent diligence I would wear you down." He slipped an arm around her shoulders as they continued deeper into the garden. "You know, Serenity, your looks are deceptive. You look like a delicate flower, so fragile a man's almost afraid to touch you for fear you'll break, but you're really amazingly strong." He gave her a brief squeeze. "You never stumble, darling. I've been waiting for a year to catch you, but you never stumble."

"My moods and temper would have driven you over the edge, Tony." Sighing, she leaned against his shoulder. "I could never be what you needed, and if I tried to mold myself into something else, it wouldn't have worked. We'd have ended up hating each other."

"I know. I've known for a long time, but I didn't want to admit it." He let out a long breath. "When you left for Brittany, I knew it was over. That's why I came to see you; I had to see you one more time." His words sounded so final that she looked up in surprise.

"But we'll see each other again, Tony; we're still friends. I'll be coming back soon."

He stopped again and met her eyes, the silence growing long between them. "Will you, Serenity?" Turning, he led her back toward the lights of the château.

The sun was warm on her bare shoulders as Serenity said her goodbyes to Tony the next morning. He had already made his farewells to the countess and Christophe, and Serenity had walked with him from the coolness of the main hall to the warmth of the flagstone courtyard. The little red Renault waited for him, his luggage already secured in the boot, and he glanced at it briefly before turning to her, taking both of her hands in his.

"Be happy, Serenity." His grip tightened, then relaxed on her hands. "Think of me sometimes."

"Of course I'll think of you, Tony. I'll write and let you know when I'll be back."

He smiled down at her, his eyes roaming over her face, as if imprinting every detail in his memory. "I'll think of you just as you are today, in a yellow dress with the sun in your hair and a castle at your back—the everlasting beauty of Serenity Smith of the golden eyes."

He lowered his mouth to hers, and she was swamped by a sudden surge of emotion, a strong premonition that she would never see him again. She threw her arms around his neck and clung to him and to the past. His lips brushed her hair before he drew her away.

"Goodbye darling." He smiled and patted her cheek.

"Goodbye, Tony. Take care." She returned his smile, determinedly battling back the tears which burned her eyes.

She watched as he walked to the car and got in, and with a wave headed down the long, winding drive. The car became a small red dot in the distance and then gradually faded from sight, and she continued to stand, allowing the silent tears to have their freedom. An arm slipped around her waist, and she turned to see her grandmother standing beside her, sympathy and understanding in the angular face.

"You are sad to see him go, *ma petite?*" The arm was comforting, and Serenity leaned her head against the slim shoulder.

"*Oui,* Grandmère, very sad."

"But you are not in love with him." It was a statement rather than a question, and Serenity sighed.

"He was very special to me." Pushing a tear from her cheek, she gave a childish sniffle. "I shall miss him very much. Now, I shall go to my room and have a good cry."

"Oui, that is wise." The countess patted her shoulder. "Few things clear the brain and cleanse the heart like a good cry." Turning, Serenity enveloped her in a hug. *"Allez, vite, mon enfant."* The countess held her close for a moment before disengaging herself. "Go shed your tears."

Serenity ran up the stone steps and entered through the heavy oak doors into the coolness of the château. Rushing toward the main staircase, she collided with a hard object. Hands gripped her shoulders.

"You must watch where you are going, *ma chérie,"* Christophe's voice mocked. "You will be running into walls and damaging your beautiful nose." She attempted to pull away, but one hand held her in place without effort as another came under her chin to tilt back her head. At the sight of brimming eyes, the mockery faded, replaced by surprise, then concern, and lastly an unfamiliar helplessness. "Serenity?" Her name was a question, the tone gentle as she had not heard it before, and the tenderness in the dark eyes broke what little composure she could still lay claim to.

"Oh, please," she choked on a desperate sob, "let me go." She struggled from his grasp, striving not to crumble completely, yet wanting to be held close by this suddenly gentle man.

"Is there something I can do?" He detained her by placing a hand on her arm.

Yes, you idiot! her brain screamed. *Love me!* "No," she said aloud, running up the stairs. "No, no, no!"

She streaked up the stairs, like a golden doe pursued

by hunters, and finding her bedroom door, she opened it, then slammed it behind her, and threw herself on her bed.

The tears had worked their magic. Finally, Serenity was able to rinse them away and face the world and whatever the future had in store. She glanced at the manila envelope which she had tossed negligently on her bureau.

"Well, I suppose it's time to see what old Barkley sent me." Serenity got up reluctantly and went over to the bureau to pick up the envelope. She threw herself down on the bed again to break the seal, dumping its contents on the spread.

There was merely a page with the firm's impressive letterhead, which brought thoughts of Tony flooding back to her mind, and another sealed envelope. She picked up the neatly typewritten page listlessly, wondering what new form the family retainer had discovered for her to fill out. As she read the letter's contents, and the totally unexpected message it contained, she sat bolt upright.

Dear Miss Smith,

Enclosed you will find an envelope addressed to you containing a letter from your father. This letter was left in my care to be given to you only if you made contact with your mother's family in Brittany. It has come to my attention through Anthony Rollins that you are now residing at the Château Kergallen in the company of your maternal grandmother, so I am entrusting same to Anthony to be delivered to you at the earliest possible date.

Had you informed me of your plans, I would have carried out your father's wishes at an earlier date. I, of course, have no knowledge of its contents, but I am sure your father's message will bring you comfort.

M. Barkley

Serenity read no farther, but put the lawyer's letter aside and picked up the message her father had left in his care. She stared at the envelope which had fallen face down on the bed, and, turning it over, her eyes misted at seeing the familiar handwriting. She broke the seal. The letter was written in her father's bold, clear hand:

My own Serenity,
When you read this your mother and I will no lon-
ger be with you, and I pray you do not grieve too
deeply, for the love we feel for you remains true
and strong as life itself.
    As I write this, you are ten years old, already
the image of your mother, so incredibly lovely that
I am already fretting about the boys I will have to
fight off one day. I watched you this morning as you
sat sedately (a most unusual occupation for you,
as I am more used to seeing you skating down the
sidewalks at a horrifying speed or sliding without
thought to bruised skin down the banisters). You
sat in the garden, with my sketch book and a pen-
cil, drawing with fierce concentration the azaleas
that bloomed there. I saw in that moment, to both
my pride and despair, that you were growing up,
and would not always be my little girl, safe in the
security your mother and I had provided for you.
I knew then it was necessary to write down events
you might one day have the need to understand.
    I will give old Barkley (a small smile appeared

on Serenity's face as she noted that the attorney
had been known by that name even so many years
ago) *instructions to hold this letter for you until
such time as your grandmother, or some member
of your mother's family, makes contact with you. If
this does not occur, there will be no need to reveal
the secret your mother and I have already kept for
more than a decade.*

*I was painting on the sidewalks of Paris in the
full glory of spring, in love with the city and needing no mistress but my art. I was very young, and,
I am afraid, very intense. I met a man, Jean-Paul
le Goff, who was impressed by my, as he put it,
raw young talent. He commissioned me to paint a
portrait of his fiancée as a wedding present to her,
and arranged for me to travel to Brittany and re-
side in the Château Kergallen. My life began the
moment I entered that enormous hall and had my
first glimpse of your mother.*

*It was not my intention to act upon the love I felt
from the first moment I saw her, a delicate angel
with hair like sunlight. I tried with all my being to
put my art first. I was to paint her; she belonged to
my patron; she belonged to the château. She was
an angel, an aristocrat with a family lineage longer than time. All these things I told myself a hundred times. Jonathan Smith, itinerant artist, had no
right to possess her in dreams, let alone reality. At
times, when I made my preliminary sketches, I believed I would die for love of her. I told myself to
go, to make some excuse and leave, but I could not
find the courage. I thank God now that I could not.*

*One night, as I walked in the garden, I came
upon her. I thought to turn away before I disturbed*

*her, but she heard me, and when she turned, I saw
in her eyes what I had not dared dream. She loved
me. I could have shouted with the joy of it, but
there were so many obstacles. She was betrothed,
honor-bound to marry another man. We had no
right to our love. Does one need a right to love,
Serenity? Some would condemn us. I pray you do
not. After much talk and tears, we defied what some
would call right and honor, and we married. Gaelle
begged me to keep the marriage a secret until she
could find the right way to tell Jean-Paul and her
mother. I wanted the world to know, but I agreed.
She had given up so much for me, I could deny
her nothing.*

*During this time of waiting, a more disturbing
problem came to light. The countess, your grandmother, had in her possession a Raphael Madonna,
displayed in prominence in the main drawing room.
It was a painting, the countess informed me, which
had been in her family for generations. Next to
Gaelle, she treasured this painting above all things.
It seemed to symbolize to her the continuity of her
family, a shining beacon remaining constant after
the hell of war and loss. I had studied this painting closely and suspected it was a forgery. I said
nothing, at first thinking perhaps the countess herself had had a copy made for her own needs. The
Germans had taken so much from her—husband,
home—that perhaps they had taken the original
Raphael, as well. When she made the announcement that she had decided to donate the painting to
the Louvre in order to share its greatness, I nearly
froze with fear. I had grown fond of this woman,
her pride and determination, her grace and dig-*

nity. *I had no desire to see her hurt, and I realized
that she believed the painting to be authentic. I
knew Gaelle would be tormented by the scandal
if the painting was dismissed as a fraud, and the
countess would be destroyed. I could not let this
happen. I offered to clean the painting in order to
examine it more critically, and I felt like a traitor.*

*I took the painting to my studio in the tower, and
under close study, I had no doubt that it was a very
well-executed copy. Even then, I do not know what
I would have done, if it had not been for the letter
I found hidden behind the frame. The letter was
a confession from the countess's first husband, a
cry of despair for the treachery he had committed.
He confessed he had lost nearly all of his posses-
sions, and those of his wife. He was deep in debt,
and having decided the Germans would defeat the
Allies, he arranged to sell the Raphael to them. He
had a copy made and replaced the original without
the countess's knowledge, feeling the money would
see him through the hardship of war, and the deal
with the Germans would keep his estates secure.
Too late, he despaired of his action, and hiding
his confession in the frame of the copy, he went to
face the men he had dealt with in the hopes of returning the money. The note ended with his telling
of his intention, and pleading for forgiveness if he
proved unsuccessful.*

*As I finished reading the letter, Gaelle came
into the studio; I had not the foresight to bolt the
door. It was impossible to hide my reaction, or the
letter, which I still held in my hand, and so I was
forced to share the burden with the one person I
most wanted to spare. I found in those moments, in*

*that secluded tower room, that the woman I loved
was endowed with more strength than most men.
She would keep the knowledge from her mother at
all costs. She felt it imperative that the countess
be shielded from humiliation and the knowledge
that the painting she so prized was but forgery. We
devised a plan to conceal the painting, to make it
appear as if it had been stolen. Perhaps we were
wrong. To this day I do not know if we did the right
thing; but for your mother, there was no other way.
And so, the deed was done.*

*Gaelle's plans to tell her mother of our marriage
were soon forced into reality. She found, to our un-
ending joy, that she carried our child, you, the fruit
of our love that would grow to be the most important treasure of our lives. When she told her mother
of our marriage and her pregnancy, the countess
flew into a rage. It was her right to do, Serenity,
and the animosity she felt for me was well deserved
in her eyes. I had taken her daughter from her without her knowledge, and in doing so, I had placed a
mark on her family's honor. In her anger, she disowned Gaelle, demanded that we leave the château
and never enter again. I believe she would have
rescinded her decision in time; she loved Gaelle
above all things. But that same day she found the
Raphael missing. Putting two and two together, she
accused me of stealing both her daughter and her
family treasure. How could I deny it? One crime
was no worse than the other, and the message in
your mother's eyes begged me to keep silent. So
I took your mother away from the château, her
country, her family, her heritage, and brought her
to America.*

*We did not speak of her mother, for it brought
only pain, and we built our life fresh with you to
strengthen our bond. And now you have the story,
and with it, forgive me, the responsibility. Perhaps
by the time you read this, it will be possible to tell
the entire truth. If not, let it remain hidden, as the
forgery was hidden, away from the world with
something infinitely more precious to conceal it.
Do what your heart tells you.*

Your loving father.

Tears had fallen on the letter since its beginning, and
now as Serenity finished reading, she wiped them away
and took a long breath. Standing, she moved over to the
window and stared down at the garden where her parents
had first revealed their love.

"What do I do?" she murmured aloud, still gripping
the letter in her hand. *If I had read this a month ago, I
would have gone straight to the countess with it, but now
I don't know,* she told herself silently.

To clear her father's name, she would have to reveal
a secret kept hidden for twenty-five years. Would the
telling accomplish anything, or would it undo whatever
good the sacrifices made by both her parents had done?
Her father had instructed her to listen to her heart, but it
was so filled with the love and anguish of his letter that
she could hear nothing, and her mind was clouded with
indecision. There was a swift, fleeting impulse to go to
Christophe, but she quickly pushed it aside. To confide
in him would only make her more vulnerable, and the
separation she must soon deal with more agonizing.

She had to think, she decided, taking several deep
breaths. She had to clear away the fog and think clearly

and carefully, and when she found an answer, she had to be sure it was the right one.

Pacing the room, she halted suddenly and began changing her clothes in a frantic rush. She remembered the freedom and openness that had come to her when she rode through the woods, and it was this sensation, she determined, slipping on jeans and shirt, that she required to ease her heart and clear her brain.

Chapter 10

The groom greeted her request to saddle Babette doubt-fully. He argued, albeit respectfully, that he had no orders from the count to go riding, and for once Serenity used her aristocratic heritage and haughtily informed him that as the countess's granddaughter, she was not to be questioned. The groom submitted, with a faint muttering of Breton, and she was soon mounted on the now-familiar mare and setting off on the path Christophe had taken on her first lesson.

The woods were quiet and comforting, and she emptied her mind in the hopes that the answer would then find room to make an appearance. She walked the mare easily for a time, finding it simple now to retain command of the animal while still feeling a part of it. She found herself no closer to resolving her problem, however, and urged Babette into a canter.

They moved swiftly, the wind blowing her hair back

from her face and engulfing her once more with the sense of freedom which she sought. Her father's letter was tucked into her back pocket, and she decided to ride to the hill overlooking the village and read it once more, hoping by then to find the wisdom to make the right decision.

A shout rang out behind her, and she turned in the saddle to see Christophe coming after her astride the black stallion. As she turned, her foot connected sharply with the mare's side, and Babette took this as a command and streaked forward in a swift gallop. Serenity was nearly unseated in surprise, and she struggled to right herself as the horse raced down the path with unaccustomed speed. At first all of her attention was given to the problem of remaining astride, not even contemplating the mechanics of halting the mare's headlong rush. Before her brain had the opportunity to communicate with her hands and give them the idea to rein in, Christophe came alongside her. Then, reaching over, he pulled back on her reins, uttering a stream of oaths in a variety of languages.

Babette came to a docile halt, and Serenity's eyes closed in relief. The next thing she knew, she was gripped around the waist and dragged from the saddle without ceremony, with Christophe's dark eyes burning into hers.

"What do you hope to accomplish by running away from me?" he demanded, shaking her like a rag doll.

"I was doing no such thing," she protested through teeth that chattered at the movement. "I must have startled the horse when I turned around." Her own anger began to replace relief. "It wouldn't have happened if you hadn't come chasing after me." She began to struggle away, but his grip increased with painful emphasis. "You're hurting me!" she stormed at him. "Why must you always hurt me?"

"You would find a broken neck more painful, *ma petite folle,*" he stated, dragging her farther down the path and away from the horses. "That is what could have happened to you. What do you mean by riding off unescorted?"

"Unescorted?" she repeated with a laugh, jerking away from him. "How quaint. Aren't women allowed to ride unescorted in Brittany?"

"Not women who have no brains," he returned with dark fury, "and who have been on a horse only twice before in their lives."

"I was going very well before you came." She tossed her head at his logic. "Now just go away and leave me alone." She watched as his eyes narrowed, and he took a step toward her. "Go away!" she shouted, backing up. "I want my privacy. I have things to think about."

"I will give you something else to think about."

He moved swiftly, gripping her behind the neck and stealing her breath with his lips. She pushed against him without success, fighting both him and the whirling dizziness which flew to her brain. Gripping her shoulders, he drew her away, his fingers digging into her flesh.

"Enough! *C'est entendu!*" He shook her again, and she saw by his face that the aristocrat had fled and there was only the man. "I want you. I want what no man has had before—and, by God, I *will* have you."

He swept her up into his arms, and she struggled with a wild, primitive fear, beating against his chest like a trapped bird beating against the bars of its cage, but his stride remained steady and sure, as though he carried a complaisant child rather than a terrified woman.

Then she was on the ground, with his body crushing down on hers, his mouth savaging hers like a man possessed, her protests making no more of a ripple than a pebble tossed into the ocean. With a swift, violent motion, her blouse was opened, and he claimed her naked skin with bruising fingers, his lovemaking filled with a desperate urgency which conquered all thought of resistance, all will to struggle.

Struggle became demand, and her mouth became mobile and seeking under his; the hands which had previously pushed him away were now pulling him closer. Drowned in the deluge of passion, she reveled in the intimacy of his masculine hardness, her body moving with the ageless rhythm of instinct beneath him. Urgent and without restraint, his hands traced trails of heat along her naked flesh, his mouth following the blaze, returning again and again to drink from hers. Each time, his thirst grew, his demands taking her into a new and timeless world, the border between heaven and hell, where only one man and one woman can exist.

Deeper and deeper he led her, until pleasure and pain merged into one spiraling sensation, one all-consuming need. Helpless under the barrage of shimmering passion, the trembling began slowly, growing more intense as the journey took her further from the known and closer to the unexperienced. With a moan mixed with fear and desire, her fingers clutched at his shoulders, as if to keep from plummeting into an eternal void.

His mouth left hers suddenly, and with his breath uneven, his cheek rested against her brow for a moment before he lifted his head and looked down at her.

"I am hurting you again, *ma petite*." He sighed and rolled off her to lie on his back. "I tossed you on the ground and nearly ravished you like a barbarian. I seem to find it difficult to control my baser instincts with you."

She sat up quickly, fumbling with the buttons of her blouse with unsteady fingers. "It's all right." She at-

tempted but failed to produce a careless-sounding voice.
"No harm done. I've often been told how strong I am.
You must learn to temper your technique a bit, though,"
she babbled on to hide the extent of her pain. "Geneviève
is more fragile than I."

"Geneviève?" he repeated, lifting himself on his elbow
to look at her directly. "What has Geneviève to do with
this?"

"With this?" she answered. "Oh, nothing. I have no
intention of saying anything to her of this. I'm quite fond
of her."

"Perhaps we should speak in French, Serenity. I am
having difficulty understanding you."

"She's in love with you, you big idiot!" she blurted out,
ignoring his request for French. "She told me; she came
asking for my advice." She controlled the short burst of
hysterical laughter which escaped her. "She asked for
my advice," she elaborated, "on how to make you see
her as a woman instead of a child. I didn't tell her what
your opinion was of me; she wouldn't have understood."

"She told you she was in love with me?" he demanded,
his eyes narrowing.

"Not by name," she said shortly, wishing the conversation had never begun. "She said she had been in love
with a man all of her life, and he regarded her as a child.
I simply told her to set him straight, tell him that she was
a woman, and… What are you laughing at?"

"You thought she spoke of me?" He was once more
flat on his back and laughing more freely than she had
ever seen. "Little Geneviève in love with me!"

"How dare you laugh at her! How can you be so callous as to make fun of someone who loves you?" He
caught her fists before they made contact with his chest.

"Geneviève did not seek you out for advice about

me, *chérie*." He continued to hold her off without effort. "She was speaking of Iann. But you have not met Iann, have you, *mon amour?*" He ignored her furious struggles and continued to speak with a wide grin. "We grew up together—Iann, Yves, and I—with Geneviève trailing along like a little puppy. Yves and I remained her 'brothers' after she grew into a woman, but it was Iann she truly loved. He has been in Paris on business for the last month, only returning home yesterday." A small jerk of his wrists brought her down on his chest. "Geneviève called this morning to tell me of their engagement. She also told me to thank you for her, and now I know why." His grin increased as amber eyes grew wide.

"She's engaged? It wasn't you?"

"Yes, she is; and no, it was not," he answered helpfully. "Tell me, *ma belle cousine,* were you jealous when you thought Geneviève to be in love with me?"

"Don't be ridiculous," she lied, attempting to remove her mouth from its proximity to his. "I would be no more jealous of Geneviève than you would be of Yves."

"Ah." In one swift movement he had reversed their positions and lay looking down at her. "Is that so? And should I tell you that I was nearly consumed with jealousy of my friend Yves, and that I very nearly murdered your American Tony? You would give them smiles that should be mine. From the moment I saw you step off the train, I was lost, bewitched, and I fought it as a man fights that which threatens to enslave him. Perhaps this slavery is freedom." His hand moved through the silk of her hair. "Ah, Serenity, *je t'aime.*"

She swallowed in the search for her voice. "Would you say that again?"

He smiled, and his mouth teased hers for a moment. "In English? I love you. I loved you from the moment I saw you, I love you infinitely more now, and I will love you for the rest of my life." His lips descended on hers, moving them with a tenderness he had never shown, lifting only when he felt the moistness of her tears. "Why do you weep?" he questioned, his brow creasing in exasperation. "What have I done?"

She shook her head. "It's only that I love you so much, and I thought..." She hesitated and let out a long breath. "Christophe, do you believe my father was innocent, or do you think me to be the daughter of a thief?"

His brow creased again with a frown, and he studied her silently. "I will tell you what I know, Serenity, and I will tell you what I believe. I know that I love you, not just the angel who stepped off the train at Lannion, but the woman I have come to know. It would make no difference if your father was a thief, a cheat, or a murderer. I have heard you speak of your father, and I have seen how you look when you tell of him. I cannot believe that a man who earned this love and devotion could have committed such a crime. This is what I believe, but it does not matter; nothing he did or did not do could change my love for you."

"Oh, Christophe," she whispered, pulling his cheek down to hers, "I've waited all my life for someone like you. There is something I must show you." She pushed him away gently, taking the letter from her pocket and handing it to him. "My father told me to listen to my heart, and now it belongs to you."

Serenity sat across from him, watching his face as he read, and she felt a deep peace, a contentment she had not known since her parents had been taken from her. Love for him filled her, along with a strong sense of security that he would help her to make the right decision. The woods were silent, tranquil, disturbed only by the whisper of wind through the leaves, and the birds that answered it. For a moment, it was a place out of time, inhabited only by man and woman.

When he had finished reading the letter, Christophe lifted his eyes from the paper and met hers. "Your father loved your mother very much."

"Yes."

He folded the letter, replacing it in its envelope, his eyes never leaving hers. "I wish I had known him. I was only a child when he came to the château, and he did not stay long."

Her eyes clung to his. "What should we do?"

He moved nearer, taking her face in his hands. "We must take the letter and show it to Grandmère."

"But they're dead, and she's alive. I love her; I don't want to hurt her."

He bent down and kissed shimmering lashes. "I love you, Serenity, for so many reasons, and you have just given me one more." He tilted her head so their eyes met again. "Listen to me now, *mon amour,* and trust me. Grandmère needs to see this letter, for her own peace of mind. She believes her daughter betrayed her, stole from her. She has lived with this for twenty-five years. This letter will set her free. She will read in your father's words the love Gaelle had for her, and, equally important, she will see the love your father had for her daughter. He was an honorable man, but he lived with the fact that his wife's mother thought him to be a thief. The time has come to set them all free."

"All right," she agreed. "If you say this is what we must do, this is what we will do."

He smiled, and taking both her hands in his, he lifted them to his lips before helping her to her feet. "Tell me,

cousine"—the familiar mocking smile was in place—
"will you always do as I say?"

"No," she answered with a vigorous shake of her head.
"Absolutely not."

"Ah, I thought not." He led her to the horses. "Life will
not be dull." He took the reins of the buckskin in his hand,
and she mounted without assistance. He frowned as he
handed her the reins. "You are disturbingly independent,
stubborn, and impulsive, but I love you."

"And you," she commented, as he moved to mount
the stallion, "are arrogant, overbearing, and irritatingly
confident, but I love you, as well."

They reached the stables. After relinquishing the
horses to a groom, they set off toward the château with
linked hands. As they approached the garden entrance,
Christophe stopped and turned to her.

"You must give this to Grandmère yourself, Serenity." He took the envelope from his pocket and handed
it to her.

"Yes, I know." She looked down at it as he placed it
in her hand. "But you will stay with me?"

"Oui, ma petite." He drew her into his arms. "I will
stay with you." His mouth met hers, and she threw her
arms around his neck until the kiss deepened, and they
were only aware of each other.

"Alors, mes enfants." The countess's words broke the
spell, and they both turned to see her watching them
from the edge of the garden. "You have decided to stop
fighting the inevitable."

"You are very clever, Grandmère," Christophe commented with a lift of his brow. "But I believe we would
have managed even without your invaluable assistance."

Elegant shoulders moved expressively. "But you might

have wasted too much time, and time is a precious commodity."

"Come inside, Grandmère. Serenity has something to show you."

They entered the drawing room, and the countess seated herself in her regular thronelike chair. "What is it you have to show me, *ma petite?*"

"Grandmère," Serenity said as she began moving in front of the countess, "Tony brought me some papers from my attorney. I didn't even bother to open them until he left, but I found when I did that they were much more important than I had anticipated." She held out the letter. "Before you read this, I want you to know I love you." The countess opened her mouth to speak, but Serenity hurried on. "I love Christophe, and before he read what I'm giving you, he told me he loved me, as well. I can't tell you how wonderful it was to know that before he saw this letter. We decided to share this with you because we love you." She handed the letter to her grandmother and then seated herself on the sofa. Christophe joined her, and he took her hand in his as they waited.

Serenity's eyes were drawn to her mother's portrait, the eyes that met hers full of joy and happiness, the expression of a woman in love. *I have found it, too, Maman,* she spoke silently, *the overwhelming joy of love, and I hold it here in my hand.*

She dropped her eyes to the joined hands, the strong bronzed fingers intertwined with the alabaster ones, the ruby ring which had been her mother's glowing against the contrasting colors. She stared at the ring on her own hand, then raised her eyes to the replica on her mother's, and she understood. The countess's movement as she rose from her chair interrupted Serenity's thoughts.

"For twenty-five years I have wronged this man, and

the daughter whom I loved." The words were soft as she turned to gaze out the window. "My pride blinded me and hardened my heart."

"You were not to know, Grandmère," Serenity replied, watching the straight back. "They wanted only to protect you."

"To protect me from the knowledge that my husband had been a thief, and from the humiliation of public scandal, your father allowed himself to be branded, and my daughter gave up her heritage." Moving back to the chair, she sank down wearily. "I sense from your father's words a great feeling of love. Tell me, Serenity, was my daughter happy?"

"You see the eyes as my father painted them." She gestured to the portrait. "She looked always as she looked then."

"How can I forgive myself for what I did?"

"Oh, no, Grandmère." Serenity rose and knelt in front of her, taking the fragile hands in her own. "I didn't give you the letter to add to your grief, but to take it from you. You read the letter; you see that they blamed you for nothing; they purposely allowed you to believe that they betrayed you. Maybe they were wrong, but it's done, and there can be no going back." She gripped the narrow hands tighter. "I tell you now that I blame you for nothing, and I beg you, for my sake, to let the guilt die."

"Ah, Serenity, *ma chère enfant.*" The countess's voice was as tender as her eyes. *"C'est bien,"* she said briskly, drawing her shoulders up straight once more. "We will remember only the happy times. You will tell me more of Gaelle's life with your father in this Georgetown, and you will bring them both close to me again, *n'est-ce pas?*"

"Oui, Grandmère."

"Perhaps one day you will take me to the house where you grew up."

"To America?" Serenity asked, deeply shocked. "Wouldn't you be afraid to travel to so uncivilized a country?"

"You are being impudent again," the countess stated regally as she rose from her chair. "I begin to believe I will come to know your father very well through you, *mignonne*." She shook her head. "When I think of what I allowed that painting to cost me! I am well pleased to be rid of it."

"You still have the copy, Grandmère," Serenity corrected. "I know where it is."

"How do you know this?" Christophe asked, speaking for the first time since they had entered the room.

She turned to him and smiled. "It was right there in the letter, but I didn't realize it at first. It was when we were sitting together just now, and you held my hand, that it came to me. Do you see this?" She held out her hand where the ruby gleamed. "It was my mother's, the same she wears in the portrait."

"I had noticed the ring in the painting," the countess said slowly, "but Gaelle had no such ring. I thought your father merely painted it to match the earrings she wore."

"She had the ring, Grandmère; it was her engagement ring. She wore it always with her wedding band on her left hand."

"But what has this to do with the copy of the Raphael?" Christophe questioned with a frown.

"In the painting she wears the ring on her right hand. My father would never have made such a mistake in detail unless he did it intentionally."

"It is possible," the countess murmured.

"I know it's there; it says so in the letter. He says he

concealed it, covered by something infinitely more precious. Nothing was more precious to him than Maman."

"Oui," the countess agreed, studying the painting of her daughter. "There could be no safer hiding place."

"I have some solution," Serenity began. "I could uncover a corner; then you could be sure."

"Non." She shook her head. *"Non,* there is no need. I would not have you mar one inch of your father's work if the true Raphael were under it." She turned to Serenity and lifted a hand to her cheek. "This painting, Christophe, and you, *mon enfant,* are my treasures now. Let it rest. It is where it belongs." She turned back to her grandchildren with a smile. "I will leave you now. Lovers should have their privacy."

She left the room with the air of a queen, and Serenity watched her in admiration. "She's magnificent, isn't she?"

"Oui," Christophe agreed easily, taking Serenity into his arms. "And very wise. I have not kissed you for more than an hour."

After he had remedied the discrepancy to their mutual satisfaction, he looked down at her with his habitual air of confidence. "After we are married, *mon amour,* I will have your portrait painted, and we will add still another treasure to the château."

"Married?" Serenity repeated with a frown. "I never agreed to marry you." She pushed away as though reluctant. "You can't just order me to do so; a woman likes to be asked." He pulled her against him and kissed her thoroughly, his lips hard and insistent.

"You were saying, *cousine?*" he asked when he freed her.

She regarded him seriously, but allowed her arms to twine around his neck. "I shall never be an aristocrat."

"Heaven forbid," he agreed with sincerity.

"We shall fight often, and I will constantly infuriate you."

"I shall look forward to it."

"Very well," she said, managing to keep a smile from her lips. "I will marry you—on one condition."

"And that is?" His brow raised in question.

"That you walk in the garden with me tonight." She drew her arms around him tighter. "I'm so tired of walking in the moonlight with other men and wishing they were you."

* * * * *

THE RIGHT PATH

Chapter 1

The sky was cloudless—the hard, perfect blue of a summer painting. A breeze whispered through the roses in the garden. Mountains were misted by distance. A scent—flowers, sea, new grass—drifted on the air. With a sigh of pure pleasure, Morgan leaned farther over the balcony rail and just looked.

Had it really only been yesterday morning that she had looked out on New York's steel and concrete? Had she run through a chill April drizzle to catch a taxi to the airport? One day. It seemed impossible to go from one world to another in only a day.

But she was here, standing on the balcony of a villa on the Isle of Lesbos. There was no gray drizzle at all, but strong Greek sunlight. There was quiet, a deep blanketing stillness that contrasted completely with the fits and starts of New York traffic. If I could paint, Morgan mused, I'd paint this view and call it *Silence*.

"Come in," she called when there was a knock on the door. After one last deep breath, she turned, reluctantly.

"So, you're up and dressed." Liz swept in, a small, golden fairy with a tray-bearing maid in her wake.

"Room service." Morgan grinned as the maid placed the tray on a glass-topped table. "I'll begin to wallow in luxury from this moment." She took an appreciative sniff of the platters the maid uncovered. "Are you joining me?"

"Just for coffee." Liz settled in a chair, smoothing the skirts of her silk and lace robe, then took a long survey of the woman who sat opposite her.

Long loose curls in shades from ash blond to honey brown fell to tease pale shoulders. Almond-shaped eyes, almost too large for the slender face, were a nearly transparent blue. There was a straight, sharp nose and prominent cheekbones, a long, narrow mouth and a subtly pointed chin. It was a face of angles and contours that many a model starved herself for. It would photograph like a dream had Morgan ever been inclined to sit long enough to be captured on film.

What you'd get, Liz mused, would be a blur of color as Morgan dashed away to see what was around the next corner.

"Oh, Morgan, you look fabulous! I'm so glad you're here at last."

"Now that I'm here," Morgan returned, shifting her eyes back to the view, "I can't understand why I put off coming for so long. *Efxaristo,*" she added as the maid poured her coffee.

"Show-off," Liz said with mock scorn. "Do you know how long it took me to master a simple Greek hello, how are you? No, never mind." She waved her hand before Morgan could speak. The symphony of diamonds and sapphires in her wedding ring caught the flash of sunlight. "Three years married to Alex and living in Athens and Lesbos, and I still stumble over the language. Thank you, Zena," she added in English, dismissing the maid with a smile.

"You're simply determined not to learn." Morgan bit enthusiastically into a piece of toast. She wasn't hungry, she discovered. She was ravenous. "If you'd open your mind, the words would seep in."

"Listen to you." Liz wrinkled her nose. "Just because you speak a dozen languages."

"Five."

"Five is four more than a rational person requires."

"Not a rational interpreter," Morgan reminded her and dug wholeheartedly into her eggs. "And if I hadn't spoken Greek, I wouldn't have met Alex and you wouldn't be *Kryios* Elizabeth Theoharis. Fate," she announced with a full mouth, "is a strange and wonderful phenomenon."

"Philosophy at breakfast," Liz murmured into her coffee. "That's one of the things I've missed about you. Actually, I'd hate to think what might have happened if I hadn't been home on layover when Alex popped up. You wouldn't have introduced us." She commandeered a piece of toast, adding a miserly dab of plum jelly. "I'd still be serving miniature bottles of bourbon at thirty thousand feet."

"Liz, my love, when something's meant, it's meant." Morgan cut into a fat sausage. "I'd love to take credit for your marital bliss, but one brief introduction wasn't responsible for the fireworks that followed." She glanced up at the cool blond beauty and smiled. "Little did I know I'd lose my roommate in less than three weeks. I've never seen two people move so fast."

"We decided we'd get acquainted after we were married." A grin warmed Liz's face. "And we have."

"Where is Alex this morning?"

"Downstairs in his office." Liz moved her shoulders absently and left half her toast untouched. "He's building another ship or something."

Morgan laughed outright. "You say that in the same tone you'd use if he were building a model train. Don't you know you're supposed to become spoiled and disdainful when you marry a millionaire—especially a foreign millionaire?"

"Is that so? Well, I'll see what I can do." She topped off her coffee. "He'll probably be horribly busy for the next few weeks, which is one more reason I'm glad you're here."

"You need a cribbage partner."

"Hardly," Liz corrected as she struggled with a smile. "You're the worst cribbage player I know."

"Oh, I don't know," Morgan began as her brows drew together.

"Perhaps you've improved. Anyway," Liz went on, concealing with her coffee cup what was now a grin, "not to be disloyal to my adopted country, but it's just so good to have my best friend, and an honest-to-God American, around."

"*Spasibo.*"

"English at all times," Liz insisted. "And I know that wasn't even Greek. You aren't translating government hyperbole at the U.N. for the next four weeks." She leaned forward to rest her elbows on the table. "Tell me the truth, Morgan, aren't you ever terrified you'll interpret some nuance incorrectly and cause World War III?"

"Who me?" Morgan opened her eyes wide. "Not a chance. Anyway, the trick is to think in the language you're interpreting. It's that easy."

"Sure it is." Liz leaned back. "Well, you're on vacation, so you only have to think in English. Unless you want to argue with the cook."

"Absolutely not," Morgan assured her as she polished off her eggs.

"How's your father?"

"Marvelous, as always." Relaxed, content, Morgan poured more coffee. When was the last time she had taken the time for a second cup in the morning? Vacation, Liz had said. Well, she was damn well going to learn how to enjoy one. "He sends you his love and wants me to smuggle some ouzo back to New York."

"I'm not going to think about you going back." Liz rose and swirled around the balcony. The lace border at the hem of her robe swept over the tile. "I'm going to find a suitable mate for you and establish you in Greece."

"I can't tell you how much I appreciate your handling things for me," Morgan returned dryly.

"It's all right. What are friends for?" Ignoring the sarcasm, Liz leaned back on the balcony. "Dorian's a likely candidate. He's one of Alex's top men and really attractive. Blond and bronzed with a profile that belongs on a coin. You'll meet him tomorrow."

"Should I tell Dad to arrange my dowry?"

"I'm serious." Folding her arms, Liz glared at Morgan's grin. "I'm not letting you go back without a fight. I'm going to fill your days with sun and sea, and dangle hordes of gorgeous men in front of your nose. You'll forget that New York and the U.N. exist."

"They're already wiped out of my mind…for the next four weeks." Morgan tossed her hair back over her shoulders. "So, satiate and dangle. I'm at your mercy. Are you going to drag me to the beach this morning? Force me to lie on the sand and soak up rays until I have a fabulous golden tan?"

"Exactly." With a brisk nod, Liz headed for the door. "Change. I'll meet you downstairs."

Thirty minutes later, Morgan decided she was going to like Liz's brand of brainwashing. White sand, blue water. She let herself drift on the gentle waves. *Too wrapped up in your work.* Isn't that what Dad said? *You're letting the job run you instead of the other way around.* Closing her eyes, Morgan rolled to float on her back. Between job pressure and the nasty breakup with Jack, she mused, I need a peace transfusion.

Jack was part of the past. Morgan was forced to admit that he had been more a habit than a passion. They'd suited each other's requirements. She had wanted an intelligent male companion; he an attractive woman whose manners would be advantageous to his political career.

If she'd loved him, Morgan reflected, she could hardly think of him so objectively, so…well, coldly. There was no ache, no loneliness. What there was, she admitted, was relief. But with the relief had come the odd feeling of being at loose ends. A feeling Morgan was neither used to nor enjoyed.

Liz's invitation had been perfectly timed. And this, she thought, opening her eyes to study that perfect sweep of sky, was paradise. Sun, sand, rock, flowers—the whispering memory of ancient gods and goddesses. Mysterious Turkey was close, separated only by the narrow Gulf of Edremit. She closed her eyes again and would have dozed if Liz's voice hadn't disturbed her.

"Morgan! Some of us have to eat at regular intervals."

"Always thinking of your stomach."

"And *your* skin," Liz countered from the edge of the water. "You're going to fry. You can overlook lunch, but not sunburn."

"All right, Mommy." Morgan swam in, then stood

on shore and shook like a wet dog. "How come you can swim and lie in the sun and still look ready to walk into a ballroom?"

"Breeding," Liz told her and handed over the short robe. "Come on, Alex usually tears himself away from his ships for lunch."

I could get used to eating on terraces, Morgan thought after lunch was finished. They relaxed over iced coffee and fruit. She noted that Alexander Theoharis was still as fascinated with his small, golden wife as he had been three years before in New York.

Though she'd brushed off Liz's words that morning, Morgan felt a certain pride at having brought them together. A perfect match, she mused, Alex had an Old World charm—dark aquiline looks made dashing by a thin white scar above his eyebrow. He was only slightly above average height but with a leanness that was more aristocratic than rangy. It was the ideal complement for Liz's dainty blond beauty.

"I don't see how you ever drag yourself away from here," Morgan told him. "If this were all mine, nothing would induce me to leave."

Alex followed her gaze across the glimpse of sea to the mountains. "But when one returns, it's all the more magnificent. Like a woman," he continued, lifting Liz's hand to kiss, "paradise demands constant appreciation."

"It's got mine," Morgan stated.

"I'm working on her, Alex." Liz laced her fingers with his. "I'm going to make a list of all the eligible men within a hundred miles."

"You don't have a brother, do you, Alex?" Morgan asked, sending him a smile.

"Sisters only. My apologies."

"Forget it, Liz."

"If we can't entice you into matrimony, Alex will have to offer you a job in the Athens office."

"I'd steal Morgan from the U.N. in a moment," Alex reminded her with a move of his shoulders. "I couldn't lure her away three years ago. I tried."

"We have a month to wear her down this time." She shot Alex a quick glance. "Let's take her out on the yacht tomorrow."

"Of course." He agreed immediately. "We'll make a day of it. Would you like that, Morgan?"

"Oh, well, I'm constantly spending the day on a yacht on the Aegean, but"—her lake-blue eyes lit with laughter—"since Liz wants to, I'll try not to be too bored."

"She's such a good sport," Liz confided to Alex.

It was just past midnight when Morgan made her way down to the beach again. Sleep had refused to come. Morgan welcomed the insomnia, seeing it as an excuse to walk out into the warm spring night.

The light was liquid. The moon was sliced in half but held a white, gleaming brightness. Cypresses which flanked the steps down to the beach were silvered with it. The scent of blossoms, hot and pungent during the day, seemed more mysterious, more exotic, by moonlight.

From somewhere in the distance, she heard the low rumble of a motor. A late-night fisherman, she thought, and smiled. It would be quite an adventure to fish under the moon.

The beach spread in a wide half circle. Morgan dropped both her towel and wrap on a rock, then ran into the water. Against her skin it was so cool and silky that she toyed with the idea of discarding even the brief bikini. Better not, she thought with a low laugh. No use tempting the ghosts of the gods.

Though the thought of adventure appealed to her, she kept to the open bay and suppressed the urge to explore the inlets. They'd still be there in the daylight, she reminded herself. She swam lazily, giving her strokes just enough power to keep her afloat. She hadn't come for the exercise.

Even when her body began to feel the chill, she lingered. There were stars glistening on the water, and silence. Such silence. Strange, that until she had found it, she hadn't known she was looking for it.

New York seemed more than a continent away; it seemed centuries away. For the moment, she was content that it be so. Here she could indulge in the fantasies that never seemed appropriate in the rush of day-to-day living. Here she could let herself believe in ancient gods, in shining knights and bold pirates. A laugh bubbled from her as she submerged and rose again. Gods, knights, and pirates...well, she supposed she'd take the pirate if she had her pick. Gods were too bloodthirsty, knights too chivalrous, but a pirate...

Shaking her head, Morgan wondered how her thoughts had taken that peculiar turn. It must be Liz's influence, she decided. Morgan reminded herself she didn't want a pirate or any other man. What she wanted was peace.

With a sigh, she stood knee-deep in the water, letting the drops stream down her hair and skin. She was cold now, but the cold was exhilarating. Ignoring her wrap, she sat on the rock and pulled a comb from its pocket and idly ran it through her hair. Moon, sand, water. What more could there be? She was, for one brief moment, in total harmony with her own spirit and with nature's.

Shock gripped her as a hand clamped hard over her mouth. She struggled, instinctively, but an arm was banded around her waist—rough cloth scraping her naked skin. Dragged from the rock, Morgan found herself molded against a solid, muscular chest.

Rape? It was the first clear thought before the panic. She kicked out blindly as she was pulled into the cover of trees. The shadows were deep there. Fighting wildly, she raked with her nails wherever she could reach, feeling only a brief satisfaction at the hiss of an undrawn breath near her ear.

"Don't make a sound." The order was in quick, harsh Greek. About to strike out again, Morgan felt her blood freeze. A glimmer of knife caught the moonlight just before she was thrust to the ground under the length of the man's body. "Wildcat," he muttered. "Keep still and I won't have to hurt you. Do you understand?"

Numb with terror, Morgan nodded. With her eyes glued to his knife, she lay perfectly still. *I can't fight him now,* she thought grimly. *Not now, but somehow, somehow I'll find out who he is. He'll pay.*

The first panic was gone, but her body still trembled as she waited. It seemed an eternity, but he made no move, no sound. It was so quiet, she could hear the waves lapping gently against the sand only a few feet away. Over her head, through the spaces in the leaves, stars still shone. *It must be a nightmare,* she told herself. *It can't be real.* But when she tried to shift under him, the pressure of his body on hers proved that it was very, very real.

The hand over her mouth choked her breath until vague colors began to dance before her eyes. Morgan squeezed them tight for a moment to fight the faintness. Then she heard him speak again to a companion she couldn't see.

"What do you hear?"

"Nothing yet—in a moment." The voice that answered was rough and brisk. "Who the devil is she?"

"It doesn't matter. She'll be dealt with."

The roaring in her ears made it difficult to translate the Greek. Dealt with? she thought, dizzy again from fear and the lack of air.

The second man said something low and furious about women, then spat into the dirt.

"Just keep your ears open," Morgan's captor ordered. "And leave the woman to me."

"Now."

She felt him stiffen, but her eyes never left the knife. He was gripping it tighter now, she saw the tensing of his fingers on the handle.

Footsteps. They echoed on the rock steps of the beach. Hearing them, Morgan began to struggle again with the fierce strength of panic and of hope. With a whispered oath, he put more of his weight on her. He smelt faintly of the sea. As he shifted she caught a brief glimpse of his face in a patchy stream of moonlight. She saw dark, angular features, a grim mouth, and narrowed jet eyes. They were hard and cold and ruthless. It was the face of a man prepared to kill. *Why?* She thought as her mind began to float. I don't even know him.

"Follow him," he ordered his companion. Morgan heard a slight stirring in the leaves. "I'll take care of the woman."

Morgan's eyes widened at the sharp glimmer of the blade. She tasted something—bitter, copper—in her throat, but didn't recognize it as terror. The world spun to the point of a pin, then vanished.

The sky was full of stars, silver against black. The sea whispered. Against her back, the sand was rough. Morgan rose on her elbow and tried to clear her head. Fainted? Good God, had she actually fainted? Had she simply fallen asleep and dreamed it all? Rubbing her fingers against her temple, she wondered if her fantasies about pirates had caused her to hallucinate.

A small sound brought her swiftly to her feet. No, it had been real, and he was back. Morgan hurled herself at the shadow as it approached. She'd accepted the inevitability of death once without a struggle. This time, he was going to have a hell of a fight on his hands.

The shadow grunted softly as she struck, then Morgan found herself captured again, under him with the sand scraping her back.

"*Diabolos!* Be still!" he ordered in furious Greek as she tried to rip at his face.

"The hell I will!" Morgan tossed back in equally furious English. She fought with every ounce of strength until he pinned her, spread-eagle beneath him. Breathless, fearless in her rage, she stared up at him.

Looking down, he studied her with a frown. "You're not Greek." The statement, uttered in surprised and impatient English, stopped her struggles. "Who are you?"

"None of your business." She tried, and failed, to jerk her wrists free of his hold.

"Stop squirming," he ordered roughly, as his fingers clamped down harder. He wasn't thinking of his strength or her fragility, but that she wasn't simply a native who had been in the wrong place at the wrong time. His profession had taught him to get answers and adjust for complications. "What were you doing on the beach in the middle of the night?"

"Swimming," she tossed back. "Any idiot should be able to figure that out."

He swore, then shifted as she continued to struggle beneath him. "Damn it, be still!" His brows were lowered, not in anger now but concentration. "Swimming," he repeated as his eyes narrowed again. He'd watched her walk out of the sea—perhaps it was as innocent as that. "American," he mused, ignoring Morgan's thrashing. Weren't the Theoharises expecting an American woman? Of all the ill-timed… "You're not Greek," he murmured again.

"Neither are you," Morgan said between clenched teeth.

"Half." His thoughts underwent some rapid readjustments. The Theoharises' American houseguest, out for a moonlight swim—he'd have to play this one carefully or there'd be hell to pay. Quite suddenly, he flashed her a smile. "You had me fooled. I thought you could understand me."

"I understand perfectly," she retorted. "And you won't find it an easy rape now that you don't have your knife out."

"Rape?" Apparently astonished, he stared at her. His laughter was as sudden as the smile. "I hadn't given that much thought. In any case, Aphrodite, the knife was never intended for you."

"Then what do you mean by dragging me around like that? Flashing a knife in my face and nearly suffocating me?" Fury was much more satisfying than fear, and Morgan went with it. "Let me go!" She pushed at him with her body, but couldn't nudge him.

"In a moment," he said pleasantly. The moonlight played on her skin, and he enjoyed it. A fabulous face, he mused, now that he had time to study it. She'd be a woman accustomed to male admiration. Perhaps charm would distract her from the rather unique aspect of their meeting. "I can only say that what I did was for your own protection."

"Protection!" she flung back at him and tried to wrench her arms free.

"There wasn't time for amenities, fair lady. My apologies if my...technique was unrefined." His tone seemed to take it for granted that she would understand. "Tell me, why were you out alone, sitting like Lorelei on the rock and combing your hair?"

"That's none of your business." His voice had dropped, becoming low and seductive. The dark eyes had softened and appeared depthless. She could almost believe she had imagined the ruthlessness she'd glimpsed in the shadows. But she felt the light throbbing where his fingers had gripped her flesh. "I'm going to scream if you don't let me go."

Her body was tempting now that he had time to appreciate it, but he rose with a shrug. There was still work to be done that night. "My apologies for your inconvenience."

"Oh, is that right?" Struggling to her feet, Morgan began to brush at the sand that clung to her skin. "You have your nerve, dragging me off into the bushes, smothering me, brandishing a knife in my face, then apologizing like you've just stepped on my toe." Suddenly cold, she wrapped her arms around herself. "Just who are you and what was this all about?"

"Here." Stooping, he picked up the wrap he had dropped in order to hold her off. "I was bringing this to you when you launched your attack." He grinned as she shrugged into the wrap. It was a pity to cover the lengthy, intriguing body. "Who I am at the moment isn't relevant. As for the rest"—again the smooth, easy shrug—"I can't tell you."

"Just like that?" With a quick nod, Morgan turned and stalked to the beach steps. "We'll see what the police have to say about it."

"I wouldn't if I were you."

The advice was quiet, but vibrated with command. Hesitating, Morgan turned at the base of the steps to study him. He wasn't threatening now. What she felt wasn't fear, but his authority. He was quite tall, she noticed suddenly. And the moonlight played tricks with his face, making it almost cruel one moment, charming the next. Now it held all the confidence of Lucifer regrouping after the Fall.

Looking at him, she remembered the feel of hard, wiry muscles. He was standing easily, hands thrust into the pockets of jeans. The aura of command fit him perfectly. His smile didn't disguise it, nor did his casual stance. Damn pirates, she thought, feeling a quick twinge. Only lunatics find them attractive. Because she felt vulnerable, Morgan countered with bravado.

"Wouldn't you?" She lifted her chin and walked back to him.

"No," he answered mildly. "But perhaps, unlike me, you look for complications. I'm a simple man." He took a long, searching look of her face. *This is not,* he decided instantly, *a simple woman.* Though in his mind he cursed her, he went on conversationally. "Questions, reports to fill out, hours wasted on red tape. And then, even if you had my name"—he shrugged and flashed the grin again—"no one would believe you, Aphrodite. No one."

She didn't trust that grin—or the sultry way he called her by the goddess's name. She didn't trust the sudden warmth in her blood. "I wouldn't be so sure," Morgan began, but he cut her off, closing the slight distance between them.

"And I didn't rape you." Slowly, he ran his hands down her hair until they rested on her shoulders. His fingers didn't bite into her flesh now, but skimmed lazily. She had the eyes of a witch, he thought, and the face of a goddess. His time was short, but the moment was not to be missed. "Until now, I haven't even given in to the urge to do this."

His mouth closed over hers, hot and stunningly sweet. She hadn't been prepared for it. She pushed against him, but it was strictly out of reflex and lacked strength. He was a man who knew a woman's weakness. Deliberately, he brought her close, using style rather than force.

The scent of the sea rose to surround her, and heat— such a furnace heat that seemed to come from within and without at the same time. Almost leisurely, he explored her mouth until her heart thudded wildly against the quick, steady beat of his. His hands were clever, sliding beneath the wide sleeves of her robe to tease and caress the length of her arms, the slope of her shoulders.

When her struggles ceased, he nibbled at her lips as if he would draw out more taste. Slow, easy. His tongue tempted hers then retreated, then slipped through her parted lips again to torment and savor. For a moment, Morgan feared she would faint for a second time in his arms.

"One kiss," he murmured against her lips, "is hardly a criminal offense." She was sweeter than he had imagined and, he realized as desire stirred hotly, deadlier. "I could take another with little more risk."

"No." Coming abruptly to her senses, Morgan pushed away from him. "You're mad. And you're madder still if you think I'm going to let this go. I'm going—" She broke off as her hand lifted to her throat in a nervous gesture. The chain which always hung there was missing. Morgan glanced down, then brought her eyes back to his, furious, glowing.

"What have you done with my medal?" she demanded. "Give it back to me."

"I'm afraid I don't have it, Aphrodite."

"I want it back." Bravado wasn't a pose this time; she was livid. She stepped closer until they were toe to toe. "It's not worth anything to you. You won't be able to get more than a few drachmas for it."

His eyes narrowed. "I didn't take your medal. I'm not a thief." The temper in his voice was cold, coated with control. "If I were going to steal something from you, I would have found something more interesting than a medal."

Her eyes filled in a rush, and she swung out her hand to slap him. He caught her wrist, adding frustration to fury.

"It appears the medal is important," he said softly, but his hand was no longer gentle. "A token from a lover?"

"A gift from someone I love," Morgan countered. "I wouldn't expect a man like you to understand its value." With a jerk, she pulled her wrist from his hold. "I won't forget you," she promised, then turned and flew up the stairs.

He watched her until she was swallowed by the darkness. After a moment he turned back to the beach.

Chapter 2

The sun was a white flash of light. Its diamonds skimmed the water's surface. With the gentle movement of the yacht, Morgan found herself half-dozing.

Could the moonlit beach and the man have been a dream? she wondered hazily. Knives and rough hands and sudden draining kisses from strangers had no place in the real world. They belonged in one of those strange, half-remembered dreams she had when the rush and demands of work and the city threatened to become too much for her. She'd always considered them her personal release valve. Harmless, but absolutely secret—something she'd never considered telling Jack or any of her co-workers.

If it hadn't been for the absence of her medal, and the light trail of bruises on her arms, Morgan could have believed the entire incident had been the product of an overworked imagination.

Sighing, she shifted her back to the sun, pillowing her

head on her hands. Her skin, slick with oil, glistened. Why was she keeping the whole crazy business from Liz and Alex? Grimacing, she flexed her shoulders. They'd be horrified if she told them she'd been assaulted. Morgan could all but see Alex placing her under armed guard for the rest of her stay on Lesbos. He'd make certain there was an investigation—complicated, time-consuming, and in all probability fruitless. Morgan could work up a strong hate for the dark man for being right.

And what, if she decided to pursue it, could she tell the police? She hadn't been hurt or sexually assaulted. There'd been no verbal threat she could pin down, not even the slimmest motivation for what had happened. And what had happened? she demanded of herself. A man had dragged her into the bushes, held her there for no clear reason, then had let her go without harming her.

The Greek police wouldn't see the kiss as a criminal offense. She hadn't been robbed. There was no way on earth to prove the man had taken her medal. And damn it, she added with a sigh, as much as she'd like to assign all sorts of evil attributes to him, he just didn't fit the role of a petty thief. Petty anything, she thought grudgingly. Whatever he did, she was certain he did big...and did well.

So what was she going to do about it? True, he'd frightened and infuriated her—the second was probably a direct result of the first—but what else was there?

If and when they caught him, it would be his word against hers. Somehow, Morgan thought his word would carry more weight.

So I was frightened—my pride took a lump. She shrugged and shifted her head on her hands. It's not worth upsetting Liz and Alex. Midnight madness, she mused.

Another strange adventure in the life and times of Morgan James. File it and forget it.

Hearing Alex mount the steps to the sun deck, Morgan rested her chin on her hands and smiled at him. On the lounger beside her, Liz stirred and slept on.

"So, the sun has put her to sleep." Alex mounted the last of the steps, then settled into the chair beside his wife.

"I nearly dozed off myself." With a yawn, Morgan stretched luxuriously before she rolled over to adjust the lounger to a sitting position. "But I didn't want to miss anything." Gazing over the water, she studied the clump of land in the distance. The island seemed to float, as insubstantial as a mist.

"Chios," Alex told her, following her gaze. "And"—he gestured, waiting for her eyes to shift in the direction of his—"the coast of Turkey."

"So close," Morgan mused. "It seems as though I could swim to it."

"At sea, the distance can be deceiving." He flicked a lighter at the end of a black cigarette. The fragrance that rose from it was faintly sweet and exotic. "You'd have to be a hardy swimmer. Easy enough with a boat, though. There are some who find the proximity profitable." At Morgan's blank expression, Alex laughed. "Smuggling, innocence. It's still popular even though the punishment is severe."

"Smuggling," she murmured, intrigued. Then the word put her in mind of pirates again and her curious expression turned into a frown. A nasty business, she reminded herself, and not romantic at all.

"The coast," Alex made another gesture, sweeping, with the elegant cigarette held between two long fingers. "The many bays and peninsulas, offshore islands, inlets. There's simple access from the sea to the interior."

She nodded. Yes, a nasty business—they weren't talking about French brandy or Spanish lace. "Opium?"

"Among other things."

"But Alex." His careless acceptance caused her frown to deepen. Once she'd sorted it through, Morgan's own sense of right and wrong had little middle ground. "Doesn't it bother you?"

"Bother me?" he repeated, taking a long, slow drag on the cigarette. "Why?"

Flustered with the question, she sat up straighter. "Aren't you concerned about that sort of thing going on so close to your own home?"

"Morgan." Alex spread his hands in an acceptance of fate. The thick chunk of gold on his left pinky gleamed dully in the sunlight. "My concern would hardly stop what's been going on for centuries."

"But still, with crime practically in your own backyard…" She broke off, thinking about the streets of Manhattan. Perhaps she was the pot calling the kettle black. "I supposed I'd thought you'd be annoyed," she finished.

His eyes lit with a touch of amusement before he shrugged. "I leave the matter—and the annoyance—to the patrols and authorities. Tell me, are you enjoying your stay so far?"

Morgan started to speak again, then consciously smoothed away the frown. Alex was Old World enough not to want to discuss unpleasantries with a guest. "It's wonderful here, Alex. I can see why Liz loves it."

He flashed her a grin before he drew in strong tobacco. "You know Liz wants you to stay. She's missed you. At times, I feel very guilty because we don't get to America to see you often enough."

"You don't have to feel guilty, Alex." Morgan pushed

on sunglasses and relaxed again. After all, she reflected, smuggling had nothing to do with her. "Liz is happy."

"She'd be happier with you here."

"Alex," Morgan began with a smile for his indulgence of his wife. "I can't simply move in as a companion, no matter how much both of us love Liz."

"You're still dedicated to your job at the U.N.?" His tone had altered slightly, but Morgan sensed the change. It was business now.

"I like my work. I'm good at it, and I need the challenge."

"I'm a generous employer, Morgan, particularly to one with your capabilities." He took another long, slow drag, studying her through the mist of smoke. "I asked you to come work for me three years ago. If I hadn't been"—he glanced down at Liz's sleeping figure—"distracted"—he decided with a mild smile—"I would have taken more time to convince you to accept."

"Distracted?" Liz pushed her sunglasses up to her forehead and peered at him from under them.

"Eavesdropping," Morgan said with a sniff. A uniformed steward set three iced drinks on the table. She lifted one and drank. "Your manners always were appalling."

"You have a few weeks yet to think it over, Morgan." Tenacity beneath a smooth delivery was one of Alex's most successful business tactics. "But I warn you, Liz will be more persistent with her other solution." He shrugged, reaching for his own drink. "And I must agree—a woman needs a husband and security."

"How very Greek of you," Morgan commented dryly.

His grin flashed without apology. "I'm afraid one of Liz's candidates will be delayed. Dorian won't join us until tomorrow. He's bringing my cousin Iona with him."

"Marvelous." Liz's response was drenched in sarcasm. Alex sent her a frown.

"Liz isn't fond of Iona, but she's family." The quiet look he sent his wife told Morgan the subject had been discussed before. "I have a responsibility."

Liz took the last glass with a sigh of acceptance. Briefly she touched her hand to his. "We have a responsibility," she corrected. "Iona's welcome."

Alex's frown turned into a look of love so quickly, Morgan gave a mock groan. "Don't you two ever fight? I mean, don't you realize it isn't healthy to be so well balanced?"

Liz's eyes danced over the rim of her glass. "We have our moments, I suppose. A week ago I was furious with him for at least—ah, fifteen minutes."

"That," Morgan said positively, "is disgusting."

"So," Alex mused, "you think a man and woman must fight to be...healthy?"

Shaking back her hair, Morgan laughed. "*I* have to fight to be healthy."

"Morgan, you haven't mentioned Jack at all. Is there a problem?"

"Liz." Alex's disapproval was clear in the single syllable.

"No, it's all right, Alex." Taking her glass, Morgan rose and moved to the rail. "It's not a problem," she said slowly. "At least I hope it's not." She stared into her drink, frowning, as if she wasn't quite sure what the glass contained. "I've been running on this path—this very straight, very defined path. I could run it blindfolded." With a quick laugh, Morgan leaned out on the rail to let the wind grab at her hair. "Suddenly, I discovered it wasn't a path, but a rut and it kept getting deeper. I decided to change course before it became a pit."

"You always did prefer an obstacle course," Liz murmured. But she was pleased with Jack's disposal, and took little trouble to hide it.

The sea churned in a white froth behind the boat. Morgan turned from her study of it. "I don't intend to fall at Dorian's feet, Liz—or anyone else you might have in mind—just because Jack and I are no longer involved."

"I should hope not," Liz returned with some spirit. "That would take all the fun out of it."

With a sigh of exasperated affection, Morgan turned back to the rail.

The stark mountains of Lesbos rose from the sea. Jagged, harsh, timeless. Morgan could make out the pure white lines of Alex's villa. She thought it looked like a virgin offering to the gods—cool, classic, certainly feminine. Higher still was a rambling gray structure which seemed hewn from the rock itself. It faced the sea; indeed, it loomed over it. As if challenging Poseidon to claim it, it clung to the cliff. Morgan saw it as arrogant, rough, masculine. The flowering vines which grew all around it didn't soften the appearance, but added a haunted kind of beauty.

There were other buildings—a white-washed village, snuggled cottages, one or two other houses on more sophisticated lines, but the two larger structures hovered over the rest. One was elegant; one was savage.

"Who does that belong to?" Morgan called over her shoulder. "It's incredible."

Following her gaze, Liz grinned and rose to join her. "I should have known that would appeal to you. Sometimes I'd swear it's alive. Nicholas Gregoras, olive oil, and more recently, import-export." She glanced at her friend's profile. "Maybe I'll include him for dinner tomorrow if he's free, though I don't think he's your type."

Morgan gave her a dry look. "Oh? And what is my type?"

"Someone who'll give you plenty to fight about. Who'll give you that obstacle course."

"*Hmm.* You know me too well."

"As for Nick, he's rather smooth and certainly a charmer." Liz tapped a fingernail against the rail as she considered. "Not as blatantly handsome as Dorian, but he has a rather basic sort of sex appeal. Earthier, and yet…" She trailed off, narrowing her eyes she tried to pigeonhole him. "Well, he's an odd one. I suppose he'd have to be to live in a house like that. He's in his early thirties, inherited the olive oil empire almost ten years ago. Then he branched into import-export. He seems to have a flair for it. Alex is very fond of him because they go back to short pants together."

"Liz, I only wanted to know who owned the house. I didn't ask for a biography."

"These facts are part of the service." She cupped her hands around her lighter and lit a cigarette. "I want to give you a clear picture of your options."

"Haven't you got a goatherd up your sleeve?" Morgan demanded. "I rather like the idea of a small, whitewashed cottage and baking black bread."

"I'll see what I can do."

"I don't suppose it occurs to you or Alex that I'm content to be single—the modern, capable woman on her own? I know how to use a screwdriver, how to change a flat tire…"

"'Methinks she doth protest too much,'" Liz quoted mildly.

"Liz—"

"I love you, Morgan."

On a frustrated sigh, Morgan lifted her drink again. "Damn it, Liz," she murmured.

"Come on, let me have my fun," she coaxed, giving Morgan a friendly pat on the cheek. "As you said yourself, it's all up to fate anyway."

"Hoist by my own petard. All right, bring on your Dorians and your Nicks and your Lysanders."

"Lysander?"

"It's a good name for a goatherd."

With a chuckle, Liz flicked her cigarette into the churning water. "Just wait and see if I don't find one."

"Liz…" Morgan hesitated for a moment, then asked casually, "do many people use the beach where we swam yesterday?"

"*Hmm?* Oh." She tucked a pale blond strand behind her ear. "Not really. It's used by us and the Gregoras villa for the most part. I'd have to ask Alex who owns it, I've never given it any thought. The bay's secluded and only easily accessible by the beach steps which run between the properties. Oh, yes, there's a cottage Nick owns which he rents out occasionally," she remembered. "It's occupied now by an American. Stevens…no," she corrected herself. "Stevenson. Andrew Stevenson, a poet or a painter or something. I haven't met him yet." She gave Morgan a frank stare. "Why? Did you plan for an all over tan?"

"Just curious." Morgan rearranged her thoughts. If she was going to file it and forget it, she had to stop letting the incident play back in her mind. "I'd love to get a close look at that place." She gestured toward the gray villa. "I think the architect must have been just a little mad. It's fabulous."

"Use some charm on Nick and get yourself an invitation," Liz suggested.

"I might just do that." Morgan studied the villa consideringly. She wondered if Nick Gregoras was the man whose footsteps she had heard when she had been held in the bushes. "Yes, I might just."

That evening, Morgan left the balcony doors wide. She wanted the warmth and scents of the night. The house was quiet but for the single stroke of a clock that signaled the hour. For the second night in a row she was wide awake. Did people really sleep on vacations? she wondered. What a waste of time.

She sat at the small rosewood desk in her room, writing a letter. From somewhere between the house and the sea, an owl cried out twice. She paused to listen, hoping it would call again, but there was only silence. How could she describe how it felt to see Mount Olympus rising from the sea? Was it possible to describe the timelessness, the strength, the almost frightening beauty?

She shrugged, and did what she could to explain the sensation to her father on paper. He'd understand, she mused as she folded the stationery. Who understood better her sometimes whimsical streaks of fancy than the man she'd inherited them from? And, she thought with a lurking smile, he'd get a good chuckle at Liz's determination to marry her off and keep her in Greece.

She rose, stretched once, then turned and collided with a hard chest. The hand that covered her mouth used more gentleness this time, and the jet eyes laughed into hers. Her heart rose, then fell like an elevator with its cable clipped.

"*Kalespera,* Aphrodite. Your word that you won't scream, and you have your freedom."

Instinctively she tried to jerk away, but he held her still without effort, only lifting an ironic brow. He was a man who knew whose word to accept and whose word to doubt.

Morgan struggled for another moment, then finding herself outmatched, reluctantly nodded. He released her immediately.

She drew in the breath to shout, then let it out in a frustrated huff. A promise was a promise, even if it was to a devil. "How did you get in here?" she demanded.

"The vines to your balcony are sturdy."

"You climbed?" Her incredulity was laced with helpless admiration. The walls were sheer, the height was dizzying. "You must be mad."

"That's a possibility," he said with a careless smile.

He seemed none the worse for wear after the climb. His hair was disheveled, but then she'd never seen it otherwise. There was a shadow of beard on his chin. His eyes held no strain or fatigue, but rather a light of adventure that drew her no matter how hard she tried to resist. In the lamplight she could see him more clearly than she had the night before. His features weren't as harsh as she had thought and his mouth wasn't grim. It was really quite beautiful, she realized with a flood of annoyance.

"What do you want?"

He smiled again, letting his gaze roam down her leisurely with an insolence she knew wasn't contrived but inherent. She wore only a brief cinnamon-colored teddy that dipped low at the breast and rose high at the thighs. Morgan noted the look, and that he stood squarely between her and the closet where she had left her robe. Rather than acknowledge the disadvantage, she tilted her chin.

"How did you know where to find me?"

"It's my business to find things out," he answered. Silently, he approved more than her form, but her courage as well. "Morgan James," he began. "Visiting friend of Elizabeth Theoharis. American, living in New York. Unmarried. Employed at the U.N. as interpreter. You speak Greek, English, French, Italian and Russian."

She tried not to let her mouth fall open at his careless rundown on her life. "That's a very tidy summary," she said tightly.

"Thank you. I try to be succinct."

"What does any of that have to do with you?"

"That's yet to be decided." He studied her, thinking again. It might be that he could employ her talents and position for his own uses. The package was good, very good. And so, more important at the moment, was the mind.

"You're enjoying your stay on Lesbos?"

Morgan stared at him, then slowly shook her head. No, he wasn't a ruffian or a rapist. That much she was sure of. If he were a thief, which she still reserved judgment on, he was no ordinary one. He spoke too well, moved too well. What he had was a certain amount of odd charm, a flair that was hard to resist, and an amazing amount of arrogance. Under different circumstances, she might even have liked him.

"You have incredible gall," she decided.

"You continue to flatter me."

"All right." Tight-lipped, Morgan strode over to the open balcony doors and gestured meaningfully. "I gave you my word I wouldn't scream, and I didn't. But I have no intention of standing here making idle conversation with a lunatic. Out!"

With his lips still curved in a smile, he sat on the edge of the bed and studied her. "I admire a woman of her word." He stretched out jean-clad legs and crossed his feet. "I find a great deal to admire about you, Morgan.

Last night you showed good sense and courage—rare traits to find together."

"Forgive me if I'm not overwhelmed."

He caught the sarcasm, but more important, noted the change in her eyes. She wasn't as angry as she tried to be. "I did apologize," he reminded her and smiled.

Her breath came out in a long-suffering sigh. She could detest him for making her want to laugh when she should be furious. Just who the devil was he? He wasn't the mad rapist she had first thought—he wasn't a common thief. So just what was he? Morgan stopped herself before she asked—she was better off in ignorance.

"It didn't seem like much of an apology to me."

"If I make a more...honest attempt," he began with a bland sincerity that made her lips twitch, "would you accept?"

Firmly, she banked down on the urge to return his smile. "If I accept it, will you go away?"

"But I find your company so pleasant."

An irrepressible light of humor flickered in her eyes. "The hell you do."

"Aphrodite, you wound me."

"I'd like to draw and quarter you. Are you going to go away?"

"Soon." Smiling, he rose again. What was that scent that drifted from her? he wondered. It was not quite sweet, not quite tame. Jasmine—wild jasmine. It suited her. He moved to the dresser to toy with her hand mirror. "You'll meet Dorian Zoulas and Iona Theoharis tomorrow," he said casually. This time Morgan's mouth did drop. "There's little on the island I'm not aware of," he said mildly.

"Apparently," she agreed.

Now he noted a hint of curiosity in her tone. It was

what he had hoped for. "Perhaps, another time, you'll give me your impression of them."

Morgan shook her head more from bafflement than offense. "I have no intention of there being another time, or of gossiping with you. I hardly see why—"

"Why not?" he countered.

"I don't *know* you," she said in frustration. "I don't know this Dorian or Iona either. And I don't understand how you could possibly—"

"True," he agreed with a slight nod. "How well do you know Alex?"

Morgan ran a hand through her hair. Here I am, wearing little more than my dignity, exchanging small talk with a maniac who climbed in the third-story window. "Look, I'm not discussing Alex with you. I'm not discussing anyone or anything with you. Go away."

"We'll leave that for later too, then," he said mildly as he crossed back to her. "I have something for you." He reached into his pocket, then opened his hand and dangled a small silver medal by its chain.

"Oh, you did have it!" Morgan grabbed, only to have him whip it out of her reach. His eyes hardened with fury.

"I told you once, I'm no thief." The change in his voice and face had been swift and potent. Involuntarily, she took a step away. His mouth tightened at the movement before he went on in a more controlled tone. "I went back and found it in the grove. The chain had to be repaired, I'm afraid."

With his eyes on hers, he held it out again. Taking it, Morgan began to fasten it around her neck. "You're a very considerate assailant."

"Do you think I enjoyed hurting you?"

Her hands froze at the nape of her neck. There was no teasing banter in his tone now, no insolent light of amusement in his eyes. This was the man she recognized from the shadows. Waves of temper came from him, hardening his voice, burning in his jet eyes. With her hands still lifted, Morgan stared at him.

"Do you think I enjoyed frightening you into fainting, having you think I would murder you? Do you think it gives me pleasure to see there are bruises on you and know that I put them there?" He whirled away, stalking the room. "I'm not a man who makes a habit of misusing women."

"I wouldn't know about that," she said steadily.

He stopped, and his eyes came back to hers. Damn, she was cool, he thought. And beautiful. Beautiful enough to be a distraction when he couldn't afford one.

"I don't know who you are or what you're mixed up in," she continued. Her fingers trembled a bit as she finished fastening the chain, but her voice was calm and unhurried. "Frankly, I don't care as long as you leave me alone. Under different circumstances, I'd thank you for the return of my property, but I don't feel it applies in this case. You can leave the same way you came in."

He had to bank down on an urge to throttle her. It wasn't often he was in the position of having a half-naked woman order him from her bedroom three times in one evening. He might have found it amusing if he hadn't been fighting an overwhelming flood of pure and simple desire.

The hell with fighting it, he thought. A woman who kept her chin lifted in challenge deserved to be taken up on it.

"Courage becomes you, Morgan," he said coolly. "We might do very well together." Reaching out, he fingered the medal at her throat and frowned at it. With a silent oath, he tightened his grip on the chain and brought his eyes back to hers.

There was no fear in those clear blue pools now, but a light, maddening disdain. A woman like this, he thought, could make a man mad, make him suffer and ache. And by God, a woman like this would be worth it.

"I told you to go," she said icily, ignoring the sudden quick thud of her pulse. It wasn't fear—Morgan told herself she was through with fear. But neither was it the anger she falsely named it.

"And so I will," he murmured and let the chain drop. "In the meantime, since you don't offer, I take."

Once again she found herself in his arms. It wasn't the teasing, seductive kiss of the night before. Now he devoured her. No one had kissed her like this before—as if he knew every secret she hoarded. He would know, somehow, where she needed to be touched.

The hot, insistent flow of desire that ran through her left her too stunned to struggle, too hungry to reason. How could she want him? her mind demanded. How could she want a man like this to touch her? But her mouth was moving under his, she couldn't deny it. Her tongue met his. Her hands gripped his shoulders, but didn't push him away.

"There's honey on your lips, Morgan," he murmured. "Enough to drive a man mad for another taste."

He took his hand on a slow journey down her back, pressing silk against her skin before he came to the hem. His fingers were strong, callused, and as clever as a musician's. Without knowing, without caring what she did, Morgan framed his face with her hands for a moment before they dove into his hair. The muttered Greek she heard from him wasn't a love word but an oath as he dragged her closer.

How well she knew that body now. Long and lean and wiry with muscle. She could smell the sea on it, almost taste it beneath that hot demand as his mouth continued to savage hers.

The kiss grew deeper, until she moaned, half in fear of the unexplored, half in delight of the exploration. She'd forgotten who she was, who he was. There was only pleasure, a dark, heavy pleasure. Through her dazed senses she felt a struggle—a storm, a fury. Then he drew her away to study her face.

He wasn't pleased that his heartbeat was unsteady. Or that the thoughts whirling in his head were clouded with passion. This was no time for complications. And this was no woman to take risks with. With an effort, he slid his hands gently down her arms. "More satisfying than a thank you," he said lightly, then glanced with a grin toward the bed. "Are you going to ask me to stay?"

Morgan pulled herself back with a jolt. He must have hypnotized her, she decided. There was no other rational explanation. "Some other time, perhaps," she managed, as carelessly as he.

Amusement lightened his features. Capturing her hand, he kissed it formally. "I'll look forward to it, Aphrodite."

He moved to the balcony, throwing her a quick grin before he started his descent. Unable to prevent herself, Morgan ran over to watch him climb down.

He moved like a cat, confident, fearless, a shadow clinging to the stark white walls. Her heart stayed lodged in her throat as she watched him. He sprang to the ground and melted into the cover of trees without looking back. Whirling, Morgan shut the doors to the balcony. And locked them.

Chapter 3

Morgan swirled her glass of local wine but drank little. Though its light, fruity flavor was appealing, she was too preoccupied to appreciate it. The terrace overlooked the gulf with its hard blue water and scattering of tiny islands. Small dots that were boats skimmed the surface, but she took little notice of them. Most of her mind was occupied in trying to sort out the cryptic comments of her late-night visitor. The rest was involved with following the conversation around her.

Dorian Zoulas was all that Liz had said—classically handsome, bronzed, and sophisticated. In the pale cream suit, he was a twentieth-century Adonis. He had intelligence and breeding, tempered with a golden beauty that was essentially masculine. Liz's maneuvers might have caused Morgan to treat him with a polite aloofness if she hadn't seen the flashes of humor in his eyes. Morgan had realized immediately that he not only knew the way his hostess's mind worked, but had decided to play the game. The teasing challenge in his eyes relaxed her. Now she could enjoy a harmless flirtation without embarrassment.

Iona, Alex's cousin, was to Morgan's mind less appealing. Her dark, sultry looks were both stunning and disturbing. The gloss of beauty and wealth didn't quite polish over an edge that might have come from poor temperament or nerves. There was no humor in the exotic sloe eyes or pouting mouth. Iona was, Morgan mused, like a volcano waiting to erupt. Hot, smoky, and alarming.

The adjectives brought her night visitor back to her mind. They fit him just as neatly as they fit Iona Theoharis, and yet…oddly, Morgan found she admired them in the man and found them disturbing in the woman. Double standard? she wondered, then shook her head. No, the energy in Iona seemed destructive. The energy in the man was compelling. Annoyed with herself. Morgan turned from her study of the gulf and pushed aside her disturbing thoughts.

She gave Dorian her full attention. "You must find it very peaceful here after Athens."

He turned in his chair to face her. With only a smile, he intimated that there was no woman but she on the terrace—a trick Morgan found pleasant. "The island's a marvelous place…tranquil. But I thrive on chaos. As you live in New York, I'm sure you understand."

"Yes, but at the moment, tranquility is very appealing." Leaning against the rail, she let the sun play warm on her back. "I've been nothing but lazy so far. I haven't even whipped up the energy to explore."

"There's quite a bit of local color, if that's what you have in mind." Dorian slipped a thin gold case from his pocket, and opening it, offered Morgan a cigarette. At the shake of her head, he lit one for himself, then leaned back in a manner that was both relaxed and alert. "Caves and inlets, olive groves, a few small farms and flocks," he continued. "The village is very quaint and unspoiled."

"Exactly what I want." Morgan nodded and sipped her drink. "But I'm going to take it very slow. I'll collect shells and find a farmer who'll let me milk his goat."

"Terrifying aspirations," Dorian commented with a quick smile.

"Liz will tell you, I've always been intrepid."

"I'd be happy to help you with your shells." He continued to smile as his eyes skimmed her face with an approval she couldn't have missed. "But as to the goat…"

"I'm surprised you're content with so little entertainment." Iona's husky voice broke into the exchange.

Morgan shifted her gaze to her and found it took more of an effort to smile. "The island itself is entertainment enough for me. Remember, I'm a tourist. I've always thought vacations where you rush from one activity to the next aren't vacations at all."

"Morgan's been lazy for two full days," Liz put in with a grin. "A new record."

Morgan cast her a look, thinking of her nighttime activities. "I'm shooting for two weeks of peaceful sloth," Morgan murmured. *Starting today,* she added silently.

"Lesbos is the perfect spot for idleness." Dorian blew out a slow, fragrant stream of smoke. "Rustic, quiet."

"But perhaps this bit of island isn't as quiet as it appears." Iona ran a manicured nail around the rim of her glass.

Morgan saw Dorian's brows lift as if in puzzlement while Alex's drew together in disapproval.

"We'll do our best to keep it quiet during Morgan's visit," Liz said smoothly. "She rarely stays still for long, and since she's determined to this time, we'll see that she has a nice, uneventful vacation."

Morgan made some sound of agreement and managed not to choke over her drink. Uneventful! If Liz only knew.

"More wine, Morgan?" Dorian rose, bringing the bottle to her.

Iona began to tap her fingers on the arm of her wrought iron chair. "I suppose there are people who find boredom appealing."

"Relaxation," Alex said with a slight edge in his voice, "comes in many forms."

"And of course," Liz went on, skimming her hand lightly over the back of her husband's, "Morgan's job is very demanding. All those foreign dignitaries and protocol and politics."

Dorian sent Morgan an appreciative smile as he poured more wine into her glass. "I'm sure someone with Morgan's talents would have many fascinating stories to tell."

Morgan cocked a brow. It had been a long time since she had been given a purely admiring male smile—undemanding, warm without being appraising. She could learn to enjoy it. "I might have a few," she returned.

The sun was sinking into the sea. The rosy light streamed through the open balcony doors and washed the room. Red sky at night, Morgan mused. Wasn't that supposed to mean clear sailing? She decided to take it as an omen.

Her first two days on Lesbos had been a far cry from the uneventful vacation Liz had boasted of, but that was behind her now. With luck, and a little care, she wouldn't run into that attractive lunatic again.

Morgan caught a glimpse of her own smile in the mirror and hastily rearranged her expression. Perhaps when she got back to New York, she'd see a psychiatrist. When you started to find lunatics appealing, you were fast becoming one yourself. Forget it, she ordered herself firmly as she went to the closet. There were more important things to think about—like what she was going to wear to dinner.

After a quick debate, Morgan chose a drifting white dress—thin layers of crêpe de chine, full-sleeved, full-skirted. Dorian had inspired her to flaunt her femininity a bit. Jack, she recalled, had preferred the tailored look. He had often offered a stern and unsolicited opinion on her wardrobe, finding her taste both inconsistent and flighty. There might be a multicolored gypsy-style skirt hanging next to a prim business suit. He'd never understood that both had suited who she was. Just another basic difference, Morgan mused as she hooked the line of tiny pearl buttons.

Tonight she was going to have fun. It had been a long while since she'd flirted with a man. Her thoughts swung back to a dark man with tousled hair and a shadowed chin. Hold on, Morgan, she warned herself. *That* was hardly in the same league as a flirtation. Moving over, she closed the balcony doors and gave a satisfied nod as she heard the click of the lock. And that, she decided, takes care of that.

Liz glided around the salon. It pleased her that Morgan hadn't come down yet. Now she could make an entrance. For all her blond fragility, Liz was a determined woman. Loyalty was her strongest trait; where she loved, it was unbendable. She wanted Morgan to be happy. Her own marriage had given her nothing but happiness. Morgan would have the same if Liz had any say in it.

With a satisfied smile, she glanced around the salon.

The light was low and flattering. The scent of night blossoms drifting in through the open windows was the perfect touch. The wines she'd ordered for dinner would add the final prop for romance. Now, if Morgan would cooperate…

"Nick, I'm so glad you could join us." Liz went to him, holding out both hands. "It's so nice that we're all on the island at the same time for a change."

"It's always a pleasure to see you, Liz," he returned with a warm, charming smile. "And a relief to be out of the crowds in Athens for a few weeks." He gave her hands a light squeeze, then lifted one to his lips. His dark eyes skimmed her face. "I swear, you're lovelier every time I see you."

With a laugh, Liz tucked her arm through his. "We'll have to invite you to dinner more often. Did I ever thank you properly for that marvelous Indian chest you found me?" Smiling, she guided him toward the bar. "I adore it."

"Yes, you did." He gave her hand a quick pat. "I'm glad I was able to find what you had in mind."

"You never fail to find the perfect piece. I'm afraid Alex wouldn't know an Indian chest from a Hepplewhite."

Nick laughed. "We all have our talents, I suppose."

"But your work must be fascinating." Liz glanced up at him with her wide-eyed smile as she began to fix him a drink. "All those treasures and all the exotic places you travel to."

"There are times it's more exciting just to be home."

She shot him a look. "You make that hard to believe, since you're so seldom here. Where was it last month? Venice?"

"A beautiful city," he said smoothly.

"I'd love to see it. If I could drag Alex away from his

ships…" Liz's eyes focused across the room. "Oh dear, it looks like Iona is annoying Alex again." On a long breath, she lifted her eyes to Nick's. Seeing the quick understanding, she gave a rueful smile. "I'm going to have to play diplomat."

"You do it charmingly, Liz. Alex is a lucky man."

"Remind him of that from time to time," she suggested. "I'd hate for him to take me for granted. Oh, here comes Morgan. She'll keep you entertained while I do my duty."

Following Liz's gaze, Nick watched as Morgan entered the room. "I'm sure she will," was his murmured reply. He liked the dress she wore, the floating white that was at once alluring and innocent. She'd left her hair loose so that it fell over her shoulders almost as if it had come off a pillow. Quite beautiful, he thought as he felt the stir. He'd always had a weakness for beauty.

"Morgan." Before Morgan could do any more than smile her hello at Liz, Liz took her arm. "You'll keep Nick happy for a moment, I have a job to do. Morgan James, Nicholas Gregoras." With the quick introduction, Liz was halfway across the room.

Morgan stared in stunned silence. Nick lifted her limp hand to his lips. "You," she managed in a choked whisper.

"Aphrodite, you're exquisite. Even fully dressed."

With his lips lingering over her knuckles, he met her eyes. His were dark and pleased. Regaining her senses, Morgan tried to wrench her hand free. Without changing expression, Nick tightened his grip and held her still.

"Careful, Morgan," he said mildly. "Liz and her guest will wonder at your behavior. And explanations would"— he grinned, exactly as she remembered—"cause them to wonder about your mental health."

"Let go of my hand," she said quietly and smiled with her lips only. "Or I swear, I'll deck you."

"You're magnificent." Making a small bow, he released her. "Did you know your eyes literally throw darts when you're annoyed?"

"Then I've the pleasure of knowing you're riddled with tiny holes," she returned. "Let me know when one hits the heart, *Mr.* Gregoras."

"Nick, please," he said in a polished tone. "We could hardly start formalities now after all we've...been through together."

Morgan gave him a brilliant smile. "Very well, Nick, you odious swine. What a pity this isn't the proper time to go into how detestable you are."

He inclined his head. "We'll arrange for a more appropriate opportunity. Soon," he added with the faintest hint of steel. "Now, let me get you a drink."

Liz breezed up, pleased with the smiles she had seen exchanged. "You two seem to be getting along like old friends."

"I was just telling Mr. Gregoras how enchanting his home looks from the sea." Morgan sent him a quick but lethal glance.

"Yes, Morgan was fascinated by it," Liz told him. "She's always preferred things that didn't quite fit a mold, if you know what I mean."

"Exactly." Nick let his eyes sweep over Morgan's face. A man could get lost in those eyes, he thought, if he wasn't careful. Very careful. "Miss James has agreed to a personal tour tomorrow afternoon." He smiled, watching her expression go from astonishment to fury before she controlled it.

"Marvelous!" Pleased, Liz beamed at both of them.

"Nick has so many treasures from all over the world. His house is just like Aladdin's cave."

Smiling, Morgan thought of three particularly gruesome wishes, all involving her intended host. "I can't wait to see it."

Through dinner, Morgan watched, confused, then intrigued by Nick's manner. This was not the man she knew. This man was smooth, polished. Gone was the intensity, the ruthlessness, replaced by an easy warmth and charm.

Nicholas Gregoras, olive oil, import-export. Yes, she could see the touches of wealth and success—and the authority she'd understood from the first. But command sat differently on him now, with none of the undertones of violence.

He could sit at the elegant table, laughing with Liz and Alex over some island story with the gleam of cut crystal in his hand. The smoky-gray suit was perfectly tailored and fit him with the same ease as the dark sweatshirt and jeans she'd first seen him in. His arrogance had a more sophisticated tone now. All the rough edges were smoothed.

He seemed relaxed, at home—with none of that vital, dangerous energy. How could this be the same man who had flourished a knife, or climbed the sheer wall to her balcony?

Nick handed her a glass of wine and she frowned. But he was the same man, she reminded herself. And just what game was he playing? Lifting her eyes, Morgan met his. Her fingers tightened on the stem of the glass. The look was brief and quickly veiled, but she saw the inner man. The force was vital. If he was playing games, she thought, sipping her wine to calm suddenly tight nerves, it wasn't a pleasant one. And she wanted no part of it—or of him.

Turning to Dorian, Morgan left Nick to Iona. Intelligent, witty, and with no frustrating mysteries, Dorian was a more comfortable dinner companion. Morgan fell into the easy exchange and tried to relax.

"Tell me, Morgan, don't you find the words of so many languages a bit crowded in the mind?"

She toyed with her moussaka, finding her stomach too jittery to accept the rich sauce. Damn the man for interfering even with her appetite. "I do my thinking in one at a time," she countered.

"You take it too lightly," Dorian insisted. "It's an accomplishment to be proud of. Even a power."

"A power?" Her brows drew together for a moment, then cleared as she smiled. "I suppose it is, though I'd never really thought about it. It just seemed too limiting to only be able to communicate and think in one language, then once I got started, I couldn't seem to stop."

"Having the language, you'd be at home in many countries."

"Yes, I guess that's why I feel so—well, easy here."

"Alex tells me he's trying to entice you into his company." With a smile, Dorian toasted her. "I've drafted myself as promoter. Working with you would add to the company benefits."

Iona's rich laughter floated across the table. "Oh, Nicky, you say the most ridiculous things."

Nicky, Morgan thought with a sniff. I'll be ill any minute. "I think I might enjoy your campaign," Morgan told Dorian with her best smile.

"Take me out on your boat tomorrow, Nicky. I simply must have some fun."

"I'm sorry, Iona, not tomorrow. Perhaps later in the

week." Nick softened the refusal with the trace of a finger down her hand.

Iona's mouth formed a pout. "I might die of boredom by later in the week."

Morgan heard Dorian give a quiet sigh. Glancing over, she noted the quick look of exasperation he sent Iona. "Iona tells me she ran into Maria Popagos in Athens last week." The look of exasperation was gone, and his voice was gentle. "She has what—four children now, Iona?"

They treat her like a child, Morgan thought with distaste. And she behaves like one—a spoiled, willful, not quite healthy child.

Through the rest of the meal, and during coffee in the salon, Morgan watched Iona's moods go from sullen to frantic. Apparently used to it, or too good mannered to notice, Dorian ignored the fluctuations. And though she hated to give him the credit for it, so did Nick. But Morgan noted, with a flutter of sympathy, that Alex grew more distracted as the evening wore on. He spoke to his cousin in undertones as she added more brandy to her glass. Her response was a dramatic toss of her head before she swallowed the liquor and turned her back on him.

When Nick rose to leave, Iona insisted on walking with him to his car. She cast a look of triumph over her shoulder as they left the salon arm-in-arm. Now who, Morgan mused, was that aimed at? Shrugging, she turned back to Dorian and let the evening wind down naturally. There would be time enough to think things through when she was alone in her room again.

Morgan floated with the dream. The wine had brought sleep quickly. Though she had left the balcony doors securely locked, the night breeze drifted through the windows. She sighed, and shifted with its gentle caress on her skin. It was a soft stroking, like a butterfly's wing. It teased across her lips then came back to warm them. She stirred with pleasure. Her body was pliant, receptive. As the phantom kiss increased in pressure, she parted her lips. She drew the dream lover closer.

Excitement was sleepy. The tastes that seeped into her were as sweet and as potent as the wine that still misted her brain. With a sigh of lazy, languid pleasure, she floated with it. In the dream, her arms wrapped around the faceless lover—the pirate, the phantom. He whispered her name and deepened the kiss as his hands drew down the sheet that separated them. Rough fingers, familiar fingers, traced over her skin. A body, too hard, too muscular for a dream, pressed against hers. The lazy images became more tangible, and the phantom took on form. Dark hair, dark eyes, and a mouth that was grimly beautiful and oh, so clever.

Warmth became heat. With a moan, she let passion take her. The stroking along her body became more insistent at her response. Her mouth grew hungry, demanding. Then she heard the breathy whisper of a Greek endearment against her ear.

Suddenly, the filmy curtain of sleep lifted. The weight on her body was real, achingly real—and achingly familiar. Morgan began a confused struggle.

"The goddess awakes. More's the pity."

She saw him in the shaft of moonlight. Her body was alive with needs, her mind baffled with the knowledge that he had induced them. "What are you doing!" she demanded, and found her breathing was quick and ragged. His mouth had been on hers, she knew. She could still taste him. And his hands… "This is the limit! If you think for one minute I'm going to sit still for you crawling into my bed while I'm sleeping—"

"You were very agreeable a moment ago."

"Oh! What a despicable thing to do."

"You're very responsive," Nick murmured, and traced her ear with his fingertip. Beneath his hand he could feel the thunder of her heartbeat. He knew, though he fought to slow it, that his own beat as quickly. "It seemed to please you to be touched. It pleased me to touch you."

His voice had lowered again, as she knew it could—dark, seductive. The muscles in her thighs loosened. "Get off of me," she ordered in quick defense.

"Sweet Morgan." He nipped her bottom lip—felt her tremble, felt a swift rush of power. It would be so easy to persuade her...and so risky. With an effort, he gave her a friendly smile. "You only postpone the inevitable."

She kept her eyes level as she tried to steady her breathing. Something told her that if all else he had said had been lies, his last statement was all too true. "I didn't promise not to scream this time."

He lifted a brow as though the possibility intrigued him. "It might be interesting to explain this...situation to Alex and Liz. I could claim I was overcome with your beauty. It has a ring of truth. But you won't scream in any case."

"Just what makes you so sure?"

"You'd have given me away—or tried to by now—if you were going to." Nick rolled aside.

Sitting up, Morgan pushed at her hair. Did he always have to be right? she wondered grimly. "What do you want now? And how the hell did you get in this time? I locked..." Her voice trailed off as she saw the balcony doors were wide open.

"Did you think a lock would keep me out?" With a laugh, Nick ran a finger down her nose. "You have a lot to learn."

"Now, you listen to me—"

"No, save the recriminations for later. They're understood in any case." Absently, he rubbed a lock of her hair between his thumb and forefinger. "I came back to make certain you didn't develop a convenient headache that would keep you from coming to the house tomorrow. There are one or two things I want to discuss with you."

"I've got a crate full of things to discuss with you," Morgan hissed furiously. "Just what were you doing that night on the beach? And who—"

"Later, Aphrodite. I'm distracted at the moment. That scent you wear, for instance. It's very…" He lifted his eyes to hers, "alluring."

"Stop it." She didn't trust him when his voice dropped to that tone. She didn't trust him at all, she reminded herself and gave him a level look. "What's the purpose behind that ridiculous game you were playing tonight?"

"Game?" His eyes widened effectively. "Morgan, my love, I don't know what you're talking about. I was quite natural."

"Natural be damned."

"No need to swear at me," he said mildly.

"There's every need," she countered. How could he manage to be charming under such ridiculous circumstances? "You were the perfect guest this evening," Morgan went on, knocking his hand aside as he began to toy with the thin strap of her chemise. "Charming—"

"Thank you."

"And false," she added, narrowing her eyes.

"Not false," Nick disagreed. "Simply suitable, considering the occasion."

"I suppose it would have looked a bit odd if you'd pulled a knife out of your pocket."

His fingers tightened briefly, then relaxed. She wasn't

going to let him forget that—and he wasn't having an easy time blanking out that moment she had gone limp with terror beneath him. "Few people have seen me other than I was tonight," he murmured, and began to give the texture of her hair his attention. "Perhaps it's your misfortune to count yourself among them."

"I don't want to see you *any* way, from now on."

Humor touched his eyes again as they shifted to hers. "Liar. I'll pick you up tomorrow at one."

Morgan tossed out a phrase commonly heard in the less elite portions of Italy. Nick responded with a pleased laugh.

"*Agapetike,* I should warn you, in my business I've had occasion to visit some Italian gutters."

"Good, then you won't need a translation."

"Just be ready." He let his gaze sweep down her, then up again. "You might find it easier to deal with me in the daylight—and when you're more adequately attired."

"I have no intention of dealing with you at all," Morgan began in a furious undertone. "Or of continuing this ridiculous charade by going with you tomorrow."

"Oh, I think you will." Nick's smile was confident and infuriating. "You'd find yourself having a difficult time explaining to Liz why you won't come when you've already expressed an interest in my home. Tell me, what was it that appealed to you about it?"

"The insanity of the architecture."

He laughed again and took her hand. "More compliments. I adore you, Aphrodite. Come, kiss me goodnight."

Morgan drew back and scowled. "I certainly will not."

"You certainly will." In a swift movement he had her pinned under him again. When she cursed him, he laughed and the insolence was back. "Witch," he murmured. "What mortal can resist one?"

His mouth came down quickly, lingering until she had stopped squirming beneath him. Gradually, the force went out of the kiss, but not the power. It seeped into her, so that she couldn't be sure if it was hers or his. Then it was only passion—clean and hot and senseless. On a moan, Morgan accepted it, and him.

Feeling the change in her, Nick relaxed a moment and simply let himself enjoy.

She had a taste that stayed with him long after he left her. Each time he touched her he knew, eventually, he would have to have it all. But not now. Now there was too much at stake. She was a risk, and he had already taken too many chances with her. But that taste…

He gave himself over to the kiss knowing the danger of letting himself become vulnerable, even for a moment, by losing himself in her. If she hadn't been on the beach that night. If he hadn't had to reveal himself to her. Would things have been different than they were now? he wondered as desire began to claw at him. Would he have been able to coax her into his arms, into his bed, with a bit of flair and a few clever words? If they had met for the first time tonight, would he have wanted her this badly, this quickly?

Her hands were in his hair. He found his mouth had roamed to her throat. Her scent seemed to concentrate there, and the taste was wild and dangerous. He lived with danger and enjoyed it—lived by his wits and won. But this woman, this feeling she stirred in him, was a risk he could calculate. Yet it was done. There was no changing the course he had to take. And no changing the fact that she was involved.

He wanted to touch her, to tear off that swatch of silk

she wore and feel her skin warm under his hand. He dared not. He was a man who knew his own limitations, his own weaknesses. Nick didn't appreciate the fact that Morgan James had become a weakness at a time when he could least afford one.

Murmuring his name, Morgan slid her hands beneath the loose sweatshirt, to run them over the range of muscle. Nick felt need shoot like a spear, white-tipped, to the pit of his stomach. Using every ounce of will, he banked down on it until it was a dull ache he could control. He lifted his head and waited for those pale, clouded blue eyes to open. Something dug into his palm, and he saw that he had gripped her medal in his hand without realizing it. Nick had to quell the urge to swear, then give himself a moment until he knew he could speak lightly. "Sleep well, Aphrodite," he told her with a grin. "Until tomorrow."

"You—" She broke off, struggling for the breath and the wit to hurl abuse at him.

"Tomorrow," Nick repeated as he brought her hand to his lips.

Morgan watched him stride to the balcony, then lower himself out of sight. Lying perfectly still, she stared at the empty space and wondered what she had gotten herself into.

Chapter 4

The house was cool and quiet in the mid-morning hush. Gratefully, Morgan accepted Liz's order to enjoy the beach. She wanted to avoid Iona's company, and though she hated to admit it, she didn't think she could handle Liz's carefree chatter about the dinner party. Liz would have expected her to make some witty observations about Nick that Morgan just didn't feel up to. Relieved that Dorian had business with Alex, and wouldn't feel obliged to keep her company, she set out alone.

Morgan wanted the solitude—she did her best thinking when she was alone. In the past few days she had accumulated quite a bit to think about. Now she decided to work it through one step at a time.

What had Nicholas Gregoras been doing that night on the beach? He'd had the scent of the sea on him, so it followed that he had been out on the water. She remembered the sound of a motor. She'd assumed it belonged to a fisherman but Nick was no fisherman. He'd been desperate not to be seen by someone…desperate enough to have been carrying a knife. She could still see the look on his face as she had lain beneath him in the shadows of the cypress. He'd been prepared to use the knife.

Somehow the knowledge that this was true disturbed her more now than it had when he'd been a stranger. Kicking bad-temperedly at a stone, she started down the beach steps.

And who had been with him? Morgan fretted. Someone had followed his orders without any question. Who had used the beach steps while Nick had held her prisoner in the shadows? Alex? The man who rented Nick's cottage? Frustrated, Morgan slipped out of her shoes and began to cross the warm sand. Why would Nick be ready to kill either one of them rather than be discovered by them? By anyone, she corrected. It could have been a servant of one of the villas, a villager trespassing.

One question at a time, Morgan cautioned herself as she kicked idly at the sand. First, was it logical to assume that the footsteps she had heard were from someone who had also come from the sea? Morgan thought it was. And second, she decided that the person must have been headed to one of the villas or a nearby cottage. Why else would they have used that particular strip of beach? Logical, she concluded, walking aimlessly. So why was Nick so violently determined to go unseen?

Smuggling. It was so obvious. So logical. But she had continued to push the words aside. She didn't want to think of him involved in such a dirty business. Somewhere, beneath the anger and resentment she felt for him, Morgan had experienced a totally different sensation. There was something about him—something she couldn't really pinpoint in words. Strength, perhaps. He was the kind of man you could depend on when no one else could—or would—help. She wanted to trust him. There was no logic to it, it simply was.

But was he a smuggler? Had he thought she'd seen something incriminating? Did the footsteps she'd heard belong to a patrol? Another smuggler? A rival? If he'd believed her to be a threat, why hadn't he simply used the knife on her? If he were a cold-blooded killer…no. Morgan shook her head at the description. While she could almost accept that Nick would kill, she couldn't agree with the adjective. And that led to hundreds of other problems.

Questions and answers sped through her mind. Stubborn questions, disturbing answers. Morgan shut her eyes on them. I'm going to get some straight answers from him this afternoon, she promised herself. It was his fault she was involved. Morgan dropped to the sand and brought her knees to her chest. She had been minding her own business when he had literally dragged her into it. All she had wanted was a nice, quiet vacation.

"Men!"

"I refuse to take that personally."

Morgan spun her head around and found herself staring into a wide, friendly smile.

"Hello. You seem to be angry with my entire gender." He rose from a rock and walked to her. He was tall and very slender, with dark gold curls appealingly disarrayed around a tanned face that held both youth and strength. "But I think it's worth the risk. I'm Andrew Stevenson." Still smiling, he dropped to the sand beside her.

"Oh." Recovering, Morgan returned the smile. "The poet or the painter? Liz wasn't sure."

"Poet," he said with a grimace. "Or so I tell myself." Glancing down, she saw the pad he held. It was dog-eared and covered with a fine, looping scribble. "I've interrupted your work, I'm sorry."

"On the contrary, you've given me a shot of inspiration. You have a remarkable face."

"I think," Morgan considered, "that's a compliment."

"Dear lady, yours is a face a poet dreams of." He let his eyes roam it for a moment. "Do you have a name, or are you going to vanish in a mist and leave me bewitched?"

"Morgan." The fussy compliment, delivered with bland sincerity made her laugh. "Morgan James, and are you a good poet, Andrew Stevenson?"

"I can't say no." Andrew continued to study her candidly. "Modesty isn't one of my virtues. You said Liz. I assume that's Mrs. Theoharis. You're staying with them?"

"Yes, for a few weeks." A new thought crossed her mind. "You're renting Nicholas Gregoras's cottage?"

"That's right. Actually, it's a free ride." Though he set down the pad, he began to trace patterns in the sand as if he couldn't keep his hands quite still. "We're cousins." Andrew noted the surprise on her face. His smile deepened. "Not the Greek side. Our mothers are related."

"Oh, so his mother's American." This at least explained his ease with the language.

"A Norling of San Francisco," he stated with a grin for the title. "She remarried after Nick's father died. She's living in France."

"So, you're visiting Lesbos and your cousin at the same time."

"Actually, Nick offered me the retreat when he learned I was working on an epic poem—a bit Homeric, you see." His eyes were blue, darker than hers, and very direct on her face. Morgan could see nothing in the open, ingenuous look to link him with Nick. "I wanted to stay on

Lesbos awhile, so it worked out nicely. The home of Sappho. The poetry and legend have always fascinated me."

"Sappho," Morgan repeated, turning her thoughts from Nick. "Oh, yes, the poetess."

"The Tenth Muse. She lived here, in Mitilini." His gaze, suddenly dreamy, swept down the stretch of beach. "I like to think Nick's house is on the cliff where she hurled herself into the sea, desperate for Phaon's love."

"An interesting thought." Morgan looked up to where a portion of a gray stone wall was visible. "And I suppose her spirit floats over the house searching for her love." Somehow, she liked the idea and smiled. "Lord knows, it's the perfect house for a poetic haunting."

"Have you been inside?" Andrew asked her, his tone as dreamy as his eyes now. "It's fantastic."

"No, I'm getting a personal tour this afternoon." Morgan kept her voice light as she swore silently in several languages.

"A personal tour?" Abruptly direct again, Andrew tilted his head, with brows lifted in speculation. "You must have made quite an impression on Nick. But then," he added with a nod, "you would. He sets great store by beauty."

Morgan gave him a noncommittal smile. He could hardly know that it wasn't her looks or charm that had secured the invitation. "Do you often write on the beach? I can't keep away from it myself." Morgan hesitated briefly, then plunged. "I came down here a couple of nights ago and swam by moonlight."

There was no shock or anxiety in his eyes at this information. Andrew grinned. "I'm sorry I missed that. You'll find me all over this part of the island. Here, up on the cliffs, in the olive groves. I go where the mood strikes me."

"I'm going to do some exploring myself." She thought wistfully of a carefree hour in the inlets.

"I'm available if you'd like a guide." His gaze skimmed over her face again, warm and friendly. "By now, I know this part of the island as well as a native. If you find you want company, you can usually find me wandering around or in the cottage. It isn't far."

"I'd like that." A gleam of amusement lit her eyes. "You don't happen to keep a goat, do you?"

"Ah—no."

Laughing at his expression, Morgan patted his hand. "Don't try to understand," she advised. "And now I'd better go change for my tour."

Andrew rose with her and captured her hand. "I'll see you again." It was a statement, not a question. Morgan responded to the gentle pressure.

"I'm sure you will; the island's very small."

Andrew smiled as he released her hand. "I'd rather call it kismet." He watched Morgan walk away before he settled back on his rock, facing the sea.

Nicholas Gregoras was very prompt. By five minutes past one, Morgan found herself being shoved out the door by an enthusiastic Liz. "Have fun, darling, and don't hurry back. Nick, Morgan will adore your house; all those winding passages and the terrifying view of the sea. She's very courageous, aren't you, Morgan?"

"I'm practically stalwart," she muttered while Nick grinned.

"Well, run along and have fun." Liz shooed them out the door as if they were two reluctant children being sent to school.

"You should be warned," Morgan stated as she slid into Nick's car, "Liz considers you a suitable candidate for my hand. I think she's getting desperate picturing me as her unborn child's maiden aunt."

"Aphrodite." Nick settled beside her and took her hand. "There isn't a male alive who could picture you as anyone's maiden aunt."

Refusing to be charmed, Morgan removed her hand from his, then studied the view out the side window. "I met your poet in residence this morning on the beach."

"Andrew? He's a nice boy. How did you find him?"

"Not like a boy." Turning back to Nick, Morgan frowned. "He's a very charming man."

Nick lifted a brow fractionally. "Yes, I suppose he is. Somehow, I always think of him as a boy, though there's barely five years between us." He moved his shoulders. "He does have talent. Did you charm him?"

"'Inspire' was his word," she returned, annoyed.

Nick flashed her a quick grin. "Naturally. One romantic should inspire another."

"I'm not a romantic." The conversation forced her to give him a great deal more of her attention than she had planned. "I'm very practical."

"Morgan, you're an insatiable romantic." Her annoyance apparently amused him, because a smile continued to hover on his mouth. "A woman who combs her hair on a moonlit beach, wears filmy white, and treasures a valueless memento thrives on romance."

Uncomfortable with the description, Morgan spoke coolly. "I also clip coupons and watch my cholesterol."

"Admirable."

She swallowed what might have been a chuckle. "You, Nicholas Gregoras, are a first-rate bastard."

"Yes. I hate to be second-rate at anything."

Morgan flounced back in her seat, but lost all resentment as the house came into full view. "Oh, Lord," she murmured. "It's wonderful!"

It looked stark and primitive and invulnerable. The second story lashed out over the sea like an out-stretched arm—not offering payment, but demanding it. None of the power she had felt out at sea was diminished at close range. The flowering shrubs and vines which trailed and tangled were placed to disguise the care of their planting. The result was an illusion of wild abandon. Sleeping Beauty's castle, she thought, a century after she pricked her finger.

"What a marvelous place." Morgan turned to him as he stopped the car at the entrance. "I've never seen anything like it."

"That's the first time you've smiled at me and meant it." He wasn't smiling now, but looking at her with a trace of annoyance. He hadn't realized just how much he'd wanted to see that spontaneous warmth in her eyes—directed at him. And now that he had, he wasn't certain what to do about it. With a quick mental oath, Nick slid from the car.

Ignoring him, Morgan climbed out and tried to take in the entire structure at once. "You know what it looks like," she said, half to herself. "It looks like Zeus hurled a lightning bolt into the mountain and the house exploded into existence."

"An interesting theory." Nick took her hand and started up the stone steps. "If you'd known my grandfather, you'd realize how close that is to the truth."

Morgan had primed herself to begin hurling questions and demanding explanations as soon as they had arrived. When she stepped into the entrance hall, she forgot everything.

Wide and speckled in aged white, the hall was spo-

radically slashed with stark colors from wall hangings
and primitive paintings. On one wall, long spears were
crossed—weapons for killing, certainly, but with an ancient dignity she had to admire. The staircase leading to
the upper floors arched in a half circle with a banister of
dark, unvarnished wood. The result was one of earthy
magnificence. It was far from elegant, but there was a
sense of balance and savage charm.

"Nicholas." Turning a full circle, Morgan sighed. "It's
really wonderful. I expect a cyclops to come stalking
down the stairs. Are there centaurs in the courtyard?"

"I'll take you through, and we'll see what we can do."
She was making it difficult for him to stick to his plan.
She wasn't supposed to charm him. That wasn't in the
script. Still, he kept her hand in his as he led her through
the house.

Liz's comparison to Aladdin's cave was completely
apt. Room after room abounded with treasures—Venetian
glass, Fabergé boxes, African masks, Native American
pottery, Ming vases. All were set together in a hodge-
podge of cultures. What might have seemed like a museum was instead a glorious clutter of wonders. As the
house twisted and turned, revealing surprise after surprise, Morgan became more fascinated. Elegant Wa-
terford crystal was juxtaposed with a deadly-looking
seventeenth-century crossbow. She saw exquisite porcelain and a shrunken head from Ecuador.

Yes, the architect was mad, she decided, noting lintels
with wolves' heads or grinning elves carved into them.
Wonderfully mad. The house was a fairy tale—not the
tame children's version, but with all the whispering shadows and hints of gremlins.

A huge curved window on the top floor gave her the
sensation of standing suspended on the edge of the cliff.

It jutted out, arrogantly, then fell in a sheer drop into the sea. Morgan stared down, equally exhilarated and terrified.

Nick watched her. There was a need to spin her around and seize, to possess while that look of dazzled courage was still on her face. He was a man accustomed to taking what he wanted without a second thought. She was something he wanted.

Morgan turned to him. Her eyes were still alive with the fascination of the sea and hints of excited fear. "Andrew said he hoped this was the cliff where Sappho hurled herself into the sea. I'm ready to believe it."

"Andrew's imaginative."

"So are you," she countered. "You live here."

"Your eyes are like some mythological lake," he murmured. "Translucent and ethereal. I should call you Circe rather than Aphrodite." Abruptly, he gripped her hair in his hand, tugging it until her face was lifted to his. "I swear you're more witch than goddess."

Morgan stared at him. There was no teasing in his eyes this time, no arrogance. What she saw was longing. And the longing, more than passion, seduced her. "I'm only a woman, Nicholas," she heard herself say.

His fingers tightened. His expression darkened. Then even as she watched, his mood seemed to shift. This time, he took her arm rather than her hand. "Come, we'll go down and have a drink."

As they entered the salon, Morgan reasserted her priorities. She had to get answers—she *would* get answers. She couldn't let a few soft words and a pair of dark eyes make her forget why she'd come. Before she could speak, however, a man slipped into the doorway.

He was small, with creased, leather skin. His hair was gray with age, but thick. So were his arms—thick and muscled. He made her think of a small-scaled, very efficient tank. His moustache was a masterpiece. It spread under his nose to drop free along the sides of his mouth, reaching his chin in two flowing arches. He smiled, showing several gaps in lieu of teeth.

"Good afternoon." He spoke in respectful Greek, but his eyes were dancing.

Intrigued, Morgan gave him an unsmiling stare. *"Yiasou."*

"Stephanos, Miss James. Stephanos is my, ah, caretaker."

The checkerboard grin widened at the term. "Your servant, my lady." He bowed, but there was nothing deferential in the gesture. "The matter we discussed has been seen to, Mr. Gregoras." Turning to Nick, the old man spoke with exaggerated respect. "You have messages from Athens."

"I'll tend to them later."

"As you wish." The small man melted away. Morgan frowned. There had been something in the exchange that wasn't quite what it should be. Shaking her head, she watched Nick mix drinks. It wasn't Nick's relationship with his servants that she was interested in.

Deciding that plunging head first was the most direct route, Morgan leaped. "What were you doing on the beach the other night?"

"I rather thought we'd concluded I was assaulting you." His voice was very mild.

"That was only part of the evening's entertainment." She swallowed and took another dive. "Had you been smuggling?"

To his credit, Nick hesitated only briefly. As his back was to her, Morgan didn't see his expression range from surprise to consideration. A very sharp lady, he mused. Too damn sharp.

"And how did you come by such an astonishing conclusion?" He turned to hand her a delicate glass.

"Don't start that charade with me," Morgan fumed, snatching the glass. "I've seen you stripped." She sat down and aimed a level stare.

Nick's mouth twitched. "What a fascinating way you have of putting things."

"I asked if you were a smuggler."

Nick sat across from her, taking a long study of her face as he ticked off possibilities. "First, tell me why you think I might be."

"You'd been out on the water that night. I could smell the sea on you."

Nick gazed down into the liquid in his glass, then sipped. "It's fanciful, to say the least, that my being out on the water equals smuggling."

Morgan ground her teeth at the cool sarcasm and continued. "If you'd been out on a little fishing trip, you'd hardly have dragged me into the trees waving a knife."

"One might argue," he murmured, "that fishing was precisely my occupation."

"The coast of Turkey is very convenient from this part of the island. Alex told me smuggling was a problem."

"Alex?" Nick repeated. There was a quick, almost imperceptible change in his expression. "What was Alex's attitude toward smuggling?"

Morgan hesitated. The question had broken into her well-thought-out interrogation. "He was…resigned, like one accepts the weather."

"I see." Nick swirled his drink as he leaned back. "And did you and Alex discuss the intricacies of the procedure?"

"Of course not!" she snapped, infuriated that he had cleverly turned the interrogation around on her. "Alex would hardly be intimate with such matters. But," she continued, "I think you are."

"Yes, I can see that."

"Well?"

He sent her a mildly amused smile that didn't quite reach his eyes. "Well what?"

"Are you going to deny it?" She wanted him to, Morgan realized with something like a jolt. She very, very badly wanted him to deny it.

Nick considered her for a moment. "If I deny it, you won't believe me. It's easy to see you've already made up your mind." He tilted his head, and now the amusement crept into his eyes. "What will you do if I admit it?"

"I'll turn you over to the police." Morgan took a bold sip of her drink. Nick exploded with laughter.

"Morgan what a sweet, brave child you are." He leaned over to take her hand before she could retort. "You don't know my reputation, but I assure you, the police would think you mad."

"I could prove—"

"What?" he demanded. His eyes were steady on hers, probing. The polished veneer was slowly fading. "You can't prove what you don't know."

"I know that you're not what you pretend to be." Morgan tried to pull her hand from his, but he held it firm. "Or maybe it's more accurate to say you're something you pretend not to be."

Nick watched her in silence, torn between annoyance and admiration. "Whatever I am, whatever I'm not, has nothing to do with you."

"No one wishes more than I that that was the truth."

Battling a new emotion, he sat back and studied her

over the rim of his glass. "So your conclusions that I might be involved in smuggling would prompt you to go to the police. That wouldn't be wise."

"It's a matter of what's right." Morgan swallowed, then blurted out what was torturing her mind. "The knife— would you have used it?"

"On you?" he asked, his eyes as expressionless as his voice.

"On anyone."

"A general question can't be given a specific answer."

"Nicholas, for God's sake—"

Nick set down his drink, then steepled his fingers. His expression changed, and his eyes were suddenly dangerous. "If I were everything you seem to think, you're incredibly brave or incredibly foolish to be sitting here discussing it with me."

"I think I'm safe enough," she countered and straightened her shoulders. "Everyone knows where I am."

"I could always dispose of you another time if I considered you an obstacle." Morgan's eyes flickered with momentary fear, quickly controlled. It was one more thing he could admire her for.

"I can take care of myself."

"Can you?" he murmured, then shrugged as his mood shifted again. "Well, in any case, I have no intention of wasting beauty especially when I intend to enjoy its benefits. Your talents could be useful to me."

Her chin shot up. "I have no intention of being your tool. Smuggling opium is a filthy way to make money. It's a far cry from crossing the English Channel with French silks and brandy."

"With mists curling and eye-patched buccaneers?" Nick countered with a smile. "Is that how your practical mind sees it, Morgan?"

She opened her mouth to retort, but found herself smiling. "I refuse to like you, Nicholas."

"You don't have to like me, Morgan. Like is too tame for my tastes in any case." Outwardly relaxed, he picked up his glass again. "Don't you like your drink?"

Without taking her eyes from his, Morgan set it down. "Nicholas, I only want a straight answer—I deserve one. You're perfectly right that I can't go to the police, no matter what you tell me. You really have nothing to fear from me."

Something flashed in his eyes at her final statement, then was quickly banked. He considered his options before he spoke. "I'll tell you this much, I am—concerned with smuggling. I'd be interested to know of any conversations you might hear on the subject."

Frowning, Morgan rose to wander the room. He was making it difficult for her to remember the straight and narrow path of right and wrong. The path took some confusing twists and turns when emotions were involved. Emotions! She brought herself up short. No, no emotions here. She had no feelings toward him.

"Who was with you that night?" Keep to the plan, she told herself. Questions and answers. Save the introspection for later. "You were giving someone orders."

"I thought you were too frightened to notice." Nick sipped at his drink.

"You were speaking to someone," Morgan went on doggedly. "Someone who did precisely what you told him without question. Who?"

Nick weighed the pros and cons before he answered. With her mind she'd figure it out for herself soon enough. "Stephanos."

"That little old man?" Morgan stopped in front of Nick

and stared down. Stephanos was not Morgan's image of a ruthless smuggler.

"That little old man knows the sea like a gardener knows a rose bush." He smiled at her incredulous expression. "He also has the advantage of being loyal. He's been with me since I was a boy."

"How convenient all this is for you." Depressed, Morgan wandered to a window. She was getting her answers, but she discovered they weren't the ones she wanted. "A home on a convenient island, a convenient servant, a convenient business to ease distribution. Who passed by the grove that night whom you wanted to avoid?"

Frightened or not, he thought angrily, she'd been far too observant. "That needn't concern you."

Morgan whirled. "You got me into this, Nicholas. I have a right to know."

"Your rights end where I say they do." He rose as his temper threatened. "Don't push me too far, Morgan. You wouldn't like the results. I've told you all I intend to for now. Be content with it."

She backed away a step, furious with herself for being frightened. He swore at the movement, then gripped her shoulders.

"I have no intention of harming you, damn it. If I had, there's already been ample opportunity. What do you picture?" he demanded, shaking her. "Me cutting your throat or tossing you off a cliff?"

Her eyes were dry and direct, more angry now than frightened. "I don't know what I picture."

Abruptly he realized he was hurting her. Cursing himself, he eased the grip to a caress. He couldn't keep letting her get under his skin this way. He couldn't let it matter what she thought of him. "I don't expect you to trust me," he said calmly. "But use common sense. Your involvement was a matter of circumstance, not design. I don't want to see you hurt, Morgan. That much you can take as the truth."

And that much she believed. Intrigued, she studied his face. "You're a strange man, Nicholas. Somehow, I can't quite see you doing something as base as smuggling opium."

"Intuition, Morgan?" Smiling, Nick tangled his fingers in her hair. It was soft, as he remembered, and tempting. "Are you a woman who believes in her intuition, or in her reason?"

"Nicholas—"

"No. No more questions or I'll have to divert you. I'm very"—a frown hovered, then flashed into a grin— "very susceptible to beauty. You have a remarkable supply. Coupled with a very good mind, the combination is hard to resist." Nick lifted the medal at her throat, examined it, then let it fall before he moved back from her. "Tell me, what do you think of Dorian and Iona?"

"I resent this. I resent all of this." Morgan spun away from him. He shouldn't be allowed to affect her so deeply, so easily, then switch off like a light. "I came to Lesbos to get away from pressures and complications."

"What sort of pressures and complications?"

She turned back to him, eyes hot. "They're my business. I had a life before I went down to that damned beach and ran into you."

"Yes," he murmured and picked up his drink. "I'm sure you did."

"Now, I find myself tossed into the middle of some grade-B thriller. I don't like it."

"It's a pity you didn't stay in bed that night, Morgan." Nick drank deeply, then twirled his glass by the stem. "Maybe I'm Greek enough to say the gods didn't will it so. For the moment your fate's linked with mine and there's nothing either of us can do about it."

She surprised him by laying a hand on his chest. He didn't like the way his heart reacted to the touch. Needs... he couldn't need. Wants were easily satisfied or ignored, but needs ate at a man.

"If you feel that way, why won't you give me a straight answer?"

"I don't choose to." His eyes locked on hers, cementing her to the spot. In them she saw desire—his and a mirror of her own. "Take me for what I am, Morgan."

She dropped her hand. Frightened not of him now, but of herself. "I don't want to take you at all."

"No?" He pulled her close, perversely enjoying her resistance. "Let's see just how quickly I can make a liar of you."

She could taste anger on his mouth, and just as clearly she could taste need. Morgan stopped resisting. The path of right and wrong took a few more confusing twists when she was in his arms. Whoever, whatever he was, she wanted to be held by him.

Her arms wound around his neck to draw him closer. She heard him murmur something against her mouth; the kiss held a savageness, a demand she was answering with equal abandon.

Had this passion always been there, sleeping inside her? It wasn't asleep any longer. The force of it had her clinging to him, had her mouth urgent and hungry against his. Something had opened inside her, letting him pour through. His hands were in her hair, then running down her back in a swift stroke of possession. She arched against him as if daring him to claim her—taunting him to try.

Somehow she knew, as her body fit truly to his, that

they would come back to each other, again and again, against their will, against all reason. She might fight it from moment to moment, but there would be a time. The knowledge filled her with hunger and fear.

"Morgan." Her name wrenched from him on a sigh of need. "I want you—by the gods, I want you. Come, stay here with me tonight. Here, where we can be alone."

His mouth was roaming her face. She wanted to agree. Her body was aching to agree to anything—to everything. Yet, she found herself drawing back. "No."

Nick lifted his face. His expression was amused and confident. "Afraid?"

"Yes."

His brows rose at the unexpected honesty, then drew together in frustration. The look in her eyes made it impossible for him to press his advantage. "*Diabolos,* you're an exasperating woman." He strode away and poured more liquor into his glass. "I could toss you over my shoulder, haul you up to the bedroom, and be done with it."

Though her legs were watery, Morgan forced herself to remain standing. "Why don't you?"

He whirled back, furious. She watched as he slowly pulled out the control. "You're more accustomed to a wine and candlelight seduction, I imagine. Soft promises. Soft lies." Nick drank deep, then set down his glass with a bang. "Is that what you want from me?"

"No." Morgan met his fury steadily while her hand reached instinctively for the medal at her throat. "I don't want you to make love to me."

"Don't take me for a fool!" He took a step toward her, then stopped himself. Another step and neither of them would have a choice. "Your body betrays you every time I touch you."

"That has nothing to do with it," she said calmly. "I don't want you to make love to me."

He waited a beat until the desire and frustration could be tamed a bit. "Because you believe I'm an opium smuggler?"

"No," she said, surprising both of them. She felt her strength waver a moment, then told him the truth. "Because I don't want to be one of your amusements."

"I see." Carefully, Nick dipped his hands into his pockets. "I'd better take you back before you discover I find nothing amusing in lovemaking."

A half-hour later, Nick slammed back into the house. His temper was foul. He stalked into the salon, poured himself another drink, and slumped into a chair. Damn the woman, he didn't have the time or patience to deal with her. The need for her was still churning inside him like a pain, sharp and insistent. He took a long swallow of liquor to dull it. Just physical, he told himself. He'd have to find another woman—any other woman—and release some of the tension.

"Ah, you're back." Stephanos entered. He noted the black temper and accepted it without comment. He'd seen it often enough in the past. "The lady is more beautiful than I remembered." Nick's lack of response left him unperturbed. He moved to the bar and poured himself a drink. "How much did you tell her?"

"Only what was necessary. She's sharp and remarkably bold." Nick eyed the liquid in his glass with a scowl. "She accused me flat out of smuggling." At Stephanos's cackle of laughter, Nick drained more liquor. "Your sense of humor eludes me at the moment, old man."

Stephanos only grinned. "Her eyes are sharp—they linger on you." Though Nick made no response, Stephanos's grin remained. "Did you speak to her of Alex?"

"Not at length."

"Is she loyal?"

"To Alex?" Nick frowned into his drink. "Yes, she would be. Where she cares, she'd be loyal." He set down the glass, refusing to give in to the urge to hurl it across the room. "Getting information out of her won't be easy."

"You'll get it nonetheless."

"I wish to hell she'd stayed in bed that night," Nick said savagely.

The gap-toothed grin appeared before Stephanos tossed back the drink in one long swallow. He let out a wheezy sigh of appreciation. "She lingers in your mind. That makes you uncomfortable." He laughed loud and long at Nick's scowl, then sighed again with the effort of it. "Athens is waiting for your call."

"Athens can fry in hell."

Chapter 5

Morgan's frame of mind was as poor as Nick's when she entered the Theoharis villa. Somewhere on the drive back from Nick's she had discovered that what she was feeling wasn't anger. It wasn't fear or even resentment. In a few days Nick had managed to do something Jack hadn't done in all the months she had known him. He'd hurt her.

It had nothing to do with the bruises that were already fading on her arms. This hurt went deeper, and had begun before she had even met him. It had begun when he had chosen the life he was leading.

Nothing to do with me. Nothing to do with me, Morgan told herself again and again. But she slammed the front door as she swept into the cool white hall. Her plans to go immediately to her room before she could snarl at anyone were tossed to the winds by a call and a wave from Dorian.

"Morgan, come join us."

Fixing on a smile, Morgan strolled out to the terrace. Iona was with him sprawled on a lounge in a hot-pink playsuit that revealed long, shapely legs but covered her arms with white lace cuffs at the wrists. She sent Morgan a languid greeting, then went back to her sulky study of the gulf. Morgan felt the tension hovering in the air and wondered if it had been there before or if she had brought it with her.

"Alex is on a transatlantic call," Dorian told her as he held out a chair. "And Liz is dealing with some domestic crisis in the kitchen."

"Without an interpreter?" Morgan asked. She smiled, telling herself Nick wasn't going to ruin her mood and make her as sulky as Alex's cousin.

"It's ridiculous." Iona gestured for Dorian to light her cigarette. "Liz should simply fire the man. Americans are habitually casual with servants."

"Are they?" Morgan felt her back go up at the slur on her friend and her nationality. "I wouldn't know."

Iona's dark eyes flicked over her briefly. "I don't imagine you've had many dealings with servants."

Before Morgan could retort, Dorian stepped in calmly. "Tell me, Morgan, what did you think of Nick's treasure trove?"

The expression in his eyes asked her to overlook Iona's bad manners, and told her something she'd begun to suspect the night before. He's in love with her, she mused, and felt a stab of pity. With an effort, Morgan relaxed her spine. "It's a wonderful place, like a museum without being regimented or stiff. It must have taken him years to collect all those things."

"Nick's quite a businessman," Dorian commented. Another look passed between him and Morgan. This time she saw it was gratitude. "And, of course, he uses his knowledge and position to secure the best pieces for himself."

"There was a Swiss music box," she remembered. "He said it was over a hundred years old. It played *Für Elise*." Morgan sighed, at ease again. "I'd kill for it."

"Nick's a generous man—when approached in the proper manner." Iona's smile was sharp as a knife. Morgan turned her head and met it.

"I wouldn't know anything about that either," she said coolly. Deliberately, she turned back to Dorian. "I met Nick's cousin earlier this morning."

"Ah, yes, the young poet from America."

"He said he wanders all over this part of the island. I'm thinking of doing the same myself. It's such a simple, peaceful place. I suppose that's why I was so stunned when Alex said there was a problem with smuggling."

Dorian merely smiled as if amused. Iona stiffened. As Morgan watched, the color drained from her face, leaving it strained and cold and anything but beautiful. Surprised by the reaction, Morgan studied her carefully. Why, she's afraid, she realized. Now why would that be?

"A dangerous business," Dorian commented conversationally. Since his eyes were on Morgan, Iona's reaction went unnoticed by him. "But common enough—traditional in fact."

"An odd tradition," Morgan murmured.

"The network of patrols is very large, I'm told, and closely knotted. As I recall, five men were killed last year, gunned down off the Turkish coast." He lit a cigarette of his own. "The authorities confiscated quite a cache of opium."

"How terrible." Morgan noticed that Iona's pallor increased.

"Just peasants and fishermen," he explained with a

shrug. "Not enough intelligence between them to have organized a large smuggling ring. It's rumored the leader is brilliant and ruthless. From the stories passed around in the village, he goes along on runs now and then, but wears a mask. Apparently, not even his cohorts know who he is. It might even be a woman." He flashed a grin at the idea. "I suppose that adds an element of romance to the whole business."

Iona rose and dashed from the terrace.

"You must forgive her." Dorian sighed as his eyes followed her. "She's a moody creature."

"She seemed upset."

"Iona's easily upset," he murmured. "Her nerves…"

"You care for her quite a lot."

His gaze came back to lock on Morgan's before he rose and strode to the railing.

"I'm sorry, Dorian," Morgan began immediately. "I didn't mean to pry."

"No, forgive me." He turned back and the sun streamed over his face, gleaming off the bronzed skin, combing through his burnished gold hair. Adonis, Morgan thought again, and for the second time since she had come to Lesbos wished she could paint. "My feelings for Iona are… difficult and, I had thought, more cleverly concealed."

"I'm sorry," Morgan said again, helplessly.

"She's spoiled, willful." With a laugh, Dorian shook his head. "What is it that makes one person lose his heart to another?"

Morgan looked away at the question. "I don't know. I wish I did."

"Now I've made you sad." Dorian sat back down beside Morgan and took her hands. "Don't pity me. Sooner or later, what's between Iona and me will be resolved. I'm a patient man." He smiled then, his eyes gleaming with confidence. "For now, we'll talk of something else. I have to confess, I'm fascinated by the smuggling legends."

"Yes. It is interesting. You said the rumor is that no one, not even the men who work for him, know who the leader is."

"That's the story. Whenever I'm on Lesbos, I keep hoping to stumble across some clue that would unmask him."

Morgan murmured something as her thoughts turned uncomfortably to Nick. "Yet you don't seem terribly concerned about the smuggling itself."

"Ah, the smuggling." Dorian moved his shoulders. "That's something for the authorities to worry about. But the thrill of the hunt, Morgan." His eyes gleamed as they moved past her. "The thrill of the hunt."

"You wouldn't believe it!" Liz bustled out and plopped into a chair. "A half-hour with a temperamental Greek cook. I'd rather face a firing squad. Give me a cigarette, Dorian." Her smile and everyday complaint made the subject of smuggling absurd. "So tell me, Morgan, how did you like Nick's house?"

Pink streaks joined sky and sea as dawn bloomed. The air was warm and moist. After a restless night, it was the best of beginnings.

Morgan strolled along the water's edge and listened to the first serenading of birds. This was the way she had planned to spend her vacation—strolling along the beach, watching sunrises, relaxing. Isn't that what her father and Liz had drummed into her head?

Relax, Morgan. Get off the treadmill for a while. You never give yourself any slack.

She could almost laugh at the absurdity. But then, neither Liz nor her father had counted on Nicholas Gregoras.

He was an enigma, and she couldn't find the key. His involvement in smuggling was like a piece of a jigsaw puzzle that wouldn't quite fit. Morgan had never been able to tolerate half-finished puzzles. She scuffed her sandals in the sand. He was simply not a man she could categorize, and she wanted badly to shake the need to try.

On the other hand, there was Iona. Morgan saw the puzzle there as well. Alex's sulky cousin was more than a woman with an annoying personality. There was some inner agitation—something deep and firmly rooted. And Alex knows something of it, she mused. Dorian, too, unless she missed her guess. But what? And how much? Iona's reaction to talk of smuggling had been a sharp contrast to both Alex's and Dorian's. They'd been resigned—even amused. Iona had been terrified. Terrified of discovery? Morgan wondered. But that was absurd.

Shaking her head, Morgan pushed the thought aside. This morning she was going to do what she had come to Greece to do. Nothing. At least, nothing strenuous. She was going to look for shells, she decided, and after rolling up the hem of her jeans, splashed into a shallow inlet.

They were everywhere. The bank of sand and the shallow water were glistening with them. Some had been crushed underfoot or beaten smooth by the slow current. Crouching, she stuffed the pockets of her jacket with the best of them.

She noticed the stub of a black cigarette half-buried in the sand. So, Alex comes this way, she thought with a smile. Morgan could see Liz and her husband strolling hand in hand through the shallows.

As the sun grew higher, Morgan became more engrossed. If only I'd brought a tote, she thought, then shrugged and began to pile shells in a heap to retrieve later. She'd have them in a bowl on her windowsill at home. Then, whenever she was trapped indoors on a cold, rainy afternoon, she could look at them and remember Greek sunshine.

There were dozens of gulls. They flapped around her, circled, and called out. Morgan found the high, piercing sound the perfect company for a solitary morning. As the time passed, she began to find that inner peace she had experienced so briefly on the moonlit beach.

The hunt had taken her a good distance from the beach. Glancing up, she saw, with pleasure, the mouth of a cave. It wasn't large and was nearly hidden from view, but she thought it was entitled to an exploration. With a frown for her white jeans, Morgan decided to take a peek inside the entrance and come back when she was more suitably dressed. She moved to it with the water sloshing up to her calves. Bending down, she tugged another shell from its bed of sand. As her gaze swept over toward the cave, her hand froze.

The face glistened white in the clear water. Dark eyes stared back at her. Her scream froze in her throat, locked there by terror. She had never seen death before—not unpampered, staring death. Morgan stepped back jerkily, nearly slipping on a rock. As she struggled to regain her balance, her stomach heaved up behind the scream so that she could only gag. Even through the horror, she could feel the pressure of dizziness. She couldn't faint, not here, not with that only a foot away. She turned and fled.

She scrambled and spilled over rocks and sand. The only clear thought in her head was to get away. On a dead run, breath ragged, she broke from the concealment of the inlet out to the sickle of beach.

Hands gripped her. Blindly, Morgan fought against them with the primitive fear that the thing in the inlet had risen up and come after her.

"Stop it! Damn it, I'll end up hurting you again. Morgan, stop this. What's wrong with you?"

She was being shaken roughly. The voice pierced the first layer of shock. She stared and saw Nick's face. "Nicholas?" The dizziness was back and she went limp against him as waves of fear and nausea wracked her. Trembling, she couldn't stop the trembling, but knew she'd be safe now. He was there. "Nicholas," she managed again as though his name alone was enough to shield her.

Nick caught her tighter and shook her again. Her face was deathly pale, her skin clammy. He'd seen enough of horror to recognize it in her eyes. In a moment, he knew, she'd faint or be hysterical. He couldn't allow either.

"What happened?" he demanded in a voice that commanded an answer.

Morgan opened her mouth, but found she could only shake her head. She buried her face against his chest in an attempt to block out what she had seen. Her breath was still ragged, coming in dry sobs that wouldn't allow for words. She'd be safe now, she told herself as she fought the panic. He'd keep her safe.

"Pull yourself together, Morgan," Nick ordered curtly, "and tell me what happened."

"Can't…" She tried to burrow herself into him.

In one quick move he jerked her away, shaking her. "I said tell me." His voice was cold, emotionless. He knew only one way to deal with hysteria, and her breath was still rising in gasps.

Dazed by the tone of his voice, she tried again, then jolted, clinging to him when she heard the sound of footsteps.

"Hello. Am I intruding?" Andrew's cheerful voice came from behind her, but she didn't look back. The trembling wouldn't stop.

Why was he angry with her? Why wasn't he helping her? The questions whirled in her head as she tried to catch her breath. Oh, God, she needed him to help her.

"Is something wrong?" Andrew's tone mirrored both concern and curiosity as he noted Nick's black expression and Morgan's shaking form.

"I'm not sure." Nick forced himself not to curse his cousin and spoke briefly. "Morgan was running across the beach. I haven't been able to get anything out of her yet." He drew her away, his fingers digging roughly in her skin as she tried to hold firm. She saw nothing in his face but cool curiosity. "Now, Morgan"—there was an edge of steel now—"tell me."

"Over there." Her teeth began to chatter as the next stage of reaction set in. Swallowing, she clamped them together while her eyes pleaded with him. His remained hard and relentless on hers. "Near the cove." The effort of the two short sentences swam in her head. She leaned toward him again. "Nicholas, please."

"I'll have a look." He grabbed her arms, dragging them away from him, wishing he didn't see what she was asking of him—knowing he couldn't give it to her.

"Don't leave, please!" Desperate, she grabbed for him again only to be shoved roughly into Andrew's arms.

"Damn it, get her calmed down," Nick bit off, tasting his own fury. She had no right—no right to ask for things he couldn't give. He had no right—no right to want to give them to her. He swore again, low and pungent under his breath as he turned away.

"Nicholas!" Morgan struggled out of Andrew's arms, but Nick was already walking away. She pressed a hand to her mouth to stop herself from calling him again. He never looked back.

Arms encircled her. Not Nick's. She could feel the gentle comfort of Andrew as he drew her against his chest. Her fingers gripped his sweater. Not Nick. "Here now." Andrew brought a hand to her hair. "I had hoped to entice you into this position under different circumstances."

"Oh, Andrew." The soft words and tender stroking had the ice of shock breaking into tears. "Andrew, it was so horrible."

"Tell me what happened, Morgan. Say it fast. It'll be easier then." His tone was quiet and coaxing as he stroked her hair. Morgan gave a shuddering sigh.

"There's a body at the mouth of the cave."

"A body!" He drew her back to stare into her face. "Good God! Are you sure?"

"Yes, yes, I saw—I was…" She covered her face with her hands a moment until she thought she could speak.

"Easy, take it easy," he murmured. "And let it come out."

"I was collecting shells in the inlet. I saw the cave. I was going to peek inside, then I…" She shuddered once, then continued. "Then I saw the face—under the water."

"Oh, Morgan." He drew her into his arms again and held her tight. He didn't say any more, but in silence gave her everything she had needed. When the tears stopped, he kept her close.

Nick moved rapidly across the sand. His frown deepened as he saw Morgan molded in his cousin's arms. As he watched, Andrew bent down to kiss her hair. A small fire leaped inside him that he smothered quickly.

"Andrew, take Morgan up to the Theoharis villa and phone the authorities. One of the villagers has had a fatal accident."

Nodding, Andrew continued to stroke Morgan's hair. "Yes, she told me. Terrible that she had to find it." He swallowed what seemed to be his own revulsion. "Are you coming?"

Nick looked down as Morgan turned her face to his. He hated the look in her eyes as she stared at him—the blankness, the hurt. She wouldn't forgive him easily for this. "No, I'll stay and make sure no one else happens across it. Morgan…" He touched her shoulders, detesting himself. There was no response, her eyes were dry now, and empty. "You'll be all right. Andrew will take you home."

Without a word, Morgan turned her face away again.

His control slipped a bit as Nick shot Andrew a hard glance. "Take care of her."

"Of course," Andrew murmured, puzzled by the tone. "Come on, Morgan, lean on me."

Nick watched them mount the beach steps. When they were out of sight, he went back to search the body.

Seated in the salon, her horror dulled with Alex's best brandy, Morgan studied Captain Tripolos of Mitilini's police department. He was short, with his build spreading into comfortable lines that stopped just short of fat. His gray hair was carefully slicked to conceal its sparseness. His eyes were dark and sharp. Through the haze of brandy and shock, Morgan recognized a man with the tenacity of a bulldog.

"Miss James." The captain spoke in quick, staccato English. "I hope you understand, I must ask you some questions. It is routine."

"Couldn't it wait?" Andrew was stationed next to Morgan on the sofa. As he spoke he slipped an arm around her shoulders. "Miss James has had a nasty shock."

"No, Andrew, it's all right." Morgan laid her hand over his. "I'd rather be done with it. I understand, Captain."

She gave him a straight look which he admired. "I'll tell you whatever I can."

"Efxaristo." He licked the end of his pencil, settled himself in his chair, and smiled with his mouth only. "Perhaps you could start by telling me exactly what happened this morning, from the time you arose."

Morgan began to recount the morning as concisely as she could. She spoke mechanically, with her hands limp and still in her lap. Though her voice trembled once or twice, Tripolos noted that her eyes stayed on his. She was a strong one, he decided, relieved that she wasn't putting him to the inconvenience of tears or jumbled hysterics.

"Then I saw him under the water." Morgan accepted Andrew's hand with gratitude. "I ran."

Tripolos nodded. "You were up very early. Is this your habit?"

"No. But I woke up and had an impulse to walk on the beach."

"Did you see anyone?"

"No." A shudder escaped, but her gaze didn't falter. She went up another notch in Tripolos's admiration. "Not until Nicholas and Andrew."

"Nicholas? Ah, Mr. Gregoras." He shifted his eyes to where Nick sprawled on a sofa across the room with Alex and Liz. "Had you ever seen the…deceased before?"

"No." Her hand tightened convulsively on Andrew's as the white face floated in front of her eyes. With a desperate effort of will, she forced the image away. "I've only been here a few days and I haven't been far from the villa yet."

"You're visiting from America?"

"Yes."

He made a quiet cluck of sympathy. "What a pity a murder had to blight your vacation."

"Murder?" Morgan repeated. The word echoed in her head as she stared into Tripolos's calm eyes. "But I thought...wasn't it an accident?"

"No." Tripolos glanced idly down at his notepad. "No, the victim was stabbed—in the back," he added with distaste. It was as if he considered murder one matter and back-stabbing another. "I hope I won't have to disturb you again." He rose and bowed over her hand. "Did you find many shells this morning, Miss James?"

"Yes I—I gathered quite a few." She felt compelled to reach in her jacket pocket and produce some. "I thought they were...lovely."

"Yes." He smiled, then turned to the others. "I regret we will have to question everyone on their whereabouts from last evening to this morning. Of course," he continued with a shrug, "we will no doubt find the murder was a result of a village quarrel, but with the body found so close to both villas..." He trailed off as he pocketed his pad and pencil. "One of you might recall some small incident that will help settle the matter."

Settle the matter? Morgan thought on a wave of hysteria. Settle the matter. But a man's dead. I'm dreaming. I must be dreaming.

"Easy, Morgan," Andrew whispered in her ear. "Have another sip." Gently, he urged the brandy back to her lips.

"You have our complete cooperation, Captain," Alex stated, and rose. "It isn't pleasant for any of us to have such a thing happen so near our homes. It's particularly upsetting that a guest of mine should have found the man."

"I understand, of course." Tripolos nodded wearily, rubbing a hand over his square chin. "It would be less confusing if I spoke with you one at a time. Perhaps we could use your office?"

"I'll show you where it is." Alex gestured to the door. "You can speak to me first if you like."

"Thank you." Tripolos gave the room a general bow before retreating behind Alex. Morgan watched his slow, measured steps. He'd haunt a man to the grave, she thought, and shakily swallowed the rest of the brandy.

"I need a drink," Liz announced, moving toward the liquor cabinet. "A double. Anyone else?"

Nick's eyes skimmed briefly over Morgan. "Whatever you're having." He gestured with his hand, signaling Liz to refill Morgan's glass.

"I don't see why he has to question us." Iona moved to the bar, too impatient to wait for Liz to pour. "It's absurd. Alex should have refused. He has enough influence to avoid all of this." She poured something potent into a tall glass and drank half of it down.

"There's no reason for Alex to avoid anything." Liz handed Nick his drink before splashing another generous portion of brandy into Morgan's glass. "We have nothing to hide. What can I fix you, Dorian?"

"Hide? I said nothing about hiding," Iona retorted as she swirled around the room. "I don't want to answer that policeman's silly questions just because *she* was foolish enough to stumble over some villager's body," she said, gesturing toward Morgan.

"A glass of ouzo will be fine, Liz," Dorian stated before Liz could fire a retort. His gaze lit on Iona. "I hardly think we can blame Morgan, Iona. We'd have been questioned in any case. As it is, she's had to deal with finding the man as well as the questions. Thank you, Liz," he added as she placed a glass in his hand and shot him a grim smile.

"I cannot stay in this house today." Iona prowled the room, her movements as jerky as a nervous finger on a trigger. "Nicky, let's go out in your boat." She stopped and dropped to the arm of his chair.

"The timing's bad, Iona. When I'm finished here, I have paperwork to clear up at home." He sipped his drink and patted her hand. His eyes met Morgan's briefly, but long enough to recognize condemnation. Damn you, he thought furiously, you have no right to make me feel guilty for doing what I have to do.

"Oh, Nicky." Iona's hand ran up his arm. "I'll go mad if I stay here today. Please, a few hours on the sea?"

Nick sighed in capitulation while inside he fretted against a leash that was too long, and too strong, for him to break. He had reason to agree, and couldn't let Morgan's blank stare change the course he'd already taken. "All right, later this afternoon."

Iona smiled into her drink.

The endless questioning continued. Liz slipped out as Alex came back in. And the waiting went on. Conversation came in fits and starts, conducted in undertones. As Andrew left the room for his conference, Nick wandered to Morgan's new station by the window.

"I want to talk to you." His tone was quiet, with the steel under it. When he put his hand over hers, she jerked it away.

"I don't want to talk to you."

Deliberately, he slipped his hands into his pockets. She was still pale. The brandy had steadied her but hadn't brought the color back to her cheeks. "It's necessary, Morgan. At the moment, I haven't the opportunity to argue about it."

"That's your problem."

"We'll go for a drive when the captain's finished. You need to get away from here for a while."

"I'm not going anywhere with you. Don't tell me what

I need now." She kept her teeth clamped and spoke without emotion. "I needed you then."

"Damn it, Morgan." His muttered oath had all the power of a shout. She kept her eyes firmly on Liz's garden. Some of the roses, she thought dispassionately, were overblown now. The hands in his pockets were fists, straining impotently. "Don't you think I know that? Don't you think I—" He cut himself off before he lost control. "I couldn't give you what you needed—not then. Don't make this any more impossible for me than it is."

She turned to him now, meeting his fury with frost. "I have no intention of doing that." Her voice was as low as his but with none of his vibrating emotion. "The simple fact is I don't want anything from you now. I don't want anything to do with you."

"Morgan…" There was something in his eyes now that threatened to crack her resolve. Apology, regret, a plea for understanding where she'd never expected to see one. "Please, I need—"

"I don't care what you need," she said quickly, before he could weaken her again. "Just stay away from me. Stay completely away from me."

"Tonight," he began, but the cold fury in her eyes stopped him.

"Stay away," Morgan repeated.

She turned her back on him and walked across the room to join Dorian. Nick was left with black thoughts and the inability to carry them out.

Chapter 6

Morgan was surprised she'd slept. She hadn't been tired when Liz and Alex had insisted she lie down, but had obeyed simply because her last words with Nick had sapped all of her resistance. Now as she woke she saw it was past noon. She'd slept for two hours.

Groggy, heavy-eyed, Morgan walked into the bath to splash cool water on her face. The shock had passed, but the nap had brought her a lingering weariness instead of refreshment. Beneath it all was a deep shame—shame that she had run, terrified, from a dead man. Shame that she had clung helplessly to Nick and been turned away. She could feel even now that sensation of utter dependence—and utter rejection.

Never again, Morgan promised herself. She should have trusted her head instead of her heart. She should have known better than to ask or expect anything from a man like him. A man like him had nothing to give. You'd always find hell if you looked to a devil. And yet…

And yet it had been Nick she had needed, and trusted—him she had felt safe with the moment his arms had come around her. My mistake, Morgan thought grimly, and studied herself in the mirror over the basin. There were still some lingering signs of shock—the pale cheeks and too wide eyes, but she felt the strength returning.

"I don't need him," she said aloud, wanting to hear the words. "He doesn't mean anything to me."

But he's hurt you. Someone who doesn't matter can't hurt you.

I won't let him hurt me again, Morgan promised herself. Because I won't ever go to him again, I won't ever ask him again, no matter what.

She turned away from her reflection and went downstairs.

Even as she entered the main hall, Morgan heard the sound of a door closing and footsteps. Glancing behind her, she saw Dorian.

"So, you've rested." He came to her and took her hand. In the gesture was all the comfort and concern she could have asked for.

"Yes. I feel like a fool." At his lifted brow, Morgan moved her shoulders restlessly. "Andrew all but carried me back up here."

With a low laugh, he slipped an arm around her shoulders and led her into the salon. "You American women—do you always have to be strong and self-reliant?"

"I always have been." She remembered weeping in Nick's arms—clinging, pleading—and straightened her spine. "I have to depend on myself."

"I admire you for it. But then, you don't make a habit of stumbling over dead bodies." He cast a look at her pale cheeks and gentled his tone. "There, it was foolish of me to remind you. Shall I fix you another drink?"

"No— No, I've enough brandy in me as it is." Morgan managed a thin smile and moved away from him.

Why was it she was offered a supporting arm by everyone but the one who mattered? No, Nick couldn't matter, she reminded herself. She couldn't let him matter, and she didn't need a supporting arm from anyone.

"You seem restless, Morgan. Would you rather be alone?"

"No." She shook her head as she looked up. His eyes were calm. She'd never seen them otherwise. There'd be strength in him, she thought, and wished bleakly it had been Dorian she had run to that morning. Going to the piano, she ran a finger over the keys. "I'm glad the captain's gone. He made me nervous."

"Tripolos?" Dorian drew out his cigarette case. "I doubt he's anything to worry about. I doubt even the killer need worry," he added with a short laugh. "The Mitilini police force isn't known for its energy or brilliance."

"You sound as if you don't care if the person who killed that man is caught."

"Village quarrels mean nothing to me," he countered. "I'm concerned more with the people I know. I don't like to think you're worried about Tripolos."

"He doesn't worry me," she corrected, frowning as he lit a cigarette. Something was nagging at the back of her mind, struggling to get through. "He just has a way of looking at you while he sits there, comfortable and not quite tidy." She watched the column of smoke curl up from the tip of the long, black cigarette. With an effort, Morgan shook off the feeling of something important, half remembered. "Where is everyone?"

"Liz is with Alex in his office. Iona's gone on her boat ride."

"Oh, yes, with Nicholas." Morgan looked down at her hands, surprised that they had balled into fists. Deliberately, she opened them. "It must be difficult for you."

"She needed to escape. The atmosphere of death is hard on her nerves."

"You're very understanding." Disturbed and suddenly headachy, Morgan wandered to the window. "I don't think I would be—if I were in love."

"I'm patient, and I know that Nick means less than nothing to her. A means to an end." He paused for a moment, before he spoke again, thoughtfully. "Some people have no capacity for emotion—love or hate."

"How empty that would be," Morgan murmured.

"Do you think so?" He gave her an odd smile. "Somehow, I think it would be comfortable."

"Yes, comfortable perhaps but…" Morgan trailed off as she turned back. Dorian was just lifting the cigarette to his lips. As Morgan's eyes focused on it, she remembered, with perfect clarity, seeing the stub of one of those expensive brands in the sand, only a few yards from the body. A chill shot through her as she continued to stare.

"Morgan, is something wrong?" Dorian's voice broke through so that she blinked and focused on him again.

"No, I—I suppose I'm not myself yet. Maybe I'll have that drink after all."

She didn't want it, but needed a moment to pull her thoughts together. The stub of a cigarette didn't have to mean anything, she told herself as Dorian went to the bar. Anyone from the villa could have wandered through that inlet a dozen times.

But the stub had been fresh, Morgan remembered—half in, half out of the sand, unweathered. The birds hadn't picked at it. Surely if someone had been that close to the body, they would have seen. They would have seen, and they would have gone to the police. Unless...

No, that was a ridiculous thought, she told herself as she felt a quick tremor. It was absurd to think that Dorian might have had anything to do with a villager's murder. Dorian or Alex, she thought as that sweet, foreign smoke drifted over her.

They were both civilized men—civilized men didn't stab other men in the back. Both of them had such beautiful, manicured hands and careful manners. Didn't it take something evil, something cold and hard to kill? She thought of Nick and shook her head. No, she wouldn't think of him now. She'd concentrate on this one small point and work it through to the end.

It didn't make any sense to consider Dorian or Alex as killers. They were businessmen, cultured. What possible dealings could they have had with some local fisherman? It was an absurd thought, Morgan told herself, but couldn't quite shake the unease that was creeping into her. There'd be a logical explanation, she insisted. There was always a logical explanation. She was still upset, that was all. Blowing some minor detail out of proportion.

Whose footsteps were on the beach steps that first night? a small voice insisted. Who was Nick hiding from? Or waiting for? That man hadn't been killed in a village quarrel, her thoughts ran on. She hadn't believed it for a moment, any more than she'd really believed the man had died accidentally. Murder... smuggling. Morgan closed her eyes and shuddered.

Who was coming in from the sea when Nick had held her in the shadow of the cypress? Nick had ordered Stephanos to follow him. Alex? Dorian? The dead man perhaps? She jolted when Dorian offered her the snifter.

"Morgan, you're still so pale. You should sit."

"No...I guess I'm still a little jumpy, that's all." Morgan cupped the snifter in both hands but didn't drink. She would ask him, that was all. She would simply ask him if he'd been to the inlet. But when her eyes met his, so calm, so concerned, she felt an icy tremor of fear. "The inlet—" Morgan hesitated, then continued before her courage failed her. "The inlet was so beautiful. It seemed so undisturbed." But so many shells had been crushed underfoot, she remembered abruptly. Why hadn't she thought of that before? "Do you—do a lot of people go there?"

"I can't speak for the villagers," Dorian began, watching as she perched on the arm of a divan. "But I'd think most of them would be too busy with their fishing or in the olive groves to spend much time gathering shells."

"Yes." She moistened dry lips. "But still, it's a lovely spot, isn't it?"

Morgan kept her eyes on his. Was it her imagination, or had his eyes narrowed? A trick of the smoke that wafted between them? Her own nerves?

"I've never been there," Dorian said lightly. "I suppose it's a bit like a native New Yorker never going to the top of the Empire State Building." Morgan's gaze followed his fingers as he crushed out the cigarette in a cut-glass ashtray. "Is there something else, Morgan?"

"Something—no." Hastily, she looked back up to meet his eyes. "No, nothing. I suppose like Iona, the atmosphere's getting to me, that's all."

"Small wonder." Sympathetic, he crossed to her. "You've been through too much today, Morgan. Too much talk of death. Come out in the garden," he suggested. "We'll talk of something else."

Refusal was on the tip of her tongue. She didn't know why, only that she didn't want to be with him. Not then.

Not alone. Even as she cast around for a reasonable excuse, Liz joined them.

"Morgan, I'd hoped you were resting."

Grateful for the interruption, Morgan set down her untouched brandy and rose. "I rested long enough." A quick scan of Liz's face showed subtle signs of strain. "You look like you should lie down awhile."

"No, but I could use some air."

"I was just taking Morgan out to the garden." Dorian touched a hand to Liz's shoulder. "You two go out and relax. Alex and I have some business we should clear up."

"Yes." Liz lifted her hand to his. "Thank you, Dorian. I don't know what Alex or I would have done without you today."

"Nonsense." He brushed her cheek with his lips. "Go, take your mind off this business."

"I will. See if you can get Alex to do the same." The plea was light, but unmistakable before Liz hooked her arm through Morgan's.

"Dorian." Morgan felt a flush of shame. He'd been nothing but kind to her, and she'd let her imagination run wild. "Thank you."

He lifted a brow at the gratitude, then smiled and kissed her cheek in turn. He smelt of citrus groves and sunshine. "Sit with the flowers for a while, and enjoy."

As he walked into the hall, Liz turned and headed toward the garden doors. "Should I order us some tea?"

"Not for me. And stop treating me like a guest."

"Good Lord, was I doing that?"

"Yes, ever since—"

Liz shot Morgan a quick look as she broke off, then grimaced. "This whole business really stinks," Liz stated inelegantly, and plopped down on a marble bench.

Surrounded by the colors and scents of the garden,

isolated from the house and the outside world by vines, Morgan and Liz frowned at each other.

"Damn, Morgan, I'm so sorry that you had to be the one. No, don't shrug and try to look casual," she ordered as Morgan did just that. "We've known each other too long and too well. I know what it must have been like for you this morning. And I know how you must be feeling right now."

"I'm all right, Liz." She chose a small padded glider and curled her legs under her. "Though I'll admit I won't be admiring seashells for a while. Please," she continued as Liz's frown deepened. "Don't do this. I can see that you and Alex are blaming yourselves. It was just—just a horrible coincidence that I happened to take a tour of that inlet this morning. A man was killed; someone had to find him."

"It didn't have to be you."

"You and Alex aren't responsible."

Liz sighed. "My practical American side knows that, but…" She shrugged, then managed to smile. "But I think I'm becoming a bit Greek. You're staying in my house." Liz lit a cigarette resignedly as she rose to pace the tiny courtyard.

A black cigarette, Morgan noticed with a tremor of anxiety—slim and black. She'd forgotten Liz had picked up the habit of occasionally smoking one of Alex's brand.

She stared up into Liz's oval, classic face, then shut her eyes. She must be going mad if she could conceive, even for an instant, that Liz was mixed up in smuggling and back-stabbing. This was a woman she'd known for years—lived with. Certainly if there was one person she knew as well as she knew herself, it was Liz.

But how far—how far would Liz go to protect the man she loved?

"And I have to admit," Liz went on as she continued to pace, "though it sticks me in the same category as Iona, that policeman made me nervous. He was just too"—she searched for an adjective—"respectful," she decided. "Give me a good old American grilling."

"I know what you mean," Morgan murmured. She had to stop thinking, she told herself. If she could just stop thinking, everything would be all right again.

"I don't know what he expected to find out, questioning us that way." Liz took a quick, jerky puff, making her wedding ring flash with cold, dazzling light.

"It was just routine, I suppose." Morgan couldn't take her eyes from the ring—the light, the stones. Love, honor, and obey—forsaking all others.

"And creepy," Liz added. "Besides, none of us even knew this Anthony Stevos."

"The captain said he was a fisherman."

"So is every second man in the village."

Morgan allowed the silence to hang. Carefully, she reconstructed the earlier scene in the salon. What were the reactions? If she hadn't been so dimmed with brandy and shock, would she have noticed something? There was one more person she'd seen lighting one of the expensive cigarettes. "Liz," she began slowly, "don't you think Iona went a little overboard? Didn't she get a bit melodramatic about a few routine questions?"

"Iona thrives on melodrama," Liz returned with grim relish. "Did you see the way she fawned all over Nick? I don't see how he could bear it."

"He didn't seem to mind," Morgan muttered. No, not yet, she warned herself. You're not ready to deal with that yet. "She's a strange woman," Morgan continued. "But this morning…" And yesterday, she remembered.

"Yesterday when I spoke of smuggling… I think she was really afraid."

"I don't think Iona has any genuine feelings," Liz said stubbornly. "I wish Alex would just cross her off as a bad bet and be done with it. He's so infuriatingly conscientious."

"Strange, Dorian said almost the same thing." Morgan plucked absently at an overblown rose. It was Iona she should concentrate on. If anyone could do something deadly and vile, it was Iona. "I don't see her that way."

"What do you mean?"

"Iona." Morgan stopped plucking at the rose and gave Liz her attention. "I see her as a woman of too many feelings rather than none at all. Not all healthy certainly, perhaps even destructive—but strong, very strong emotions."

"I can't abide her," Liz said with such unexpected venom, Morgan stared. "She upsets Alex constantly. I can't tell you how much time and trouble and money he's put into that woman. And he gets nothing back but ingratitude, rudeness."

"Alex has very strong family feelings," Morgan began. "You can't protect him from—"

"I'd protect him from anything," Liz interrupted passionately. "Anything and anyone." Whirling, she hurled her cigarette into the bushes where it lay smoldering. Morgan found herself staring at it with dread. "Damn," Liz said in a calmer tone. "I'm letting all this get to me."

"We all are." Morgan shook off the sensation of unease and rose. "It hasn't been an easy morning."

"I'm sorry, Morgan, it's just that Alex is so upset by all this. And as much as he loves me, he just isn't the kind of man to share certain areas with me. His trouble—his business. He's too damn Greek." With a quick laugh, she shook her head. "Come on, sit down. I've vented my spleen."

"Liz, if there were something wrong—I mean, something really troubling you, you'd tell me, wouldn't you?"

"Oh, don't start worrying about me now." Liz nudged Morgan back down on the glider. "It's just frustrating when you love someone to distraction and they won't let you help. Sometimes it drives me crazy that Alex insists on trying to keep the less-pleasant aspects of his life away from me."

"He loves you," Morgan murmured and found she was gripping her hands together.

"And I love him."

"Liz…" Morgan took a deep breath and plunged. "Do you and Alex walk through the inlet often?"

"Hmmm?" Obviously distracted, Liz looked back over her shoulder as she walked toward her bench. "Oh, no, actually, we usually walk on the cliffs—if I can drag him away from his office. I can't think when's the last time I've been near there. I only wish," she added in a gentler tone, "I'd been with you this morning."

Abruptly and acutely ashamed at the direction her thoughts had taken, Morgan looked away. "I'm glad you weren't. Alex had his hands full enough with one hysterical female."

"You weren't hysterical," Liz corrected in a quiet voice. "You were almost too calm by the time Andrew brought you in."

"I never even thanked him." Morgan forced herself to push doubts and suspicions aside. They were as ugly as they were ridiculous. "What did you think of Andrew?"

"He's a very sweet man." Sensing Morgan's changing mood, Liz adjusted her own thoughts. "He appeared to put himself in the role of your champion today." She smiled, deliberately looking wise and matronly. "I'd say he was in the first stages of infatuation."

"How smug one becomes after three years of marriage."

"He'd be a nice diversion for you," Liz mused, unscathed. "But he's from the genteel-poor side of Nick's family. I rather fancy seeing you set up in style. Then again," she continued as Morgan sighed, "he'd be nice company for you…for a while."

Dead on cue, Andrew strolled into the courtyard. "Hello. I hope I'm not intruding."

"Why, no!" Liz gave him a delighted smile. "Neighboring poets are always welcome."

He grinned, a flash of boyishness. With that, he went up several notches on Liz's list. "Actually, I was worried about Morgan." Bending over, he cupped her chin and studied her. "It was such an awful morning, I wanted to see how you were doing. I hope you don't mind." His eyes were dark blue, like the water in the bay—and with the same serenity.

"I don't." She touched the back of his hand. "At all. I'm really fine. I was just telling Liz I hadn't even thanked you for everything you did."

"You're still pale."

His concern made her smile. "A New York winter has something to do with that."

"Determined to be courageous?" he asked with a tilted smile.

"Determined to do a better job of it than I did this morning."

"I kind of liked the way you held on to me." He gave her hand a light squeeze. "I want to steal her for an evening," he told Liz, shifting his gaze from Morgan's face.

"Can you help me convince her a diversion is what she needs?"

"You have my full support."

"Come have dinner with me in the village." He bent down to Morgan again. "Some local color, a bottle of ouzo, and a witty companion. What more could you ask for?"

"What a marvelous idea!" Liz warmed to Andrew and the scheme. "It's just what you need, Morgan."

Amused, Morgan wondered if she should just let them pat each other on the back for a while. But it was what she needed—to get away from the house and the doubts. She smiled at Andrew. "What time should I be ready?"

His grin flashed again. "How about six? I'll give you a tour of the village. Nick gave me carte blanche with his Fiat while I'm here, so you won't have to ride on an ass."

Because her teeth were tight again, Morgan relaxed her jaw. "I'll be ready."

The sun was high over the water when Nick set his boat toward the open sea. He gave it plenty of throttle, wanting the speed and the slap of the wind.

Damn the woman! he thought on a new surge of frustration. Seething, he tossed the butt of a slender black cigarette into the churning waves. If she'd stay in bed instead of wandering on beaches at ridiculous hours, all of this could have been avoided. The memory of the plea in her voice, the horror in her eyes flashed over him. He could still feel the way she had clung to him, needing him.

He cursed her savagely and urged more speed from the motor.

Shifting his thoughts, Nick concentrated on the dead man. Anthony Stevos, he mused, scowling into the sun. He knew the fisherman well enough—what he had oc-

casionally fished for—and the Athens phone number he
had found deep inside Stevos's pants pocket.

Stevos had been a stupid, greedy man, Nick thought
dispassionately. Now he was a dead one. How long would
it take Tripolos to rule out the village brawl and hit on
the truth? Not long enough, Nick decided. He was going
to have to bring matters to a head a bit sooner than he
had planned.

"Nicky, why are you looking so mean?" Iona called to
him over the motor's roar. Automatically, he smoothed
his features.

"I was thinking about that pile of paperwork on my
desk." Nick cut the motor off and let the boat drift in its
own wake. "I shouldn't have let you talk me into taking
the afternoon off."

Iona moved to where he sat. Her skin glistened, oiled
slick, against a very brief bikini. Her bosom spilled over
in invitation. She had a ripe body, rounded and full and
arousing. Nick felt no stir as she swung her hips moving toward him.

"*Agapetikos,* we'll have to take your mind off business matters." She wound herself into his lap and pressed
against him.

He kissed her mechanically, knowing that, after the
bottle of champagne she'd drunk, she'd never know the
difference. But her taste lingered unpleasantly on his lips.
He thought of Morgan, and with a silent, furious oath,
crushed his mouth against Iona's.

"*Mmm.*" She preened like a stroked cat. "Your mind
isn't on your paperwork now, Nicky. Tell me you want
me. I need a man who wants me."

"Is there a man alive who wouldn't want a woman
such as you?" He ran a hand down her back as her mouth
searched greedily for his.

"A devil," she muttered with a slurred laugh. "Only a devil. Take me, Nicky." Her head fell back, revealing eyes half closed and dulled by wine. "Make love to me here, in the open, in the sun."

And he might have to, he thought with a grinding disgust in his stomach. To get what he needed. But first, he would coax what he could from her while she was vulnerable.

"Tell me, *matia mou,*" he murmured, tasting the curve of her neck while she busily undid the buttons of his shirt. "What do you know of this smuggling between Lesbos and Turkey?"

Nick felt her stiffen, but her response—and, he knew, her wits—were dulled by the champagne. In her state of mind, he thought, it wouldn't take much more to loosen her tongue. She'd been ready to snap for days. Deliberately, he traced his tongue across her skin and felt her sigh.

"Nothing," she said quickly and fumbled more desperately at his buttons. "I know nothing of such things."

"Come, Iona," he murmured seductively. She was a completely physical woman, one who ran on sensations alone. Between wine and sex and her own nerves, she'd talk to him. "You know a great deal. As a businessman"—he nipped at her earlobe—"I'm interested in greater profit. You won't deny me a few extra drachmas, will you?"

"A few million," she murmured, and put her hand on his to show him what she wanted. "Yes, there's much I know."

"And much you'll tell me?" he asked. "Come, Iona. You and the thought of millions excite me."

"I know the man that stupid woman found this morning was murdered because he was greedy."

Nick forced himself not to tense. "But greed is so difficult to resist." He went with her as she stretched full length on the bench. "Do you know who murdered him, Iona?" She was slipping away from him, losing herself to the excess of champagne. On a silent oath, Nick nipped at her skin to bring her back.

"I don't like murder, Nicky," she mumbled, "and I don't like talking to the police even more." She reached for him, but her hands fumbled. "I'm tired of being used," she said pettishly, then added, "Perhaps it's time to change allegiance. You're rich, Nicky. I like money. I need money."

"Doesn't everyone?" Nick asked dryly.

"Later, we'll talk later. I'll tell you." Her mouth was greedy on his. Forcing everything from his mind, Nick struggled to find some passion, even the pretense of passion, in return. God, he needed a woman; his body ached for one. And he needed Iona. But as he felt her sliding toward unconsciousness, he did nothing to revive her.

Later, as Iona slept in the sun, Nick leaned over the opposite rail and lit a cigarette from the butt of another. The clinging distaste both infuriated and depressed him. He knew that he would have to use Iona, be used by her—if not this time, then eventually. He had to tap her knowledge to learn what he wanted to know. It was a matter of his own safety—and his success. The second had always been more important to him than the first.

If he had to be Iona's lover to gain his own end, then he'd be her lover. It meant nothing. Swearing, he drew deeply on the cigarette. It meant nothing, he repeated. It was business.

He found he wanted a shower, a long one, something to cleanse himself of the dirt which wouldn't wash away.

Years of dirt, years of lies. Why had he never felt imprisoned by them until now?

Morgan's face slipped into his mind. Her eyes were cold. Flinging the cigarette out to sea, he went back to the wheel and started the engine.

Chapter 7

During a leisurely drink after a leisurely tour, Morgan decided the village was perfect. White-washed houses huddled close together, some with pillars, some with arches, still others with tiny wooden balconies. The tidiness, the freshness of white should have lent an air of newness. Instead, the village seemed old and timeless and permanent.

She sat with Andrew at a waterfront *kafenion,* watching the fishing boats sway at the docks, and the men who spread their nets to dry.

The fishermen ranged from young boys to old veterans. All were bronzed, all worked together. There were twelve to each net—twenty-four hands, some wrinkled and gnarled, some smooth with youth. All strong. As they worked they shouted and laughed in routine companionship.

"Must have been a good catch," Andrew commented.

He watched Morgan's absorption with the small army of men near the water's edge.

"You know, I've been thinking." She ran a finger down the side of her glass. "They all seem so fit and sturdy. Some of those men are well past what we consider retirement age in the States. I suppose they'll sail until they die. A life on the water must be a very satisfying existence." Pirates…would she ever stop thinking of pirates?

"I don't know if any of these people think much about satisfaction. It's simply what they do. They fish or work in Nick's olive groves. They've been doing one or the other for generations." Toying with his own drink, Andrew studied them too. "I do think there's a contentment here. The people know what's expected of them. If their lives are simple, perhaps it's an enviable simplicity."

"Still, there's the smuggling," Morgan murmured.

Andrew shrugged. "It's all part of the same mold, isn't it? They do what's expected of them and earn a bit of adventure and a few extra drachmas."

She shot him a look of annoyed surprise. "I didn't expect that attitude from you."

Andrew looked back at her, both brows raised. "What attitude?"

"This—this nonchalance over crime."

"Oh, come on, Morgan, it's—"

"Wrong," she interrupted. "It should be stopped." Morgan swallowed the innocently clear but potent ouzo.

"How do you stop something that's been going on for centuries in one form or another?"

"It's current form is ugly. I should think the men of influence like Alex and…Nicholas, with homes on the island, would put pressure on whoever should be pressured."

"I don't know Alex well enough to comment," Andrew

mused, filling her glass again. "But I can't imagine Nick getting involved in anything that didn't concern himself or his business."

"Can't you?" Morgan murmured.

"If that sounds like criticism, it's not." He noted he had Morgan's full attention, but that her eyes were strangely veiled. "Nick's been very good to me, lending me the cottage and the money for my passage. Lord knows when I'll be able to pay him back. And it irks quite a bit to have to borrow, but poetry isn't the most financially secure career."

"I think I read somewhere that T.S. Eliot was a bank teller."

Andrew returned her understanding smile with a wry grimace. "I could work out of Nick's California office." He shrugged and drank. "His offer wasn't condescending, just absentminded. It's rough on the ego." He looked past her, toward the docks. "Maybe my ship will come in."

"I'm sure it will, Andrew. Some of us are meant to follow dreams."

His gaze came back to her. "And artists are meant to suffer a bit, rise beyond the more base needs of money and power?" His smile was brittle, his eyes cool. "Let's order." Morgan watched him shake off the mood and smile with his usual warmth. "I'm starved."

The evening sky was muted as they finished their meal. There were soft, dying colors flowing into the western sea. In the east, it was a calm, deep violet waiting for the first stars. Morgan was content with the vague glow brought on by spiced food and Greek ouzo. There was intermittent music from a mandolin. Packets of people shuffled in and out of the café, some of them breaking into song.

Their waiter cum proprietor was a wide man with a

thin moustache and watery eyes. Morgan figured the eyes could be attributed to the spices and cook smoke hanging in the air. American tourists lifted his status. Because he was impressed with Morgan's easily flowing Greek, he found opportunities to question and gossip as he hovered around their table.

Morgan toyed with a bit of *psomaki* and relaxed with the atmosphere and easy company. She'd found nothing but comfort and good will in the Theoharis villa, but this was something different. There was an earthier ambience she had missed in Liz's elegant home. Here there would be lusty laughter and spilled wine. As strong as Morgan's feelings were for both Liz and Alex, she would never have been content with the lives they led. She'd have rusted inside the perpetual manners.

For the first time since that morning, Morgan felt the nagging ache at the base of her skull begin to ease.

"Oh, Andrew, look! They're dancing." Cupping her chin on her hands, Morgan watched the line of men hook arms.

As he finished up the last of a spicy sausage, Andrew glanced over. "Want to join in?"

Laughing, she shook her head. "No, I'd spoil it—but you could," she added with a grin.

"You have," Andrew began as he filled her glass again, "a wonderful laugh. It's rich and unaffected and trails off into something sensuous."

"What extraordinary things you say, Andrew." Morgan smiled at him, amused. "You're an easy man to be with. We could be friends."

Andrew lifted his brows. Morgan was surprised to find her mouth briefly captured. There was a faint taste of the island on him—spicy and foreign. "For starters." At her stunned expression, he leaned back and grinned.

"That face you're wearing doesn't do great things for my ego, either." He pulled a pack of cigarettes out of his jacket pocket, then dug for a match. Morgan stopped staring at him to stare at the thin black box.

"I didn't know you smoked," she managed after a moment.

"Oh, not often." He found a match. The tiny flame flared, flickering over his face a moment, casting shadows, mysteries, suspicions. "Especially since my taste runs to these. Nick takes pity on me and leaves some at my cottage whenever he happens by. Otherwise, I suppose I'd do without altogether." When he noticed Morgan's steady stare, he gave her a puzzled smile. "Something wrong?"

"No." She lifted her glass and hoped she sounded casual. "I was just thinking—you'd said you roam all over this part of the island. You must have been in that inlet before."

"It's a beautiful little spot." He reached over for her hand. "Or it was. I guess I haven't been there in over a week. It might be quite a while before I go back now."

"A week," Morgan murmured.

"Don't dwell on it, Morgan."

She lifted her eyes to his. They were so clear, so concerned. She was being a fool. None of them—Alex, Dorian, Andrew—none of them were capable of what was burning into her thoughts. How was she to know that some maniac from the village hadn't had a taste for expensive tobacco and back-stabbing? It made more sense, a great deal more sense than her ugly suspicions.

"You're right." She smiled again and leaned toward him. "Tell me about your epic poem."

"Good evening, Miss James, Mr. Stevenson."

Morgan twisted her head and felt the sky cloud over. She looked up into Tripolos's pudgy face. "Hello, Captain."

If her greeting lacked enthusiasm, Tripolos seemed unperturbed. "I see you're enjoying a bit of village life. Do you come often?"

"This is Morgan's first trip," Andrew told him. "I convinced her to come out to dinner. She needed something after this morning's shock."

Tripolos clucked sympathetically. Morgan noted the music and laughter had stilled. The atmosphere in the café was hushed and wary.

"Very sensible," the captain decided. "A young lady must not dwell on such matters. I, unfortunately, must think of little else at the moment." He sighed and looked wistfully at the ouzo. "Enjoy your evening."

"Damn, damn, *damn!*" she muttered when he walked away. "Why does he affect me this way? Every time I see him, I feel like I've got the Hope diamond in my pocket."

"I know what you mean." Andrew watched people fall back to create a path for Tripolos. "He almost makes you wish you had something to confess."

"Thank God, it's not just me." Morgan lifted her glass again, noticed her hands were trembling, and drained it. "Andrew," she began in calm tones, "unless you have some moral objection, I'm going to get very drunk."

Sometime later, after learning Andrew's views on drinking were flexible, Morgan floated on a numbing cloud of ouzo. The thin light of the moon had replaced the colors of sunset. As the hour grew later, the café crowd grew larger, both in size and volume. Music was all strings and bells. If the interlude held a sheen of unreality, she no longer cared. She'd had enough of reality.

The waiter materialized with yet another bottle. He set it on the table with the air of distributing a rare wine.

"Busy night," Morgan commented, giving him a wide if misty, smile.

"It is Saturday," he returned, explaining everything.

"So, I've chosen my night well." She glanced about, seeing a fuzzy crush of people. "Your customers seem happy."

He followed her survey with a smug smile, wiping a hand on his apron. "I feared when the Mitilini captain came, my business would suffer, but all is well."

"The police don't add to an atmosphere of enjoyment. I suppose," she added slowly, "he's investigating the death of that fisherman."

He gave Morgan a quick nod. "Stevos came here often, but he was a man with few companions. He was not one for dancing or games. He found other uses for his time." The waiter narrowed his eyes. "My customers do not like to answer questions." He muttered something uncomplimentary, but Morgan wasn't sure if it was directed at Stevos or Tripolos.

"He was a fisherman," she commented, struggling to concentrate on the Greek's eyes. "But it appears his comrades don't mourn him."

The waiter moved his shoulders eloquently, but she saw her answer. There were fishermen, and fishermen. "Enjoy your evening, *kyrios*. It is an honor to serve you."

"You know," Andrew stated when the waiter drifted to another table, "it's very intimidating listening to all that Greek. I couldn't pick up on it. What was he saying?"

Not wanting to dwell on the murder again, Morgan merely smiled. "Greek males are red-blooded, Andrew, but I explained that I was otherwise engaged for this evening." She locked her hands behind her head and looked up at the stars. "Oh, I'm glad I came. It's so lovely. No murders—no smuggling tonight. I feel marvelous, Andrew. When can I read some of your poetry?"

"When your brain's functioning at a normal level." Smiling, he tilted more ouzo into her glass. "I think your opinion might be important."

"You're a nice man." Morgan lifted her glass and studied him as intensely as possible. "You're not at all like Nicholas."

"What brought that on?" Andrew frowned, setting the bottle back down again.

"You're just not." She held out her glass. "To Americans," she told him. "One hundred percent pure."

After tapping her glass with his, Andrew drank and shook his head. "I have a feeling we weren't toasting the same thing."

She felt Nick begin to push into her thoughts and she thrust him away. "What does it matter? It's a beautiful night."

"So it is." His finger traced lightly over the back of her hand. "Have I told you how lovely you are?"

"Oh, Andrew, are you going to flatter me?" With a warm laugh, she leaned closer. "Go ahead, I love it."

With a wry grin, he tugged her hair. "You're spoiling my delivery."

"Oh, dear…how's this?" Morgan cupped her chin on her hands again and gave him a very serious stare.

On a laugh, Andrew shook his head. "Let's walk for a while. I might find a dark corner where I can kiss you properly."

Rising, he helped Morgan to her feet. She exchanged a formal and involved good-night with the proprietor before Andrew could navigate her away from the crowd.

Those not gathered in the *kafenion* were long since in bed. The white houses were closed and settled for the night. Now and then a dog barked, and another answered. Morgan could hear her own footsteps echo down the street.

"It's so quiet," she murmured. "All you can really hear is the water and the night itself. Ever since that first morning when I woke up on Lesbos, I've felt as if I belonged. Nothing that's happened since has spoiled that for me. Andrew." She whirled herself around in his arms and laughed. "I don't believe I'm *ever* going home again. How can I face New York and the traffic and the snow again? Rushing to work, rushing home. Maybe I'll become a fisherman, or give in to Liz and marry a goatherd."

"I don't think you should marry a goatherd," Andrew said practically, and drew her closer. Her scent was tangling his senses. Her face, in the moonlight, was an ageless mystery. "Why don't you give the fishing a try? We could set up housekeeping in Nick's cottage."

It would serve him right, her mind muttered. Lifting her mouth, Morgan waited for the kiss.

It was warm and complete. Morgan neither knew nor cared if the glow was a result of the kiss or the liquor. Andrew's lips weren't demanding, weren't urgent and possessive. They were comforting, requesting. She gave him what she could.

There was no rocketing passion—but she told herself she didn't want it. Passion clouded the mind more successfully than an ocean of ouzo. She'd had enough of hunger and passions. They brought pain with disillusionment. Andrew was kind, uncomplicated. He wouldn't turn away when she needed him. He wouldn't give her sleepless nights. He wouldn't make her doubt her own strict code of right and wrong. He was the knight—a woman was safe with a knight.

"Morgan," he murmured, then rested his cheek on her hair. "You're exquisite. Isn't there some man I should consider dueling with?"

Morgan tried to think of Jack, but could form no clear picture. There was, however, a sudden, atrociously sharp image of Nick as he dragged her close for one of his draining kisses.

"No," she said too emphatically. "There's no one. Absolutely no one."

Andrew drew her away and tilted her chin with his finger. He could see her eyes in the dim glow of moonlight. "From the strength of your denial, I'd say my competition's pretty formidable. No"—he laid a finger over her lips as she started to protest—"I don't want to have my suspicions confirmed tonight. I'm selfish." He kissed her again, lingering over it. "Damn it, Morgan, you could be habit forming. I'd better take you home while I remember I'm a gentleman and you're a very drunk lady."

The villa shimmered white under the night sky. A pale light glowed in a first-floor window for her return.

"Everyone's asleep," Morgan stated unnecessarily as she let herself out of the car. Andrew rounded the hood. "I'll have to be very quiet." She muffled irrepressible giggles with a hand over her mouth. "Oh, I'm going to feel like an idiot tomorrow if I remember any of this."

"I don't think you'll remember too much," Andrew told her as he took her arm.

Morgan managed the stairs with the careful dignity of someone who no longer feels the ground under her feet. "It would never do to disgrace Alex by landing on my face in the foyer. He and Dorian are *so* dignified."

"And I," Andrew returned, "will have to resume my

drive with the utmost caution. Nick wouldn't approve if I ran his Fiat off a cliff."

"Why, Andrew." Morgan stood back and studied him owlishly. "You're almost as sloshed as I am."

"Not quite, but close enough. However"—he let out a long breath and wished he could lie down—"I conducted myself with the utmost restraint."

"Very nicely done." She went off into a muffled peal of giggles again. "Oh, Andrew." She leaned against him so heavily that he had to shift his balance to support her. "I did have a good time—a wonderful time. I needed it more than I realized. Thank you."

"In you go." He opened the door and gave her a nudge inside. "Be careful on the stairs," he whispered. "Should I wait and listen for the sounds of an undignified tumble?"

"Just be on your way and don't take the Fiat for a swim." She stood on her toes and managed to brush his chin with her lips. "Maybe I should make you some coffee."

"You'd never find the kitchen. Don't worry, I can always park the car and walk if worse comes to worst. Go to bed, Morgan, you're weaving."

"That's you," she retorted before she closed the door.

Morgan took the stairs with painful caution. The last thing she wanted to do was wake someone up and have to carry on any sort of reasonable conversation. She stopped once and pressed her hands to her mouth to stop a fresh bout of giggles. Oh, it felt so good, so good not to be able to think. But this has to stop, she told herself firmly. No more of this, Morgan, straighten up and get upstairs before all is discovered.

She managed to pull herself to the top landing, then had to think carefully to remember in which direction her room lay. To the left, of course, she told herself with a shake of the head. But which way is left, for God's sake? She spent another moment working it out before she crept down the hall. She gripped the doorknob, then waited for the door to stop swaying before she pushed it open.

"Ah, success," she murmured, then nearly spoiled it by stumbling over the rug. Quietly, she shut the door and leaned back against it. Now, if she could just find the bed. A light switched on, as if by magic. She smiled absently at Nick.

"*Yiasou*, you seem to be a permanent fixture."

The fury in his eyes rolled off the fog as she stepped unsteadily out of her shoes.

"What the hell have you been up to?" he demanded. "It's nearly three o'clock in the morning!"

"Oh, how rude of me not to have phoned to tell you I'd be late."

"Don't get cute, damn it, I'm not in the mood." He stalked over to her and grabbed her arms. "I've been waiting for you half the night, Morgan, I…" His voice trailed off as he studied her. His expression altered from fury to consideration then reluctant amusement. "You're totally bombed."

"Completely," she agreed, and had to take a deep breath to keep from giggling again. "You're so observant, Nicholas."

Amusement faded as her hand crept up his shirt front. "How the hell am I supposed to have a rational conversation with a woman who's seeing two of everything?"

"Three," she told him with some pride. "Andrew's only up to two. I quite surpassed him." Her other hand slid up to toy with one of his buttons. "Did you know you have wonderful eyes. I've never seen eyes so dark. Andrew's are blue. He doesn't kiss anything like you do. Why don't you kiss me now?"

He tightened his grip for a moment, then carefully released her. "So, you've been out with young Andrew." He wandered the room while Morgan swayed and watched him.

"*Young* Andrew and I would have asked you to join us, but it just slipped our minds. Besides, you can be really boring when you're proper and charming." She had a great deal of trouble with the last word and yawned over it. "Do we have to talk much longer? My tongue's getting thick."

"I've had about enough of being proper and charming myself," he muttered, picking up a bottle of her scent and setting it down again. "It serves its purpose."

"You do it very well," she told him and struggled with her zipper. "In fact, you're nearly perfect at it."

"Nearly?" His attention caught, he turned in time to see her win the battle with the zipper. "Morgan, for God's sake, don't do that now. I—"

"Yes, except you do slip up from time to time. A look in your eyes—the way you move. I suppose it's convincing all around if I'm the only one who's noticed. Then again, it might be because everyone else knows you and expects the inconsistency. Are you going to kiss me or not?" She dropped the dress to the floor and stepped out of it.

He felt his mouth go dry as she stood, clad only in a flimsy chemise, watching him mistily. Desire thudded inside him, hot, strong, and he forced himself back to what she was saying.

"Noticed what?"

Morgan made two attempts to pick up the dress. Each time she bent, the top of the chemise drifted out to show the swell of her breasts. Nick felt the thud lower to his stomach. "Noticed what?" she repeated as she left the dress where it was. "Oh, we're back to that. It's definitely the way you move."

"Move?" He struggled to keep his eyes on her face and away from her body. But her scent was already clouding his brain, and her smile—her smile challenged him to do something about it.

"It's like a panther," Morgan told him, "who knows he's being hunted and plans to turn the attack to his advantage when he's ready."

"I see." He frowned, not certain he liked her analogy. "I'll have to be more careful."

"Your problem," Morgan said cheerfully. "Well, since you don't want to kiss me, I'll say good-night, Nicholas. I'm going to bed. I'd see you down your vine, but I'm afraid I'd fall off the balcony."

"Morgan, I need to talk to you." He moved quickly and took her arm before she could sink onto the bed. That, he knew, would be too much pressure for any man. But she lost her already uncertain balance and tumbled into his arms. Warm and pliant, she leaned against him, making no objection as he molded her closer.

"Have you changed your mind?" she murmured, giving him a slow, sleepy-eyed smile. "I thought of you when Andrew kissed me tonight. It was very rude of me—or of you, I'm not sure which. Perhaps I'll think of Andrew if you kiss me now."

"The hell you will." He dragged her against him, teetering on the edge. Morgan let her head fall back.

"Try me," she invited.

"Morgan—the hell with all of it!"

Helplessly, he devoured her mouth. She was quickly and totally boneless, arousing him to desperation by simple surrender. Desire was a fire inside him, spreading dangerously.

For the first time, he let himself go. He could think of nothing, nothing but her and the way her body flowed in his hands. She was softer than anything he'd ever hoped to know. So soft, she threatened to seep into him, become a part of him before he could do anything to prevent it. The need was raging, overpowering, taking over the control he'd been master of for as long as he could remember. But now, he burned to forfeit it.

With her, everything could be different. With her, he'd be clean again. Could she turn back the clock?

He could feel the brush of the bedspread against his thigh and knew, in one movement, he could be on it with her. Then nothing would matter but that he had her—a woman. But it wasn't any woman he wanted. It had been her since the first night she had challenged him on that deserted beach. It had been her since the first time those light, clear eyes had dared him. He was afraid—and he feared little—that it would always be her.

Mixed with the desire came a quick twist of pain. With a soft oath, he pulled her away, keeping his grip firm on her arms.

"Pay attention, will you?" His voice was rough and unsteady, but she didn't seem to notice. She smiled up at him and touched his cheek with her palm.

"Wasn't I?"

He checked the urge to shake her and spoke calmly. "I need to talk to you."

"Talk?" She smiled again. "Do we have to talk?"

"There are things I need to tell you—this morning…" He fumbled with the words, no longer certain what he wanted to say, what he wanted to do. How could her scent be stronger than it had been a moment ago? He was drowning in it.

"Nicholas." Morgan sighed sleepily. "I drank an incredible amount of ouzo. If I don't sleep it off, I may very well die. I'm sure the body only tolerates a certain amount of abuse. I've stretched my luck tonight."

"Morgan." His breath was coming too quickly. His own pulse like thunder in his ears. He should let her go, he knew. He should simply let her go—for both their sakes. But his arms stayed around her. "Straighten up and listen to me," he demanded.

"I'm through listening." She gave a sleepy, sultry laugh. "Through listening. Make love with me or go."

Her eyes were only slits, but the clear, mystical blue pulled him in. No struggle, no force would drag him out again. "Damn you," he breathed as they fell onto the bed. "Damn you for a witch."

It was all hell smoke and thunder. He couldn't resist it. Her body was as fluid as wine—as sweet and as potent. Now he could touch her wherever he chose and she only sighed. As his mouth crushed possessively on hers, she yielded, but in yielding held him prisoner. Even knowing it, he was helpless. There'd be a payment—a price in pain—for succumbing to the temptation. He no longer cared for tomorrows. Now, this moment, he had her. It was enough.

He tore the filmy chemise from her, too anxious, too desperate, but she made no protest as the material ripped away. On a groan of need, he devoured her.

Tastes—she had such tastes. They lingered on his tongue, spun in his head. The crushed wild honey of her mouth, the rose-petal sweetness of her skin, drove him to search for more, and to find everything. He wasn't gentle—he was long past gentleness, but the quiet moans that came from her spoke of pleasure.

Words, low and harsh with desire, tumbled from him. He wasn't certain if he cursed her again or made her hundreds of mad promises. For the moment, it was all the same. Needs ripped through him—needs he understood, needs he'd felt before. But there was something else, something stronger, greedier. Then his flesh was against her flesh, and everything was lost. Fires and flames, a furnace of passion engulfed him, driving him beyond control, beyond reason. She was melting into him. He felt it as a tangible ache but had no will to resist.

Her hands were hot on his skin, her body molten. He could no longer be certain who led and who followed. Beneath his, her mouth was soft and willing, but he tasted her strength. Under him, her body was pliant, unresisting, but he felt her demand. Her skin would be white, barely touched by the sun. He burned to see it, but saw only the glimmer of her eyes in the darkness.

Then she pulled his mouth back to hers and he saw nothing, nothing but the blur of raging colors that were passion. The wild, sweet scent of jasmine seeped into him, arousing, never soothing, until he thought he'd never smell anything else.

With a last force of will, he struggled for sanity. He wouldn't lose himself in her—to her. He couldn't. Without self-preservation he was nothing, vulnerable. Dead.

Even as he took her in a near violent rage, he surrendered.

Chapter 8

The sunlight that poured through the windows, through the open balcony doors, throbbed and pulsed in Morgan's head. With a groan she rolled over, hoping oblivion would be quick and painless. The thudding only increased. Morgan shifted cautiously and tried for a sitting position. Warily she opened her eyes then groaned at the flash of white morning sun. She closed them again in self-preservation. Slowly, gritting her teeth for courage, she allowed her lids to open again.

The spinning and whirling which had been enjoyable the night before, now brought on moans and mutters. With queasy stomach and aching eyes, she sat in the center of the bed until she thought she had the strength to move. Trying to keep her head perfectly still, she eased herself onto the floor.

Carelessly, she stepped over her discarded dress and found a robe in the closet. All she could think of were ice packs and coffee. Lots of coffee.

Then she remembered. Abruptly, blindingly. Morgan whirled from the closet to stare at the bed. It was empty—maybe she'd dreamed it. Imagined it. In useless defense she pressed her hands to her face. No dream. He had been there, and everything she remembered was real. And she remembered…the anger in his eyes, her own misty, taunting invitation. The way his mouth had pressed bruisingly to hers, her own unthinking, abandoned response.

The passion—it had been all she had thought it would be. Unbearable, wonderful, consuming. He'd cursed her. She could remember his words. Then he had taken her places she'd never even glimpsed before. She'd given him everything, then mindlessly challenged him to take more. She could still feel those taut, tensing muscles in his back, hear that ragged, desperate breathing at her ear.

He had taken her in fury, and it hadn't mattered to her. Then he had been silent. She had fallen asleep with her arms still around him. And now he was gone.

On a moan, Morgan dropped her hands to her sides. Of course he was gone. What else did she expect? The night had meant nothing to him—less than nothing. If she hadn't had so much to drink…

Oh, convenient excuse, Morgan thought on a wave of disgust. She still had too much pride to fall back on it. No, she wouldn't blame the ouzo. Walking to the bed, she picked up the torn remains of her chemise. She'd wanted him. God help her, she cared for him—too much. No, she wouldn't blame the ouzo. Balling the chemise in her fist, Morgan hurled it into the bottom of the closet. She had only herself to blame.

With a snap, Morgan closed the closet door. It was over, she told herself firmly. It was done. It didn't have to mean any more to her than it had to Nick. For a moment, she leaned her forehead against the smooth wooden panel and fought the urge to weep. No, she wouldn't cry over him. She'd never cry over him. Straightening, Morgan told herself it was the headache that was making her feel so weak and weepy. She was a grown woman, free to give herself, to take a man, when and where she chose. Once she'd gone down and had some coffee, she'd be able to put everything in perspective.

She swallowed the threatening tears and walked to the door.

"Good morning, *kyrios*." The tiny maid greeted Morgan with a smile she could have done without. "Would you like your breakfast in your room now?"

"No, just coffee." The scent of food didn't agree with her stomach or her disposition. "I'll go down for it."

"It's a beautiful day."

"Yes, beautiful." With her teeth clenched, Morgan moved down the hall.

The sound of crashing dishes and a high-pitched scream had Morgan gripping the wall for support. She pressed her hand to her head and moaned. Did the girl have to choose this morning to be clumsy!

But when the screaming continued, Morgan turned back. The girl knelt just inside the doorway. Scattered plates and cups lay shattered over the rug where the food had splattered.

"Stop it!" Leaning down, Morgan grabbed her shoulders and shook Zena out of self-defense. "No one's going to fire you for breaking a few dishes."

The girl shook her head as her eyes rolled. She pointed a trembling finger toward the bed before she wrenched herself from Morgan's hold and fled.

Turning, Morgan felt the room dip and sway. A new nightmare crept in to join the old. With her hand gripping the doorknob; she stared.

A shaft of sunlight spread over Iona as she lay on her back, flung sideways across the bed. Her head hung over the edge, her hair streaming nearly to the floor. Morgan shook off the first shock and dizziness and raced forward. Though her fingers trembled, she pressed them to Iona's throat. She felt a flutter, faint, but she felt it. The breath she hadn't been aware she'd held came out in a rush of relief. Moving on instinct, she pulled Iona's unconscious form until she lay back on the bed.

It was then she saw the syringe lying on the tumbled sheets.

"Oh, my God."

It explained so much. Iona's moodiness, those tight, jerky nerves. She'd been a fool not to suspect drugs before. She's overdosed, Morgan thought in quick panic. What do I do? There must be something I'm supposed to do.

"Morgan—dear God!"

Turning her head only, Morgan looked at Dorian standing pale and stiff in the doorway. "She's not dead," Morgan said quickly. "I think she's overdosed—get a doctor—an ambulance."

"Not dead?"

She heard the flat tone of his voice, heard him start to come toward her. There was no time to pamper his feelings. "Do it quickly!" she ordered. "There's a pulse, but it's faint."

"What's Iona done now?" Alex demanded in a tone of strained patience. "The maid's hysterical, and—oh, sweet Lord!"

"An ambulance!" Morgan demanded as she kept her fingers on Iona's pulse. Perhaps if she kept them there, it would continue to beat. "In the name of God, *hurry!*" She turned then in time to see Alex rush from the room as

Dorian remained frozen. "There's a syringe," she began with studied calm. She didn't want to hurt him, but continued as his gaze shifted to her. His eyes were blank. "She must have o.d.'d. Did you know she used drugs, Dorian?"

"Heroin." And a shudder seemed to pass through him. "I thought it had stopped. Are you sure she's—"

"She's alive." Morgan gripped his hand as he came to the bed. A wave of pity washed over her—for Iona, for the man whose hand she held in her own. "She's alive, Dorian. We'll get help for her."

His hand tightened on hers for a moment so that Morgan had to choke back a protest. "Iona," he murmured. "So beautiful—so lost."

"She's not lost, not yet!" Morgan said fiercely. "If you know how to pray, pray that we found her in time."

His eyes came back to Morgan's, clear, expressionless. She thought as she looked at him she'd never seen anything so empty. "Pray," he said quietly. "Yes, there's nothing else to be done."

It seemed to take hours, but when Morgan watched the helicopter veer off to the west, the morning was still young. Iona, still unconscious, was being rushed to Athens. Dorian rode with her and the doctor while Alex and Liz began hurried preparations for their own flight.

Still barefoot and in her robe, Morgan watched the helicopter until it was out of sight. As long as she lived, she thought, she'd never forget that pale, stony look on Dorian's face—or the lifeless beauty on Iona's. With a shudder, she turned away and saw Alex just inside the doorway.

"Tripolos," he said quietly. "He's in the salon."

"Oh, not now, Alex." Overcome with pity, she held

out both hands as she went to him. "How much more can you stand?"

"It's necessary." His voice was tight with control and he held her hands limply. "I apologize for putting you through all this, Morgan—"

"No." She interrupted him and squeezed his hands. "Don't treat me that way, Alex. I thought we were friends."

"*Diabolos*," he murmured. "Such friends you have. Forgive me."

"Only if you stop treating me as though I were a stranger."

On a sigh, he slipped his arm around her shoulders. "Come, we'll face the captain."

Morgan wondered if she would ever enter the salon without seeing Captain Tripolos seated in the wide, high-back chair. She sat on the sofa as before, faced him, and waited for the questions.

"This is difficult for you," Tripolos said at length. "For all of you." His gaze roamed over the occupants of the room, from Morgan to Alex to Liz. "We will be as discreet as is possible, Mr. Theoharis. I will do what I can to avoid the press, but an attempted suicide in a family as well known as yours…" He let the rest trail off.

"Suicide," Alex repeated softly. His eyes were blank, as if the words hadn't penetrated.

"It would seem, from the preliminary report, that your cousin took a self-induced overdose. Heroin. But I hesitate to be more specific until the investigation is closed. Procedure, you understand."

"Procedure."

"You found Miss Theoharis, Miss James?"

Morgan gave a quick, nervous jolt at the sound of her name, then settled. "No, actually, the maid found her. I went in to see what was wrong. Zena had dropped the tray and was carrying on...when I went in I saw Iona."

"And you called for an ambulance?"

"No." She shook her head, annoyed. He knew Alex had called, but wanted to drag the story from her piece by piece. Resigned, Morgan decided to accommodate him. "I thought at first she was dead—then I felt a pulse. I got her back into bed."

"Back into bed?"

Tripolos's tone had sharpened, ever so faintly, but Morgan caught it. "Yes, she was half out of it, almost on the floor. I wanted to lay her down." She lifted her hands helplessly. "I honestly don't know what I wanted to do, it just seemed like the right thing."

"I see. Then you found this?" He held up the syringe, now in a clear plastic bag.

"Yes."

"Did you know your cousin was a user of heroin, Mr. Theoharis?"

Alex stiffened at the question. Morgan saw Liz reach out to take his hand. "I knew Iona had a problem—with drugs. Two years ago she went to a clinic for help. I thought she had found it. If I had believed she was still... ill," he managed. "I wouldn't have brought her into my home with my wife and my friend."

"Mrs. Theoharis, were you unaware of Miss Theoharis's problem?"

Morgan heard the breath hiss out between Alex's teeth, but Liz spoke quickly. "I was perfectly aware of it." Alex's head whipped around but she continued calmly. "That is, I was aware that my husband arranged for her to have treatment two years ago, though he tried to shield me." Without looking at him, Liz covered their joined hands with her free one.

"Would you, Mr. Theoharis, have any notion where your cousin received her supply?"

"None."

"I see. Well, since your cousin lives in Athens, perhaps it would be best if I worked with the police there, in order to contact her close friends."

"Do what you must," Alex said flatly. "I only ask that you spare my family as much as possible."

"Of course. I will leave you now. My apologies for the intrusion, yet again."

"I must phone my family," Alex said dully when the door closed behind Tripolos. As if seeking comfort, his hand went to his wife's hair. Then he rose and left without another word.

"Liz," Morgan began. "I know it's a useless phrase, but if there's anything I can do…"

Liz shook her head. She shifted her eyes from the doorway back to her friend's. "It's all so unbelievable. That she's lying there, so near death. What's worse, I never liked her. I made no secret of it, but now…" She rose and walked to the window. "She's Alex's family, and he feels that deeply. Now, in his heart, he's responsible for whatever happens to her. And all I can think of is how cold I was to her."

"Alex is going to need you." Morgan rose and walked over to put a hand on her shoulder. "You can't help not liking her, Liz. Iona isn't an easy person to like."

"You're right, of course." With a deep breath Liz turned and managed a weak smile. "It's been a hell of a vacation so far, hasn't it? No, don't say anything." She squeezed Morgan's hand. "I'm going to see if Alex needs me. There'll be arrangements to be made."

The villa was silent as Morgan went up to change. As she buttoned her shirt, she stood by the terrace doors, staring out at the view of garden, sea, and mountain. How could it be that so much ugliness had intruded in such a short time? she wondered. Death and near death. This wasn't the place for it. But even Paradise named its price, she thought, and turned away.

The knock on her door was quiet. "Yes, come in."

"Morgan, am I disturbing you?"

"Oh, Alex." As she looked up, Morgan's heart welled with sympathy. The lines of strain and grief seemed etched into his face. "I know how horrible all this is for you, and I don't want to add to your problems. Perhaps I should go back to New York."

"Morgan." He hesitated for a moment. "I know it's a lot to ask, but I don't do it for myself. For Liz. Will you stay for Liz? Your company is all I can give her for a time." He released Morgan's hands and moved restlessly around the room. "We'll have to fly to Athens. I can't say how long—until Iona is well or—" He broke off as if he wasn't yet prepared for the word. "I'll have to stay with my family for a few days. My aunt will need me. If I could send Liz back knowing you'd be here with her, it would make it so much easier."

"Of course, Alex. You know I will."

He turned and gave her a phantom of a smile. "You're a good friend, Morgan. We'll have to leave you for at least a day and a night. After that, I'll send Liz back. I can be sure she'll leave Athens if you're here." With a sigh, he took her hand absently. "Dorian might choose to stay in Athens as well. I believe he…has feelings for Iona I didn't realize before. I'll ask Nick to look after you while we're gone."

"No." She bit her tongue on the hurried protest. "No, really, Alex, I'll be fine. I'm hardly alone, with the servants in the house. When will you leave?"

"Within the hour."

"Alex, I'm sure it was an accident."

"I'll have to convince my aunt of that." He held out his hands, searching his own palms for a moment. "Though as to what I believe…" His look had hardened when he lifted his eyes again. "Iona courts disaster. She feeds on misery. I'll tell you now, because I won't ever be able to speak freely to anyone else. Not even Liz." His face was a grim mask now. Cold. "I detest her." He spit the words out as if they were poison. "Her death would be nothing but a blessing to everyone who loves her."

When Alex, Liz, and Dorian were gone, Morgan left the villa. She needed to walk—needed the air. This time she avoided her habit of heading for the beach. She was far from ready for that. Instead, she struck out for the cliffs, drawn to their jagged, daring beauty.

How clean the air was! Morgan wanted no floral scents now, just the crisp tang of the sea. She walked without destination. Up, only up, as if she could escape from everything if she could only get higher. If the gods had walked here, she thought, they would have come to the cliffs, to hear the water beat against rock, to breathe the thin, pure air.

She saw, to her pleasure, a scruffy, straggly goat with sharp black eyes. He stared at her a moment as he gnawed on a bit of wild grass he'd managed to find growing in between the rocks. But when she tried to get closer, he scrambled up, lightly, and disappeared over the other side of the cliff.

With a sigh, Morgan sat down on a rock perched high above the water. With some surprise, she saw tiny blue-headed flowers struggling toward the sun out of a crevice hardly wider than a thumbnail. She touched them, but couldn't bring herself to pluck any. Life's everywhere, she realized, if you only know where to look.

"Morgan."

Her hand closed over the blooms convulsively at the sound of his voice. She opened it slowly and turned her head. Nick was standing only a short distance away, his hair caught by the breeze that just stirred the air. In jeans and a T-shirt, his face unshaven, he looked more like the man she had first encountered. Undisciplined. Unprincipled. Her heart gave a quick, bounding leap before she controlled it.

Without a word, Morgan rose and started down the slope.

"Morgan." He caught her quickly, then turned her around with a gentleness she hadn't expected from him. Her eyes were cool, but beneath the frost, he saw they were troubled. "I heard about Iona."

"Yes, you once told me there was little that happened on the island you didn't know."

Her toneless voice slashed at him, but he kept his hands easy on her arms. "You found her."

She wouldn't let that uncharacteristic caring tone cut through her defenses. She could be—would be—as hard and cold as he had been. "You're well informed, Nicholas."

Her face was unyielding, and he didn't know how to begin. If she would come into his arms, he could show her. But the woman who faced him would lean on no one. "It must have been very difficult for you."

She lifted a brow, as though she were almost amused. "It was easier to find someone alive than to find someone dead."

He winced at that—a quick jerk of facial muscles, then dropped his hands. She'd asked him for comfort once, and now that he wanted to give it, needed to give it, it was too late. "Will you sit down?"

"No, it's not as peaceful here as it was."

"Stop slashing at me!" he exploded, grabbing her arms again.

"Let me go."

But the faint quaver in her voice told him something her words hadn't. She was closer to her own threshold than perhaps even she knew. "Very well, if you'll come back to the house with me."

"No."

"Yes." Keeping a hand on her arm, Nick started up the rough path. "We'll talk."

Morgan jerked her arm but his grip was firm. He propelled her up the rough path without looking at her. "What do you want, Nicholas? More details?"

His mouth thinned as he pulled her along beside him. "All right. You can tell me about Iona if you like."

"I don't like," she tossed back. They were already approaching the steps to his house. Morgan hadn't realized they were so close. What devil had prompted her to walk that way? "I don't want to go with you."

"Since when have I cared what you want?" he asked bitterly and propelled her through the front door. "Coffee," he demanded as Stephanos appeared in the hall.

"All right, I'll give you the details," Morgan raged as she whirled inside the door of the salon. "And then, by God, you'll leave me be! I found Iona unconscious, hardly alive. There was a syringe in bed with her. It seems she was an addict." She paused, unaware that her breath was starting to heave. "But you knew that, didn't you, Nicholas? You know all manner of things."

She'd lost all color, just as she had when she'd run

across the beach and into his arms. He felt a twinge, an ache, and reached out for her.

"Don't touch me!" Nick's head jerked back as if she'd slapped him. Morgan pressed her hands against her mouth and turned away. "Don't touch me."

"I won't put my hands on you," Nick managed as they balled into fists. "Sit down, Morgan, before you keel over."

"Don't tell me what to do." Her voice quavered, and she detested it. Making herself turn back, she faced him again. "You have no right to tell me what to do."

Stephanos entered, silent, watchful. As he set the coffee tray down, he glanced over at Morgan. He saw, as Nick couldn't, her heart in her eyes. "You'll have coffee, miss," he said in a soft voice.

"No, I—"

"You should sit." Before Morgan could protest, Stephanos nudged her into a chair. "The coffee's strong."

Nick stood, raging at his impotence as Stephanos clucked around her like a mother hen.

"You'll have it black," he told her. "It puts color in your cheeks."

Morgan accepted the cup, then stared at it. "Thank you."

Stephanos gave Nick one long, enigmatic look, then left them.

"Well, drink it," Nick ordered, furious that the old man had been able to hack through her defenses when he felt useless. "It won't do you any good in the cup."

Because she needed to find strength somewhere, Morgan drank it down quickly. "What else do you want?"

"Damn it, Morgan, I didn't bring you here to grill you about Iona."

"No? You surprise me." Steadier, she set the cup aside

and rose again. "Though why anything you do should surprise me, I don't know."

"There's nothing too vile you wouldn't attribute to me, is there?" Ignoring the coffee, Nick strode to the bar. "Perhaps you think I killed Stevos and left the body for you to find."

"No," she said calmly, because she could speak with perfect truth. "He was stabbed in the back."

"So?"

"You'd face a man when you killed him."

Nick turned away from the bar, the glass still empty in his hand. His eyes were black now, as black as she'd ever seen them. There was passion in them barely, just barely, suppressed. "Morgan, last night—"

"I won't discuss last night with you." Her voice was cold and final, cutting through him more accurately than any blade.

"All right, we'll forget it." This time he filled the glass. He'd known there would be a price to pay; somehow he hadn't thought it would be quite so high. "Would you like an apology?"

"For what?"

He gave a short laugh as his hand tightened on the glass. He tossed back the liquor. "God, woman, you've a streak of ice through you I hadn't seen."

"Don't talk to me of ice, Nicholas." Her voice rose with a passion she'd promised herself she wouldn't feel. "You sit here in your ancestral home, playing your dirty chess games with lives. I won't be one of your pawns. There's a woman barely alive in an Athens hospital. You make your money feeding her illness. Do you think you're remote from the blame because you cross the strait in the dead of night like some swashbuckling pirate?"

Very carefully, he set down the glass and turned. "I know what I am."

She stared at him until her eyes began to fill again. "So do I," she whispered. "God help me."

Turning, she fled. He didn't go after her.

Moments later, Stephanos came back into the room. "The lady's upset," he said mildly.

Nick turned his back to fill his glass again. "I know what the lady is."

"The past two days have been difficult for her." He clucked his tongue. "She came to you for comfort?"

Nick whirled but managed to bite back the words. Stephanos watched calmly. "No, she didn't come to me. She'd go to the devil himself before she came to me again." With an effort, he controlled the rage and his tone. "And it's for the best, I can't let her interfere now. As things stand, she'll be in the way."

Stephanos caressed his outrageous moustache and whistled through his teeth. "Perhaps she'll go back to America."

"The sooner the better," Nick muttered and drained his glass. At the knock on the door, he swore. "See who the hell it is and get rid of them if you can."

"Captain Tripolos," Stephanos announced a few moments later. There was a gleam in his eye as he melted out of sight.

"Captain." Nick fought off the need to swear again. "You'll join me for coffee?"

"Thank you." Tripolos settled into a chair with a few wheezes and sighs. "Was that Miss James I just saw going down the cliff path?"

"Yes." With some effort, Nick prevented his knuckles from whitening against the handle of the pot. "She was just here."

Both men watched each other with what seemed casual interest. One was Morgan's panther—the other a crafty bear.

"Then she told you about Miss Theoharis."

"Yes." Nick offered the cream. "A nasty business, Captain. I intend to call Athens later this morning to see what news there is. Is Iona's condition why you're here?"

"Yes. It's kind of you to see me, Mr. Gregoras. I know you are a very busy man."

"It's my duty to cooperate with the police, Captain," Nick countered as he sat back with his coffee. "But I don't know how I can help you in this case."

"As you were with Miss Theoharis all of yesterday afternoon, I hoped you could shed some light on her frame of mind."

"Oh, I see." Nick sipped his coffee while his mind raced with possibilities. "Captain, I don't know if I can help you. Naturally, Iona was distressed that the man's murder was practically on her doorstep. She was edgy—but then, she often is. I can't say I saw anything different in her."

"Perhaps you could tell me what you did on your boat trip?" Tripolos suggested. "If Miss Theoharis said anything which seemed to indicate she was thinking of suicide?"

Nick lifted a brow. "We weren't overly engaged in conversation."

"Of course."

Nick wondered how long they could continue to fence. He decided to execute a few flourishes of his own. "I will say that Iona seemed a trifle nervous. That is, as I said, however, a habitual trait. You'll find that the people who know her will describe Iona as a…restive woman. I can say with complete honesty that it never entered my mind that she was contemplating suicide. Even now, to be candid, I find the idea impossible."

Tripolos settled back comfortably. "Why?"

Generalities, Nick concluded, would suffice. "Iona's too fond of herself to seek death. A beautiful woman, Captain, and one greedy for life's pleasures. It's merely an opinion, you understand. You know much more about this sort of thing." He shrugged. "My opinion is that it was an accident."

"An accident, Mr. Gregoras, is unlikely." He was fishing for a reaction, and Nick gave him another curious lift of brow. "There was too much heroin in her system for any but an amateur to take by mistake. And Miss Theoharis is no stranger to heroin. The marks of the needle tell a sad story."

"Yes, I see."

"Were you aware that Miss Theoharis was an addict?"

"I didn't know Iona very well, Captain. Socially, of course, but basically, she's a cousin of a friend—a beautiful woman who isn't always comfortable to be around."

"Yet you spent the day with her yesterday."

"A beautiful woman," Nick said again, and smiled. "I'm sorry I can't help you."

"Perhaps you'd be interested in a theory of mine."

Nick didn't trust those bland eyes but continued to smile. "Of course."

"You see, Mr. Gregoras," Tripolos went on. "If it was an accident, and if your instincts are correct, there is only one answer."

"One answer?" Nick repeated then allowed his expression to change slowly. "Do you mean you think someone attempted to…murder Iona?"

"I'm a simple policeman, Mr. Gregoras." Tripolos

looked plumply humble. "It is my nature to look at such matters from a suspicious point of view. May I be frank?"

"By all means," Nick told him, admiring the captain's plodding shrewdness. Frank be damned, Nick mused, he's going to try to give me enough rope to hang myself.

"I am puzzled, and as a man who knows the Theoharis family well, I would like your opinion."

"Whatever I can do."

Tripolos nodded. "I will tell you first—and of course, you understand this cannot leave this room?"

Nick merely inclined his head and sipped his coffee.

"I will tell you Anthony Stevos was part of a smuggling ring operating on Lesbos."

"I must admit, the thought had crossed my mind." Amused, Nick took out a box of cigarettes, offering one to Tripolos.

"It's no secret that a group has been using this island's nearness to Turkey to smuggle opium across the strait." Tripolos admired the thin wisp of elegant tobacco before he bent closer to Nick for a light.

"You think this Stevos was murdered by one of his cohorts?"

"That is my theory." Tripolos drew in the expensive smoke appreciatively. "It is the leader of this group that is my main concern. A brilliant man, I am forced to admit." Reluctant respect crossed his face. "He is very clever and has so far eluded any nets spread for his capture. It is rumored he rarely joins in the boat trips. When he does, he is masked."

"I've heard the rumors, naturally," Nick mused behind a mist of smoke. "I put a great deal of it down to village gossip and romance. A masked man, smuggling—the stuff of fiction."

"He is real, Mr. Gregoras, and there is nothing romantic about back-stabbing."

"No, you're quite right."

"Stevos was not a smart man. He was being watched in hopes he would lead us to the one we want. But…" As was his habit, Tripolos let the sentence trail off.

"I might ask, Captain, why you're telling me what must be police business."

"As an important man in our community," Tripolos said smoothly, "I feel I can take you into my confidence."

The old fox, Nick thought, and smiled. "I appreciate that. Do you think this masked smuggler is a local man?"

"I believe he is a man who knows the island." Tripolos gave a grim smile in return. "But I do not believe he is a fisherman."

"One of my olive pickers?" Nick suggested blandly, blowing out a stream of smoke. "No, I suppose not."

"I believe," Tripolos continued, "from the reports I have received on Miss Theoharis's activities in Athens, that she is aware of the identity of the man we seek."

Nick came to attention. "Iona?"

"I am of the opinion that Miss Theoharis is very involved in the smuggling operation. Too involved for her own safety. If…when," he amended, "she comes out of her coma, she'll be questioned."

"It's hard for me to believe that Alex's cousin would be a part of something like that." *He's getting entirely too close,* Nick realized, and swore silently at the lack of time. "Iona's a bit untamed," he went on, "but smuggling and murder. I can't believe it."

"I am very much afraid someone tried to murder Miss Theoharis because she knew too much. I will ask you, Mr. Gregoras, as one who is acquainted with her, how far would Miss Theoharis have gone for love—or for money?"

Nick paused as if considering carefully while his mind raced at readjustments to plans already formed. "For love, Captain, I think Iona would do little. But for money"— he looked up—"for money, Iona could justify anything."

"You are frank," Tripolos nodded. "I am grateful. Perhaps you would permit me to speak with you again on this matter. I must confess"—Tripolos's smile was sheepish, but his eyes remained direct—"it is a great help to discuss my problems with a man like yourself. It allows me to put things in order."

"Captain, I'm glad to give you any help I can, of course." Nick gave him an easy smile.

For some time after Tripolos left, Nick remained in his chair. He scowled at the Rodin sculpture across the room as he calculated his choices.

"We move tonight," he announced as Stephanos entered.

"It's too soon. Things are not yet safe."

"Tonight," Nick repeated and shifted his gaze. "Call Athens and let them know about the change in plan. See if they can't rig something up to keep this Tripolos off my back for a few hours." He laced his fingers together and frowned. "He's dangled his bait, and he's damn well expecting me to bite."

"It's too dangerous tonight," Stephanos insisted. "There's another shipment in a few days."

"In a few days, Tripolos will be that much closer. We can't afford to have things complicated with the local police now. And I have to be sure." Jet eyes narrowed, and his mouth became a grim line. "I haven't gone through all this to make a mistake at this point. I have to speed things up before Tripolos starts breathing down the wrong necks."

Chapter 9

The cove was blanketed in gloom. Rocks glistened, protecting it from winds—and from view. There was a scent—lush wet leaves, wild blossoms that flourished in the sun and hung heavy at night. But somehow it wasn't a pleasant fragrance. It smelt of secrets and half-named fears.

Lovers didn't hold trysts there. Legend said it was haunted. At times, when a man walked near enough on a dark, still night, the voices of spirits murmured behind the rocks. Most men took another route home and said nothing at all.

The moon shed a thin, hollow light over the face of the water, adding to rather than detracting from the sense of whispering stillness, of mystic darkness. The water itself sighed gently over the rocks and sand. It was a passive sound, barely stirring the air.

The men who gathered near the boat were like so

many shadows—dark, faceless in the gloom. But they were men, flesh and blood and muscle. They didn't fear the spirits in the cove.

They spoke little, and only in undertones. A laugh might be heard from time to time, quick and harsh in a place of secrets, but for the most part they moved silently, competently. They knew what had to be done. The time was nearly right.

One saw the approach of a new shadow and grunted to his companion. Stealthily, he drew a knife from his belt, gripping its crude handle in a strong, work-worn hand. The blade glittered dangerously through the darkness. Work stopped; men waited.

As the shadow drew closer, he sheathed the knife and swallowed the salty taste of fear. He wouldn't have been afraid to murder, but he was afraid of this man.

The thick, sturdy fingers trembled as they released the knife. "We weren't expecting you."

"I do not like to always do the expected." The answer was in brisk Greek as a pale finger of moonlight fell over him. He wore black—all black, from lean black slacks to a sweater and leather jacket. Lean and tall, he might have been god or devil.

A hood concealed both his head and face. Only the gleam of dark eyes remained visible—and deadly.

"You join us tonight?"

"I am here," he returned. He wasn't a man who answered questions, and no more were asked. He stepped aboard as one used to the life and sway of boats.

It was a typical fishing vessel. Its lines were simple. The decks were clean but rough, the paint fresh and black. Only the expense and power of its motor separated it from its companions.

Without a word, he crossed the deck, ignoring the men

who fell back to let him pass. They were hefty, muscled men with thick wrists and strong hands. They moved away from the lean man as if he could crush them to bone with one sweep of his narrow hand. Each prayed the slitted eyes would not seek him out.

He placed himself at the helm, then gazed casually over his shoulder. At the look, the lines were cast off. They would row until they were out to sea and the roar of the motor would go unnoticed.

The boat moved at an easy pace, a lone speck in a dark sea. The motor purred. There was little talk among the men. They were a silent group in any case, but when the man was with them, no one wanted to speak. To speak was to bring attention to yourself—not many dared to do so.

He stared out into the water and ignored the wary glances thrown his way. He was remote, a figure of the night. His hood rippled in the salt-sprayed wind—a carefree, almost adventurous movement. But he was still as a stone.

Time passed; the boat listed with the movement of the sea. He might have been a figurehead. Or a demon.

"We are short-handed." The man who had greeted him merged with his shadow. His voice was low and coarse. His stomach trembled. "Do you wish me to find a replacement for Stevos?"

The hooded head turned—a slow, deliberate motion. The man took an instinctive step in retreat and swallowed the copper taste that had risen to his throat.

"I will find my own replacement. You would all do well to remember Stevos." He lifted his voice on the warning as his eyes swept the men on deck. "There is no one who cannot be…replaced." He used a faint emphasis on the final word, watching the dropping of eyes with satisfaction. He needed their fear, and he had it. He could smell it on them. Smiling beneath the hood, he turned back to the sea.

The journey continued, and no one else spoke to him—or about him. Now and then a sailor might cast his eyes toward the man at the helm. The more superstitious crossed themselves or made the ancient sign against evil. When the devil was with them, they knew the full power of fear. He ignored them, treated them as though he were alone on the boat. They thanked God for it.

Midway between Lesbos and Turkey, the motor was shut off. The sudden silence resounded like a thunderclap. No one spoke as they would have done if the figure hadn't been at the helm. There were no crude jokes or games of dice.

The boat shifted easily in its own wake. They waited, all but one swatting in the cool sea breeze. The moon winked behind a cloud, then was clear again.

The motor of an approaching boat was heard as a distant cough, but the sound grew steadier, closer. A light signaled twice, then once again before the glow was shut off. The second motor, too, gave way to silence as another fishing vessel drifted alongside the first. The two boats merged into one shadow.

The night was glorious—almost still and silvered by the moon. Men waited, watching that dark, silent figure at the helm.

"The catch is good tonight," a voice called out from the second boat. The sound drifted, disembodied over the water.

"The fish are easily caught while sleeping."

There was a short laugh as two men leaned over the side and hauled a dripping net, pregnant with fish, onto the deck. The vessel swayed with the movement, then steadied.

The hooded man watched the exchange without word or gesture. His eyes shifted from the second vessel to the pile of fish lying scattered and lifeless on the deck. Both motors roared into life again and separated; one to the east, one to the west. The moon glimmered white. The breeze picked up. The boat was again a lone speck on a dark sea.

"Cut them open."

The men looked up sharply into the slitted eyes. "Now?" one of them dared to ask. "Don't you want them taken to the usual place?"

"Cut them open," he repeated. His voice sent a chill through the quiet night. "I take the cache with me."

Three men knelt beside the fish. Their knives worked swiftly and with skill while the scent of blood and sweat and fear prickled the air. A small pile of white packets grew as they were torn from the bellies of fish. The mutilated corpses were tossed back into the sea. No one would bring that catch to their table.

He moved quickly but without any sense of hurry, slipping packets into the pockets of his jacket. To a man they scrambled back from him, as if his touch might bring death—or worse. Satisfied, he gave them a brief survey before he resumed his position at the helm.

Their fear brought him a grim pleasure. And the cache was his for the taking. For the first time, he laughed—a long, cold sound that had nothing to do with humor. No one spoke, in even a whisper, on the journey back.

Later, a shadow among shadows, he moved away from the cove. He was wary that the trip had gone so easily, exhilarated that it was done. There had been no one to question him, no one with the courage to follow, though he was one man and they were many. Still, as he crossed the strip of beach, he moved with caution, for he wasn't a fool. He had more than just a few frightened fishermen to consider. And he would have more to deal with before he was done.

The walk was long, and steep, but he took it at an easy pace. The hollow call of an owl caused him to pause only briefly to scan the trees and rocks through the slits in the mask. From his position, he could see the cool white lines of the Theoharis villa. He stood where he was a moment—watching, thinking. Then he spun away to continue his climb.

He moved over rocks as easily as a goat—walking with a sure, confident stride in the darkness. He'd covered that route a hundred times without a light. And he kept clear of the path—a path meant men. He stepped around the rock where Morgan had sat that morning, but he didn't see the flowers. Without pausing, he continued.

There was a light in the window. He'd left it burning himself before he had set out. Now for the first time he thought of comfort—and a drink to wash the taste of other men's fear from his throat.

Entering the house, he strode down the corridor and entered a room. Carelessly, he dumped the contents of his pockets on an elegant Louis XVI table, then removed his hood with a flourish.

"Well, Stephanos." Nick's teeth flashed in a grin. "The fishing was rich tonight."

Stephanos acknowledged the packets with a nod. "No trouble?"

"One has little trouble with men who fear the air you breathe. The trip was as smooth as a whore's kiss." Moving away, he poured two drinks and handed one to his companion. The sense of exhilaration was still on him—

the power that comes from risking death and winning.
He drained his drink in one swallow. "A seedy crew,
Stephanos, but they do their job. They're greedy, and"—
he lifted the hood, then let it fall on the cache of opium,
black on white—"terrified."

"A terrified crew is a cooperative one," Stephanos
commented. He poked a stubby finger at the cache of
opium. "Rich fishing indeed. Enough to make a man
comfortable for a long time."

"Enough to make him want more," Nick stated with
a grin. "And more. *Diabolos,* the smell of fish clings to
me." He wrinkled his nose in disgust. "Send our cache
to Athens, and see they send a report to me of its purity.
I'm going to wash off this stink and go to bed."

"There's a matter you might be interested in."

"Not tonight." Nick didn't bother to turn around. "Save
your gossip for tomorrow."

"The woman, Nicholas." Stephanos saw him stiffen
and pause. There was no need to tell him which woman.
"I learned she doesn't go back to America. She stays here
while Alex is in Athens."

"Diabolos!" Nick swore and turned back into the
room. "I can't be worried about a woman."

"She stays alone until Alex sends his lady back."

"The woman is not my concern," he said between
his teeth.

As was his habit, Stephanos sniffed the liquor to add to
his appreciation. "Athens was interested," he said mildly.
"Perhaps she could still be of use."

"No." Nick took an agitated turn around the room.
Nerves that had been cold as ice began to thaw. Damn
her, he thought, she'll make me careless even thinking
of her. "That woman is more trouble than use. No," he

repeated as Stephanos lifted his brows. "We'll keep her out of it."

"Difficult, considering—"

"We'll keep her out of it," Nick repeated in a tone that made Stephanos stroke his moustache.

"As you wish, *kyrios*."

"Go to the devil." Annoyed with the mock respectful tone, Nick picked up his glass, then set it down again. "She's no use to us," he said with more calm. "More of a stumbling block. We'll hope she keeps her elegant nose inside the villa for a few days."

"And if she pokes her elegant nose out?" Stephanos inquired, enjoying his liquor.

Nick's mouth was a grim line. "Then I'll deal with her."

"I think perhaps," he murmured as Nick strode from the room, "she has already dealt with you, old friend." He laughed and poured himself another drink. "Indeed, the lady's dealt you a killing blow."

After he had bathed, Nick couldn't settle. He told himself it was the excess energy from the night, and his success. But he found himself standing at his window, staring down at the Theoharis villa.

So she was alone, he thought, asleep in that big soft bed. It meant nothing to him. He'd climbed that damn wall to her room for the last time. He'd gone there the night before on impulse, something he'd known better than to do. He'd gone to see her, with some mad idea of justifying his actions to her.

Fool, he called himself as his hands curled tight around the stone railing. Only a fool justifies what he does. He'd gone to her and she'd taunted him, driven him to give up something he had no business giving up. His heart. Damn her, she'd wrenched it out of him.

His grip tightened as he remembered what it had been

like to have her—to taste her and fill himself with her. It had been a mistake, perhaps the most crucial one he'd ever made. It was one matter to risk your life, another to risk your soul.

He shouldn't have touched her, Nick thought on yet another wave of anger. He'd known it even as his hands had reached for her. She hadn't known what she was doing, drunk on the ouzo Andrew had bought her. Andrew— he felt a moment's rage and banked it. There'd been moments when he hated Andrew, knowing he'd kissed her. Hated Dorian because Morgan had smiled at him. And Alex because he could touch her in friendship.

And, he knew, Morgan would hate him for what had passed between them that night. Hadn't he heard it in the icy words she'd flung at him? He'd rather have handed her his own knife than to have the words of a woman slash at him that way. She would hate him for taking her when she was vulnerable—while that damn medal hung around her neck. And she would hate him for what he was.

On a rising wave of temper, Nick whirled away from the window. Why should it concern him? Morgan James would slip out of his life like a dream in only a few weeks in any case. He'd chosen his path before, long before he'd seen her. It was his way. If she hated him for what he was, then so be it. He wouldn't allow her to make him feel dirty and soiled.

If she'd touched his heart, he could deal with it. Sprawling into a chair, Nick scowled into the darkness. He would deal with it, he promised himself. After all he'd done, and all he'd faced, no blue-eyed witch would take him under.

Morgan felt completely alone. The solitude and silence she had so prized only a few days before now weighed down on her. The house was full of servants, but that brought her no comfort, no company. Alex and Liz and Dorian were gone. She wandered listlessly through the morning as she had wandered restlessly through the night. The house felt like a prison—clean and white and empty. Trapped inside it, she was too vulnerable to her own thoughts.

And because her thoughts centered too often on Nick, she found the idea of lying in the bed they had shared too painful. How could she sleep in peace in a place where she could still feel his hands on her, his lips ruthlessly pressing on hers? How could she sleep in a room that seemed to carry that faint sea-smell that so often drifted from him?

So she couldn't sleep, and her thoughts—and needs—haunted her. What could have happened to her to cause her to love such a man? And how long could she fight it? If she surrendered to it, she'd suffer for the rest of her life.

Knowing she was only adding to her own depression, Morgan changed into a bathing suit and headed for the beach.

It was ridiculous to be afraid of the beach, afraid of the house, she told herself. She was here to enjoy both for the next three weeks. Locking herself in her room wouldn't change anything that had happened.

The sand glistened, white and brilliant. Morgan found that on facing it again, the horror didn't materialize. Tossing aside her wrap, she ran into the sea. The water would ease the weariness, the tension. And maybe, just maybe, she would sleep tonight.

Why should she be keeping herself in a constant state of nerves over the death of a man she didn't even know? Why should she allow the harmless stub of a cigarette to haunt her? It was time to accept the simple explanations and keep her distance. The man had been killed as a result of a village brawl, and that was that. It had nothing to do with her, or anyone she knew. It was tragic, but it wasn't personal.

She wouldn't think about Iona, she told herself. She wouldn't think about smuggling or murders or—here she hesitated a moment and dived under a wave—Nicholas. For now, she wouldn't think at all.

Morgan escaped. In a world of water and sun, she thought only of pleasures. She drifted, letting the tension sink beneath the waves. She'd forgotten, in her own misery, just how clean and alive the water made her feel. For a few moments she would go back to that first day, to that feeling of peace she'd found without even trying.

Liz was going to need her in the next day or two. And Morgan wouldn't be any help at all if she were haggard and tense. Yes, tonight she'd sleep—she'd had enough of nightmares.

More relaxed than she had been in days, Morgan swam back toward shore. The sand shifted under her feet with the gentle current. Shells dotted the shoreline, clean and glistening. She stood and stretched as the water lapped around her knees. The sun felt glorious.

"So Helen rises from the sea."

Lifting her hand, Morgan shielded her eyes and saw Andrew. He sat on the beach by her towel, watching her.

"It's easy to understand how she set kingdoms at odds." He stood and moved to the water's verge to join her. "How are you, Morgan?"

"I'm fine." She accepted the towel he handed her and rubbed it briskly over her hair.

"Your eyes are shadowed. A blue sea surrounded by clouds." He traced her cheek with a fingertip. "Nick told me about Iona Theoharis." He took her hand and led her back to the white sand. Dropping the towel, Morgan sat beside him. "It's a bit soon for you to have to handle something like that, Morgan, I'm sorry you had to be the one to find her."

"It seems to be a talent of mine." She shook her head. "I'm much better today, really." Smiling, she touched his cheek. "Yesterday I felt…actually I don't think I felt much of anything yesterday. It was like I was watching everything through a fisheye lens. Everything was distorted and unreal. Today it's real, but I can cope with it."

"I suppose that's nature's way of cushioning the senses."

"I feel this incredible sorrow for Alex and Liz—and for Dorian." She leaned back on her elbows, wanting to feel the sun as it dried the water on her skin. "It's so hard on them, Andrew. It leaves me feeling helpless." She turned her face to his, pushing at her streaming hair. "I hope this doesn't sound hard, but I feel, after these past two days, I think I've just realized how glad I am to be alive."

"I'd say that's a very healthy, very normal reaction." He, too, leaned back on his elbows, narrowing his eyes against the sun as he studied her.

"Oh, I hope so. I've been feeling guilty about it."

"You can't be guilty about wanting to live, Morgan."

"No. Suddenly I realized how much I want to do. How much I want to see. Do you know, I'm twenty-six, and this is the first time I've been anywhere? My mother died when I was a baby and my father and I moved to New York from Philadelphia. I've never seen anything else." As drops of water trickled down her skin, she shook her damp hair back. "I can speak five languages, and this is the first time I've been in a country where English isn't needed. I want to go to Italy and France." She turned to face him more directly. Her eyes, though still shadowed, were huge with adventure. "I want to see Venice and ride in a gondola. I want to walk on the Cornish moors and on the Champs d'élysées." She laughed and it felt marvelous. "I want to climb mountains."

"And be a fisherman?" He smiled and laid a hand over hers.

"Oh, I did say that, didn't I?" She laughed again. "I'll do that, too. Jack always said my taste was rather eclectic."

"Jack?"

"He's a man I knew back home." Morgan found the ease with which she put him in the past satisfying. "He was in politics. I think he wanted to be king."

"Were you in love with him?"

"No, I was used to him." She rolled her eyes and grinned. "Isn't that a terrible thing to say?"

"I don't know—you tell me."

"No," she decided. "Because it's the truth. He was very cautious, very conventional, and, I'm sorry to say, very boring. Not at all like…" Her voice trailed off.

Andrew followed her gaze and spotted Nick at the top of the cliff. He stood, legs apart, hands thrust in his pockets, staring down at them. His expression was unreadable in the distance. He turned, without a wave or a sign of greeting, and disappeared behind the rocks.

Andrew shifted his gaze back to Morgan. Her expression was totally readable.

"You're in love with Nick."

Morgan brought herself back sharply. "Oh, no. No, of course not. I hardly know him. He's a very disagreeable man. He has a brutal temper, and he's arrogant and bossy and without any decent feelings. He shouts."

Andrew took in this impassioned description with a

lifted brow. "We seem to be talking about two different people."

Morgan turned away, running sand through her fingers. "Maybe. I don't like either one of them."

Andrew let the silence hang a moment as he watched her busy fingers. "But you're in love with him."

"Andrew—"

"And you don't want to be," he finished, looking thoughtfully out to sea. "Morgan, I've been wondering, if I asked you to marry me, would it spoil our friendship?"

"What?" Astonished, she spun her head back around. "Are you joking?"

Calmly, he searched her face. "No, I'm not joking. I decided that asking you to bed would put a strain on our friendship. I wondered if marriage would. Though I didn't realize you were in love with Nick."

"Andrew," she began, uncertain how to react. "Is this a question or a proposal?"

"Let's take the question first."

Morgan took a deep breath. "An offer of marriage, especially from someone you care for, is always flattering to the ego. But egos are unstable and friendships don't require flattery." Leaning over, she brushed his mouth with hers. "I'm very glad you're my friend, Andrew."

"Somehow I thought that would be your reaction. I'm a romantic at heart." Shrugging, he gave her a rueful smile. "An island, a beautiful woman with a laugh like a night wind. I could see us setting up house in the cottage. Fires in the winter, flowers in the spring."

"You're not in love with me, Andrew."

"I could be." Taking her hand, he turned it palm up and studied it. "It isn't your destiny to fall in love with a struggling poet."

"Andrew—"

"And it isn't mine to have you." Smiling again, he kissed her hand. "Still, it's a warm thought."

"And a lovely one. Thank you for it."

He nodded before he rose. "I might decide Venice offers inspiration." Andrew studied the protruding section of the gray stone wall before turning back to her. "Maybe we'll see each other there." He smiled, the flashing boyish smile, and Morgan felt a twinge of regret. "Timing, Morgan, is such an essential factor in romance."

She watched him cross the sand and mount the steps before she turned back to the sea.

Chapter 10

The villa whispered and trembled like an old woman. Even after all her promises to herself that morning, Morgan couldn't sleep. She rolled and tossed in her bed, frantically bringing herself back from dreams each time she started to drift off. It was too easy for Nick to slip into her mind in a dream. Through sheer force of will, Morgan had blocked him out for most of the day. She wouldn't surrender to him now, for only a few hours sleep.

Yet awake and alone, she found herself remembering the inlet—the face under the water, the slim black stub of a cigarette. And Iona, pale and barely alive, with her thick mane of hair streaming nearly to the floor.

Why was it she couldn't rid herself of the thought that one had something to do with the other?

There was too much space, too much quiet in the villa to be tolerated in solitude. Even the air seemed hot and oppressive. As fatigue began to take over, Morgan found herself caught between sleep and wakefulness, that vulnerable land where thoughts can drift and tease.

She could hear Alex's voice, cold and hard, telling her that Iona would be better off dead. There were Dorian's eyes, so calm, so cool, as he lifted a thin black cigarette to his lips. Andrew smiling grimly as he waited for his ship to come in. Liz vowing passionately that she would protect her husband from anyone and anything. And the knife blade, so sharp and deadly. She knew without seeing that Nick's hand gripped the handle.

On a half scream, Morgan sat up and willed herself awake. No, she wouldn't sleep, not alone. She didn't dare.

Before giving herself time to think, she rose and slipped on jeans and a shirt. The beach had given her peace that afternoon. Maybe it would do the same for her tonight.

Outside, she found the openness comforting. There were no walls here or empty rooms. There were stars and the scent of blossoms. She could hear the cypress leaves whisper. The feeling of dread slid from her with every step. She headed for the beach.

The moon was nearly full now, and white as bone. The breeze off the water was degrees cooler than the air had been in her room. She followed the path without hesitation, without fear. Some instinct told her nothing would harm her that night.

After rolling up her pants legs, she stood, letting the water lap over her ankles, warm and silky. Gratefully, she breathed in the moist sea air and felt it soothe her. She stretched her arms toward the stars.

"Will you never learn to stay in bed?"

Morgan spun around to find herself face-to-face with Nick. Had he already been there? she wondered. She hadn't heard him walk behind her. Straightening, she eyed him coolly. Like her, he wore jeans and no shoes. His shirt hung unbuttoned over his bare chest. What madness was it, she wondered, that made her long to go to him. Whatever madness drew her to him, she suppressed.

"That's not your concern." Morgan turned her back on him.

Nick barely prevented himself from yanking her back around. He'd been standing sleepless at his window when he'd seen her leave the house. Almost before he had known what he was doing, he was coming down the beach steps to find her. And it was ice, that same ice, she greeted him with.

"Have you forgotten what happens to women who wander night beaches alone?" The words rang with mockery as he tangled his fingers in her hair. He'd touch her if he chose, he thought furiously. No one would stop him.

"If you plan to drag me around this time, Nicholas, I warn you, I'll bite and scratch."

"That should make it interesting." His fingers tightened as she tossed her head to dislodge his grip. "I'd think you'd have had your fill of beaches today, Aphrodite. Or are you expecting Andrew again?"

She ignored the taunt and the peculiar thrill that came whenever he called her by that name. "I'm not expecting anyone. I came here to be alone. If you'd go away, I could enjoy myself."

Hurting, wanting, Nick spun her around. His fingers bruised her skin so that she made a surprised sound of pain before she could clamp it down. "Damn you, Morgan, don't push me any more. You'll find me a different breed from young Andrew."

"Take your hands off me." She managed to control her voice to a hard, cold steadiness. Her eyes glimmered with frost as they stared into his. She wouldn't cower before him again, and she wouldn't yield. "You'd do well to take lessons from Andrew"—deliberately, she tossed her head and smiled—"or Dorian on how to treat a woman."

Nick swore with quick Greek expertise. Unable to do otherwise, he gripped her tighter, but this time she made no sound. Morgan watched as the dark fury took total command of his face. He was half devil now, violent, with barely a trace of the man others knew. It gave her a perverse enjoyment to know she had driven him to it.

"So you offer yourself to Dorian as well?" He bit off the words as he fought to find some hold on his control. "How many men do you need?"

A flood of fury rose, but she stamped it down. "Isn't it strange, Nicholas," she said calmly, "how your Greek half seems to take over when you're angry? I simply can't see how you and Andrew can be related, however remotely."

"You enjoy leading him on, don't you?" The comparison stroked his fury higher. Morgan found she was gritting her teeth to prevent a whimper at the pain. She wouldn't give him the satisfaction. "Heartless bitch," he hissed at her. "How long do you intend to dangle and tease?"

"How dare you!" Morgan pushed against him. Anger, unreasonable and full, welled up in her for all the sleepless hours he'd given her, and all the pain. "How dare you criticize me for anything! You, with the filthy games you play, and the lies. You care about *no one*—no one but yourself. I detest you and everything you are!" Wrenching free, Morgan fled into the sea, blind and senseless with rage.

"Stupid woman!" Nick tore through two sentences of furious Greek before he caught her and pulled her around. The water lapped around her hips as he shook her. When her feet slipped on the bottom, he dragged her back up. He couldn't think now, couldn't reason. His voice whipped out with the violence of his thoughts. "I'll be damned if you'll make me crawl. Damned if I'll beg for your good feelings. I do what I have to do; it's a matter of necessity. Do you think I enjoy it?"

"I don't care about your necessities or your smuggling or your murders! I don't care about anything that has to do with you. I hate you!" She took a swing at his chest and nearly submerged again. "I hate everything about you. I hate myself for ever letting you touch me!"

The words cut at him, deeper than he wanted them to. He fought not to remember what it had felt like to hold her, to press his mouth against her and feel her melt against him. "That's fine. Just keep your distance and we'll get along perfectly."

"There's nothing I want more than to keep away from you." Her eyes glittered as the words brought her a slash of pain. "Nothing I want more than to never see your face again or hear your name."

He controlled himself with an effort—for there was nothing he wanted more at that moment than to crush her against him and beg, as he'd never begged anyone, for whatever she'd give him. "Then that's what you'll have, Aphrodite. Play your games with Dorian if you like, but tread carefully with Andrew. Tread carefully, or I'll break your beautiful neck."

"Don't you threaten me. I'll see Andrew just as often as I like." Morgan pushed at her dripping hair and glared at him. "I don't think he'd appreciate your protection. He asked me to marry him."

In one swift move, Nick lifted her off her feet and dragged her against his chest. Morgan kicked out, succeeding only in drenching both of them. "What did you tell him?"

"It's none of your business." She struggled, and though she was slick as an eel in the water, his hold remained firm. "Put me *down!* You can't treat me this way."

Fury was raging in him, uncontrollable, savage. No, he wouldn't stand by and watch her with another man. "Damn you, I said what did you tell him!"

"No!" she shouted, more in anger than in fear. "I told him *no.*"

Nick relaxed his grip. Morgan's feet met the sea bottom again as he formed a brittle smile. Her face was white as chalk and he cursed himself. God, would he do nothing but hurt her? Would she do nothing but hurt him? If there weren't so many walls in his way…if he could break down even one of them, he'd have her.

"That's fine." His voice was far from steady, but she had no way of knowing it was from panic rather than temper. "I won't stand by and watch you lead Andrew along. He's an innocent yet." He released her, knowing it might be the last time he'd ever touch her. "I don't suppose you chose to tell him about the lover you left behind."

"Lover?" Morgan pushed at her hair as she took a step back. "What lover?"

Nick lifted the medallion at her neck, then let it fall before he gave into the need to rip it from her. "The one who gave you the trinket you treasure so much. When a woman carries another man's brand, it's difficult to overlook it."

Morgan closed her hand over the small piece of silver. She had thought nothing could make her more angry than she already was. She was blind and trembling with it. "Another man's brand," she repeated in a whisper. "How typical of you. No one brands me, Nicholas. No one, no matter how I love."

"Your pardon, Aphrodite," he returned coolly. "An expression only."

"My father gave me this," she tossed at him. "He gave it to me when I was eight years old and broke my arm falling out of a tree. He's the kindest and most loving person I've ever known. You, Nicholas Gregoras, are a stupid man."

She turned and darted toward the beach, but he caught her again while the water was still around her ankles. Ignoring her curses and struggles, Nick turned her to face him. His eyes bored into hers. His breath was coming in gasps, but not from rage. He needed an answer, and quickly, before he exploded.

"You don't have a lover in America?"

"I said let me *go!*" She was glorious in fury—eyes glittering, skin white as the moonlight. With her head thrown back, she dared him to defy her. In that moment he thought he would have died for her.

"Do you have a lover in America?" Nick demanded again, but his voice was quiet now.

Morgan threw up her chin. "I haven't a lover *anywhere*."

On an oath that sounded more like a prayer, Nick drew her close. The heat from his body fused through the soaked shirts as if they had been naked. Morgan's breath caught at the pressure and the sudden gleam of triumph in his eyes.

"You do now."

Capturing her mouth, he pulled her to the sand.

His lips were urgent, burning. His talk of branding raced through her head, but Morgan accepted the fire eagerly. And already he was stripping off her shirt as if he couldn't bear even the thin separation between them.

Morgan knew he would always love like this. Intensely, without thought, without reason. She gloried in it. Desire this strong took no denial. Her own fingers were busy with his shirt, ripping at the seam in her hurry to be flesh to flesh. She heard him laugh with his mouth pressed against her throat.

There was no longer any right or wrong. Needs were too great. And love. Even as passion drove her higher, Morgan knew and recognized her love. She had waited for it all of her life. With the heat building, there was no time to question how it could be Nick. She only knew it was, whatever, whoever, he was. Nothing else mattered.

When his hands found her naked breasts, he groaned and crushed his lips to hers again. She was so soft, so slender. He struggled not to bruise her, not again, but desire was wild and free in him. He'd never wanted a woman like this. Not like this. Even when he had taken her the first time, he hadn't felt this clean silver streak of power.

She was consuming him, pouring inside his mind. And the taste. Dear God, would he never get enough of the taste of her? He found her breast with his mouth and filled himself.

Morgan arched and dove her fingers into his hair. He was murmuring something, but his breathing was as ragged as hers and she couldn't understand. When his mouth was back on hers, there was no need to. She felt him tugging her jeans over her hips, but was too delirious to realize she had pulled at his first. She felt the skin stretched tight over his bones, the surprising narrowness of his body.

Then his lips and hands were racing over her—not in the angry desperation she remembered from the night before, but in unquestionable possession. There was no gentleness, but neither was there a fierceness. He took and took as though no one had a better right. Those strong lean fingers stroked down her, making her gasp out loud in pleasure, then moan in torment when they lay still.

His mouth was always busy, tongue lightly torturing, teeth taking her to the edge of control. There seemed to be no part of her, no inch he couldn't exploit for pleasure. And the speed never slacked.

Cool sand, cool water, and his hot, clever mouth—she was trapped between them. There was moonlight, rippling white, but she was a willing prisoner of the darkness. In the grove of cypresses a night bird called out—one long, haunting note. It might have been her own sigh. She tasted the sea on his skin, knew he would taste it on hers as well. Somehow, that small intimacy made her hold him tighter.

They might have been the only ones, washed ashore, destined to be lovers throughout their lives without the need for anyone else. The scent of the night wafted over her—his scent. They would always be the same to her.

Then she heard nothing, knew nothing, as he drove her beyond reason with his mouth alone.

She was grasping at him, demanding and pleading in the same breathless whispers for him to give her that final, delirious relief. But he held her off, pleasing himself, and pleasing her until she thought her body would simply implode at the pressure that was building.

With a wild, hungry kiss he silenced her while leading her closer to the edge. Though she could feel his heart racing against hers, he seemed determined to hold them there—an instant, an hour—hovering between heaven and hell.

When he drove them over, Morgan wasn't certain on which side they had fallen—only that they had fallen together.

* * *

Morgan lay quiet, cushioned against Nick's bare shoulder. The waves gently caressed her legs. In the aftermath of the demands of passion she was light and cool and stunned. She could feel the blood still pounding in his chest and knew no one, no one had ever wanted her like this. The sense of power it might have given her came as an ache. She closed her eyes on it.

She hadn't even struggled, she thought. Not even a token protest. She had given herself without thought—not in submission to his strength, but in submission to her own desires. Now, as the heat of passion ebbed, she felt the hard edge of shame.

He was a criminal—a hard, self-seeking man who trafficked in misery for profit. And she had given him her body and her heart. Perhaps she had no control over her heart, but Morgan was honest enough to know she ruled her own body. Shivering, she drew away from him.

"No, stay." Nick nuzzled in her hair as he held her against his side.

"I have to go in," she murmured. Morgan drew her body away as far as his arm would permit. "Please, let me go."

Nick shifted until his face hovered over hers. His lips were curved in amusement; his face was relaxed and satisfied. "No," he said simply. "You won't walk away from me again."

"Nicholas, please." Morgan turned her head aside. "It's late. I have to go."

He became still for a moment, then took her face firmly in his hand and turned it back to his. He saw the gleam of tears, tightly controlled, and swore. "It occurs to you suddenly that you've just given yourself to a criminal and enjoyed it."

"Don't!" Morgan shut her eyes. "Just let me go in. Whatever I've done, I've done because I wanted to."

Nick stared down at her. She was dry-eyed now, but her eyes were bleak. Swearing again, he reached for his partially dry shirt and pulled Morgan into a sitting position. Athens, he thought again, could fry in hell.

"Put this on," he ordered, swinging it over her shoulders. "We'll talk."

"I don't want to talk. There's no need to talk."

"I said we'll talk, Morgan." Nick pushed her arm into a sleeve. "I won't have you feeling guilty over what just happened." She could feel the simmering anger pulsing from him as he pulled his shirt over her breasts. "I won't have that," he muttered. "It's too much. I can't explain everything now…there are some things I won't ever explain."

"I'm not asking for explanations."

His eyes locked on hers. "You ask every time you look at me." Nick pulled a cigarette from the pocket of the shirt, then lit it. "My business in import-export has made me quite a number of contacts over the years. Some of whom, I imagine, you wouldn't approve of." He mused over this for a moment as he blew out a hazy stream of smoke.

"Nicholas, I don't—"

"Shut up, Morgan. When a man's decided to bare his soul, a woman shouldn't interrupt. God knows how dark you'll find it," he added, as he drew in smoke again. "When I was in my early, impressionable twenties, I met a man who considered me suitable for a certain type of work. I found the work itself fascinating. Danger can become addicting, like any other drug."

Yes, she thought as she stared out over the water. If nothing else, she could understand that.

"I began to—freelance." He smiled at the term, but it had little to do with humor. "For his organization. For the most part I enjoyed it. In any case, I was content with it. It's amazing that a way of life, ten years of my life should become a prison in a week's time."

Morgan had drawn her knees close to her chest while she stared out over the water. Nick laid a hand on her hair, but she still didn't look at him. He was finding it more difficult to tell her than he had imagined. Even after he'd finished, she might turn away from him. He'd be left with nothing—less than nothing. He drew hard on his cigarette, then stared at the red glow at the tip.

"Morgan, there are things I've done..." He swore briefly under his breath. "There are things I've done I wouldn't tell you about even if I were free to. You wouldn't find them pleasant."

Now she lifted her face. "You've killed people."

He found it difficult to answer when she was looking at him with tired despair in her eyes. But his voice was cool with control. "When it was necessary."

Morgan lowered her head again. She hadn't wanted to think him a murderer. If he had denied it, she would have tried to have taken him at his word. She hadn't wanted to believe he was capable of what she considered the ultimate sin. The taking of a life.

Nick scowled at the cigarette and hurled it into the sea. *I could have lied to her,* he thought furiously. *Why the hell didn't I just lie—I'm an expert at it. Because I can't lie to her,* he realized with a tired sigh. *Not anymore.* "I did what I had to do, Morgan," he said flatly. "I can't erase the way I've lived for ten years. Right or wrong, it was my choice. I can't apologize for it."

"No, I'm not asking you to. I'm sorry if it seems that way." She drew herself up again and faced him. "Please,

Nicholas, let's leave it at this. Your life's your own. You don't have to justify it to me."

"Morgan—" If she had hurled abuse at him, stabbed him with ice, he might have been able to keep silent. But he couldn't be silent while she struggled to understand. He would tell her, and the decision he'd been struggling with for days would be made. "For the last six months, I've been working on breaking the smuggling ring that runs between Turkey and Lesbos."

Morgan stared at him as though she'd never seen him before. "Breaking it? But I thought…you told me—"

"I've never told you much of anything," he said curtly. "I let you assume. It was better that way. It was necessary."

For a moment she sat quietly, trying to sort out her thoughts. "Nicholas, I don't understand. Are you telling me you're a policeman?"

He laughed at the thought, and part of his anger drained. "No, Aphrodite, spare me that."

Morgan frowned. "A spy then?"

The rest of his anger vanished. He cupped her face in his hands. She was so unbearably sweet. "You will romanticize it, Morgan, I'm a man who travels and follows orders. Be content with that, it's all I can give you."

"That first night on the beach…" At last the puzzle pieces were taking a shape she could understand. "You were watching for the man who runs the smuggling ring. That was who Stephanos followed."

Nick frowned and dropped his hands. She believed him without question or hesitation. Already she'd forgotten that he'd killed—and worse. Why, when she was making it so easy for him did he find it so hard to go on? "I had to get you out of the way. I knew he'd cross that section of beach on his way to Stevos's cottage. Stevos was eliminated because he knew, as I don't yet, the man's exact position in the organization. I think he asked for a raise and got a knife in the back."

"Who is he, Nicholas?"

"No." His eyes came back to hers. His face was hard again, unreachable. "Even if I were sure, I wouldn't tell you. Don't ask me questions I can't answer, Morgan. The more I tell you, the more dangerous your position becomes." His eyes grew darker. "I was ready to use you once, and my organization is very interested in your talent with languages, but I'm a selfish man. You're not going to be involved." His tone was final and just a little furious. "I told my associate you weren't interested."

"That's a bit presumptuous," Morgan began. She frowned until he twisted his head and looked at her again. "I'm capable of making my own decisions."

"You haven't one to make," Nick countered coolly. "And once I know for certain the identity of the head of the ring, my job's finished. Athens will have to learn how to function without me."

"You're not going to do this…" She gestured vaguely, not knowing what title to give his work. "This sort of thing anymore?"

"No." Nick stared back out to sea. "I've been in it long enough."

"When did you decide to stop?"

When I first made love with you, he thought, and nearly said it. But it wasn't quite true. There was one more thing he would have to tell her. "The day I took Iona on the boat." Nick let out an angry breath and turned to her. He had his doubts that she would forgive him for what he was going to say. "Iona's in this, Morgan, deeply."

"In the smuggling? But—"

"I can only tell you that she is, and that part of my job was to get information out of her. I took her out on the boat, fully intending to make love to her to help loosen her tongue." Morgan kept her eyes steady and he continued, growing angrier. "She was cracking under pressure. I was there to help her along. That's why someone tried to kill her."

"Kill her?" Morgan tried to keep her voice level as she dealt with what he was telling her. "But Captain Tripolos said it was attempted suicide."

"Iona would no more have committed suicide than she would have tended goats."

"No," she said slowly. "No, of course you're right."

"If I could have worked on her a little longer, I would have had all that I needed."

"Poor Alex," she murmured. "He'll be crushed if it comes out that she was mixed up in this. And Dorian…" She remembered his empty eyes and his words. *Poor Iona—so beautiful—so lost.* Perhaps he already suspected. "Isn't there something you can do?" She looked up at Nick, this time with trust. "Do the police know? Captain Tripolos?"

"Tripolos knows a great deal and suspects more." Nick took her hand now. He wanted the link badly. "I don't work directly with the police, it slows things down. At the moment," he added cheerfully, "Tripolos has me pegged as the prime suspect in a murder, an attempted murder, and sees me in the role of the masked smuggler. Lord, I'd have given him a thrill last night."

"You enjoy your work, don't you?" Morgan studied him, recognizing the light of adventure in his eyes. "Why are you stopping?"

His smile faded. "I told you I was with Iona. It wasn't the first time I used that method. Sex can be a weapon or a tool, it's a fact of life." Morgan dropped her gaze to the sand. "She'd had too much champagne to be cooperative, but there would have been another time. Since that day, I haven't felt clean." He slid his hand under her chin and lifted it. "Not until tonight."

She was studying him closely, searching. In his eyes she saw something she had only seen once before—regret, and a plea for understanding. Lifting her arms, she brought his mouth down to hers. She felt more than his lips—the heady wave of his relief.

"Morgan." He pressed her back to the sand again. "If I could turn back the clock and have this past week to live over…" He hesitated, then buried his face in her hair. "I probably wouldn't do anything differently."

"You apologize beautifully, Nicholas."

He couldn't keep his hands off her. They were roaming again, arousing them both. "This thing should come to a head tomorrow night, then I'll be at loose ends. Come away somewhere with me for a few days. Anywhere."

"Tomorrow?" She struggled to keep her mind on his words while her body heated. "Why tomorrow?"

"A little complication I caused last night. Come, we're covered with sand. Let's take a swim."

"Complication?" Morgan repeated as he hauled her to her feet. "What kind of complication?"

"I don't think our man will tolerate the loss of a shipment," he murmured as he slipped his shirt from her shoulders.

"You stole it!"

He was pulling her into the water. His blood was already pounding for her as he saw the moonlight glow white over her body. "With incredible ease." When she was past her waist, he drew her against him. The water lapped around them as he began to explore her again.

"Stephanos and I watched the connection from a safe distance on several runs." His mouth brushed over hers, then traced down to her throat. "We'd just come back from one the night I found you on the beach. Now, about those few days."

"What will you do tomorrow night?" Morgan drew back enough to stop his roaming hands and mouth. A hint of fear had worked its way in. "Nicholas, what's going to happen?"

"I'm waiting for some conclusive information from Athens. When it comes, I'll know better how to move. At any rate, I'll be there when the boat docks with its cache tomorrow night."

"Not alone?" She gripped his shoulders. "He's already killed a man."

Nick rubbed his nose against hers. "Do you worry for me, Aphrodite?"

"Don't joke!"

He heard the very real panic in her voice and spoke soothingly. "By late tomorrow afternoon, Tripolos will be brought up to date. If everything goes as planned, I can brief him personally." He smiled down at the frown on her face. "He'll gain all official credit for whatever arrests are made."

"But that's unfair!" Morgan exclaimed. "After all your work, and the time, why shouldn't you—"

"Shut up, Morgan, I can't make love to a woman who's constantly complaining."

"Nicholas, I'm trying to understand."

"Understand this." Impatience shimmered in his voice as he pulled her close again. "I've wanted you from the minute I saw you sitting on that damn rock, and I haven't begun to have enough. You've driven me mad for days. Not anymore, Aphrodite. Not anymore."

He lowered his mouth, and all else was lost.

Chapter 11

Her jeans were still damp as Morgan struggled into them laughing. "You would make me so furious I'd run into the water fully dressed."

Nick fastened the snap on his own. "The feeling was mutual."

Turning her head, she looked at him as he stood, naked to the waist, shaking what sand he could from his shirt. A gleam of mischief lit her eyes. "Oh?" Taking a step closer, Morgan ran her palms up his chest—taking her time—enjoying the hard, firm feel of it before she linked them around his neck. "Did it make you furious thinking I was wearing a token from a lover waiting for me back home?"

"No," he lied with a careless smile. Gripping his shirt in both hands, Nick hooked it around her waist to draw her closer. "Why should that concern me?"

"Oh." Morgan nipped lightly at his bottom lip. "Then perhaps you'd like to hear about Jack."

"I damn well wouldn't," he muttered before his mouth crushed down on hers. Even as her lips answered his, Nick heard the low sound of her muffled laughter. "Witch." Then he took her deeper, deeper, until her laughter was only a sigh. "Maybe you prefer me when I'm angry."

"I prefer you," she said simply, and rested her head on his shoulder.

His arms tightened, strong, possessive. Yet somehow he knew strength alone would never keep her. "Dangerous woman," Nick murmured. "I knew it the first time I held you."

With a laugh, Morgan tossed back her head. "The first time you held me, you cursed me."

"And I continue to do so." But his lips sought hers again without an oath.

"I wish there was only tonight." Suddenly, she was clinging to him with her heart racing. "No tomorrows, only now. I don't want the sun to come up."

Nick buried his face in her hair as the guilt swamped him. He'd brought her fear from the first instant. Even loving her, he could bring her nothing else. He had no right to tell her now that his heart was hers for the asking. Once he told her, she might beg him to abandon his responsibility, leave his job half finished. And he would do just as she asked, he realized…and never feel like a man again.

"Don't wish your days away, Morgan," he told her lightly. "The sun comes up tomorrow, then goes down. And when it comes up again, we'll have nothing but time."

She had to trust him, had to believe that he would be safe—that the danger he lived with would be over in little more than twenty-four hours.

"Come back with me now." Lifting her head again, Morgan gave him a smile. Her worry and fears wouldn't help him. "Come back to the villa and make love with me again."

"You tempt me, Aphrodite." Bending, he kissed both her cheeks in a gesture she found unbearably gentle and sweet. "But you're asleep on your feet. There'll be other nights. I'll take you back."

She allowed him to turn her toward the beach steps. "You might not find it as easy to leave me there alone as you think," she commented with another smile.

With a quiet laugh, he drew her closer to his side. "Not easy perhaps, but—" His head whipped up abruptly, as if he were scenting the air. Narrowed and cold, his eyes swept the darkness of the cliffs above them.

"Nicholas, what—"

But his hand clamped over her mouth as he pulled her, once again, into the shadows of the cypress. Her heart leaped to her throat as it had before, but this time Morgan didn't struggle.

"Be still and don't speak," Nick whispered. Removing his hand, he pushed her back against the trunk of a tree. "Not a sound, Morgan."

She nodded, but he wasn't looking at her. His eyes were trained on the cliffs. Standing at the edge of the covering, Nick watched and waited. Then he heard it again— the quiet scrape of boot on rock. Tensing, he strained his eyes and at last saw the shadow. So, he thought with a grim smile as he watched the black form move swiftly over the rocks, he's come for his cache. But you won't find it, Nick told the shadow silently. And I'll be like a hound on your tail.

Soundlessly, he moved back to Morgan. "Go back to

the villa and stay there." All warmth had dropped away from him. His voice was as cold as his eyes.

"What did you see?" she demanded. "What are you going to do?"

"Do as I say." Taking her arm, he pulled her toward the beach steps. "Go quickly, I haven't got time to waste. I'll lose him."

Him. Morgan felt a flutter of fear. She swallowed it. "I'm going with you."

"Don't be a fool." Impatient, Nick dragged her along. "Go back to the villa, I'll speak to you in the morning."

"No." Morgan pulled out of his hold. "I said I'm going with you. You can't stop me."

She was standing straight as an arrow, eyes blazing with a combination of fear and determination. Nick swore at her, knowing every second he stayed meant his man was farther away. "I don't have time—"

"Then you'd better stop wasting it," Morgan said calmly. "I'm coming."

"Then come," he said under his breath as he turned away from her. She won't last five minutes on the cliffs without shoes, he thought. She'd limp her way back to the villa in ten. He moved quickly up the beach steps without waiting for her. Gritting her teeth, Morgan raced after him.

As he left the steps to start his scramble up the cliff, Nick paid little attention to her. He cast his eyes to the sky and wished the night were not so clear. A cloud over the moon would allow him to risk getting closer to the man he followed. He gripped a rock and hauled himself up farther—a few pebbles loosened and skidded down. When he glanced back, he was surprised to see Morgan keeping pace with him.

Damn the woman, he thought with a twinge of reluctant admiration. Without a word, he held out his hand and pulled her up beside him. "Idiot," he hissed, wanting to shake her and kiss her all at once. "Will you go back? You don't have any shoes."

"Neither do you," Morgan gritted.

"Stubborn fool."

"Yes."

Cursing silently, Nick continued the climb. He couldn't risk the open path in the moonlight, so kept to the rocks. Though it wouldn't be possible to keep his quarry in sight, Nick knew where he was going.

Morgan clamped her teeth shut as the ball of her foot scraped against a rock. With a quick hiss of breath, she kept going. She wasn't going to whimper and be snapped at. She wasn't going to let him go without her.

On a rough ledge, Nick paused briefly to consider his options. Circling around would take time. If he'd been alone—and armed, he would have taken his chances with the narrow path now. Odds were that the man he followed was far enough ahead and confident enough to continue his journey without looking over his shoulder. But he wasn't alone, he thought on a flare of annoyance. And he had no more than his hands to protect Morgan if they were spotted.

"Listen to me," he whispered, hoping to frighten her as he grabbed her by the shoulders. "The man's killed—and killed more than once, I promise you. When he finds his cache isn't where it should be, he'll know he's being hunted. Go back to the villa."

"Do you want me to call the police?" Morgan asked calmly, though he'd succeeded very well in frightening her.

"No!" The word whipped out, no louder than a breath. "I can't afford to give up the chance to see who he is."

Frustrated, he glared at her. "Morgan, I don't have a weapon, if he—"

"I'm not leaving you, Nicholas. You're wasting time arguing about it."

He swore again, then slowly controlled his temper. "All right, damn you. But you'll do exactly as I say or I promise you, I'll knock you unconscious and shove you behind a rock."

She didn't doubt it. Morgan lifted her chin. "Let's go."

Agilely, Nick pulled himself over the ridge and onto the path. Before he could reach back to assist her, Morgan was kneeling on the hard ground beside him. He thought, as he looked into her eyes, that she was a woman men dreamed of. Strong, beautiful, loyal. Taking her hand, he dashed up the path, anxious to make up the time he'd wasted arguing with her. When he felt they'd been in the open long enough, he left the path for the rocks again.

"You know where he's going," Morgan whispered, breathing quickly. "Where?"

"A small cave near Stevos's cottage. He thinks to pick up last night's cache." He grinned suddenly. Morgan heard it in his voice. "He won't find it, and then, by God, he'll sweat. Keep low now—no more talk."

She could see the beauty of the night clearly in the moonlight. The sky was velvet, pierced with stars, flooded by the moon. Even the thin, scruffy bushes working their way through rock held an ethereal allure. The sound of the sea rose from below them, soft with distance. An owl sent up a quiet hooting music of lazy contentment. Morgan thought, if she could look, she might find more blue-headed flowers. Then Nick was pulling her over the next ridge and pressing her to the ground.

"It's just up ahead. Stay here."

"No, I—"

"Don't argue," he said roughly. "I can move faster without you. Don't move and don't make a sound."

Before she could speak, he was scrambling away, silently, half on his belly, half on his knees. Morgan watched him until he was concealed by another huddle of rocks. Then, for the first time since they had begun, she started to pray.

Nick couldn't move quickly now. If he had misjudged the timing, he'd find himself face-to-face with his quarry. He needed to save that pleasure for the following night. But to know—to know who he had been hounding for six months was a bonus Nick couldn't resist.

There were more rocks and a few trees for cover, and he used them as he skirted the dead man's rough cottage. An attempt had been made to clear the ground for a vegetable garden, but the soil had never been worked. Nick wondered idly what had become of the woman who had sometimes shared Stevos's bed and washed his shirts. Then he heard the quiet scrape of boot on rock again. Less than a hundred yards away, Nick estimated. Eyes gleaming in the darkness, he crept toward the mouth of the cave.

He could hear the movements inside, quiet, confident. Slipping behind a rock, he waited, patient, listening. The furious oath that echoed inside the cave brought Nick a rich thrill of pleasure.

Taste the betrayal, he told the man inside. And choke on it.

The movements inside the cave became louder. Nick's smile spread. He'd be searching now, Nick concluded. Looking for signs to tell him if his hiding place had been looted. But no, you haven't been robbed, Nick thought. Your little white bags were lifted from right under your nose.

He saw him then, striding out of the cave—all in black, still masked. Take it off, Nick ordered him silently. Take it off and let me see your face.

The figure stood in the shadows of the mouth of the cave. Fury flowed from him in waves. His head turned from side to side as if he were searching for something... or someone.

They heard the sound at the same instant. The shifting of pebbles underfoot, the rustling of bushes. Dear God, Morgan! Nick thought and half rose from his concealment. As he tensed, he saw the black-clad figure draw a gun and melt back into the shadows.

With his heart beating in his throat, Nick gripped the rock and prepared to lunge. He could catch the man off-guard, he thought rapidly, gain enough time to shout a warning to Morgan so that she could get away. Fear licked at him—not for himself, but at the thought that she might not run fast enough.

The bush directly across the path trembled with movement. Nick sucked in his breath to lunge.

Bony, and with more greed than wit, a dusty goat stepped forward to find a more succulent branch.

Nick sunk down behind the rock, furious that he was trembling. Though she had done nothing more than what he had told her, he cursed Morgan fiercely.

With a furious oath, the man in black stuck the gun back in his belt as he strode down the path. As he passed Nick, he whipped off his mask.

Nick saw the face, the eyes, and knew.

Morgan huddled behind the rock where Nick had shoved her, her arms wrapped around her knees. It seemed she'd already waited an eternity. She strained to hear every sound—the whisper of the wind, the sigh of leaves. Her heart hadn't stopped its painful thudding since he'd left her.

Never again, Morgan promised herself. Never again would she sit and wait. Never again would she sit helpless and trembling, on the verge of hot, useless tears. If anything happened—she clamped down on the incomplete thought. Nothing was going to happen to Nick. He'd be back any moment. But the moments dragged on.

When he dropped down beside her, she had to stifle a scream. Morgan had thought her ears were tuned to hear even the dust blow on the wind, but she hadn't heard his approach. She didn't even say his name, just went into his arms.

"He's gone," Nick told her.

The memory of that one shuddering moment of terror washed over him. He crushed his mouth to hers as though he were starving. All of her fears whipped out, one by one, until there was nothing in her but a well of love.

"Oh, Nicholas, I was so frightened for you. What happened?"

"He wasn't pleased." With a grin that was both ruthless and daring, he pulled her to her feet. "No, he wasn't pleased. He'll be on the boat tomorrow."

"But did you see who—"

"No questions." He silenced her again with his mouth, roughly, as though the adventure were only beginning. "I don't want to have to lie to you again." With a laugh, Nick drew her toward the path and the moonlight. "Now, my stubborn, courageous witch, I'll take you back. Tomorrow when your feet are too sore to stand, you'll curse me."

He wouldn't tell her any more, Morgan thought. And for now, perhaps it was best. "Share my bed tonight." She smiled as she hooked her arm around his waist. "Stay another hour with me, and I won't curse you."

Laughing, he ran a hand down her hair. "What man could resist such an ultimatum?"

Morgan awoke as a soft knock sounded at her door. The small maid peeked inside.

"Your pardon, *kyrios,* a phone call from Athens."

"Oh…thank you, Zena, I'll be right there." Rising quickly, Morgan hurried to the phone in Liz's sitting room, belting her robe as she went. "Hello?"

"Morgan, did I wake you? It's past ten."

"Liz?" Morgan tried to shake away the cobwebs. It had been dawn before she had slept.

"Do you know anyone else in Athens?"

"I'm a bit groggy." Morgan yawned, then smiled with memories. "I went for a late-night swim. It was wonderful."

"You sound very smug," Liz mused. "We'll have to discuss it later. Morgan, I feel terrible about it, but I'm going to have to stay here until tomorrow. The doctors are hopeful, but Iona's still in a coma. I can't leave Alex to cope with his family and everything else alone."

"Please, don't worry about me. I'm sorry, Liz. I know it's difficult for both of you." She thought of Iona's involvement in the smuggling and felt a fresh wave of pity. "How is Alex holding up? He seemed so devastated when he left here."

"It would be easier if the whole family didn't look to him for answers. Oh, Morgan, it's so ugly." Strain tightened her voice and Morgan heard her take a deep breath to control it. "I don't know how Iona's mother will handle it if she dies. And suicide—it just makes it harder."

Morgan swallowed the words she wanted to say. Nick

had spoken to her in confidence; she couldn't betray it even for Liz. "You said the doctors are hopeful."

"Yes, her vital signs are leveling, but—"

"What about Dorian, Liz? Is he all right?"

"Barely." Morgan heard Liz sigh again. "I don't know how I could have been so blind not to see how he felt about her. He's hardly left her bedside. If Alex hadn't bullied him, I think he might have slept in the chair beside her last night instead of going home. From the way he looks this morning, I don't think he got any sleep anyway."

"Please give him my best—and Alex, too." On a long frustrated breath she sat down. "Liz, I feel so helpless." She thought of smuggling, attempted murder and shut her eyes. "I wish there were something I could do for you."

"Just be there when I get back." Though her tone lightened, Morgan recognized the effort. "Enjoy the beach for me, look for your goatherd. If you're going to take moonlight swims, you should have some company for them." When Morgan was silent Liz continued slowly. "Or did you?"

"Well, actually…" Smiling, Morgan trailed off.

"Tell me, have you settled on a goatherd or a poet?"

"Neither."

"It must be Nick then," Liz concluded. "Imagine that—all I had to do was invite him to dinner."

Morgan lifted a brow and found herself grinning. "I don't know what you're talking about." Life was everywhere, she remembered, if you only knew where to look.

"*Mmm-hmmm.* We'll talk about it tomorrow. Have fun. The number's there if you need me for anything. Oh, there's some marvelous wine in the cellar," she added, and for the first time, the smile in her voice seemed genuine. "If you feel like a cozy evening—help yourself."

"I appreciate it, Liz, but—"

"And don't worry about me or any of us. Everything's going to be fine. I just know it. Give Nick my love."

"I will," Morgan heard herself saying.

"I thought so. See you tomorrow."

Smiling, Morgan replaced the receiver.

"And so," Stephanos finished, lovingly stroking his moustache, "after several glasses of ouzo, Mikal became more expansive. The last two dates he gave me when our man joined the fishing expedition were the last week in February and the second week in March. That doesn't include the evening we encountered Morgan James, or when you took the trip in his stead."

Smiling, Nick flipped through the reports on his desk. "And from the end of February to the first week of April, he was in Rome. Even without my stroke of luck last night, that would have ruled him out. With the phone call I just got from Athens, I'd say we've eliminated him altogether from having any part in this. Now we know our man works alone. We move."

"And you move with an easy heart?" Stephanos noted. "What did Athens say?"

"The investigation on that end is complete. He's clean. His books, his records, his phone calls and correspondence. From this end, we know he hasn't been on the island to take part in any of the runs." Nick leaned back in his chair. "I have no doubt that since our man learned of the loss of his last shipment, he'll make the trip tonight. He won't want another to slip through his fingers." He tapped idly on the papers which littered his desk. "Now that I have the information I've been waiting for, we won't keep Athens waiting any longer. We'll have him tonight."

"You were out very late last night," Stephanos commented, taking out an ugly pipe and filling it.

"Keeping tabs on me, Stephanos?" Nick inquired with a lift of brow. "I haven't been twelve for a very long time."

"You are in very good humor this morning." He continued to fill his pipe, tapping the tobacco with patient care. "You haven't been so for many days."

"You should be glad my mood's broken. But then, you're used to my moods, aren't you, old man?"

Stephanos shrugged in agreement or acceptance. "The American lady is fond of walking on the beach. Perhaps you encountered her last night?"

"You're becoming entirely too wise in your old age, Stephanos." Nick struck a match and held it over the bowl of the pipe.

"Not too old to recognize the look of a man satisfied with a night of pleasure," Stephanos commented mildly and sucked to get flame. "A very beautiful lady. Very strong."

Lighting a cigarette, Nick smiled at him. "So you've mentioned before. I'd noticed myself. Tell me, Stephanos, are you also not too old to have ideas about strong, beautiful ladies?"

Stephanos cackled. "Only the dead have no ideas about strong, beautiful ladies, Nicholas. I'm a long way from dead."

Nick flashed him a grin. "Keep your distance, old man. She's mine."

"She is in love with you."

The cigarette halted on its journey to Nick's lips. His smiled faded. Stephanos stood grinning broadly as he was pierced with one of his friend's, lancing looks. "Why do you say that?"

"Because it is true, I've seen it." He puffed enjoyably

on his pipe. "It is often difficult to see what is standing before your eyes. How much longer is she alone?"

Nick brought his thoughts back and scowled at the papers on his desk. "I'm not certain. Another day or so at least, depending on Iona's condition. In love with me," he murmured and looked back at Stephanos.

He knew she was attracted, that she cared—perhaps too much for her own good. But in love with him.... He'd never allowed himself to consider the possibility.

"She will be alone tonight," Stephanos continued blandly, appreciating Nick's stunned look. "It wouldn't do for her to wander from the villa." He puffed a few moments in silence. "If all does not go smoothly, you would want her safely behind locked doors."

"I've already spoken to her. She understands enough to listen and take care." Nick shook his head. Today of all days he had to think clearly. "It's time we invited Captain Tripolos in. Call Mitilini."

Morgan enjoyed a late breakfast on the terrace and toyed with the idea of walking to the beach. He might come, she thought. I could phone and ask him to come. No, she decided, nibbling on her lip as she remembered all he had told her. If tonight is as important as he thinks, he needs to be left alone. I wish I knew more. I wish I knew what he was going to do. What if he gets hurt or...Morgan clamped down on the thought and wished it were tomorrow.

"Kyrios." At the maid's quiet summons, Morgan gasped and spun. "The captain from Mitilini is here to speak with you."

"What?" Panic rose and Morgan swallowed it. If Nick had spoken to him, Tripolos would hardly be waiting to see her, she thought frantically. Perhaps Nick wasn't ready yet. What could Tripolos possibly want with her?

"Tell him I'm out," she decided quickly. "Tell him I've gone to the beach or the village."

"Very good, *kyrios*." The maid accepted her order without question, then watched as Morgan streaked from the terrace.

For the second time, Morgan climbed the steep cliff path. This time, she knew were she was going. She could see Tripolos's official car parked at the villa's entrance as she rounded the first bend. She increased her pace, running until she was certain she herself was out of view.

Her approach had been noticed, however. The wide doors of Nick's villa opened before she reached the top step. Nick came out to meet her.

"*Yiasou*. You must be in amazing shape to take the hill at that speed."

"Very funny," she panted as she ran into his arms.

"Is it that you couldn't keep away from me or is something wrong?" He held her close a moment, then drew her back just far enough to see her face. It was flushed with the run, but there was no fear in her eyes.

"Tripolos is at the villa." Morgan pressed her hand to her heart and tried to catch her breath. "I slipped out the back because I didn't know what I should say to him. Nicholas, I have to sit down. That's a very steep hill."

He was searching her face silently. Still struggling for her breath, Morgan tilted her head and returned the survey. She laughed and pushed the hair from her eyes. "Nicholas, why are you staring at me like that?"

"I'm trying to see what's standing in front of my eyes."

She laughed again. "Well, I am, you fool, but I'm going to collapse from exhaustion any minute."

With a sudden grin, Nick swept her off her feet and

into his arms. She circled his neck as his mouth came down on hers.

"What are you doing?" she asked, when he let her breathe again.

"Taking what's mine."

His lips came back to hers and lingered. Slowly, almost lazily, he began to tease her tongue with his until he felt her breath start to shudder into his mouth. He promised himself that when everything was over, he would kiss her again, just like this—luxuriously with the heat of the sun warming her skin. When the night's work was finally over, he thought, and for a moment his lips were rough and urgent. Needs rushed through him almost painfully before he banked them.

"So…" He strolled into the house, still carrying her. "The captain came to see you. He's very tenacious."

Morgan took a deep breath to bring herself back from the power of the kiss. "You said you were going to speak with him today, but I didn't know if you were ready. If you'd gotten the information you needed. And to confess and humiliate myself, I'm a coward. I didn't want to face him again."

"Coward, Aphrodite? No, that's something you're not." He laid his cheek against hers a moment, making her wonder what was going on in his head. "I called Mitilini," he continued, "I left a message for Tripolos. After our talk, he should lose all interest in you."

"I'll be devastated." He grinned and took her lips again. "Would you put me down? I can't talk to you this way."

"I'm enjoying it." Ignoring her request, he continued into the salon. "Stephanos, I believe Morgan might like something cool. She had quite a run."

"No, nothing really. *Efxaristo*." Faintly embarrassed,

she met Stephanos's checkerboard grin. When he backed out of sight, she turned her head back to Nick. "If you know who the man is who's running the smuggling, can't you just tell Captain Tripolos and have him arrested?"

"It's not that simple. We want to catch him when the cache is in his possession. There's also the matter of cleaning up the place in the hills where he keeps his goods stored before he ships them on. That part," he added with an absent interest, "I'll leave to Tripolos."

"Nicholas, what will you do?"

"What has to be done."

"Nicholas—"

"Morgan," he interrupted. Standing her on feet, he placed his hands on her shoulders. "You don't want a step-by-step description. Let me finish this without bringing you in any more than I already have."

He lowered his mouth, taking hers with uncharacteristic gentleness. He brought her close, but softly, as if he held something precious. Morgan felt her bones turn to water.

"You have a knack for changing the subject," she murmured.

"After tonight, it's the only subject that's going to interest me. Morgan—"

"A thousand pardons." Stephanos hovered in the doorway. Nick looked up impatiently.

"Go away, old man."

"Nicholas!" Morgan drew out of his arms, sending him a look of reproof. "Has he always been rude, Stephanos?"

"Alas my lady, since he took his thumb out of his mouth."

"Stephanos," Nick began in warning, but Morgan gave a peal of laughter and kissed him.

"Captain Tripolos requests a few moments of your

time, Mr. Gregoras," Stephanos said, respectfully and grinned.

"Give me a moment, then send him in, and bring the files from the office."

"Nicholas." Morgan clung to his arm. "Let me stay with you. I won't get in the way."

"No." His refusal was short and harsh. He saw the hurt flicker in her eyes and sighed. "Morgan, I can't allow it even if I wanted to. This isn't going to touch you. I can't let it touch you. That's important to me."

"You're not going to send me away," she began heatedly.

He arched a brow and looked very cool. "I'm not under the same pressure I was last night, Morgan. And I will send you away."

"I won't go."

His eyes narrowed. "You'll do precisely what I say."

"Like hell."

Fury flickered, smoldered, then vanished in a laugh. "You're an exasperating woman, Aphrodite. If I had the time, I'd beat you." To prove his point, he drew her close and touched his lips to her. "Since I don't I'll ask you to wait upstairs."

"Since you *ask*."

"Mr. Gregoras. Ah, Miss James." Tripolos lumbered into the room. "How convenient. I was inquiring for Miss James at the Theoharis villa when your message reached me."

"Miss James is leaving," Nick told him. "I'm sure you'll agree her presence isn't necessary. Mr. Adonti from Athens has asked me to speak with you on a certain matter."

"Adonti?" Tripolos repeated. Nick watched surprise and interest move across the pudgy face before his eyes became direct. "So, you are acquainted with Mr. Adonti's organization?"

"Well acquainted," Nick returned mildly. "We've had dealings over the years."

"I see." He studied Nick with a thoughtful purse of his lips. "And Miss James?"

"Miss James chose an inopportune time to visit friends," Nick said and took her arm. "That's all. If you'll excuse me, I'll just see her out. Perhaps you'd care for a drink while you're waiting." With a gesture toward the bar, Nick drew Morgan out into the hall.

"He looked impressed with the name you just dropped."

"Forget the name," Nick told her briefly. "You've never heard it."

"All right," she said without hesitation.

"What have I done to deserve this trust you give me?" he demanded suddenly. "I've hurt you again and again. I couldn't make up for it in a lifetime."

"Nicholas—"

"No." He cut her off with a shake of his head. In an uncharacteristic gesture of nerves or frustration, he dragged a hand through his hair. "There's no time. Stephanos will show you upstairs."

"As you wish," Stephanos agreed from behind them. Handing Nick a folder, he turned to the stairs. "This way, my lady."

Because Nick had already turned back to the salon, Morgan followed the old man without a word. She'd been given more time with him, she told herself. She couldn't ask for any more than that.

Stephanos took her into a small sitting room off the master bedroom. "You'll be comfortable here," he told her. "I'll bring you coffee."

"No. No, thank you, Stephanos." She stared at him, and for the second time he saw her heart in her eyes. "He'll be all right, won't he?"

He grinned at her so that his moustache quivered. "Can you doubt it?" he countered before he closed the door behind him.

Chapter 12

There was nothing more frustrating than waiting, Morgan decided after the first thirty minutes. Especially for someone who simply wasn't made for sitting still.

The little room was shaped like a cozy box and done in warm, earthy colors with lots of polished wood that gleamed in the early afternoon light. It was filled with small treasures. Morgan sat down and scowled at a Dresden shepherdess. At another time she might have admired the flowing grace of the lines, the fragility. Now she could only think that she was of no more practical use than that pale piece of porcelain. She had, in a matter of speaking, been put on the shelf.

It was ridiculous for Nick to constantly try to…shield her. Morgan's sigh was quick and impatient. Hadn't that been Liz's words when she had spoken of Alex's actions? After all, Morgan thought as she rose again, she was hardly some trembling, fainting scatterbrain who couldn't deal with whatever there was to face. She remembered trembling *and* fainting dead away in his arms. With a rueful smile, she paced to the window. Well, it wasn't as though she made a habit of it.

In any case, her thoughts ran on, he should know that she would, and could, face anything now that they were together. If he understood how she felt about him, then... but did he? she thought abruptly. She'd shown him, certainly she'd shown him in every possible way open to her, but she hadn't told him.

How can I? Morgan asked herself as she sunk into another chair. When a man had lived ten years of his life following his own rules, courting danger, looking for adventures, did he want to tie himself to a woman and accept the responsibilities of love?

He cared for her, Morgan reflected. Perhaps more than he was comfortable with. And he wanted her—more than any man had ever wanted her. But love...love wouldn't come easily to a man like Nicholas. No, she wouldn't pressure him with hers now. Even the unselfish offer of it would be pressure, she thought, when he had so much on his mind. She was only free to go on showing him, trusting him.

Even that seemed to throw him off-balance a bit, she mused, smiling a little. It was as if he couldn't quite accept that someone could see him as he was, know the way he had lived and still give him trust. Morgan wondered if he would have been more comfortable if she had pulled back from him a little after the things he had told her. He would have understood her condemnations more readily than her acceptance. Well, he'll just have to get used to it, she decided. He'll just have to get used to it because I'm not going to make it easy for him to back away.

Restless, she walked to the window. Here was a different view, Morgan thought, from one she so often looked out on from her bedroom window. Higher, more dangerous. More compelling, she thought with a quick thrill. The rocks seemed more jagged, the sea less tame. How it suited the man she'd given her heart to.

There was no terrace there, and suddenly wanting the air and sun, Morgan went through to his bedroom and opened his balcony doors. She could hear the sea hissing before she reached the rail. With a laugh, she leaned farther out.

Oh, she could live with the challenge of such a view every day, she thought, and never tire of it. She could watch the sea change colors with the sky, watch the gulls swoop over the water and back to the nests they'd built in the cliff walls. She could look down on the Theoharis villa and appreciate its refined elegance, but she would choose the rough gray stone and dizzying height.

Morgan tossed back her head and wished for a storm. Thunder, lightning, wild wind. Was there a better spot on earth to enjoy it? Laughing, she dared the sky to boil and spew out its worst.

"My God, how beautiful you are."

The light of challenge still in her eyes, Morgan turned. Leaning against the open balcony door, Nick stared at her. His face was very still, his gaze like a lance. The passion was on him, simmering, bubbling, just beneath the surface. It suited him, Morgan thought, suited those long, sharp bones in his face, those black eyes and the mouth that could be beautiful or cruel.

As she leaned back on the railing, the breeze caught at the ends of her hair. Her eyes took on the color of the sky. Power swept over her, and a touch of madness. "You want me, I can see it. Come and show me."

It hurt, Nick discovered. He'd never known, until Morgan, that desire could hurt. Perhaps it was only when you loved that your needs ached in you. How many times had he loved her last night? he wondered. And each time, it had been like a tempest in him. Now, he promised himself, this time, he would show her a different way.

Slowly, he went to her. Taking both of her hands, he lifted them, then pressed his lips to the palms. When he brought his gaze to hers, Nick saw that her eyes were wide and moved, her lips parted in surprise. Something stirred in him—love, guilt, a need to give.

"Have I shown you so little tenderness, Morgan?" he murmured.

"Nicholas…" She could only whisper his name as her pulses raged and her heart melted.

"Have I given you no soft words, no sweetness?" He kissed her hands again, one finger at a time. She didn't move, only stared at him. "And you still come to me. I'm in your debt," he said quietly in Greek. "What price would you ask me?"

"No, Nicholas, I…" Morgan shook her head, unable to speak, nearly swaying with the weakness this gentle, quiet man brought her.

"You asked me to show you how I wanted you." He put his hands to her face as if she were indeed made of Dresden porcelain, then touched his lips almost reverently to hers. A sound came from her, shaky and small. "Come and I will."

He lifted her, not with a flourish as he had on the porch, but as a man lifts something he cherishes. "Now…" He laid her down with care. "In the daylight, in my bed."

Again, he took her hand, tracing kisses over the back and palm, then to the wrist where her pulse hammered. All the while he watched her as she lay back, staring at him with something like astonished wonder.

How young she looks, Nick thought as he gently drew her finger into his mouth. And how fragile. Not a witch now, or a goddess, but only a woman. His woman. And her eyes were already clouding, her breath already trembling. He'd shown her the fire and the storm, he thought, but not once—not once had he given her spring.

Bending, he nibbled lightly at her lips, allowing his hands to touch no more than her hair.

It might have been a dream, so weak and weightless did she feel. Nick kissed her eyes closed so that Morgan saw no more than a pale red glow. Then his lips continued, over her forehead, her temples, down the line of her cheekbones—always soft, always warm. The words he whispered against her skin flowed like scented oil over her. She would have moved to bring him closer if her arms had not been too heavy to lift. Instead, she lay in the flood of his tenderness.

His mouth was at her ear, gently torturing with a trace of tongue, a murmured promise. Even as she moaned in surrender, he moved lower to taste and tease the curve of her neck. With kisses like whispers, and whispers like wine, he took her deeper. Gentleness was a drug for both of them.

Hardly touching her, he loosened the buttons of her blouse and slipped it from her. Though he felt the firm pressure of her breasts against him, he took his mouth to the slope of her shoulder instead. He could feel the strength there, the grace, and he tarried.

Morgan's eyes were closed, weighed down with gold-tipped lashes. Her breath rushed out between her lips. He knew he could watch those flickers of pleasure move over her face forever. With his hands once more buried in her hair, Nick kissed her. He felt the yielding and the hunger before he moved on.

Slowly, savoring, he took his lips down to the soft swell—circling, nibbling until he came to the tender underside of her breast. On a moan, Morgan fretted under him as if she were struggling to wake from a dream. But he kept the pace slow and soothed her with words and soft, soft kisses.

With aching gentleness he stroked his tongue over the peak, fighting a surge of desperation when he found it hot and ready. Her movements beneath him took on a rhythmic sinuousness that had the blood pounding in his brain. Her scent was there, always there on the verge of his senses even when she wasn't with him. Now he wallowed in it. As he suckled, he allowed his hands to touch her for the first time.

Morgan felt the long stroke of his hands, the quick scrape of those strong rough fingers that now seemed sensitive enough to tune violins. They caressed lightly, like a breeze. They made her ache.

Soft, slow, gentle, his mouth traveled down the center of her body, lingering here, exploring there until he paused where her slacks hugged across her stomach. When she felt him unfasten them, she trembled. She arched to help him, but Nick drew them down inch by inch, covering the newly exposed flesh with moist kisses so that she could only lie steeped in a pool of pleasure.

And when she was naked, he continued to worship her with his lips, with his suddenly gentle hands. She thought she could hear her own skin hum. The muscles in her thighs quivered as he passed over them, and her desire leaped from passive to urgent.

"Nicholas," she breathed. "Now."

"You've scratched your feet on the rocks," he murmured, pressing his lips against the ball of her foot. "It's a sin to mar such skin, my love." Watching her face, he ran his tongue over the arch. Her eyes flew open, dazed with passion. "I've longed to see you like this." His voice grew thick as his control began to slip. "With sunlight streaming over you, your hair flowing over my pillow, your body trembling for me."

As he spoke, he began the slow, aching journey back, gradually back to her lips. Needs pressed at him and demanded he hurry, but he wouldn't be rushed. He told himself he could linger over the taste and the feel of her for days.

Her arms weren't heavy now, but strong as they curled around him. Every nerve, every pore of her body seemed tuned to him. The harmony seemed impossible, yet it sung through her. His flesh was as hot and damp as hers, his breath as unsteady.

"You ask how I want you," he murmured, thrilling to her moan as he slipped into her. "Look at me and see."

His control hung by a thread. Morgan pulled his mouth to hers and snapped it.

Nick held Morgan close, gently stroking her back while her trembles eased. She clung to him, almost as much in wonder as in love. How was she to have known he had such tenderness in him? How was she to have known she would be so moved by it? Blinking back tears, she pressed her lips to his throat.

"You've made me feel beautiful," she murmured.

"You are beautiful." Tilting her head back, Nick smiled at her. "And tired," he added, tracing a thumb over the mauve smudges under her eyes. "You should sleep, Morgan, I won't have you ill."

"I won't be ill." She snuggled against him, fitting herself neatly against the curve of his body. "And there'll be time for sleeping later. We'll go away for a few days, like you said."

Twining a lock of her hair around his finger, Nick gazed up at the ceiling. A few days with her would never be enough, but he still had the night to get through. "Where would you like to go?"

Morgan thought of her dreams of Venice and Cornish moors. With a sigh, she closed her eyes and drew in Nick's scent. "Anywhere. Right here." Laughing, she propped herself on his chest. "Wherever it is, I intend to keep you in bed a good deal of the time."

"Is that so?" His mouth twitched as he tugged on her hair. "I might begin to think you have designs only on my body."

"It is a rather nice one." In a long stroke, she ran her hands down his shoulders, enjoying the feel of firm flesh and strong bone. "Lean and muscled..." She trailed off when she spotted a small scar high on his chest. A frown creased her brow as she stared at it. It seemed out of place on that smooth brown skin. "Where did you get this?"

Nick tilted his head, shifting his gaze down. "Ah, an old battle scar," he said lightly.

From a bullet, Morgan realized all at once. Horror ripped through her and mirrored in her eyes. Seeing it, Nick cursed his loose tongue.

"Morgan—"

"No, please." She buried her face against his chest and held tight. "Don't say anything. Just give me a minute."

She'd forgotten. Somehow the gentleness and beauty of their lovemaking had driven all the ugliness out of her mind. It had been easy to pretend for a little while that there was no threat. Pretending's for children, she reminded herself. He didn't need to cope with a child now. If she could give him nothing else, she would give him what was left of her strength. Swallowing fear, she pressed her lips to his chest then rolled beside him again.

"Did everything go as you wanted with Captain Tripolos?"

A strong woman, Nick thought, linking his hand with hers. An extraordinary woman. "He's satisfied with the information I've given him. A shrewd man for all his plodding technique."

"Yes, I thought he was like a bulldog the first time I encountered him."

Chuckling, Nick drew her closer. "An apt description, Aphrodite." He shifted then, reaching to the table beside him for a cigarette. "I think he's one of the few policemen I find it agreeable to work with."

"Why do you—" She broke off as she looked up and focused on the slim black cigarette. "I'd forgotten," Morgan murmured. "How could I have forgotten?"

Nick blew out a stream of smoke. "Forgotten what?"

"The cigarette." Morgan sat up, pushing at her tumbled hair. "The stub of the cigarette near the body."

He lifted a brow, but found himself distracted by the firm white breasts easily within reach. "So?"

"It was fresh, from one of those expensive brands like you're smoking." She let out an impatient breath. "I should have told you before, but it hardly makes any difference at this point. You already know who killed Stevos—who runs the smuggling."

"I never told you I did."

"You didn't have to." Annoyed with herself, Morgan frowned and missed Nick's considering look.

"Why didn't I?"

"You'd have told me if you hadn't seen his face. When you wouldn't answer me at all, I knew you had."

He shook his head as a reluctant smile touched his lips.

"*Diabolos,* it's a good thing I didn't cross you earlier in my career. I'm afraid it would have been over quickly. As it happens," he added, "I saw the cigarette myself."

"I should have known you would," she muttered.

"I can assure you Tripolos didn't miss it either."

"That damn cigarette has driven me to distraction." Morgan gave an exasperated sigh. "There were moments I suspected everyone I knew—Dorian, Alex, Iona, even Liz and Andrew. I nearly made myself sick over it."

"You don't name me." Nick studied the cigarette in his hand.

"No, I already told you why."

"Yes," he murmured, "with an odd sort of compliment I haven't forgotten. I should have eased your mind sooner, Morgan, about what I do. You might have slept better."

Leaning over, she kissed him. "Stop worrying about my sleep. I'm going to start thinking I look like a tired hag."

He slid a hand behind her neck to keep her close. "Will you rest if I tell you that you do?"

"No, but I'll hit you."

"Ah, then I'll lie and tell you you're exquisite."

She hit him anyway, a quick jab in the ribs.

"So, now you want to play rough." Crushing out his cigarette, Nick rolled her beneath him. She struggled for a moment, then eyed him narrowly.

"Do you know how many times you've pinned me down like this?" Morgan demanded.

"No, how many?"

"I'm not sure." Her smile spread slowly. "I think I'm beginning to like it."

"Perhaps I can make you like it better." He muffled her laugh with his lips.

He didn't love her gently now, but fiercely. As desperate as he, Morgan let the passion rule her. Fear that it might be the last time caused her response and demands to be urgent. She lit a fire in him.

Now, where his hands had trailed slowly, they raced. Where his mouth had whispered, it savaged. Morgan threw herself into the flames without a second thought. Her mouth was greedy, searching for his taste everywhere while her hands rushed to touch and arouse.

Her body had never felt so agile. It could melt into his one moment, then slither away to drive him to madness. She could hear his desire in the short, harsh breath, feel it in the tensing and quivering of his muscles as she roamed over them, taste it in the dampness that sheened his skin. It matched her own, and again they were in harmony.

She arched against him as his mouth rushed low— but it was more a demand than an invitation. Delirious with her own strength and power, Morgan dug her fingers into his hair and urged him to take her to that first giddy peak. Even as she cried out with it, she hungered for more. And he gave more, while he took.

But she wasn't satisfied with her own pleasure. Ruthlessly she sought to undermine whatever claim he still held to sanity. Her hands had never been so clever, or so quick. Her teeth nipped at his skin before she soothed the tiny pains with a flick of her tongue. She heard him groan and a low, sultry laugh flowed from her. His breath caught when she reached him, then came out in an oath. Morgan felt the sunlight explode into fragments as he plunged into her.

Later, much later, when he knew his time with her was nearly up, Nick kissed her with lingering tenderness.

"You're going," Morgan said, struggling not to cling to him.

"Soon. I'll have to take you back to the villa in a little while." Sitting up, he drew her with him. "You'll stay inside. Lock the doors, tell the servants to let no one in. No one."

Morgan tried to promise, and found she couldn't form the words. "When you're finished, you'll come?"

Smiling, he tucked her hair behind her ear. "I suppose I can handle your window vines again."

"I'll wait up for you and let you in the front door."

"Aphrodite." Nick pressed a kiss to her wrist. "Where's your romance?"

"Oh, God!" Morgan threw her arms around his neck and clung. "I wasn't going to say it—I promised myself I wouldn't. Be careful." Biting back tears, she pressed her face against his throat. "Please, please be careful. I'm terrified for you."

"No, don't." Feeling the dampness against his skin, he held her tighter. "Don't cry for me."

"I'm sorry." With a desperate effort, she forced back the tears. "I'm not helping you."

Nick drew her away and looked at the damp cheeks and shimmering eyes. "Don't ask me not to go, Morgan."

"No." She swallowed again. "I won't. Don't ask me not to worry."

"It's the last time," he said fiercely.

The words made her shudder, but she kept her eyes on his. "Yes, I know."

"Just wait for me." He pulled her back against him. "Wait for me."

"With a bottle of Alex's best champagne," she promised in a stronger voice.

He pressed a kiss to her temple. "We'll have some of mine now, before I take you back. A toast," he told her as he drew her away again. "To tomorrow."

"Yes." She smiled. It almost reached her eyes. "I'll drink with you to tomorrow."

"Rest a moment." With another kiss, he laid her back against the pillow. "I'll go bring some up."

Morgan waited until the door had closed behind him before she buried her face in the pillow.

Chapter 13

It was dark when she woke. Confused, disoriented, Morgan struggled to see where she was. The room was all shifting shadows and silence. There was a cover over her—something soft and light with a fringe of silk. Beneath it, she was warm and naked.

Nicholas, she thought in quick panic. She'd fallen asleep and he'd gone. On a moan, she sat up, drawing her knees to her chest. How could she have wasted those last precious moments together? How long? She thought abruptly. How long had he been gone? With trembling fingers, she reached for the lamp beside the bed.

The light eased some of her fears, but before she could climb out of bed to find a clock, she saw the note propped against the lamp. Taking it, Morgan studied the bold, strong writing. *Go back to sleep* was all it said.

How like him, she thought, and nearly laughed. Morgan kept the note in her hand, as if to keep Nick close, as she rose to look for her clothes. It didn't take her long to discover they were gone.

"The louse!" Morgan said aloud, forgetting the tender thoughts she had only moments before. So, he wasn't taking any chances making certain she stayed put. Naked, hands on her hips, she scowled around the room. Where the devil does he think I'd go? she asked herself. I have no way of knowing where he is…or what he's doing, she thought on a fresh flood of worry.

Wait. Suddenly cold, Morgan pulled the cover from the bed and wrapped herself in it. All I can do is wait.

The time dripped by, minute by endless minute. She paced, then forced herself to sit, then paced again. It would be morning in only a few more hours, she told herself. In the morning, the wait would be over. For all of them.

She couldn't bear it, she thought in despair one moment. She had to bear it, she told herself the next. Would he never get back? Would morning never come? On a sound of fury, she tossed the cover aside. She might have to wait, Morgan thought grimly as she marched to Nick's closet. But she'd be damned if she'd wait naked.

Nick shifted the muscles in his shoulders and blocked out the need for a cigarette. Even the small light would be dangerous now. The cove was bathed in milky moonlight and silence. There would be a murmur now and then from behind a rock. Not from a spirit, but from a man in uniform. The cove still held secrets. Lifting his binoculars, Nick again scanned the sea.

"Any sign?" Tripolos seemed remarkably comfortable in his squat position behind a rock. He popped a tiny mint into his mouth and crunched quietly. Nick merely shook his head and handed the glasses to Stephanos.

"Thirty minutes," Stephanos stated, chewing on the stem of his dead pipe. "The wind carries the sound of the motor."

"I hear nothing." Tripolos gave the old man a doubtful frown.

Nick chuckled as the familiar feeling of excitement rose. "Stephanos hears what others don't. Just tell your men to be ready."

"My men are ready." His gaze flicked over Nick's profile. "You enjoy your work, Mr. Gregoras."

"At times," Nick muttered, then grinned. "This time, by God."

"And soon it's over," Stephanos said from beside him.

Nick turned his head to meet the old man's eyes. He knew the statement covered more than this one job, but the whole of what had been Nick's career. He hadn't told him, but Stephanos knew. "Yes," he said simply, then turned his eyes to the sea again.

He thought of Morgan and hoped she was still asleep. She'd looked so beautiful—and so exhausted when he'd come back into the room. Her cheeks had been damp. Damn, he couldn't bear the thought of her tears. But he'd felt a wave of relief that she'd been asleep. He didn't have to see her eyes when he left her.

She's safer there than if I'd taken her back, Nick told himself. With luck, she'd still be asleep when he got back and then he'd have spared her hours of worry. Stashing her clothes had been an impulse that had eased his mind. Even Morgan wouldn't go wandering around without a stitch on her back.

His grin flashed again. If she woke and looked for them, she'd curse him. The idea gave him a moment's pleasure. He could see her, standing in the center of his room with only the moonlight covering her as she raged.

He felt the low aching need in the pit of his stomach, and promised himself he'd keep her just that way—naked fire—until the sun went down again.

Lifting the binoculars, he scanned the dark sea. "They're coming."

The moon threw the boat into silhouette. A dozen men watched her approach from clumps of rock and shadows. She came in silence, under the power of oars.

She was secured with little conversation and a few deft movements of rope. There was a scent Nick recognized. The scent of fear. A fresh bubble of excitement rose, though his face was deadly calm. He's there, Nick thought. And we have him.

The crew left the boat to gather in the shadows of the beach. A hooded figure moved to join them. At Nick's signal, the cove was flooded with light. The rocks became men.

"In the King's name," Tripolos stated grandly, "this vessel will be searched for illegal contraband. Put up your weapons and surrender."

Shouts and the scrambling of men shattered the glass-like quiet of the cove. Men seeking to escape, and men seeking to capture tangled in the sudden chaos of sound and light. Gunfire shocked the balmy air. There were cries of pain and fury.

The smugglers would fight with fist and blade. The battle would be short, but grim. The sounds of violence bounced hollowly off the rocks and drifted out on the air.

Nick saw the hooded figure melt away from the confusion and streak from the cove. Swearing, he raced after it, thrusting his gun back in his belt. A burly form collided with him as another man sought escape. Each swore at the obstacle, knowing the only choice was to remove it.

Together, they rolled over the rocks, away from the

noise and the light. Thrown into darkness, they tumbled
helplessly until the ground leveled. A blade glistened,
and Nick grasped the thick wrist with both hands to halt
its plunge to his throat.

The crack of shots had Morgan springing up from her
chair. Had she heard, or just imagined? she wondered as
her heart began to thud. Could they be so close? As she
stared into the darkness, she heard another shot, and the
echo. Fear froze her.

He's all right, she told herself. He'll be here soon, and
it'll be over. I know he's all right.

Before the sentence had finished racing through her
mind, she was running down the steps and out of the
villa.

Telling herself she was only being logical, Morgan
headed for the beach. She was just going to meet him.
He'd be coming along any minute, and she would see for
herself that he wasn't hurt. Nick's jeans hung loosely at
her hips as she streaked down the cliff path. Her breath
was gasping now, the only sound as her feet padded on
the hard dirt. Morgan thought it would almost be a relief
to hear the guns again. If she heard them, she might be
able to judge the direction. She could find him.

Then, from the top of the beach steps, she saw him
walking across the sand. With a sob of shuddering relief,
she flew down them to meet him.

He continued, too intent on his own thoughts to note
her approach. Morgan started to shout his name, but the
word strangled in her throat. She stopped running. Not
Nicholas, she realized as she stared at the hooded figure. The moves were wrong, the walk. And he'd have
no reason to wear the mask. Even as her thoughts began
to race, he reached up and tore off the hood. Moonlight
fell on golden hair.

Oh God, had she been a fool not to see it? Those calm, calm eyes—too calm, she thought frantically. Had she ever seen any real emotion in him? Morgan took a step in retreat, looking around desperately for some cover. But he turned. His face hardened as he saw her.

"Morgan, what are you doing out here?"

"I—I wanted to walk." She struggled to sound casual. There was no place for her to run. "It's a lovely night. Almost morning, really." As he advanced on her she moistened her lips and kept talking. "I didn't expect to see you. You surprised me. I thought—"

"You thought I was in Athens," Dorian finished with a smile. "But as you see, I'm not. And, I'm afraid, Morgan, you've seen too much." He held up the hood, dangling it a moment before he dropped it to the sand.

"Yes." There was no use dissembling. "I have."

"It's a pity." His smile vanished as though it had never been. "Still, you could be useful. An American hostage," he said thoughtfully as he scanned her face. "Yes, and a woman." Grabbing her arm, Dorian began to pull her across the sand.

She jerked and struggled against his hold. "I won't go with you."

"You have no choice"—he touched the handle of his knife—"unless you prefer to end up as Stevos did."

Morgan swallowed as she stumbled across the beach. He said it so casually. *Some people have no capacity for emotion—love, hate.* He hadn't been speaking of Iona, Morgan realized, but himself. He was as dangerous as any animal on the run.

"You tried to kill Iona too."

"She'd become a nuisance. Greedy not only for money, but to hold me. She thought to blackmail me into marriage." He gave a quick laugh. "I had only to tempt her with the heroin. I had thought the dose I gave her was enough."

Purposely, Morgan fell to her knees as though she'd tripped. "You would have finished her that morning if I hadn't found her first."

"You have a habit of being in the wrong place." Roughly, Dorian hauled her to her feet. "I had to play the worried lover for a time—dashing back and forth between Lesbos and Athens. A nuisance. Still, if I'd been allowed one moment alone with her in the hospital…" Then he shrugged, as if the life or the death of a woman meant nothing. "So, she'll live and she'll talk. It was time to move in any case."

"You lost your last shipment," Morgan blurted out, desperate to distract him from his hurried pace toward the beach steps. If he got her up there—up there in the rocks…and the dark.…

Dorian froze and turned to her. "How do you know this?"

"I helped steal it," she said impulsively. "Your place in the hills, the cave—"

The words choked off as his hand gripped her throat. "So you've taken what's mine. Where is it?"

Morgan shook her head.

"Where?" Dorian demanded as his fingers tightened.

A god, she thought staring into his face as the moonlight streamed over it. He had the face of a god. Why hadn't she remembered her own thought that gods were bloodthirsty? Morgan put a hand to his wrist as if in surrender. His fingers eased slightly.

"Go to hell."

Swiftly, he swept the back of his hand across her face, knocking her to the sand. His eyes were a calm empty blue as he looked down at her. "You'll tell me before I'm through with you. You'll beg to tell me. There'll be time," he continued as he walked toward her, "when we're off the island."

"I'll tell you nothing." With the blood singing in her ears, Morgan inched away from him. "The police know who you are, there isn't a hole big enough for you to hide in."

Reaching down, he grabbed her by the hair and hauled her painfully to her feet. "If you prefer to die—"

Then she was free, going down to her knees again as Dorian stumbled back and fell onto the sand.

"Nick." Dorian rubbed the blood from his mouth as his gaze traveled up. "This is a surprise." It dropped again to the revolver Nick held in his hand. "Quite a surprise."

"Nicholas!" Scrambling up, Morgan ran to him. He never looked at her. His arm was rigid as iron when she gripped it. "I thought—I was afraid you were dead."

"Get up," he told Dorian with a quick gesture of the gun. "Or I'll put a bullet in your head while you lie there."

"Were you hurt?" Morgan shook his arm, wanting some sign. She'd seen that cold hard look before. "When I heard the shots—"

"Only detained." Nick pushed her aside, his gaze fixed on Dorian. "Get rid of the gun. Toss it over there." He jerked his head and leveled his own revolver. "Two fingers. If you breathe wrong, you won't breathe again."

Dorian lifted out his gun in a slow, steady motion and tossed it aside. "I have to admit you amaze me, Nick. It's been you who's been hounding me for months."

"My pleasure."

"And I would have sworn you were a man concerned only with collecting his trinkets and making money. I've always admired your ruthlessness in business—but it

seems I wasn't aware of *all* of your business." One graceful brow rose. "A policeman?"

Nick gave a thin smile. "I answer to one man only,"
he said quietly. "Adonti." The momentary flash of fear in
Dorian's eyes gave him great pleasure. "You and I might
have come to this sooner. We nearly did last night."

A shadow touched Dorian's face briefly, then was
gone. "Last night?"

"Did you think it was only a goat who watched you?"
Nick asked with a brittle laugh.

"No." Dorian gave a brief nod. "I smelled something
more—foolish of me not to have pursued it."

"You've gotten careless, Dorian. I took your place on
your last run and made your men tremble."

"You," Dorian breathed.

"A rich cache," Nick added, "according to my associates in Athens. It might have been over for you then,
but I waited until I was certain Alex wasn't involved. It
was worth the wait."

"Alex?" Dorian laughed with the first sign of true pleasure. "Alex wouldn't have the stomach for it. He thinks
only of his wife and his ships and his honor." He gave
Nick a thoughtful glance. "But it seems I misjudged you.
I thought you a rich, rather singleminded fool, a bit of a
nuisance with Iona this trip, but hardly worth a passing
thought. My congratulations on your talent for deceit,
and"—he let his gaze travel and rest on Morgan—"your
taste."

"Efxaristo."

Morgan watched in confusion, then in terror, as Nick
tossed his gun down to join Dorian's. They lay side by
side, black and ugly, on the white sand.

"It's my duty to turn you over to Captain Tripolos and
the Greek authorities." Calmly, slowly, Nick drew out a

knife. "But it will be my pleasure to cut out your heart for putting your hands on my woman."

"*No!* Nicholas, don't!"

Nick stopped Morgan's panicked rush toward him with a terse command. "Go back to the villa and stay there."

"Please," Dorian interrupted with a smile as he got to his feet. "Morgan must stay. Such an interesting development." He pulled out his own knife with a flourish. "She'll be quite a prize for the one who lives."

"Go," Nick ordered again. His hand tensed on the knife. He was half Greek, and Greek enough to have tasted blood when he had seen Dorian strike her. Morgan saw the look in his eyes.

"Nicholas, you can't. He didn't hurt me."

"He left his mark on your face," he said softly, and turned the knife in his hand. "Stay out of the way."

Touching her hand to her cheek, she stumbled back.

They crouched and circled. As she watched, the knives caught the moonlight and held it. Glittering silver, dazzling and beautiful.

At Dorian's first thrust, Morgan covered her mouth to hold back a scream. There was none of the graceful choreography of a staged fight. This was real and deadly. There were no adventurous grins or bold laughs with the thrusts and parries. Both men had death in his eyes. Morgan could smell the sweat and the sweet scent of blood from both of them.

Starlight dappled over their faces, giving them both a ghostly pallor. All she could hear was the sound of their breathing, the sound of the sea, the sound of steel whistling through the air. Nick was leading him closer to the surf—away from Morgan. Emotion was frozen in him. Anger, such anger, but he knew too much to let it escape. Dorian fought coldly. An empty heart was its own skill.

"I'll pleasure myself with your woman before the night's over," Dorian told him as blade met blade. His lips curved as he saw the quick, naked fury in Nick's eyes.

Morgan watched with horror as a bright stain spread down Nick's sleeve where Dorian had slipped through his guard. She would have screamed, but there was no breath in her. She would have prayed, but even her thoughts were frozen.

The speed with which they came together left her stunned. One moment they were separate, and the next they were locked together as one tangled form. They rolled to the sand, a confusion of limbs and knives. She could hear the labored breathing and grunted curses. Then Dorian was on top of him. Morgan watched, numb with terror, as he plunged his knife. It struck the sand, a whisper away from Nick's face. Without thought, Morgan fell on the guns.

Once, the revolver slipped through her wet hands, back onto the sand. Gritting her teeth, she gripped it again. As she knelt, she aimed toward the entwined bodies. Coldly, willing herself to do what she had always despised, she prepared to kill.

A cry split the air, animal and primitive. Not knowing which one of them it had been torn from, Morgan clutched the gun with both hands and kept it aimed on the now motionless heap in the sand. She could still hear breathing—but only from one. If Dorian stood up, she swore to herself, and to Nick, that she would pull the trigger.

A shadow moved. She heard the labored breathing and pressed her lips together. Against the trigger, her finger shook lightly.

"Put that damn thing down, Morgan, before you kill me."

"Nicholas." The gun slipped from her nerveless hand.

He moved to her, limping a little. Reaching down, he drew her to her feet. "What were you doing with the gun, Aphrodite?" he said softly, when he felt her tremble under his hands. "You couldn't have pulled the trigger."

"Yes." Her eyes met his. "I could."

He stared at her for a moment and saw she was speaking nothing less than the truth. With an oath, he pulled her against him. "Damn it, Morgan, why didn't you stay in the villa? I didn't want this for you."

"I couldn't stay in the house, not after I heard the shooting."

"Yes, you hear shooting, so naturally you run outside."

"What else could I do?"

Nick opened his mouth to swear, then shut it again. "You've stolen my clothes," he said mildly. He wouldn't be angry with her now, he promised himself as he stroked her hair. Not while she was shaking like a leaf. But later, by God, later…

"You took mine first." He couldn't tell if the sound she made was a laugh or a sob. "I thought…" Suddenly, she felt the warm stickiness against her palm. Looking down, she saw his blood on her hand. "Oh, God, Nicholas, you're hurt!"

"No, it's nothing, I—"

"Oh, damn you for being macho and stupid. You're *bleeding!*"

He laughed and crushed her to him again. "I'm not being macho and stupid, Aphrodite, but if it makes you happy, you can nurse all of my scratches later. Now, I need a different sort of medicine." He kissed her before she could argue.

Her fingers gripped at his shirt as she poured everything she had into that one meeting of lips. Fear drained from her, and with it, whatever force had driven her. She went limp against him as his energy poured over her.

"I'm going to need a lot of care for a very long time," he murmured against her mouth. "I might be hurt a great deal more seriously than I thought. No, don't." Nick drew her away as he felt her tears on his cheeks. "Morgan, don't cry. It's the one thing I don't think I can face tonight."

"No, I won't cry," she insisted as the tears continued to fall. "I won't cry. Just don't stop kissing me. Don't stop." She pressed her mouth to his. As she felt him, warm and real against her, the tears and trembling stopped.

"Well, Mr. Gregoras, it seems you intercepted Mr. Zoulas after all."

Nick swore quickly, but without heat. Keeping Morgan close, he looked over her head at Tripolos. "Your men have the crew?"

"Yes." Lumbering over, he examined the body briefly. He noted, without comment, that there was a broken arm as well as the knife wound. With a gesture, he signaled one of his men to take over. "Your man is seeing to their transportation," he went on.

Nick kept Morgan's back to the body and met Tripolos's speculative look calmly. "It seems you had a bit of trouble here," the captain commented. His gaze drifted to the guns lying on the sand. He drew his own conclusions. "A pity he won't stand trial."

"A pity," Nick agreed.

"You dropped your gun in the struggle to apprehend him, I see."

"It would seem so."

Tripolos stooped with a wheeze and handed it back to him. "Your job is finished?"

"Yes, my job is finished."

Tripolos made a small bow. "My gratitude, Mr Gregoras." He smiled at the back of Morgan's head. "And my congratulations."

Nick lifted a brow in acknowledgment. "I'll take Miss James home now. You can reach me tomorrow if necessary. Good night, Captain."

"Good night," Tripolos murmured and watched them move away.

Morgan leaned her head against his shoulder as they walked toward the beach steps. Only a few moments before she had fought to keep from reaching them. Now they seemed like the path to the rest of her life.

"Oh, look, the stars are going out." She sighed. There was nothing left, no fear, no anxiety. No more doubts. "I feel as if I've waited for this sunrise all my life."

"I'm told you want to go to Venice and ride on a gondola."

Morgan glanced up in surprise, then laughed. "Andrew told you."

"He mentioned Cornwall and the Champs d'élysées as well."

"I have to learn how to bait a hook, too," she murmured. Content, she watched as day struggled with night.

"I'm not an easy man, Morgan."

"*Hmm?* No," she agreed fervently. "No, you're not."

He paused at the foot of the steps and turned her to face him. The words weren't easy for him now. He wondered why he had thought they would be. "You know the worst of me already. I'm not often gentle, and I'm demanding. I'm prone to black, unreasonable moods."

Morgan smothered a yawn and smiled at him. "I'd be the last one to disagree."

He felt foolish. And, he discovered, afraid. Would a woman accept words of love when she had seen a man kill? Did he have any right to offer them? Looking down, he saw her, slim and straight in his clothes—jeans that hung over her hips—a shirt that billowed and hid small, firm breasts and a waist he could nearly span with his hands. Right or wrong, he couldn't go on without her.

"Morgan…"

"Nicholas?" Her smile became puzzled as she fought off a wave of weariness. "What is it?"

His gaze swept back to hers, dark, intense, perhaps a little desperate.

"Your arm," she began and reached for him.

"No! *Diabolos.*" Gripping her by the shoulders, he shook her. "It's not my arm, listen to me."

"I am listening," she tossed back with a trace of heat. "What's wrong with you?"

"This." He covered her mouth with his. He needed the taste of her, the strength. When he drew her away, his hands had gentled, but his eyes gleamed.

With a sleepy laugh, she shook her head. "Nicholas, if you'll let me get you home and see to your arm—"

"My arm's a small matter, Aphrodite."

"Not to me."

"Morgan." Nick stopped her before she could turn toward the steps again. "I'll make a difficult and exasperating husband, but you won't be bored." Taking her hands, he kissed them as he had on his balcony. "I love you enough to let you climb your mountains, Morgan. Enough to climb them with you if that's what you want."

She wasn't tired now, but stunned into full alertness. Morgan opened her mouth, but found herself stupidly unable to form a word.

"Damn it, Morgan, don't just stare at me." Frustration and temper edged his voice. "Say yes, for God's sake!" Fury flared in his eyes. "I won't let you say no!"

His hands were no longer in hers, but gripping her arms again. She knew, any moment, he would start shaking her. But there was more in his eyes than anger. She saw the doubts, the fears, the fatigue. Love swept into her, overwhelmingly.

"Won't you?" she murmured.

"No." His fingers tightened. "No, I won't. You've taken my heart. You won't leave with it."

Lifting a hand, she touched his cheek, letting her finger trace over the tense jaw. "Do you think I could climb mountains without you, Nicholas?" She drew him against her and felt his shudder of relief. "Let's go home."

* * * * *